NOVELS BY GORDON GLASCO

The Days of Eternity
Second Nature

SLOW
THROUGH
EDEN

~~~~~~~~~~~~~~~~~~~~~~~~~~

Gordon Glasco

POSEIDON PRESS

New York London Toronto Sydney Tokyo Singapore

POSEIDON PRESS

SIMON & SCHUSTER BUILDING
ROCKEFELLER CENTER
1230 AVENUE OF THE AMERICAS
NEW YORK, NEW YORK 10020

DESIGNED BY KAROLINA HARRIS
MANUFACTURED IN THE UNITED STATES OF AMERICA

1 3 5 7 9 10 8 6 4 2

LIBRARY OF CONGRESS CATALOGING IN PUBLICATION DATA
IS AVAILABLE

ISBN: 0-671-62305-2

Acknowledgments

W I T H special thanks to my publisher, Ann Patty, and to my agent, Jane Rotrosen.

And to Dr. Alexander Gancarz, Jr., Division Leader of Isotope and Nuclear Chemistry Division, Los Alamos National Laboratory, who kept my neutrons going in the right direction.

And to Julie Langston, for her French and German translations.

And to Trevor Hawkins, M.D., an excellent physician.

For Dan Anthony and my brother, Joseph Glasco

Some natural tears they dropped, but wiped them soon;
The World was all before them, where to choose
Their place of rest, and Providence their guide.
They hand in hand with wandering steps and slow,
Through Eden took their solitary way.

—MILTON, *Paradise Lost*

Prologue

"ZERO minus one minute!" the voice crackled over the loudspeaker.

Far across the desert, the shot tower glowed under the steady white beam of a seachlight, looking like a child's toy in the vast desert expanse. To the north, still veiled in mist, the Oscura peaks were like black paper cutouts against the retreating clouds. Katherine looked up. The rain had stopped, and the sweet odor of wet sagebrush hung in the air. Off to the south, above the San Andres mountains, two stars were visible, links in Andromeda's chain.

"Fifty-eight . . . fifty-seven . . . !" the voice counted off the passing seconds.

A faint gust of wind passed over Katherine's face like a cold hand. She drew back the damp hair clinging to her cheek. The beam of light at Ground Zero resembled a compass needle pointing to the heart of a vast empty darkness. She stared at it, aware of her isolation, wondering at the distance she had traveled to come to this: a barren mound of indurated clay in a remote American desert named, with prophetic cruelty, the Dead Man's Way.

"Fifty-three . . . fifty-two . . . !"

She drew the welder's glasses over her eyes, as instructed, turned her back to the shot tower and knelt down on the crusted earth. In this pivotal moment of her research career, a new awareness was dawning in Katherine. She had spent twenty-five years—two-thirds of her life—racing to reach this very place, this particular moment, and now, having arrived, she felt helpless. She did not know, none of them knew what they had made out there in the desert.

"Forty-three . . . forty-two . . . !"

The opening words of the prayer for divine protection that she had recited every night as a child in Berlin came back to her: O Gott, du bist mein Herr, wenn du auf meinem Weg . . .

With sudden panic, she searched her memory for the words that followed.

"Thirty-one . . . thirty . . . !"

She would give anything now for the chance to turn back the clock and choose another career for herself!

"Twenty-eight . . . twenty-seven . . ."

Covering her ears with her hands did little to drown out the relentless drone of the passing seconds. After spending her life trying to prove to herself and to the world that the power of human knowledge was limitless, all she had done was to come full circle, back to the ignorance of childhood—to the impotence of blind faith and the gratuitous mercy of God's providence.

"Twenty-three . . . twenty-two!"

Again, she tried to recall her childhood prayer, but without success. She wanted to weep, thinking of the disaster she had made of her life. Though she had realized the impossible dream of discovering some of the secrets of the physical universe, she could not remember the simple words of a child's prayer.

"Nineteen . . . eighteen . . . !"

As she lowered herself to the ground and turned her back to the tower, she closed her eyes and prayed, with all the enormous power of her heart, for failure.

"Twelve . . . eleven . . . !"

If the scientific work of her lifetime now succeeded, she would be forced as a woman and as a mother to commit yet another monstrous betrayal.

"Eight . . . seven . . . !"

As she reached back in her mind, trying to imagine where it had all started, she remembered that August afternoon in Germany twenty-five years ago, when the train from Berlin had pulled into the station at Göttingen and she had looked out at the ancient brick walls of the university for the first time . . . the afternoon she had met David and made the choice that changed her life.

ONE

1

THE conductor moved along the corridor of the second-class railway carriage, stopping at each compartment to announce the train's next stop. He spoke politely, acknowledging the occupants' social standing with a slight bow. It was understood nowadays that proper people, those who belonged to the real aristocracy, traveled second class. Only the nouveaux riches, the upstarts who had profited from the war, traveled first. The curtains were drawn across the corridor windows of the carriage's third compartment. Quietly, the conductor drew back the door. Seated opposite two women was a neatly moustached, middle-aged military officer. The conductor saw the officer's silver epaulets, the Iron Cross First Class suspended from his collar, and recognized at once the cherry red trouser stripes of the Führerstab, that one mark of distinction that the Great General Staff had quietly held onto from the old days. Instinctively, he snapped his heels together. "Herr Major," he said with reverence and a rush of nostalgic pride. "In fünf Minuten sind wir in Göttingen."

Major Eric von Steiner looked up, surprised by the conductor's recognition of his rank, then realized that the man was, of course, young enough to have served in the Great War. "Besten Dank," he said, thinking to himself of the countless wretched young soldiers who had been deprived of promising military careers after the war and forced to seek menial employment. The conductor's gaze, he saw, had come to rest on the newspaper lying on the seat beside him—and the headline smeared across the front page: FRANCE DEMANDS IMMEDIATE REPARATION PAYMENTS; DEUTSCHE MARK FALLS. In a reflex of shame and anger, von Steiner quickly placed his hand over the headline. "The train, is it on time?" he asked.

"Ten minutes late, Herr Major." Pretending to fuss with the tickets in his hand, the conductor turned his gaze to the two handsomely dressed women opposite the major—obviously the major's wife and daughter.

The older woman's modest ankle-length brown dress, her veiled and feathered hat, reminded him of the old Germany during the Kaiser's reign. His eye rested on the beautiful young woman seated next to the window, fidgeting with the pages of a book. The two women's resemblance was striking—the same straight thin nose, the same pale blue eyes and long blonde hair, which both wore rolled in an old-fashioned knot behind the head. "Frau Major." He bowed. "Fräulein." He bowed again and reached for the sliding door.

Major von Steiner lowered his eyes and kept silent for a moment, listening to the rhythmical beat of steel against steel. Click clack, click clack, click clack . . .like a clock, he thought, ticking away these last few minutes before Göttingen—before Katherine leaves. He looked up at his daughter turning the pages of her mathematics text. Framed in the sunny window, her profile reminded him of Elizabeth's profile twenty years ago—the summer in Berlin when they met and married. He smiled to himself, observing the haphazard strands of hair dangling loose about Katherine's neck. Unlike Elizabeth, Katherine had never been tempted by feminine vanities. Living in a world of books since childhood, she was more like a boy than a girl—except that a boy would not have been content to ignore the world around him. A son, if he had had one, would have been a soldier like his father. He glanced at his hand resting on the newspaper headline and thought with anger and bitterness of the Weimar government's spineless capitulation and the monstrous Allied revenge he himself had witnessed two years ago at Versailles.

The train slowed. He looked again at Katherine serenely reading her textbook. Nineteen years old, he thought, and completely ignorant of the sinking world she now faces. "And another thing, Katherine," he said, breaking the silence and returning to the list of rules he had been giving her when the conductor interrupted. "Your mother and I will expect you to write home each week and report the progress of your studies. I will want to know what friends you have made and where you spend your leisure hours."

"Yes, Papa," said Katherine, keeping her eyes on her book to avoid him.

He gave a soft sigh of resignation. God knows, he loved her and had always wanted the very best for her, but she had set impossible goals for herself. It was absurd to think that she could succeed in a profession completely dominated by men. But from childhood she had wanted, more than anything, to become a scientist. Perhaps the fault was his; she had always wanted to be the son that he never had, and she had spent the better part of her youth trying to win his respect and admiration. Little did she know that he would have been more than content if she had modeled herself after her mother. He glanced at his wife on the opposite seat, hurrying to finish the scarf she had been knitting for Katherine. Elizabeth, except for a brief stab at a career as a pianist, had not been tempted by ambition.

As the train clattered over a siding, Göttingen's medieval redbrick walls came into view. "There is one thing more we have not discussed, Katherine—and that's the young men you will meet at the university. They are not like young men you have known at the university in Berlin— or the Prussian boys you grew up with in Grünewald."

"I know that, Papa," Katherine said, but her gaze was turned on the town that was quickly closing around them: the high slate-roofed buildings of the Georg Augustus University; and below, clustered behind the town's crenellated medieval walls, the maze of Göttingen's ancient brick and timbered Fachwerkhäuser.

"You have had no experience with men," she heard her father say, but his words evaporated in the heat of her excitement. She recognized at once the dome and steeples of Göttingen's four famous churches, the Vierkirchenblick.

"It's places like this where young radicals get their start, and you will find yourself surrounded by Bolsheviks and Jews."

Bolsheviks and Jews: they were the scapegoats her father had found to take the blame for Germany's catastrophic war, and his hatred of them had become an obsession. It was the Jews, he was fond of saying, who had sold Germany out to the Allies at Versailles; the Jews who were now profiting from the Weimar Republic's bankrupt economy.

She pushed her father's prejudice from her mind and looked out at Göttingen's landmarks. "Mother, look!" she exclaimed, pointing toward a Gothic belfry soaring up above the roofs at the western end of town. "That tall one is St. James!"

"By Christmas," she heard her father saying, "your mother and I will know if you will continue your studies here in Göttingen."

Katherine turned to gape at him. "Christmas? What do you mean, Papa!"

"When you come home for the holidays, I will decide whether or not you can return for a second semester," he said.

"I have been accepted for the entire year. Christmas is only four months away!"

"The deutsche mark, Katherine, is on the verge of collapse." He shifted his weight on the seat and glanced at her mother. "You know very well the financial problems your mother and I now face. Last February, when you applied for admission to the Institute, the value of the deutsche mark had not declined. It now stands at seventy-five to the dollar."

She sat forward, panicky. "What are you saying, Papa?"

"I'm saying that, for now at least, I can only afford to pay for your studies until Christmas. I've therefore instructed my bank in Berlin to pay your tuition fees and your room and board for only the first semester. Moreover, I have instructed the bank to transfer fifteen thousand Marks to the account I have opened for you at the Deutsche Bank here in Göttingen. Fifteen thousand will be enough to pay your living expenses until Christmas."

There was a deafening screech of brakes as the train abruptly stopped. "And you tell me this only now, Papa!" she shouted over the noise.

"Katherine," her mother cautioned.

"I cannot afford to gamble money on an investment that may very well fail, Katherine!" he said with sudden anger. "Four months will be plenty of time for you to prove yourself. After that, my decision will be based on your academic record and your personal behavior."

She thought of the letter she had received last month from Max Born, the new director of Göttingen's Second Physics Institute: "Your experimental interpretations of Niels Bohr's spectral light emission theory were both original and promising, and I now look forward, Fräulein von Steiner, to your joining us as a student of experimental physics at the Second Physics Institute."

Her father went on. "I have written to Otto Hugenholtz, the university chancellor, and he has agreed to report to me once a month on your progress."

She looked up with surprise. "You did what?"

"You heard me, Katherine. I said that Chancellor Hugenholtz will keep me informed about your progress."

"Papa, this is a university, not a kindergarten, and I'm not a child!"

"Nonetheless, I will rely on the reports I receive from Herrn Hugenholtz."

She closed her textbook and sighed, thinking of the lengths he had gone to to keep watch on her at the University of Berlin. Though she could never prove it, she was certain that he had paid some of her fellow students to spy on her. "You don't even know the man," she added.

"Otto Hugenholtz is a friend of General von Seechkt, my Reichswehr commander," he said, "and he was glad to assent to my request."

Katherine thought of the years she had spent living in the overpowering shadow of her father. No matter how much she had talked about a career for herself in science, he had always assumed that she would either marry a man of his choice or remain at home for the rest of her life. It was only after her mother intervened on her behalf that he had allowed her to enroll as a student of physics at the University of Berlin, and only after she presented him with a fait accompli that he had allowed her to carry out her graduate studies in Göttingen.

With a feeling of helpless dismay, she looked down at the mathematics textbook in her hand, wondering if it was really love that had bound her so closely to her father all these years, or merely her need for his respect and admiration.

"The truth is, Papa, you really don't want me to succeed," she said.

"Collect your things, Katharine," Elizabeth said, rising. "We are almost there."

The major stood up, dropped his newspaper and reached for his officer's cap in the overhead rack. "You will have four months to prove yourself."

In his impenetrable gray eyes, Katherine saw the familiar steel door of resolution slam shut. As the train lumbered into the station, she turned away in frustration and stared at the people outside on the platform—at the excited young faces of the university students waiting for their arriving friends. She had dreamed of this moment for three years, and now the joy of it was spoiled. "The fact is, Papa," she said, "what you really want is for me to marry some dismal officer of your defeated Reichswehr. And failing that, you'd be satisfied if I lived out the rest of my life—like you, the Kaiser, and his Grand Imperial Army—in the humiliation of my own defeat." She hated what she was saying even before the words were out of her mouth.

"That will do, young lady!" Elizabeth exclaimed. As the train lurched to a halt, her mother was thrust forward against her father. Ashen-faced, clutching Elizabeth's shoulders, he asked, "Are you all right?"

She nodded, "Yes," and looked up at him with embarrassment and grief.

"I will go ahead," he smiled and touched her cheek. "Müller left Berlin with the car in plenty of time. I told him to drive the baggage directly to the villa, then bring the car to the station." As he pushed open the compartment door and stepped out into the corridor, he looked back.

The expression of helplessness that Katherine saw in his eyes frightened her. Quickly, she stood up to apologize. "Papa, forgive me. I didn't mean what I said."

"I will look for Müller and meet you in front of the station," he said, and he turned away down the corridor.

Avoiding her mother's eyes, Katherine reached for the book she had dropped in the seat.

"That was very cruel of you," said Elizabeth, "cruel and unthinking."

"I will not live in the past, Mama! I will not live the rest of my life like Papa! I have a future!"

"Listen to me, child!" Elizabeth let go of the baggage and grabbed hold of Katherine's arms as she started past her for the door. "Try to understand! Your father lectures you because he is afraid for you! And he's afraid because he loves you!"

"He loves me as a child, Mutti. He does not respect me as a woman. And if he had his way, I would remain a child."

"I beg of you, Katherine, don't hurt your father like this! Be patient. These things take time."

"Patient? How long should I be patient? Should I be patient like you— patient for the rest of my life?"

The question brought a look of stinging recognition to her mother's eyes. She quickly turned to collect her baggage and knitting case from the seat. "We must go. The train will not stand here forever," she said and hurried off down the corridor.

Katherine followed, turning over in her mind the old question that had troubled her since childhood, when she first discovered her mother's "little secret," as she called it. At nineteen, her mother had faced the choice between love, marriage, and children, and a career as a concert pianist. Back then, at the turn of the century, knowing that it was impossible to have both, she had chosen the security of marriage over the uncertainty of a career. Only later, when it was too late, had she come to realize that she had sacrificed a talent that was priceless.

With the assistance of the porter, Elizabeth preceded Katherine down the steps and into the milling crowd on the platform. "Don't linger behind, Katherine," she said with alarm. "We must stay together."

"Yes, Mama," Katherine replied.

Students laden with bags and bundles swarmed in noisy groups over the platform, greeting one another with carefree cheer. A young man wearing a threadbare jacket hurried past. He looked back at Katherine and their eyes locked, but only for an instant, for the smile and the look of amazement that came over his face made her lower her eyes. It was her clothes, she knew, that amused him. Compared to the other girls on the platform, who wore short colorful dresses in the modern style, she looked ridiculously old-fashioned in the prim ankle-length dress her mother had insisted she wear for her arrival. Nearby, a girl with brightly painted lips stood smoking a cigarette, breezily chatting with two young foreigners. Fighting shame and envy, Katherine dropped back to put distance between herself and her elegant but turn-of-the-century mother. At the far end of the platform she caught sight of her father patiently making his way through the students gathered around the station entrance, looking conspicous and anachronistic in his medaled and braided, gray and silver, Imperial Prussian Guard's uniform.

At the door leading into the station lobby, he paused to buy another newspaper, the *Völkischer Beobachter,* a virulently anti-Semitic propaganda sheet published in Bavaria by the new National Socialist German Workers' Party. She had seen copies of the paper in her father's study at home and had been surprised to hear him repeat the Party's call for a national revolution. The Nazi Party is the answer to Germany's problems, she had heard him once say, and Adolf Hitler is the man for Germany's future.

Outside the station, Katherine caught sight of Müller waiting beside her father's old Maybach limousine.

"I trust you had a comfortable journey, Frau Major," said Müller as he doffed his cap and bowed. "I delivered Fräulein Katherine's bags to the villa, just as the major ordered." Here Müller gave a quick glance in Katherine's direction.

She read at once the look of mockery in his eyes and saw, at the same time, that her parents had failed to observe the man's silent communication.

"Müller tells me the villa is in the old part of town," the major said, worriedly folding his newspaper.

"Good!" exclaimed Katherine. "I'm glad it's in the old town, Papa."

Müller smiled as she stooped to enter the car. Taking her usual place in the seat next to her mother, she thought of the endless rides she had been forced to endure with Ernst Müller. This, she thought with relief, will be the last time I will have to ride in the same car with the failed sergeant, Ernst Müller!

Katherine sighed. The chauffeur's monstrous little game had started one afternoon in October, two years ago, when she returned home from the university and went to her bedroom to undress and bathe. She had forgotten to close the door, and she was already naked when she looked up and saw Müller staring at her from the darkness of the hallway. She had not told her parents, afraid to talk of such intimate things with them, afraid they would think that the fault was hers, not Müller's. Then too, as far as her father was concerned, Müller could do no wrong. The man had served in the trenches during the war, a Frontkämpfer as her father always said with pride, and he had suffered gas poisoning at the Marne. Out of pity or guilt, or both, her father had hired him as a chauffeur. And though her father would never admit it, Müller, she was sure, was responsible for his interest in the Nazi Party.

The car turned into a small cobblestone square crowded with pedestrians and cyclists. Müller broke the silence. "They tell me, Herr Major, this is the local Marktplatz. And that, Frau Major,"—he pointed with his thumb and chuckled—"is the so-called Goosegirl fountain." Katherine recognized at once the famous fountain statue of the smiling peasant girl and her pet goose.

Katherine sat back, thinking of the dream that had brought her to Göttingen—to win a doctorate in experimental physics from the Second Physics Institute: the door to a career as an atomic physicist. Only now, at the door's threshold, she wondered if her father might not be right, if she might not have dreamed a dream beyond her reach. This, after all, was Weimar Germany, and she was a woman.

Ahead, she read the street sign, Lange Geismarstrasse—the street where her villa was located—and felt as if she were approaching the edge of a cliff. Behind lay the strangling jungle of her adolescence, and ahead the open air of freedom and womanhood.

She took a deep breath.

As they turned the corner, the shops gave way to stately, private homes. She saw by the look on her father's face that he approved. Every fourth or fifth house along the street was a half-timbered medieval Fachwerkhaus, ornamented with a carved balcony or a loggia, all relics of a far more cheerful and lusty age. Searching the doors and porches for number 18, she found herself praying that the villa her father had chosen for her would be one of the whimsical Fachwerkhäuser. Herr Roland Freisler, her father's solicitor in Berlin who had arranged her boarding accomodations, had given his assurances that Frau Reichshauer's villa was one of the most desirable villas in town.

"Number eighteen, Herr Major," Müller said, as he drew up before the imposing façade of an ancient two-story gothic Fachwerkhaus.

2

KATHERINE could scarcely contain her excitement. She followed her father out of the car and stood scanning the high gabled façade with its leaded-glass oriel windows.

The major brought the iron knocker down with a portentous thud against the massive wooden door.

"Fix your hair, dear," Elizabeth said as the door swung open.

"Ah!" A tiny woman in a gray cotton smock and soiled white apron stood framed in the doorway. Her small dark eyes darted over the major's uniform, then came to rest on Elizabeth and Katherine. "We've been expecting you," she beamed, absently wiping her hands on the apron.

Nonplussed by the woman's familiarity, the major cleared his throat. "Good afternoon. Would you inform Frau Reichshauer that Major von Steiner, his wife, and daughter have arrived?"

"I am Frau Reichshauer, Herr Major von Steiner," she said and laughed, as she effortlessly swung open the massive door. "Do, all of you, come in."

"May I present my wife," the major said, and stepped back for Elizabeth to pass.

"Welcome to Welchzeckhaus, Frau von Steiner," said Frau Reichshauer, extending her hand with gracious warmth.

As Elizabeth took the proffered hand, the major looked at her with surprise. "Thank you, Frau Reichshauer," Elizabeth smiled. "And this is our daughter, Katherine."

With an expression of open welcome, Frau Reichshauer extended both hands. "Please come in, Katherine, we've been waiting for your arrival."

Katherine saw that the quick dark eyes had instantly evaluated her and approved. "Thank you," she said, feeling an immediate connection in the warmth of the old woman's hands. As she entered the high rib-vaulted hallway, she caught sight of her two large bags at the foot of the staircase leading to the second floor.

"Please come," Frau Reichshauer said, "we'll have tea in my study." With energetic steps, she led them past the ancient wooden staircase, down the long hallway lit from above by a leaded glass window.

Frau Reichshauer opened a door at the far end of the hallway. "Forgive the clutter," she said, "this is my own little sanctuary. The rest of the house belongs to my boarders."

Elizabeth paused to admire a colorful enamelled drinking glass resting

on a table outside the door. "This glass, Frau Reichshauer, is it a Rhein-
ischer Humpen, by chance?"

"Indeed! It belonged to my great-grandfather," said the old lady, beaming with pleasure. "Please! Come in!"

Katherine followed her parents into the room and drew up just inside
the door to stare at the amazing clutter of furniture: small tables covered
with framed photographs and assorted bibelots, bookcases filled with old
leather-bound books, and on the far side of the room, under the lace-
curtained window, a huge turn-of-the-century grand piano.

Frau Reichshauer hurried to clear stacks of papers from a silk-uphol-
stered Biedermeier sofa. "Do sit down, Herr Major von Steiner," she
said, pointing to an overstuffed armchair. "That chair is the most comfortable. And Katherine, please come sit here on the sofa with your
mother."

"I understand, Frau Reichshauer," said the major, declining to sit,
"that you have two other boarders."

"As of four days ago, I have only one other boarder," Frau Reichshauer
replied, settling herself on a plain, straight-backed chair.

"One?" Elizabeth looked at the major with alarm.

"Yes, Frau von Steiner, only one. The other young lady who was to
board with us was forced to remain in England."

"You're saying that Katherine will be the only female boarder."

Katherine held her breath and quickly glanced from her mother to her
father.

"That is not unusual here in Göttingen," Frau Reichshauer smiled.
"Few women, as you know, are accepted into the university. And since
the villas are all private houses, it is quite common for a young woman
to find herself the only female boarder. Our accommodations are quite
separate, and I have always assumed that any young man or woman who
is prepared to accept the rigorous academic demands of the university is,
at the same time, a responsible young adult."

"I see," said Elizabeth with dismay.

Katherine's heart sank, for her mother had made a particular issue of
her having a fellow female boarder.

"The other boarder is an American gentleman by the name of David
Linz," Frau Reichshauer went on, oblivious to Elizabeth's alarm. "Herr
Linz is a second-year student at the Institute; and Katherine, I'm sure,
will find him a valuable and delightful companion during her stay here
at Welchzeckhaus."

Katherine saw that Frau Reichshauer had failed to observe the exchange of shocked looks between her father and mother. She glanced down at her hands, waiting for the inevitable question.

"Welchzeckhaus?" the major asked.

"That is the name the townspeople have given to this house, Herr Major."

"A Polish name, I take it," said Elizabeth with forced pleasantry.

"That is correct." Innocently warming to Elizabeth's interest, Frau Reichshauer went on. "Welchzeckhaus has belonged to my family since the sixteenth century. The name was given to the house by the townspeople in the seventeenth century." She smiled pensively. "I'm afraid, however, that I am the end of the Welchzeck line. My brothers are both dead, and my husband and I had only a daughter. Sadly, our Sarah died during the first year of the war . . ." She suddenly stopped speaking, aware of the tense silence that had fallen. "How thoughtless of me!" she exclaimed. "It is Katherine's future, not my past, that we should be concerned with." She leaned forward, "Tell me, dear, how old are you?"

"Nineteen."

"And you want to be a scientist."

The statement on Frau Reichshauer's lips sounded curiously simple and unthreatening. "Yes."

"An experimental physicist, they tell me."

"How did you know?"

"Your reputation has preceded you, my dear Katherine." She beamed. "I've heard Herr Linz, your fellow boarder, speak of the research papers you sent to the Institute with your application. He tells me you have great promise."

The old woman's warm encouragement reignited Katherine's hope.

Katherine glanced at her father. "I want to be a scientist more than anything, Frau Reichshauer, and I will do everything in my power to make a success of my studies," Katherine said, then blushed at the naked presumption of her statement.

Frau Reichshauer smiled. "This habit of dreaming, Katherine—you are not, I assure you, alone. Everyone who comes here has a dream. And you must not be afraid if your dream seems impossible. For every great thing that happens in this world always begins with an impossible dream."

The major broke in irritably. "Regarding Katherine's daily routine here, Frau Reichshauer. I assume that you have rules governing the behavior of your male boarder."

"Some, but not many, Herr Major. I believe most strongly in both the art and the science of personal responsibility—in teaching young people to make choices for themselves." As she spoke, the door opened and a uniformed maid entered with a silver tray and tea service. Wordlessly, without acknowledgment from Frau Reichshauer, she placed the tray on the coffee table and withdrew. "My rules apply to the public, not to the private rooms of Welchzeckhaus. Breakfast is served at seven, a light lunch at noon, and a simple but wholesome supper at six o'clock."

Behind Frau Reichshauer, Katherine observed her father turn away and begin weaving a path through the clutter of furniture. He paused to pick up and examine a framed photograph on one of the tables: a photo of a tall fair-haired gentleman in a frock coat, carrying a top hat and a cane.

"Now," said Frau Reichshauer pleasantly, "would you care for tea, Frau von Steiner?"

"Why—yes, please," replied Elizabeth, studying the major's expression.

He returned the photograph to the table and moved on toward the breakfront against the far wall.

"Tea, Herr Major von Steiner?" Frau Reichshauer asked, intent on pouring a second cup of tea.

"No. Nothing, thank you."

"Katherine?"

"Yes, please." She saw that her father had moved closer to the breakfront and was peering through the glass.

When her father finally spoke, his voice was edged with suspicion. "I've been told, gnädige Frau, that your husband was a businessman," he said.

"That is correct. He took over my family's garment business following the deaths of my two brothers. They were both killed in France in 1914, at the outbreak of the war. My husband died of a stroke two years ago, during the last year of the war."

As Katherine raised the teacup to her lips, she saw that the color had drained from her mother's face. Then she caught sight of the object her father had been gazing at in the breakfront: standing alone on the second shelf, a small brass seven-branch candlestick: a Jewish menorah.

Katherine lowered her teacup to its saucer, Elizabeth cleared her throat, and the major broke the silence. "There remains the question of Katherine's accommodations, Frau Reichshauer."

Katherine's heart collapsed. At supper last night he had said that her stay in Göttingen would depend on his inspection and approval of her accommodations.

"Ah. Yes, of course." Frau Reichshauer stood up. "Please come this way; I will show you the room I have prepared for Katherine." She opened the door and stood back, waiting.

"I must, of course, judge for myself," said the major.

As Elizabeth returned her teacup to the table and stood up, Katherine shot her a look of appeal.

"I understand, Herr Major," said Frau Reichshauer. "The first year is as difficult for the parents as it is for the students." She motioned for the major to follow her into the hallway. "The public rooms are on the first floor, the private rooms on the second."

"Mutti!" Katherine whispered frantically as Elizabeth reached the door. But her mother ignored her and kept moving.

Katherine hurried after her parents as Frau Reichshauer led the way down the hallway, describing the features of the public rooms. When her parents turned to follow Frau Reichshauer up the staircase, Katherine read in her father's silence the resolute evidence of his decision. She had been the victim of his anti-Semitism once before—when he refused to allow her to attend Professor Albert Einstein's lecture on special relativity at the University of Berlin.

As Frau Reichshauer started down the carpeted second-floor hallway, she said, lowering her voice to a reverential whisper, "Herr Linz is in his room studying," and pointed to an open door on their right.

As Katherine reached the open door of Herr Linz's room, she paused to get a glimpse of his room. Surrounded by books stacked against the wall, he sat at his desk, busily writing, with his back to the door. Suddenly, as her eye came to rest on his curly black hair, he stirred. Before she could move on, he turned and, for an instant, arrested by his handsome unshaven face and his dark penetrating gaze, she contined to stare at him. The irritable question she saw in his face gave way to surprise; then he smiled.

"Katherine!" her father called out from the far end of the hallway.

Herr Linz's smile broadened to a knowing grin.

The feeling of pleasure that came over her was new and unfamiliar. Remembering her father's warning about the men she would meet in Göttingen, she left his door and hurried toward the room at the far end of the hallway into which her parents had vanished with Frau Reichshauer.

"The room originally belonged to my daughter," the landlady was saying as Katherine drew up to the door and caught her breath, startled by the sunlight falling through the leaded panes of the huge oriel window.

As the major surveyed the room, Katherine quietly entered and joined her mother beside the four-poster bed with its embroidered white summer coverlet.

"Whatever Fräulein von Steiner does not like in the room can, of course, be put in storage," added Frau Reichshauer.

As she watched her father move through the room, pretending to examine each object on each table, each chair, and each cushion, Katherine found herself hating his show of concern. "The room is lovely, Papa," she murmured.

He seemed not to hear her, for he had stopped to stare at an old photo hanging from a satin cord above the bureau. A chill ran up her back. The photo showed a smiling old man holding an infant in his arms. Quaintly perched on the crown of his head was a black Fedora, and draped over the shoulders of his black frock coat was fringed Jewish prayer shawl.

"The child, Frau Reichshauer, is she your daughter?" he asked.

"My daughter and her great-grandfather. It was taken the morning of Sarah's presentation at Göttingen's synagogue, Herr Major."

"I see."

To fill the sudden silence, Elizabeth said, "The frame is quite handsome, Frau Reichshauer."

Fighting an impulse to run from the room, Katherine watched the old woman move toward the window. The sunlight through the beveled leaded panes broke in a prism across her face. She spoke, finally. "The photo will, of course, be removed, Herr Major."

He started toward the door. "If you will recall, Frau Reichshauer," he said in a businesslike voice, "it was my solicitor Herr Roland Freisler, who made the arrangements for Katherine's room and board here." He cleared his throat. "And when Herr Freisler made the downpayment for the first five months, he told you that payment for the rest of the year would be forthcoming, pending my personal inspection of the accommodations."

"Papa, please don't," Katherine whispered.

The major ignored her. "The accommodations, I'm afraid, are not what I had in mind for Katherine. Her mother and I are not prepared to accept the fact that she would be the only female boarder."

In a misery of shame, Katherine broke in. "I like the room, Papa!"

"Katherine," Elizabeth scolded.

"Come along now," her father started for the door, "we will look for other accommodations."

"You needn't waste your time, Herr Major," said Frau Reichshauer. "By now, all the available rooms in Göttingen have been taken."

"Do as Papa says, Katherine," Elizabeth pleaded, as she hurriedly joined the major in the hallway. "We will talk things over in the car."

Her mother's submissiveness ignited Katherine's anger. "Talk what over in the car, Mutter?" she shouted. "My entire career? I will never be accepted again if I leave now!"

"Do as you are told," the major commanded. He took hold of Elizabeth's arm and quickly guided her down the hallway.

The frustration that Katherine had held at bay up to now suddenly engulfed her. She saw only the end of her dream. Her voice broke. "I cannot go back."

Frau Reichshauer reached up and grasped her shoulder. "I am so sorry for you, child." As she hurried from the room, her voice suddenly filled the hallway. "The truth is, Herr Major, it is not my accommodations that offend you, it is my religion."

Terrified, Katherine held back for a moment. Her parents were standing at the top of the staircase, their faces frozen in shock.

"It is your daughter who is paying the price for your foolish prejudice, Herr Major!" Frau Reichshauer exclaimed, passing Herr Linz's open door. As the old woman bore down on them, the major and Elizabeth quickly vanished down the stairs.

Knowing that Herr Linz had heard everything, certain that he was watching, Katherine looked away as she passed his open door. Dreading the scene that awaited her below, she went down the staircase slowly, one step at a time. At the foot of the staircase she paused, hearing her father's angry voice from the direction of Frau Reichshauer's study.

The old woman's words brought to Katherine's mind all the little retreats she had made in her life up to now—the endless surrenders that had made her the coward that she was. At the thought of the defeat now awaiting her if she returned to Berlin, she turned, took a deep breath, and began walking toward the study, wondering if she would find the courage to confront her father once she got there.

When she reached the open study door, her father gestured angrily for her to leave the room. When she did not move, the major said, "You will go to the car, Katherine, and you will wait there with Müller. When I have finished my business with Frau Reichshauer, we shall leave."

But Katherine's gaze was riveted on her mother, who had turned to stare at the huge concert grand piano. She saw something suddenly rise and fall in her mother's pale blue eyes: a tiny flame of regret.

Stepping into the room, she said, finally, "I cannot leave Göttingen, Papa. I have worked too hard to be accepted at the Institute."

"Go to the car, Katherine," he ordered.

She heard the note of startled uncertainty in his voice. "If I leave Göttingen now, Papa, they will not let me come back."

"You're quite right, my dear," said Frau Reichshauer. "They will not give you a second chance."

The major turned his anger on the old woman. "You have no right to give advice to my daughter!"

Elizabeth hurried to take his arm. "Never mind, Eric," she pleaded. "We will go now."

"I want to discuss with you, Frau Reichshauer," he went on, "the money I have paid you for my daughter's room and board."

Mortified, Katherine took a step backward toward the door. "Papa," she gasped. The wave of shame that swept over her drowned what little courage she had mustered. "Forgive me, Frau Reichshauer," she said, and in confusion, she turned to leave.

Herr Linz stood in the door, blocking her way. She came to an abrupt halt and caught her breath.

"You're Katherine von Steiner, aren't you?" he asked.

"Yes," she replied.

He grinned. "I've been waiting for six months to meet you."

"Waiting to meet me? I don't understand."

"The experimental work you've been doing in Berlin is exactly the kind of thing I've been looking for here. I'm a theoretical physicist."

Still smiling, he turned to her father. "Herr Major, is it not?" he asked. "Or did I hear Frau Reichshauer incorrectly?"

His German was fluent, but Katherine detected an American accent.

"I take it you're departing, Herr Major," Linz went on. "But before you leave and deprive us of your daughter, I believe you owe Frau Reichshauer an apology."

Katherine felt her pulse begin to race at his fearless confidence. She watched her father, waiting for his response.

Nonplussed, the major turned to Frau Reichshauer. "Who is this young man?"

Herr Linz was much taller than she had imagined, inches taller than her father.

"Linz is the name," came the reply before Frau Reichshauer could speak. "I'm a boarder here at Welchzeckhaus, and I think you owe Frau Reichshauer an apology, Herr Major."

"An apology?" The major's eyebrows shot up.

"Yes, Herr Major. An apology. I overheard what Frau Reichshauer said upstairs in the hallway."

"Young man, I have done nothing whatever to warrant the outburst you heard upstairs! If you will excuse us—" Seeing that he had left his officer's cap in one of the chairs, the major went to retrieve it.

Katherine tried to swallow, but her mouth was dry.

"Before you go, Herr Major," Frau Reichshauer said from across the room, "we must conclude the question of the money you have paid in advance for Katherine's room and board. I made it quite clear to your solicitor in Berlin that the money was not refundable. The terms of the agreement were set down in writing."

At that, the major's face went scarlet with rage. "Then, meine Frau, you may keep the money!" he shouted.

With Elizabeth obediently clinging to his arm, the major started past the insolent young American.

Seeing that Katherine was prepared to follow, Linz stepped forward to block the major's way. "You must forgive my intruding on your plans, Herr Major," he said, "but you have no right to force your daughter to leave Göttingen."

"I beg your pardon." The major stepped back with a look of shocked indignation.

"You're being unfair, sir," said Linz. "Your daughter is a brilliant scientist. If she leaves Göttingen now, she will never be able to come back."

"That's none of your concern, young man," said the major, starting around Linz toward the door.

But again, Linz blocked his way. "I'm sorry, Herr Major, but you're wrong. I know the work your daughter was doing in Berlin, and it's very much my concern that she be allowed to stay in Göttingen."

The major's voice shook with indignation. "It's out of the question, sir. Let me pass."

"Herr Linz," Katherine cautioned, glancing with confusion at her father.

"This is impossible. Katherine, come." The major pushed his way past Linz, then turned just outside the door.

Linz stepped forward and spoke to Katherine. "The choice is yours to make, not your father's."

"I'm sorry, Herr Linz. I must go."

As she passed him, he read in her eyes the excruciating feeling of defeat.

He followed, keeping pace behind her. "You'd be a fool to give up what you started in Berlin and leave Göttingen," he said.

She thought of the three lonely years she had worked as an undergraduate to win admission into the Institute, and came to a halt.

"You're an American, Herr Linz, and you don't understand. Here in Germany, there are loyalties to be kept—now more than ever."

"You mean, to your father?"

Her mouth was dry. She tried to swallow.

"Tell me," he said with a challenging smile, "you're beautiful, you're intelligent—what are you afraid of?"

She tried to formulate a reply, but the answer to his question, she realized, lay just beyond her reach.

"It's your father, isn't it?" he said. "You've lived in his shadow all your life, and you've never dared to disobey him."

It was true. Stubborn and self-willed as she was, she had never dared to openly disobey her father.

"You don't understand, Herr Linz," she said, hurrying to escape. "I have no choice."

"Choice!" exclaimed Linz. "Choice, Katherine, is the one thing you do have!"

She drew up just inside the door. Outside, her parents stood beside the Maybach's open passenger door. With gentle solicitude, her mother reached up to adjust her father's uniform collar. Bleached by the bright sunlight, they looked like figures she had once seen in Berlin's costume museum: relics of the past. She had seen this same scene before, she realized, the afternoon her father left home to accompany the military delegation to Paris for the signing of Germany's surrender at Versailles— her mother hovering to console him, Müller loading the baggage. It seemed, suddenly, that the prison she had vowed to escape now lay in front of her, and behind lay all the freedom of her visions—all the impossible dreams. Her father caught sight of her inside the door. Drawn by the small gesture of his right hand, she stepped out into the cobblestoned street.

Her mother had bent down to enter the car. She looked back. "Come, dear, we have a long drive ahead of us."

"Come along, Katherine," said her father patiently, as if encouraging a small child.

Emerging from under the trunk door, Müller looked up and smiled from behind the grotesque camouflage of his black walrus moustache. This time, the smile was triumphant.

She felt something that had been holding her for a long time suddenly snap. She said, quietly, "Now take the bags out."

Müller looked as if she had spoken to him in a foreign language.

"I said, take the bags out."

Her father's cheek quivered. "Don't be foolish, Katherine, get in."

"I'm not going with you, Papa," she said. "I'm not going back to Berlin."

Katherine felt a rush of liberating anger. "Do as I tell you, Müller. Take the bags out."

Bewildered, he glanced at the major for reassurance.

At that, the major reached up to finger the Iron Cross around his neck. "Tell her to do as I say, Elizabeth."

"I'm staying here, Mutti," she said, "with or without Papa's help. If it's only for four months, I will have my four months. My room and board have been paid until Christmas, I've been accepted by the Institute, and I won't leave."

"You must obey!" the major called out.

"Must, Papa? Why must I? I've done nothing but obey you all my life. Look at me! What am I . . . ?" The palsied squeak in her voice answered the question for them all.

"Come along, Katherine," Elizabeth said.

"No, Mutti. If I go back, I will never leave and I will end up no different from you. This is the chance of a lifetime, and I will not let it pass by."

A look of horrified recognition came over her mother's face. She left the car door and came forward. "Katherine is right, Eric."

The resolution in her mother's voice took him by surprise. For a moment, glancing with astonishment between the two of them, he seemed to hesitate. "Don't be ridiculous, Elizabeth," he said. "What she's asking is impossible."

"Impossible or not, she has the chance now to make a career for herself, and you must let her stay. I beg of you, Eric. If not for Katherine's sake, then for mine."

Elizabeth reached out and took hold of the major's arm. "Christmas is only four months away, Eric," said Elizabeth. "It's not forever."

The major took a step backward and reached out, helplessly, for the open car door. "Very well, then." He turned to Katherine. "I will agree to your staying in Göttingen, but only on certain conditions. First, you must promise to find another villa."

The feeling of relief that came over Katherine was like a reprieve from a death sentence. "I will do everything I can to find another villa, Papa," she said.

"And second, you must promise not to involve yourself with your fellow boarder here at Welchzeckhaus. Herr Linz is one of those young men I warned you about, Katherine. He is a Jew, like Frau Reichshauer, and I do ñot want you associating with him."

"All right, Papa," she said.

"It's clear that Herr Linz has plans to involve himself in your studies, Katherine. But if I hear that you are associating with him, I will force you to leave Göttingen."

"You have nothing to fear, Papa," she said. "There is no reason for me to involve myself with Herr Linz."

"I will rely on the reports I receive from Herr Hugenholtz," he said, "and if you fail to keep your promises, I will know about it. Do you understand me?"

"Yes, Papa. I understand."

As Elizabeth came forward, Katherine saw in her eyes a tiny flicker of compassion. With outstretched arms, she hurried to meet her mother halfway.

"It may take time," Elizabeth whispered in her ear, "but one day Papa will be very proud of you." She drew back, quickly took out the money she had in her purse, and pressed it into her hand. "I will make Papa give you the money you need, I promise."

As she hurried back to the car, the major turned to Müller with a look of helpless surrender. "Take the bags out."

Obediently, he removed the bags from the Maybach's trunk and started forward.

"Don't go in," Katherine said with all the contempt she could summon into her voice. "Just leave the bags outside."

From the passenger window her father looked out, his face a mask of fear and defeat.

As she turned and walked toward the bags Müller had left beside the door, the car's motor gave a grudging sputter, then started.

For a moment, she stood at the open door to her new home and watched her father's huge old Maybach lumber off down the cobblestoned street . . . taking with it, she realized, all the certainties of childhood, and leaving behind nothing but two old-fashioned bags.

Then she turned and went in.

3

"OH! And one more thing!" Frau Adler called out as Katherine turned to leave the crowded registry office. "It's not on your class schedule, Fräulein von Steiner, but Professor Wilhelm Schwab will be giving the 'Welcoming Lecture' next Friday! It will be held at three o'clock in the second-floor amphitheater, and all first-year students are expected to attend!"

"I'll be there, of course. Thank you!"

The ground-floor hallway of the Second Physics Institute was crowded with students hurrying to their first lectures. Katherine paused outside the registry office to check the clock at the far end of the hallway: 11:34. If she hurried, there would be time enough to visit the second-floor library before her twelve-thirty lunch with Frau Reichshauer.

Caught up in the exhilaration of her new-found freedom, she started off briskly toward the staircase leading to the second floor. It's official, she thought with amazement: I'm a student at the Second Physics Institute!

"Katherine! Wait up!" A familiar voice broke through her reverie as she reached the foot of the staircase.

Before she could turn to meet David Linz, she remembered her father's words of the previous afternoon and the promise she had made not to involve herself with Herr Linz.

"Katherine!" He came up, breathless with excitement, handsome in his brown tweed jacket. "I've been searching everywhere for you!"

"It's been a busy morning, Herr Linz. I had to register for my fall lectures."

"I was hoping to give you a tour of the Institute this morning, but Frau Reichshauer said you left the villa before breakfast."

"Yes. I had an early appointment with Professor Hilbert." She looked around at the students hurrying past them down the hallway, wondering if she was already being watched. "You must excuse me," she said. "I have a hundred things to do before lunch."

"Have you had a chance to see much of the Institute yet?"

"No. Not yet."

"In that case, I should give you a tour of the place."

She looked around again at the faces hurrying past them. In Berlin, she had never succeeded in identifying who it was her father had paid to spy on her. "Perhaps tomorrow. I'm in a bit of a rush right now."

"But what could be more important on your first day than learning the Institute's layout?"

"I'm sorry, Herr Linz, but there isn't time."

"My name is David," he said. "I would prefer that you call me David."

She let go of the bannister and picked up speed. "You must excuse me, David. I've promised to meet Frau Reichshauer for lunch at twelve thirty."

He caught up as she reached the second-floor landing. "But it's only eleven thirty-five, Katherine. I can show you everything in fifteen minutes."

It was useless, she realized, trying to evade him. "All right, then. But a short tour, please."

He took her arm as she turned down the crowded second-floor hallway. "We'll start with the second-floor lecture rooms and labs," he said. "Then I'll show you the physics lab where you'll be doing your experiments."

"Yes, I'd like to see the physics lab." She wanted to remove her arm, but he was holding it too tightly.

"This door on your left—" He pointed to an unmarked door. "That's the room where Professors Born, Franck, and Hilbert hold their seminar on matter every Thursday. It's offered by invitation; only the top students at the Institute attend."

She remembered hearing about the seminar while still in Berlin. "Yes," she said. "I know of it."

"If you're lucky enough to get an invitation, your future's assured at the Institute." He looked at her and smiled. "But best of all, it brings you the recognition of your peers."

"From what I've heard in Berlin, it's almost impossible for a first-year student to get an invitation to the seminar."

"Difficult, but not impossible. As a rule, first-year students are not invited to attend. But rules are meant to be broken." He smiled again with boyish playfulness. "It's too soon, of course, to make predictions, but with your academic record there's every chance you could get an invitation to the seminar. If not this semester, then next."

She looked down at his hand on her arm, wondering if she should tell him how doubtful her second semester was. But she would be forced to explain the promises she had made to her father, and she had known David for less than twenty-four hours. "I gather you've been invited to the seminar," she said.

"Yes. I was lucky enough to receive one my first year."

"In that case, you must have arrived in Göttingen with a reputation," she said.

"Actually, I was a complete unknown when I arrived, and that was the hardest thing of all." He tightened his grip on her arm to guide her around a group of chatting students. "To get an invitation to the seminar on matter, you have to have the recommendation of a member in good standing. It took me two weeks to meet all my colleagues at the Institute, but I finally found someone to recommend me. It was the physicist Wolfgang Pauli."

"Ah, yes," she said, thinking of her reluctance to meet new people. "I've heard of Professor Pauli."

He drew up before an open door on their right. "This is the physics lab," he said.

She looked up at the word *Physiklaboratorium* written in old German script above the door.

"It's all right," he said, and let go of her arm. "We can go in."

Through the open door, she saw to her relief that the laboratory was deserted.

She followed him into a long rectangular room furnished with three polished wooden worktables. The equipment—Geiger counters, banks of electronic devices, X-ray tubes, a cloud chamber, and brown glass bottles of purified metals—was arranged along the tables in neat rows. Four tall uncurtained windows looked out over the Bunsenstrasse and the small park opposite the Institute. She started forward to examine the Geiger counters on the center table.

"You're probably familiar with most of our equipment," he said, "but we've made a few new additions."

She gaped at the array of new Geiger counters. In comparison to her university laboratory in Berlin, the equipment here was breathtaking. "It's wonderful," she said. "It's everything I imagined it would be."

"Good. I'm glad you like it. This is where you'll be spending most of the next three years."

She thought again of the uncertain future that was awaiting her and moved on.

"There's been talk here, Katherine, about the master's thesis you wrote in Berlin on spectral light emissions," he said. "They say you've proved that the electron is a particle."

"That's not true, David. I merely showed that it sometimes behaves like a particle."

He followed her as she moved down the aisle between the worktables. "I've been working with the electron myself," he said. "In fact, I'm planning to write my doctoral thesis on the theoretical structure of the electron."

"I know," she said. "Frau Reichshauer told me."

"It's only a theory, but I believe that Niels Bohr is wrong about his jumping quantum electrons. I think the electron can be described as both a wave and particle."

She caught sight of the gleaming array of X-ray tubes at the end of the table. "It may be only a coincidence," she said, "but when I ran those X-ray spectral line experiments in Berlin, I came to the same conclusion. Sometimes the electron seemed to behave like a particle and sometimes like a wave. It was very disconcerting."

He followed, keeping pace behind her. "I know all about your experiments with light emissions," he said.

"You amaze me, David. I've been here less than twenty-four hours, and you seem to know everything about me."

"As I told you yesterday, I've been following your work with the electron since last February, when you applied for admission to the Institute."

The close proximity of his body brought back the feeling of pleasure she had experienced yesterday outside his room. "Funny," she said. "I never dreamed that I was known outside my university laboratory in Berlin."

"Oh, yes. You're famous here." He laughed again. "At least with me."

He moved still closer. "I know this sounds presumptuous," he said, "but what I'm really interested in is the structure of the atom's nucleus. If we could solve the problem of the electron's structure, I think we could find a key to open the door into the nucleus."

She could feel his breath against her neck. "That's true," she said. "The electron is the key to everything."

"If my wave-particle theory is right, it could open the door to a whole new universe," he said. "There's a tremendous amount of energy locked inside the atom's nucleus, and if we could break through the electron's barrier we might possibly make use of it."

She thought of the impossible dream she had dreamed as a student in

Berlin. "If physics could find the key to open the door into the nucleus, it would give the world a completely new kind of energy."

"And it would be the same energy that lights the sun and the stars," he said.

The feeling of his breath against her neck was like a warm caress. "It was a hope of playing some part in making such discoveries that brought me to Göttingen," she said. "I know they will be made and that they will change the world, but I wonder whether they will take place in our lifetime."

"I think they will, Katherine. There are breakthroughs in physics every day, and at the rate we're going it will be only a few years before we solve the problem of the atom's nucleus. Certainly, it will happen in our lifetime."

Linz's audacity astonished her. She had often thought about the possibility of unlocking the atom's nucleus, but she had never dared to assert that she would ever make such a discovery herself. "If you're right, David," she said, "it would be like another Copernican revolution. It would change the world forever."

Again, he moved closer. "You and I are lucky to be studying physics right now," he said.

"The way you talk, everything seems possible."

"Everything is possible. But so far, my thesis is only a theory. And unless I find experimental proof for it, the whole thing will be meaningless."

"The Institute is filled with talented experimental physicists, David," she said. "You should have no trouble finding someone to do the experiments for you."

"It isn't just a question of talent," he said. "It's a question of vision. And vision is not something you can find in a textbook. It's a gift. I think you're the one who could carry out the experimental side of my doctoral thesis."

Again, with panic, she remembered the promise she had made to her father. "But that's ridiculous," she said. "I'm only a first-year student."

"What difference does that make? If you agreed to collaborate on my thesis, it would only mean that you would have the advantage of choosing your doctoral thesis a year ahead of the other first-year students."

It was true, and she could taste the opportunity like a temptation. "It's impossible," she said.

"But why?"

"I can't make this kind of choice, David. I've been here for only twenty-four hours, and it's too soon to know what kind of experiments I will do . . ." She left off as two students hurried into the lab, chatting animatedly.

"There's no hurry," he said. "I don't have to submit my thesis until November."

She remembered what he had said about the seminar on matter and wondered to herself at the impossible deadlines she now faced. "You must forgive me," she said. "It's almost lunchtime and Welchzeckhzaus is a fifteen-minute walk from here." Without waiting for a reply, she left him standing in front of the crystal spectrometer and started down the aisle toward the door.

"But what about the rest of our tour?" he called after her. "You haven't seen the library yet!"

For a moment, she could only think of her escape. "I can't tour the Institute today, David. Maybe tomorrow!" she said and hurried out into the hallway.

The exhilaration of her new-found freedom had gone, and her future, she realized, was now hopelessly entangled with the past she had left behind in Berlin.

She stopped at the top of the stairs and looked down at the empty stairwell below her. In all her fantasies, she had never imagined that her future as a scientist could be threatened by anything so small and petty as her father's anti-Semitism.

4

"DAMN!" David exclaimed as he hurried into the Institute. The clock at the end of the deserted ground-floor hallway read 3:46. Schwab hated people wandering in late to his lectures, and he was now forty-six minutes late! He took the steps up to the second floor two at a time. It had taken him most of the afternoon to do the simplest thing—fill a fountain pen with ink and giftwrap a box.

He came to a breathless halt outside the lecture hall.

Wilhelm Schwab's deep sonorous voice came booming through the door. "The pleasing beauty that the poet sees in the design of nature around him is the work of human imagination, but the ordered physical structure of the universe that the scientist sees is the result of intelligent observation!"

David quietly drew the door open and slipped into the back aisle. Dressed in his formal cutaway and winged-tipped collar, the old Professor Emeritus of experimental physics had turned away to chalk a diagram of Rutherford's classical atom on the blackboard behind him. Moving quickly, David hurried along the aisle and took a seat at the far end of the last row.

Schwab turned back from the board and smiled patiently at his captive audience of first-, second-, and third-year students. "The fashion nowadays among physicists is to seek answers in the imagination for what they cannot physically observe through experiment . . ."

David took a deep breath and sat forward. He could see only five women in the audience, all second- and third-year students. Then he caught sight of her—between two first-year students midway down the row where he sat. He smiled. Dressed in her outdated gray wool dress, with her blonde hair tied in a knot behind her head, she looked like a classical German Rhinemaiden. He sat back, fingering the box in his jacket pocket, and wondered if his gift of an American Schaeffer fountain pen would help break through her defenses. Outside of sharing meals with him at Welchzeckhaus, she had been avoiding him for the last four days—ever since last Monday, when he gave her a brief tour of the physics lab and asked her to collaborate on his doctoral thesis.

". . . I am speaking, of course," Schwab went on, "of the fashionable new science of quantum mechanics that has spread like a contagion through Europe following the Great War."

David glanced again at Katherine, wondering if she was shocked by what she was hearing. The old man's contempt for Niels Bohr's "quantum" description of the atom was famous. For ten years, ever since the publication of Einstein's General Theory of Relativity, Schwab had refused to abandon the classical physics he had taught for half a century here in Göttingen.

"The laws of science are derived from physical observation and physical proof!" Schwab exclaimed, reaching his peroration. "They are not merely the product of logical or creative wishful thinking!"

David looked down at the cheap gift-wrap Frau Reichshauer had given him for his package. In the small sleepless hours of last night, while he lay in bed wondering how he could break through Katherine's self-imposed isolation, he had thought about the old-fashioned fountain pen she had brought with her from Berlin. Then, like a missing term in an equation, he had remembered the pen his father had given him as a parting gift. It had remained in its black leather box for over a year, unused and, for all practical purposes, brand-new. He had opened the box only once: that afternoon on the ship's deck, as the *Bremen* steamed past the Statue of Liberty and he looked out at the New York skyline, he hoped, for the last time.

"And now," said Schwab, "as we begin a new academic year, I think we should welcome the first-year members of the Second Physics Institute." With a magnanimous gesture of welcome, he brought his ancient hands together and set off a chain reaction of applause.

David joined in and, to reinforce his encouragement of Katherine, whistled.

As she turned to look in his direction, an expression of surprise came over her beautiful face, just as he had hoped.

He grinned and waved.

Schwab stepped forward and signaled for silence. "Now in the few minutes remaining," he announced, smiling, "I think we should get acquainted with our new colleagues!"

David glanced again at Katherine, and saw that she had lowered her head and was staring at her folded hands. At supper last night she had spoken about the dread she always felt when she was called on to speak in public; and he had mentioned, in passing, Schwab's habit of questioning the students in the last row. She had obviously arrived late and had failed to get a seat in the center of the hall.

"Let's begin with the young man in the tweed jacket." Schwab pointed to a dark-haired fellow with thick gold-framed glasses. "Yes, you, young man. What is your name?"

The young man's reply was inaudible.

"Speak up! You must learn to speak up!"

"Schräder. Emil Schräder, Herr Professor."

"Good. Now give us a description of that troublesome little thing we've been talking about. Describe an atom for us, Schräder, if you can."

"An atom, Herr Professor—" Schräder hesitated, seeing the amused second- and third-year faces below him. "An atom is the smallest, the most elementary substance in the physical universe."

Laughter erupted around the room at the young man's schoolboy definition.

"Go on, Herr Schräder," said Schwab, enjoying the student's misery. "Now describe this smallest, most elementary substance in the universe!"

Schräder fidgeted with his pencil for a moment. "An atom is made up of a positively charged nucleus of protons, Herr Professor; and outside the nucleus, rings of negatively charged electrons." Again, he hesitated, waiting for laughter. There was none. He gained courage. "The mass of the atom is contained in the proton nucleus. The electrons move about the nucleus in orbits, and their orbital positions around the nucleus are determined by the size of their electrical charge. When an electron shifts its position to an orbit closer to the nucleus, energy is released in the form of light—photons. In structure and behavior," he added, "the atom can be compared to the solar system, with its planets in predetermined orbits around the sun."

"Thank you, Schräder." Schwab gave a satisfied smile at the young man's orthodox description. "Now . . ." He scanned the anxious first-year faces and pointed midway along the last row. "The young lady wearing the gray dress, do you agree with Schräder's description of the atom?"

Katherine looked up and made a nervous gesture to inquire if Schwab had directed his question at her.

"Yes, Fräulein, you!"

She said in a shaky voice, "I have nothing to add, Herr Professor."

"First, Fräulein, tell us your name!"

"Katherine von Steiner, Herr Professor."

"Tell us, Fräulein von Steiner, do you agree with Schräder's description of the atom?" the old man asked.

The second- and third-year students had turned around to search out the timid female voice in the last row.

She said, "It is the accepted description, Herr Professor."

Taking advantage of her embarrassment, Schwab called out, "We did not hear you, Fräulein!"

"Herr Schräder gave the accepted classical description, Herr Professor."

Two young men whispering together in the row below Katherine suddenly sniggered. Mentally, David shot a thought to Katherine across the room: Just tell the old fart you agree with Schräder and be done with it!

Schwab gave a patient, fatherly smile. "And do you agree with Schräder's classical description, Fräulein?"

For a moment, she stared in silence at the young men who had sniggered. Then, when she spoke again, her voice was decisive and audible. "No, Herr Professor, I do not agree with Herr Schräder's description."

"Indeed, Fräulein?" Schwab's eyebrows shot up. "Then perhaps you will explain why you disagree."

David sat back as Katherine lowered her eyes pensively for a moment. Unlike himself, it was her habit to weigh her words before speaking.

"Herr Schräder's description of the atom does not agree with the experimental evidence we now have, Herr Professor," she said. "In general, it does not agree with the work of Professors Einstein and Planck here in Germany, Professors Compton and Simon in America, or Professors Bohr, Kramers, and Slater in Denmark. Incomplete as it may be, all the recent experimental evidence indicates that Dr. Rutherford's solar model of the atom is grossly inaccurate. Moreover, if you apply the laws of classical dynamics to Rutherford's atom, you will find that it is, in fact, a physical impossibility . . ." She left off as a murmur rolled through the hall.

Schwab stepped in, "In other words, you would agree with Dr. Bohr's quantum description of the atom, the airy mental gymnastics we've been hearing from Denmark?"

Anger flamed in Katherine's eyes. "I agree with the proven evidence that has been published in recent years as a result of Professor Bohr's experimental work with spectral light emissions. I also agree with the theoretical conclusions we've been forced to draw from the experimental evidence proving the validity of Einstein's theories of general and special relativity. Most recently, the experimental evidence proving that the electron does not emit energy in the form of electromagnetic waves, but in discrete, random, and unpredeterminable quanta of light." She glanced up and caught David's eye. "I can speak, Herr Professor, from personal observation," she said. "Each different atom, from the simplest hydrogen atom to the more complex carbon and nitrogen atoms, emits its light with unique and distinct colors. Such agreement between theory and experiment cannot be the result of imaginative mental gymnastics, Herr Professor. So, based on experimental evidence, we can now say with absolute scientific certainty that the Rutherford solar-model description of the atom is inaccurate."

Faced with the astonished stares of the students around her she seemed, for a moment, to lose courage.

Then she forced herself to go on. "And we can also say that the mechanical laws of classical physics no longer adequately account for the behavior of the electron around the nucleus. Moreover, given the invisible scale of atomic processes, the time has come for scientists to stop asking what the atom looks like and start asking what the atom does . . .

"I believe the time has come for scientists to give up the search for a physical model of the atom and find a new mathematical description to account for its motion and its matter."

Her words brought back to David the thrill he had felt when he described his wave-particle theory of the electron and they spoke of unlocking the energy contained in the nucleus of the atom. He sat back, waiting for Schwab's defense.

It came in the form of mocking sarcasm. "If we are to believe Fräulein von Steiner," he said, "then we are wasting our time here." The patronizing smile that played around his mouth brought a nervous ripple of laughter.

Schwab stepped free from his lectern. "If we are to believe what Fräulein von Steiner says," he went on, "then we live in a universe without cause and effect, the motion of the stars and planets is nothing more than a series of random accidents, and the science of physics is nothing but a game of roulette!"

Raising her voice above a burst of open laughter, Katherine angrily retorted, "We have been forced before, have we not, Herr Professor, to rethink the world we live in?" She caught David's eye across the room. "After all, there were those who wanted to burn Copernicus as a heretic."

Schwab gave a patient, long-suffering sigh. "Do you believe in God, Fräulein von Steiner?" he asked.

Taken off guard, she looked around, suddenly bewildered. "Yes, Professor," she replied, retreating. "I believe in God."

"Then do you believe that the physical universe is the result of a divine game of chance?"

Her reply was lost under the laughter.

With a show of checking his watch fob, Schwab turned back to the lectern. "If my clock is not a victim of relativity, I believe we have gone over time. For those of you who will attend my lecture next week, we will review the history of classical thermodynamics . . ."

To avoid the crowd, David left his seat and hurried along the back aisle. As he reached the door, Katherine turned to look at him. Reading the remorse in her pale blue eyes, he pushed the door open and started down the deserted hallway. At the top of the staircase he stepped back against the wall to wait for her.

"Someone should warn her about Hirschfeld, too!" one of the second-year students called back to a colleague. "With looks like that, it would be a crime if she didn't make it through the first term."

David caught sight of Katherine as she came toward him, keeping close to the opposite wall, trying to avoid the stares of the students around her. "Katherine!" he called to her, but she ignored him and turned down the staircase. He caught up with her on the landing. "Congratulations!" he said in English. "You were terrific!"

She kept moving as she answered, in German, "I made a fool of myself."

"It was Schwab you made a fool of."

"I should have agreed with Schräder. I've made an enemy of Professor Schwab."

"Forget it. Schwab has no influence. That's the last you'll see of him." Two second-year students ahead of them on the staircase looked back with indignation. He laughed and lifted his voice. "Wilhelm Schwab is an academic fossil!" he exclaimed in English. "The old fart still believes there's a Kaiser!"

His impulsive irreverence brought a smile from Katherine. "Even so, I should have kept silent."

"You said what you believe. And what's more, you were right." He turned with her down the first-floor hallway in the direction of the building's entrance.

"I should keep my opinions to myself," she said. "If I fail even one course this first term, it's back to Berlin."

He suddenly saw a new opening through the walls of her reserve. "If you had Max Born on your side, no one would dare give you a failing mark." As they reached the door, he took hold of her arm and drew her to a halt. "How would you like to meet Born?" he asked.

She looked up at him with doubtful surprise. "Meet Professor Born?"

He grinned. "Sure! Why not?"

He gripped her arm to keep her from moving on. "I spoke to him yesterday and I reminded him about the papers you sent with your application. He said he would be glad to meet with you."

She opened her mouth to speak, but jostled by the students pressing from behind she allowed herself to be carried forward through the door. When he caught up, she had turned up the tree-lined sidewalk fronting the Institute, heading toward the Bürgerstrasse and the Old Town. She raised her hand to shade her eyes from the bright afternoon sunlight and said with sudden anxiety, "Why do you insist on involving yourself like this with my studies, David?"

"I've already told you. I think you're the one to do the experimental side of my doctoral thesis."

"And I've already told you that it's impossible." She looked around at the students passing them on the sidewalk and picked up speed. "Please forgive me, David. I must go now."

He thought of her flight last Monday morning from the physics lab. "I don't understand you, Katherine," he said. "I know you think I'm right about the wave-particle behavior of the electron, and this could be the chance of a lifetime for both of us. Who knows, maybe a Nobel Prize."

Wondering at his self-confidence, she shifted her books from her left to her right arm and tried to hurry ahead of him.

On a sudden impulse, he said in English, "Aside from the fact that I think you're a damn good scientist, I also think you're a beautiful woman. I said so the first day we met."

"Please speak German, David," she said, and looked away, rattled. "I don't understand your English."

He conceded the language, but not the argument. "You've been avoiding me for four days, Katherine, and I want to know if I've done something to offend you."

"No. You've done nothing to offend me." She made a quick right turn into the broad, busy Bürgerstrasse.

His frustration overtook him. "It's something to do with your father, isn't it? And the fact that I'm a Jew."

She slowed down abruptly and looked off toward the small wooded park on the opposite side of the street. "It was a mistake," she said, "my staying at Welchzeckhaus."

"Why? Because of me?"

"You're an American, David, and you don't understand what it means to be German."

"What's my being an American got to do with you and me?" he asked.

"You weren't in Germany during the war, and you don't know what's happening here now."

"Maybe not. But I do know that I've tried without success to make a friend of you."

"There's something I haven't told you, David." She sighed and looked down at the sidewalk. "My father has paid for my room and board at Welchzeckhaus only until Christmas."

"Until Christmas!"

"Yes. And when I go home for the holidays, he will decide if I can continue with my second semester."

"That's only four months!"

"If I don't do as he says, he will cut off all my money and I will have to go back to Berlin."

"What do you mean, do as he says?"

She walked in silence for a moment, cradling her books against her breast. "Before he left Göttingen, Papa placed some conditions on my staying here for my second semester." She hesitated and looked away.

"Go on. I'm listening."

"First of all, I must find another villa to room and board at."

He moved up alongside her. "And second?" he asked.

She sighed again. "Second, I must avoid any involvement, either personal or academic, with you."

It was his turn to keep silent.

"You made Papa furious the afternoon we arrived, David," she said. "It's stupid, I know, but he blames everything that has happened to Germany since the war on the Jews. He says that the Jewish bankers are responsible for the depression we are in, and he thinks that it was the Jewish politicians who sold out to the Allies at Versailles. He knows you're a Jew, David, and he has forbidden me to associate with you. Papa booked my room at Welchzeckhaus through his solicitor in Berlin, and he had no idea when we arrived that the villa was owned by a Jew."

"But that's no excuse for punishing you, Katherine. The mistake was his, not yours."

"What Papa is doing to me is wrong, I know," she said, "but he's not to blame for the hatred he now feels. He's an old-fashioned soldier, and for him the surrender at Versailles was a catastrophe."

"Hatred is hatred, Katherine, and there's no justification for it."

"You would have to be German to understand my father, David. For men like him, the Kaiser could do no wrong and he has found it impossible to blame Germany for the war."

"So he's made a scapegoat of Germany's Jews."

"Yes."

Her capacity for loyalty amazed him. He kept silent, and as they reached the corner of the Nikolaistrasse, she left the sidewalk and made a quick dash through the traffic toward the opposite side of the street.

He caught up as she turned north. "Germany started the war, Katherine, and she must take responsibility for her own disaster."

"That's easier said than done, David. For Papa, blaming Germany for the war would be like blaming God for natural disasters."

He thought of his own father in America and the way he blamed David for his choice of science as a career. "You love your father, don't you?" he said.

"I love the man, David, not his foolish prejudice. He has been a good father to me and he has suffered a lot since the end of the war. I owe him my loyalty now more than ever."

"It sounds like you're mistaking pity for love," he said.

"That's not true," she said a little too quickly. "It's a question of compassion."

Again, he walked in silence for a moment, thinking of his own father. An old-fashioned orthodox Jew, the old man had never forgiven him for choosing science over religion. "So it's money you're being threatened with," he said.

"Yes. It costs money to study in Göttingen and I have none of my own."

"You're not alone with this problem, Katherine," he said. "It was the same for me, my first year at the Institute. I ran out of money before the first term was finished, and I had to get a job selling shoes until my Rockefeller grant came through."

"It's pointless to think I could get a job, David. Unemployment in Germany is at a record high, and women are the last to be hired."

"But if you can hang on till Christmas, there's every chance you'll be able to get a government grant for your second term."

She picked up speed again as they passed the church of St. Nicholas. "A government grant would be impossible," she said. "The Weimar regime is almost bankrupt, and the government is not financing graduate studies in physics."

"You haven't asked for a grant. And with Max Born on your side, anything is possible."

She said with sudden vehemence, "I came here to get my doctorate in experimental physics, David, and I will not let anything turn me away from that. We cannot have anything more to do with each other." Without waiting for a reply, she made a quick right turn into the commercial section of the Lange Geismarstrasse.

By the time he caught up with her again, anger had overtaken his frustration. He said, keeping one step behind her, "You're crazy if you think I'm going to give up trying to convince you to work on my doctoral thesis. You're the only one I know who could carry out the experiments, and I will not let anything turn me away from that."

For a moment, she stared in silence at the ancient stone wall separating the old town from the new. Then she said, "I think your wave-particle theory is brilliant, David, and I'd like to work with you on it. But if I involve myself with you and my father finds out about it, he will force me to leave Göttingen."

"How would he find out? Berlin is four hundred miles away."

"Before we left Berlin, he wrote to Chancellor Hugenholtz and made arrangements for him to send regular reports on me."

"Reports?" he asked. "What kind of reports?"

"On the way I spend my free time and the kinds of friends I make."

Again, she picked up speed and left him behind.

He overtook her at the corner of the Weender Strasse where she was stalled by the bicycle traffic heading into the Old Town. He took hold of her arm, firmly. "Before you came here, I knew you were a brilliant experimental physicist. But what I didn't know was that we share the same vision of the future."

"Please, David," she pleaded, trying to free her arm, "let me go!"

"Not only that, I didn't know how beautiful you would be."

"You are destroying everything!" she shouted. "For both of us!"

He kept on as they continued together, walking through the granite rubble of a medieval wall. "Don't you understand that we're looking for the same thing!"

She started off down the shop-lined Weender Strasse, moving against the crowd of oncoming pedestrians, not noticing that she was forcing people to step aside for her.

Again, he caught up and reached out to take hold of her arm. "I'm learning more about the contradictions of matter and motion walking with you than I would from Professor Klein," he said. "By the way, where are you going?"

"Back to Welchzeckhaus."

"Then we're heading in the wrong direction," he said, looking up at the Marktplatz tower. He thought of the famous student tavern in the winecellars under the tower. "You've been here six days, you know, and you haven't even visited the Ratskeller."

"I've had other things to think about besides taverns."

"But the Ratskeller is where all the great scientific breakthroughs have been made—over warm steins of sweet dunkles Bier."

She tugged at his hand around her arm. "You're making a terrible mistake, David," she said and looked up fearfully at the ancient brick tower above them.

"Maybe," he said.

As they started across the square toward the Rathaus, he felt the tense resistance in the muscles of her arm suddenly relax.

5

GRATEFUL for the isolated corner table, Katherine took another sip from her stein of dunkles Bier. The Ratskeller's Dunkles was sweet—sweeter than the Dortmunder her father drank at home in Berlin. She sat back and surveyed the huge ancient cellar: the crowded tables, the graffiti scrawled on the grimy walls, and the low ceiling with its massive smoke-blackened rafters. Across the room, David left the bar where he had gone to buy cigarettes and began threading his way back through the tables. She sipped her beer again, feeling conspicuous in the prim dress she was wearing.

Again, David stopped to greet friends, three men she recognized as second-year physics students and a middle-aged man in a sober blue business suit.

David smiled as he drew on his cigarette. His dark eyes sparkled, he rose to his full height, and his deep laughter broke above the noise in the room. She watched him, envying his American spontaneity, his easy self-confidence, his innocent capacity for trust, as he leaned down to speak to the middle-aged gentleman. He spoke intently, gesturing with his cigarette for emphasis, then looked up and pointed in her direction. When the gentleman turned to stare at her, she averted her eyes.

Her gaze rested again on the smoke-blackened rafter above their table: on the student motto someone had painted there in old German calligraphy. "Extra Göttingen non est vita." She repeated the words to herself in German, "Outside Göttingen there is no life."

With a wave, David left the gentleman and hurried back to their table. Throwing his leg over his stool, he sat down. "You're in," he said in English.

She sighed, frustrated by his impulsive use of the incomprehensible American vernacular. "I'm in?" she asked. "I don't understand."

"That man I spoke to, do you know who he is?"

The darting excitement in his eyes alarmed her. She knew from photographs, at least, that the man was not Max Born. "No, I don't, David. Who is he?"

"That's James Franck, the physicist."

She sat back and gazed in awe at the famous experimental physicist. Along with Born and Hilbert, Franck was one of the Institute's triumvirate of world-renowned atomic scientists.

David hurried on, "He wants to read the research paper you sent from Berlin."

First Born, and now Franck. Dumbfounded, she opened her mouth to speak, but could say nothing.

Beaming, he took a sip from his stein. "Franck is one of the three professors who runs the seminar on matter," he said, "and if he likes the work you've been doing, it could be the basis for an invitation."

She recovered her composure and said with unconcealed anger, "And did you tell him that I will be forced to leave Göttingen if you continue to involve yourself in my studies?"

He took a long exasperated drag on his cigarette. "If you make good marks in your classes and show promise as an experimental physicist, nobody can force you to leave Göttingen, Katherine."

"It costs money to live here, David!"

"So? If Born and Franck approve of your experiments, all you will have to do is submit a formal application to the Institute's board of rectors for a grant."

The naïveté of his optimism amazed her. "This is Weimar Germany, not the United States. I'm a woman, not a man, and I've already told you that academic grants are virtually impossible to obtain."

Sipping his beer, he smiled at her playfully over his stein. "Nothing in Göttingen is impossible."

She remembered Frau Reichshauer's description of David last Monday at lunch: A veritable Wunderkind, she had called him. "For you that may be true, David. But not for me. I'm only here on borrowed time."

"What I'm saying is, with a little courage and determination you can make anything happen."

"Could you make money appear from nowhere?" she asked.

"Yes. Anything."

She smiled and sipped her beer. "I have met Americans before in Berlin, David, but I have never met an American like you."

"What do you mean, like me?"

"Impulsive, reckless, and self-confident."

He replaced his stein on the table and sighed. The look of pain that streaked across his eyes was the same look she had seen that first afternoon in the hallway at Welchzeckhaus. "It's unscientific, you know," he said, "to jump to conclusions. You know next to nothing about me."

"That's not true," she said.

"But how could you know anything? You've spent four out of six days avoiding me."

"I know that you were born in New York City, I know that you graduated summa cum laude from Princeton University. I also know that you came to Göttingen to study quantum theory. You came without money, and you starved for a year until you won a grant from the American Rockefeller Foundation."

"You've been asking questions," he said, sheepishly.

"I questioned Frau Reichshauer my second day at Welchzeckhaus."

"Did she tell you that I'm as stubborn as a mule and I don't give up without a fight?" He sat forward and said, "Listen to me, Katherine. Max Born has been directing my thesis from the very beginning. He thinks I've ventured out on thin ice with my wave-particle descripton of the electron, but he says that it's worth a try. He showed me your Berlin papers because he knew that I would run into trouble with the experimental side of my thesis." He reached out and took hold of her hand. "He also knows that you and I are both after the same thing—to solve the problem of atomic electron structure by looking at the atom's energy transitions. What you've told me about your observations in Berlin and your plans to look at the electron's wave characteristics may open the way to a mathematical description of the atom's real structure." He gripped her hand and said with sudden feeling, "That's exactly what I've been hoping to find since my undergraduate days at Princeton. Think of it! If I have the right theory and you have the right experiments, there's no end to what we could accomplish! What you have, and what I have can make everything possible. Forget your father's money, forget all the fears you brought with you from Berlin! The future is here with us—in Göttingen!"

Katherine looked up at the people crowded around the nearby tables, and everything seemed suddenly out of focus, unreal. The sound of the chatter and the laughter around her belonged, it seemed, to a different dimension in space from her own. She breathed to clear her head, and the sudden dizzying release she felt from the alcohol was like the vertigo she had always felt in high open places.

She remembered the nightmare that had plagued her during the last year: how she had found herself standing at the edge of a black and unfathomable abyss, trapped between the unknown threat that was pursuing her from behind and the unmeasurable darkness that lay ahead of her. "For the last year," she said, "since I decided to come to Göttingen, I've had a dream. It's always the same dream. It's nighttime, and I'm running through a forest. Someone, or something—I never know what it is—is following me. I come into a clearing, and I find myself on the edge of a steep cliff. I know that there's a path down the side of the cliff, but I can't see it, and I can't bring myself to take a step forward in the darkness. I can't go back, and I can't go forward. I just stand there, knowing that I will never be able to move."

"For a scientist, fear is the worst thing of all. Nothing ever happens in science without a leap in the dark."

"I've never taken a leap in the dark." She withdrew her hand and looked away with embarrassment. "Ever," she added.

"Then how did you get here?"

The question itself was the answer. Silent for a moment, she drew circles around the lip of her stein with the tip of her finger. She heard herself say, knowing that it was a declaration of surrender, "People tell me that you're the brightest, the most promising student of theoretical physics in your class—a Wunderkind, they call you."

"Do they now? And who told you that?"

"Frau Reichshauer, for one. She says you're the first in your class."

He lowered his eyes and asked defensively, "What else did Frau Reichshauer say about me?"

"She told me you have a father living in America, but that your mother is dead." She hesitated, wondering if she was venturing into a private and forbidden area. "She also said that you never write home to your father."

"No. I don't." He reached quickly for another cigarette.

"Why? Are you not fond of your father?"

He shrugged. "Not as fond as you are of yours."

"Has your mother been dead a long time?"

"She died when I was ten, and I was raised by my father. In America, I was what they call an 'only child.' "

"And what does your father do in America—his profession, I mean?"

"He's a teacher. He teaches at a university in New York City."

"I see." As he looked away, she again saw an expresssion of pain in his eyes. "I ask questions, David, because you accused me of knowing nothing about you," she said.

He turned back and said guiltily, "I'm sorry. You're right." Shifting uncomfortably on his stool, he pointed to her stein. "By the way, how do you like the Ratskeller's Dunkles?"

"I like it. It's much sweeter than the beer my father keeps at home. The Dortmunder Pilsner he drinks in Berlin is bitter."

The word *bitter* brought a smile. He reached into his jacket pocket and brought out a small gift-wrapped box. "Congratulations," he said, and he placed the box in front of her on the table.

The sudden and unexpected gesture took her by surprise. She gazed at the gift-wrapped box—the red ribbon and bow and the gay wrapping. For lack of anything better, she said, "Congratulations for what?"

"For disobeying your father and staying in Göttingen. It's something I hope will make the next four months a little easier." He grinned shyly and lifted his stein.

"You shouldn't give me gifts, David," she said, nonplussed. "It isn't necessary."

"Necessary?" he laughed. "If it was necessary, it wouldn't be a gift! Go on. Open it."

She went on staring at the gift, feeling suddenly trapped between an old and familiar instinct to refuse and a new desire to accept.

He laughed. "What's wrong?"

As she reached out to grasp the ribbon, she recalled again her father's words on the train that afternoon: *The men you will meet here in Göttingen are not like the young men you have known in Berlin.*

Seeing her hesitation, he said, "I take it you've never received a gift from a man before."

When she looked at David's eyes, she saw no hint of sarcasm—only frank and boyish pride. She pulled the ribbon and freed the bow. As she drew back the paper, she knew at once what was inside the handsome leather case. "A fountain pen," she said, and lifted the lid.

"I saw the old one you brought from Berlin. I thought you needed a new one."

"It's beautiful, David," she said, removing the sleek black pen from its elastic bindings.

"It's a Schaeffer," he said, proudly watching her turn the pen in her fingers. "But you can use ordinary German ink." He took a small notepad from his pocket. "Here." He placed the pad in front of her on the table. "Give it a try. I've already put ink inside."

She unscrewed the cap. The point, she saw, was made of gold. Thinking of his struggle to make ends meet here in Germany, she said, "You should not have spent your money like this."

He laughed. "Forget it! It cost nothing, really!"

"Pens like this are very expensive," she said, puzzled by his sudden discomfort.

"I hope you don't expect me to take it back."

"You must."

"I can't take it back. I've already put ink in it." He smiled and pointed to the notepad. "Go ahead, try it."

She thought of the adjectives she had found to describe him over the last six days: handsome, brilliant, impulsive, reckless, unpredictable, stubborn, self-confident, innocent . . . and now foolishly generous. It was useless, she realized, to argue. She pressed the pen's point to the paper, then wrote, slowly and carefully, two English words: Thank you.

For a moment, the noise of voices and laughter around them was like silence. His hand moved across the table, slowly, but without hesitation. As the tips of his fingers came to rest on her hand, she felt a sensation of exciting warmth spill through her neck and face.

He said, "Tell me something. Tell me what you really imagine for yourself when you dream about your future."

"But I've already told you what I dream about."

"I don't mean your dreams as a scientist. I mean your dreams as a woman."

She looked up with surprise. "They are one and the same thing."

"You mean you never dream about marriage and a family?"

She hesitated, remembering what she had often secretly imagined during those fearful nights last year in Berlin, when she lay awake imagining the future as a scientist awaiting her: a future she would have to face alone, without the comforting help of any other human being. The thing she had feared most about her career as a scientist had been the loneliness of its success, for she had never imagined that success would come without single-minded determination.

She said, evasively, "Sometimes, when I'm alone, I picture what it would be like to be a wife and mother."

He moved his fingers gently over her hand. "And what do you picture for yourself?"

It was the alcohol, she was sure, that freed her to answer. "I picture a world where everything is perfect . . . a world where a man and a woman love each other with equality. Not a marriage like my parents', where love is measured by a woman's service to her husband, but a marriage where dreams can be shared."

He drew her hand toward him across the table. "Tell me this," he said. "What's the most wonderful thing you imagine for yourself when you dream about accomplishing something as a physicist? What's the most impossible thing you can imagine yourself ever achieving?"

Again, she hesitated, wondering where he was leading. "We talked about it in the lab the other day," she said. "Sometimes I picture myself as the scientist responsible for finding the key to unlock the atom's nucleus."

"Go on," he urged. "And what do you imagine yourself doing if you find the key to unlock the atom's nucleus?"

She heard herself say, "Sometimes I secretly imagine that I will find wonderful uses for the energy that's locked inside the atom's nucleus . . . the power, for instance, to light whole cities and to drive ships across the seas . . ." Before the words were out of her mouth, she heard the absurdity of her confession and felt the blood rush to her face. She looked away, ashamed of herself. She had never dared speak of such things to anyone before. "Now you see why I'm reluctant to talk about my ambitions," she said.

He nodded. "Now I'll tell you the kind of foolishness I dream about." He looked off for a moment toward the smoky ceiling, then chuckled. "At the very outer limits," he said in English, "when I let myself go the whole way and dream the impossible dream, I imagine myself as the theoretical physicist who will one day work out a complete theory of the atom's nuclear structure—a theory that will allow the world's experimental scientists, like you, to harness the atom's nuclear energies." He turned to her and smiled.

She thought of the offer he had made to collaborate on his doctoral thesis and the success that could be theirs if his theory proved to be right. Despite what she had always believed about success, it could be the beginning of a long and productive collaboration. "It's foolish of us to talk like this," she said, and withdrew her hand. "For scientists, wishful thinking does no good. We have to be realists."

"Perhaps. But all scientists secretly like to imagine the impossible dream for themselves; and the ones who don't dream impossible dreams never accomplish anything."

High up in the Town Hall tower above them, the bell began to toll the hour. "It's five o'clock," she said, "and Frau Reichshauer's Abendessen is always promptly at six."

She returned the fountain pen to the case, then looked around at the faces of the students at the nearby tables. The worst part of her father's surveillance in Berlin had been her inability to identify who was watching her. "Before we leave, David, I must ask you to promise me something."

"Promise you what?" he asked.

"Promise me you'll say nothing to anyone about our conversation here this afternoon."

"All right. I promise."

She hesitated, then said, "And promise me that after today you will stop trying to involve yourself in my studies."

He stared at the pencase and said nothing.

"We can be friends at Welchzeckhaus," she said, "but if I continue to associate with you in public, my father will find out and force me to leave Göttingen."

He shook his head and sighed. "Okay," he said. "After this, I promise not to involve myself with you outside Welchzeckhaus. I think you're making a big mistake, but in public we'll treat each other as strangers." He got to his feet. "Are you ready?"

The dizziness came back as she stood up and reached for her books. "Your dunkles Bier has made me drunk."

"One stein?" He started to take hold of her arm to guide her through the maze of crowded tables, but withdrew his and motioned her forward.

Halfway to the door, she heard a voice call out across the room, "David! Herr Linz!"

"Hello, Pauli!" he called back in English and waved to a young colleague seated at one of the crowded tables across the room.

Wolfgang Pauli, she remembered, was the physicist who had submitted David's name for membership in the seminar on matter. He made a gesture to David with his thumb and forefinger, the same American gesture of approval Katherine had sometimes seen David make when talking to other students. She looked down, suddenly ashamed of the ugly dress she was wearing, the dress her mother had bought her in Berlin. Acting on an impulse to escape, she left David behind and hurried toward the tavern door.

He caught up with her on the cellar steps outside, as she started up to the Marktplatz. "Stop worrying about those kinds of things," he said and took her arm again.

This time, she understood the meaning of his American vernacular. She smiled to herself, pleased that he could so easily read her mind.

As they came out into the market square, she caught sight of the warm gold reflection of late afternoon light from the rooftops of the ancient Fachwerkhäuser opposite them. She paused for a moment to listen to the sound of the Goosegirl fountain splashing patiently in the shadows under the ancient Town Hall, then continued on toward the southeast corner of the square. Students hurried by toward the four streets leading out of the square, homeward bound. A delicious feeling of peace came over her. She took a deep breath, feeling for the first time that she truly belonged here.

She said, as they left the square and turned down the narrow cobble-stoned Rote Strasse, "Thank you again for the beautiful gift."

"You're welcome. Take it as a sign of my belief in your future," he said.

She thought of his reluctance to talk about his father in America. "I've told you things about myself this afternoon, David, that I've never told anyone before," she said. "But you refuse to reciprocate."

"Okay," he said. "What would you like to know?"

"I'd like to know more about your father."

"He's sixty-three years old, he lives in New York, and he's a teacher," he said.

"You've told me that already."

"It goes without saying, he's also a Jew. In fact, he's a very religious Jew. He teaches Judaism. He's a Talmudic scholar at a Jewish university in New York. Yeshiva University, it's called."

"I take it you don't approve."

"He's the one who doesn't approve." Then, as if she had said something that turned a key and opened a door, he went on, impulsively. "For my father, religion and science don't mix. He wanted me to be like him, a biblical scholar, but I wanted to be a scientist. That's why we don't communciate anymore. What he wanted from me was impossible."

She smiled. "I thought impossible was a word you never used. And if you're afraid of my questions, how am I going to find the answers?"

He said nothing.

"Besides, what good is a scientist without curiosity?"

He sighed, slowing his pace. "Or a woman without intuition," he said and started again to reach for her arm.

Woman: she repeated the word to herself as they turned down the broad shop-lined Kurze Geismarstrasse. He had used the word to describe her without hesitation, she realized, and she felt an exhilarating rush of freedom.

A light went on in a window two shops ahead—a window displaying fashionable new dresses. As they drew alongside the window, she forced him to stop. "Do you like that one?" she asked, pointing at a mannequin beckoning to them from the window. The dress the mannequin wore was a stylishly tailored knee-length dress of pale blue gabardine.

"You mean, the dummy or the dress?"

"The dress, David," she chided.

He stepped back and assessed her dress. "For you, a dress like that would be a leap in the dark," he teased.

Katherine thought of the thousand Marks her mother had sent her from Berlin. "I'd like to know just how much a dress like that costs here in Göttingen," she said with a feeling of recklessness.

"I'd say two thousand, give or take a few Marks."

"Oh, much more. Closer to three, I'm sure."

He said in English, "We're standing here talking theory. We should approach the problem like serious scientists. Verify the theory with experiment."

She took a quick, apprehensive breath. "It would take only a minute to verify which of our theories is the correct one."

He hesitated, then reached out and grasped her arm. "That's true. Even less than a minute," he said, and opened the shop door for her.

6

As the bell sounded down the hallway, Professor Max Born, the director of the Second Physics Institute, turned from the blackboard and took his seat behind the desk. "At next week's lecture on quantum mechanics we will take up the subject of Henry Mosele's work with X-ray spectral lines," he said, closing his notes. "In the meantime, I want you to read Max von Laue's Nobel Prize paper on X-ray crystallography."

As the group of twenty-five students began gathering up their books and papers, David looked back from his desk and smiled at Katherine. She returned the smile and looked away, thinking of the letter she had received that morning from her father congratulating her on the report he had received from Chancellor Hugenholtz. "I am pleased with your progress," he had written, "and if you continue to maintain your good record I see no reason why you shouldn't return to Göttingen for a second semester." Warning her of the falling value of the deutsche mark, and reminding her of the promises she had made to him, he had sent another five thousand Marks to help pay her expenses until Christmas.

It was a game of chance she was playing with her future, she knew, but so far he was ignorant of her friendship with David.

"Before you go," Born called out, "I have an announcement to make!" He waited for the noise in the room to subside, then said, "Today is Friday, the eighteenth of September, and the time has come to announce this year's invitations to the seminar on matter."

Katherine sat back as a hush fell over the room. In the three weeks since her arrival, certain that she would be overlooked when the time came to issue invitations, she had tried to forget the seminar.

"First of all, let me remind you of how we go about selecting new members for the seminar," Born said. "Each year, a list of prospective candidates is drawn up by seminar members. The list is presented to myself and Professors Franck and Hilbert, and the choice of new members is then made on the basis of the candidates' academic records. This year, after careful consideration, we have decided to elect two new members." He opened a folder on his desk and took out a single sheet of paper.

Born cleared his throat, then said in a sonorous voice, "I am pleased to announce that the first invitation to the seminar on matter will be offered to the second-year student Rudolf Feis. Herr Feis is a student of theoretical physics, and his recommendation for the seminar was put forward by his colleague Ernst Kuhn."

There was an excited murmur, and then the room burst into applause.

Katherine joined in the applause, watching with admiration as Feis shyly accepted the congratulations of his colleagues.

Born waved for silence, then said, "As you know, invitations to the seminar on matter are rarely awarded to first-year students. Nonetheless, we have weighed this student's academic record and have decided to award the second invitation to a first-year student of physics. She is Katherine von Steiner, and the invitation is based on the work she did with spectral light emissions at the University of Berlin."

This time, the hush that fell over the room seemed to last for an eternity.

Unable to comprehend what she had heard, Katherine could only stare at the open textbook in front of her. It's impossible, she thought.

When she looked up, there were expressions of surprise and astonishment on the faces around her.

"Fräulein von Steiner is a student of experimental physics," said Born, "and her recommendation was put forward by her second-year colleague David Linz."

Katherine saw David had turned toward the window.

As the room once again erupted with applause, she remembered the promsise he had made not to publicly involve himself in her studies. That was two weeks ago, and since then he had gone out of his way to keep their friendship a secret.

"If the candidates accept the offer of their invitations," Born said, "the public announcement will be made in next Sunday's edition of the *Göttinger Zeitung*."

In the next instant, she thought again of the promise she had made to her father and the falling value of the deutsche mark. Without an additional loan from her father, she could not hope to survive until Christmas.

"You are to be congratulated, Fräulein von Steiner," she heard one of the students say. "Membership in the seminar on matter will now open all the doors for you at the Institute."

"Karl's right!" another student broke in. "And as a first-year student, it will bring you instant recognition!"

"Yes," she said, but all she could think of was the price she would have to pay for David's public involvement in her studies. Gathering up her books, she left her desk and joined the students making their way out the door.

Meanwhile, as David lingered at his desk, waiting for the room to empty, he looked out at the darkening sky over Göttingen, wondering how he would explain to Katherine why he had broken his promise. It was last week, when it became clear that she would be overlooked as a candidate for the seminar on matter, that he had decided to break it; he had gone to Max Born and had proposed her as a candidate for membership. It was a gamble with her future he had had to take, for without his recommendation she would have been forced to wait another year for an invitation.

As the air around him reverberated with distant thunder, he took his briefcase from the floor and hurriedly left the room.

Katherine was waiting for him when he reached the crowded hallway. "We can't talk here," she said. "There are too many people."

He could see the anger blazing in her eyes. "The physics lab is always empty at this hour," he said. "We can talk there."

She turned away without saying anything and started off down the hall.

When he entered the lab, she was standing in the aisle between the worktables. "You made a promise, and you broke it," she said.

He thought of the idiotic charade they had been forced to play these last two weeks to maintain the secrecy of their friendship: their stolen conversations in the hallways between classes; the casual encounters they had arranged in the library during lunch hour. "The promise I made to you was absurd, Katherine," he said. "Membership in the seminar is important to your success at the Institute, and if I had kept silent you would have had to wait another year for an invitation. You and I have work to do, and we can't go on pretending that we are strangers."

"What you did was unforgivable," she said. "If Papa learns that you were responsible for my invitation to the seminar, he will refuse me more funds and I will have to leave."

He started toward her at the worktables. "Your father met me once, Katherine. It's ridiculous to think that he would still remember me."

"Obviously, you don't know my father," she said as she tossed the books she was carrying on the worktable and went to the window.

He said with exasperation, "You're letting him control your life."

"There's nothing I can do," she said.

This time, it was the hopelessness in her voice that silenced him. He left the worktables and joined her at the window where she stood looking out at the approaching storm. It was the first storm of autumn, and there were dark clouds rolling down from the mountains to the northeast— from the direction of Berlin. "I don't understand you, Katherine," he said. "What is it you're really afraid of?"

"What do you mean, really afraid of?"

"You came to Göttingen with a wonderful dream, but so far you've done nothing to make it a reality."

"I'm doing everything I can, David."

"You could have made your decision about carrying out the experiments for my doctoral thesis. If you dream of becoming a great experimental physicist," he said, "you have to be prepared to take chances and trust someone besides your father."

"I can't afford to take chances, David."

"Then you will never become a scientist. You dream of the future, Katherine, but you live with your father in the past."

Suddenly, far off beyond the rooftops of the town, a ragged bolt of lightning streaked across the sky. She opened her mouth to speak, but the ominous thunder silenced her.

"The truth is, Katherine, it isn't the loss of your father's money you're afraid of," said David, thoughtfully. "It's his rejection. You're a nineteen-year-old child, Katherine, and if you don't free yourself from this need for your father's approval you will remain a child for the rest of your life."

"That isn't true!" she cried, and ran from the room.

7

KATHERINE stared at her reflection in the darkened glass of the oriel window above her desk, counting the seconds, listening to the relentless hammering of the rain against the leaded glass. As a girl, when she watched electrical storms approach in the skies over Berlin, she would calculate the distance of the approaching storm by measuring the time between the lightning and the thunder to distract herself from her terror of the storms.

She drew the collar of her velvet dressing gown close to her neck, remembering again how, during the most violent storms, she would always run to her father and take refuge in his arms.

This time, the thunder rattled the panes in the window.

She looked down at the letter she had received from him that morning.

"I am pleased with your progress," she read for the hundredth time, "and if you continue to maintain your good record I see no reason why you shouldn't return to Göttingen for a second semester."

Another bolt of lightning shimmered across the desktop, illuminating her father's monogrammed stationery. She tore the letter into four pieces, and when the thunder had passed, she looked up again at her face in the dark glass above her desk.

The words David had said to her that afternoon in the physics lab came back to her: "Katherine, it isn't the loss of your father's money you're afraid of. It's his rejection."

He was right, of course, but how could he know what it was like to grow up knowing that you could never take the place of the son your father had never had.

She had wanted more than anything to become a member of the prestigious seminar on matter; but if she accepted Born's invitation, David's recommendation would be published in the local paper and her father would learn about it in Berlin.

Again, the words David had said as she raced from the lab came back.

She held her breath as lightning struck again, pondering the goals she had set for herself in Berlin. She had come to Göttingen to become a professional scientist, nothing more, but the first discovery she had made—the very day she arrived—had nothing whatever to do with molecules or atoms.

Her eye came to rest on the leather pencase, the gift David had given her two weeks ago at the Ratskeller.

In all her wildest dreams, she had never imagined that the answers to all the important questions would be found not in the mind, but in the heart.

The truth was, she had come to Göttingen dreaming one dream and had found herself dreaming quite another. It was not part of the plan she had so carefully made for herself, but she had, for the first time in her life, fallen in love.

She looked up to see a brilliant bolt of lightning race down the sky. It forked, taking the shape of what looked like a serpent's tongue, and struck somewhere at the edge of town. Only one second passed before the thunder came.

She looked back down at the pencase on her desk, thinking of David's reckless generosity. Like herself, he had turned his back on his father to win a doctorate at the Second Physics Institute; and like her, he had come to Göttingen almost penniless.

She reached across the desk, took the pencase, and lifted its lid under the light of her desk lamp.

As she opened the case and took hold of the pen to remove it from the elastic bindings, the cushion detached itself from the case.

There, hidden under the cushion—untouched it seemed—was a folded page of yellowed stationery. A feeling of dread came over her as she stared at the cheap onionskin paper: for she could see that the handwriting on the opposite side of the paper was small and ragged—the shaky handwriting of an old person. She took the page from the pencase and unfolded it.

From the date at the top of the handwritten page—July 12, 1919—and from its two opening words, she knew at once who had written the letter.

Dear Son,

It would be senseless to pretend that I am not grieved by your decision to seek a career in Germany. You have known since the end of the war that I have been afraid of what is now happening in the country of my birth. But you are twenty-one now, and the responsibility for your future must be your own. I can only pray that in choosing science as a way of life you do not thereby reject the wisdom of your religion. I have said it often in the past: human reason can never supply all the answers in your quest for knowledge. Gifted scientist that you are, you will one day find yourself at the end of your powers to reason. Hopefully, you will then realize with humility that the answers to all the ultimate human questions can only be found in the darkness of blind faith. Be that as it may, I realize that you are leaving your home in America to free yourself from a religion whose moral, intellectual, and religious restrictions you have found intolerable, and to free yourself from an old-fashioned Jewish father who refuses to make any compromise with the wise, ancient commandments of his orthodox Judaism. I cannot say that I regret my efforts to intervene in your decision. But with all my heart, I pray that you will find in Germany and in science the peace you have failed to find here in America and in Judaism. Once again, I want to offer you what money I have as a help for your support in Göttingen. I offer it as a gift, free of any conditions. I give you this fountain pen in the hope that you will write to a loving father from the country of his birth. I pray, most especially, that you will always go with God, whatever path you choose to follow in this life.

Your loving father,

Jacob

Katherine looked up again at her face reflected in the dark glass. The letter, she realized, had remained under the pencase cushion since David left America for Germany . . . untouched and unread.

She remembered the one conversation they had had about his father and his curious reluctance to speak of their relationship.

She returned the pen and its cushion to the box, placed the letter inside, and closed the lid. By the clock on the bureau, it was 9:35. At this hour, David would be studying in his room.

Leaving her desk, she secured the belt around her dressing gown and quietly opened her door.

I will leave the pencase outside his door and say nothing about the letter, she thought as she hurried down the hallway.

Bending to place the pencase on the floor outside David's door, she heard a faint noise from inside the room: back and forth, back and forth, the rhythmical creaking of his rocking chair. To her surprise, there was no light visible through the crack under his door.

She stood listening to the steady creaking noise of David's rocking chair, and suddenly remembered the look of despair on his face that afternoon when she hurried out of the lab.

Suddenly frightened, she reached up and knocked, softly.

"Ja?" came his faint response.

A light went on in the room as she opened the door, and a chilling draught of air swept past her. "I'm sorry," she said, "I . . ." She left off, seeing the open window behind his desk.

He stood up and said with embarrassment, "Come in, Katherine."

"Forgive the intrusion," she said, softly closing the door behind her. "I came to return this to you."

"But you're not intruding." He caught sight of the pencase in her hand. "I'm sorry about the broken promise, Katherine," he said, making an awkward gesture in the air. "It was stupid of me. I knew when I went to Born that my recommendation would become public knowledge."

The guilt she saw in his dark eyes was like the confession of a small child. "I didn't come here to talk about that, David." She took a step forward and held out the pencase. "I only came to return this."

He said, ignoring the pencase, "I wanted to tell you about my recommendation, but I wasn't sure you would get the invitation, and I was afraid you would never speak to me again."

"You must open this," she said. "There's something inside you must see."

He came forward with uncertainty and took the case.

As he opened the lid and took out the letter, she hurried to explain. "It was hidden under the cushion. I found it by accident."

Another gust of wind blew a spray of rain through the open window. Watching his eyes move down the page, she read the kaleidoscope of his changing feelings: shock turned to realization, realization to fear; and finally, as he folded the letter, the fear gave way to guilt and shame.

He looked up, helplessly. "So now you know that it was a gift from my father," he said.

"Yes, David. But what I don't understand is why you have said so little about him all this time. Especially since I've told you everything about my father."

He turned away and placed the pencase and the letter on his desk. "I wanted to tell you about my father," he said, "but I thought that, being a Christian, you wouldn't understand."

"You've asked me to trust you, David. But trust works both ways."

He looked up at the window. "My father is seventy-one. He and my mother were both born in Germany . . . in East Prussia near the town of Danzig." He began walking slowly, thoughtfully, back and forth across the room. "In 1896, two years before I was born, they emigrated to America. They had been brought up as very strict Jews, but when they came to America they were forced to give up a lot of the old ways . . ."

He paused at the desk and looked down at his father's letter.

"In Germany, before the turn of the century, my father had been a well-known biblical scholar in Danzig, and when they moved to America he found a job teaching the Talmud at New York's Yeshiva University . . ."

He began pacing again.

"I was eight when my mother suffered her first stroke. She lived for a year. After she died, my father went back to the old ways—to the orthodox Judaism he had practiced in Germany . . ."

He stopped again and looked at the letter on his desk.

"It was after my mother died that he tried to force me to practice Judaism as he did. He wanted me to follow in his footsteps and become a biblical scholar, a rabbi."

As lightning struck above the nearby rooftops, he left the desk and began pacing back and forth again.

"You've read the letter, so you realize he doesn't approve of my being a scientist," he said, running his hand over his face. "Or of the fact that I came to this country to study."

She glanced at the yellow onionskin page on his desk. "He said that he's afraid of what is happening here in Germany."

"He's a prophet of doom. He thinks that Europe is heading for another war, and that Germany will again be at the center of it."

"My father thinks the same thing."

"Maybe they're right." He looked up as he passed her. "But Germany is where much of the new atomic science is being done."

He paused to look at the window, oblivious, it seemed, of the fact that it was open and the rain was blowing in on his papers. "In the year I've been here, my father has written me at least five times, offering to send money," he said. "I've never replied to his letters. I couldn't take my father's money and refuse to accept his religion along with it."

"It's the same with me," she said. "I couldn't take Papa's money and refuse to keep the promises I've made to him."

He stopped and looked at her. "It's funny," he said. "We've been plagued all along by the same problem—our loyalties to our fathers."

Another gust of wind swept through the open window, but David seemed preoccupied with some inward and, so far, unspoken pain. "I haven't talked about these things to anyone," he said, finally. "I grew up the only Jewish kid in an immigrant Christian neighborhood. I grew up both hating and loving my father. I loved him as a father, but I hated him for what he stubbornly refused to give up. I hated him for being an old Jew in a black coat." Like the lightning from the window behind him, anger exploded in his dark eyes. "I had no choice but to leave America. If I had stayed in the States, he would have been there—always—to accuse me of failing." He looked away. "Failing not him," he said, "but God."

Chilling wind and rain swept through the window, and Katherine reached up to draw the lapels of her dressing gown closer to her neck. As if realizing for the first time that the window was open, he hurried to close it. "I'm sorry," he said, looking around at the rain-soaked papers on his desk. "I must be crazy."

For a moment, the only sound in the room was that of the rain beating like tiny stones against the glass. As thunder struck again, the lamp on the desk flickered twice, then went out. Katherine blinked to focus her vision, but the darkness around her was absolute. For a moment, unable to see, she could only sense his presence in the room. In the silence, she heard the steady rhythmical sound of his breathing. Then her eyes adjusted to the darkness, and she saw his body silhouetted against the faint light from the window. As he came toward her, she moved backward until she came up against the door.

"Please stop running from me, Katherine," he murmured. "I cannot let you go."

The helplessness she heard in his voice touched her heart and moved her soul. Until now, she had thought that his confidence was invincible.

She felt the magnetic pull of their physical closeness, and this time, it drew her forward with a force she had never before experienced.

"David," she said, and touched him on the shoulder.

For a moment, startled by her unexpected gesture, he kept his face averted and said nothing. Then, as lightning illuminated the room, he turned and opened his arms.

Perhaps it was the suddenness of his own gesture, but a feeling of terrific vertigo came over her. She looked up at the faint outline of his face in the darkness, then she relaxed her body into his arms and closed her eyes.

Up to now, she had only imagined what a man's body would feel like against her own. She had never, until now, felt a man's lips touch the skin of her neck—or felt the wonderful force of a man's arms suddenly surrounding her.

8

"Now remember," said Frau Reichshauer, as she followed David and Katherine to the front door. "Today is Sunday, neither one of you has any lectures to attend, and I want you to take the entire day off."

"We're going to hike up to the Gästehaus Bürgerbräu," David said, adjusting the scarf around Katherine's neck, "and we promise not to be back before nightfall."

"Good." Frau Reichshauer stepped forward to open the door. "You've had a difficult night, my dear Katherine, and what you need is a day of sunshine and fresh air."

The old woman stepped forward and kissed Katherine gently on the forehead. "You're lucky to have a friend like David, my dear; together you will find a solution to this problem."

As they turned through the door, Frau Reichshauer handed David the brown paper bag she was carrying. "Here's a little snack I had the cook prepare for you," she said. "There're some chicken sandwiches and some apples inside."

"Thanks, Frau Reichshauer." David placed the bag inside his knapsack. "We'll stop and have a late lunch on the hillside."

She stood at the door and watched as they turned east, arm-in-arm, down the Lange Geismarstrasse. In the two weeks that had passed since Katherine accepted Professor Born's invitation to the seminar, she had waited for her father's response. Certain that her days in Göttingen were now numbered, she had opened herself to David's affections. But she was like a child trying to find her way in the darkness, for she had never allowed herself to experience the power of any man's love save her father's. Sadly, though, her voyage into the uncharted territory of masculine affections had been but a brief adventure, for last night her father had telephoned and had ordered her to return to Berlin, threatening to disown her if she again refused to obey him.

Praying that David's courage would triumph over Katherine's obedience, Frau Reichshauer watched until they turned the corner, then went in.

David and Katherine left town by way of the new Herzberger Land-strasse, then turned up the well-worn students' footpath through the forested foothills toward the Hain mountain east of Göttingen.

When David stopped to get his breath and looked back through the dense pine trees, Katherine had fallen behind. Using the limbs of the smaller trees to brace herself on the slippery carpet of dead needles, she came laboring up the steep hillside. He could hear her breath punctuating the deep forest silence.

"Don't give up!" he called to her. "It's only a few more yards!" He pointed toward a rocky limestone promontory jutting out from hillside. "We'll stop and rest up there!"

She stopped and caught her breath. "You promised a hill, David!" she called back. "Not a mountain!"

"Compared to the Zugspitze, this is a hill!" he laughed.

She shook her head and began to climb again.

He lowered his knapsack from his shoulder and rested it against the trunk of a nearby birch tree. She looked small and fragile in the oversized red plaid jacket, the baggy trousers, and the leather boots she had borrowed that morning. He wanted to go back down, take her in his arms, and carry her the rest of the way, but her exhaustion, he knew, was not from the climb. Last night, an hour after supper, she had come to him with the news she had just had from her father. In a fury of indignation, he had accused her of disgracing the von Steiner name and had ordered her to return at once to Berlin, saying that he had closed her bank account in Göttingen. Moreover, to reinforce his demands for her immediate and unconditional surrender, he had threatened to disown her if she once again disobeyed him. It was a threat she had not counted on, and it had devastated her.

"It's no longer just a question of money, David," she had said. "It's a question of losing the most important thing of all—my family."

In the small hours of the night, pondering the choices she now faced, he had realized that she had courageously taken her leap in the dark, only to find that she was now hopelessly trapped between the past she had left behind in Berlin and the future she had found here in Göttingen.

After she came to him with the news, he finally told her about the cable he had sent two weeks ago to his father in America: a cable asking to borrow eight hundred dollars. It would be enough, he had said, to support the two of them for the rest of the year.

He reached out as she came toward him. "Give me your hand," he said. "It's just a few more yards, then we'll stop and rest."

The moisture on her cheeks, he saw, was not from sweat; and when she took his hand, her fingers, though damp, were cold. "This was a mistake," she said. "I shouldn't have come."

He knew she wasn't speaking of their hike up the Hain. He gripped her hand, threw the knapsack over his shoulder, and drew her up the last few yards toward the rocky clearing beyond the trees. He could sense from the weight of her body that she had given up more than her will to climb. It was as if he was pulling against a magnetic force dragging her backward—all the forces, he realized, that still bound her to the past: her self-abnegating love of her father and a lifetime of obedience.

He thought of her reply last night, when he told her of his cable to America: "You don't know if your father will send the money; and besides, eight hundred dollars will only be enough to support yourself. Thank you for the offer, but I cannot accept."

He had tried to reason with her; but she was a hundred times more stubborn than he, and it was pointless to argue when her mind was made up.

They left the forest and came out onto the rocky clearing at the end of the tapering limestone escarpment. She had told him earlier of her fear of heights, and remembering that, he reached out and drew her close to him. "We're only a short distance from the Gästehaus," he said.

Ten feet away, where the sloping forest came to an abrupt end, she caught sight of the escarpment's precipitous cliff-face. "David," she said, and drew back.

"Relax. We'll keep to the center, away from the cliffs." Without waiting for a reply, he put his arm around her shoulder and started forward over the loose rocks. Far off, across the rolling forested hills of the Göttingerwald, the sun had just touched the top of the Weser mountains west of Göttingen, bathing the yellow limestone with a warm light.

"Where are you taking me?" she asked.

"Out there," he said, pointing toward a huge flat boulder at the end of the escarpment. "It's the place where I always stop and rest on my way up to the inn." In the pull of her shoulder against his arm he could feel her mounting terror. "From there," he said, "you can see Göttingen and the whole valley—everything."

She came to a halt and looked at the sheer cliffs on either side of the promontory.

"I can't go out there, David. I won't."

"For God's sake, Katherine! For once, trust me!"

"You brought me here on purpose, didn't you?"

"You've lived with this fear of high places long enough. If you can just see it for what it is, then maybe you can let go of it."

With a startled cry, two pigeon hawks suddenly took wing from the far end of the escarpment. Riding the wind with outstretched wings, they circled the edge of the cliff, hovered together for a moment, then glided out into the empty space above the valley.

He tightened his grip protectively around her shoulder, drew her close, and moved forward.

"David," she said, and closed her eyes.

As they came to the limestone boulder a dozen feet from the promontory's pointed end, a vast panorama suddenly opened up before them. Off to the west, the sun had just dropped behind the horizon and was peering out, like a huge golden eye, over the ragged silhouette of the Weser mountains. To the north, a bank of low gray clouds rolled toward them across the forested hills.

"This is the place," David said, and swung his knapsack from his shoulder.

The silence here brought a feeling of peace: there was only the soft steady rush of wind over the cliffs.

She stood with her head lowered, breathing heavily, unable to look up. He tightened his grip and drew her still closer. "Are you all right?" he asked.

She nodded, but kept her eyes lowered.

"You can see the whole of Göttingen from here," he said. "Sankt Alban's tower, the steeple of the Jacobikirche, the university buildings—everything. Even the Institute."

Still she did not look up.

He thought of the brief two weeks of loving affection they had shared together and the dream that was still within her reach. "I like to come up here when I have to make a decision," he said. "Like my thesis decision. It was here that I decided to stop doubting myself and accept what seemed impossible. It was here I decided to try and prove that two opposite things can be true at the same time."

She lifted her eyes, slowly, and from the expression on her face he could see that she was fighting her vertigo.

It seemed an eternity passed before she spoke. "You're right," she said. "It seems different from up here."

He thought of her paralyzing fear of her father and her refusal to trust herself. Feeling his way cautiously around her silence, he said, "It was on seeing Göttingen from up here that I finally realized that nothing is impossible, if you really want it. It was here," he added, "that I stopped being afraid of failure and decided to take a real leap in the dark."

Sensing where he was leading her, she looked back down. "If you brought me here to argue about my leaving Göttingen, David, then you're wasting your time."

He closed his fingers around her shoulder. "In the five weeks you've been here, you've done more than most students do in two years. You've gotten an invitation to the seminar on matter and you've been acknowledged by three of Göttingen's leading scientists. You can't say that you don't belong here."

"My decision to leave has nothing to do with my doubts about myself, David," she said. "I love my mother and father, and I don't want to lose them."

"I want you to look up, Katherine," he said. "I want you to see Göttingen—the whole of it, and I want you to remember what you see. I want you to dream about it for the rest of your life."

It was barely visible through the approaching mist, but he pointed with his left hand. "You see that little red building just east of St. Alban's tower. That's the Institute. From here, it doesn't look like much. But that's where your future lies."

"We can't live on dreams, David," she said and looked off toward the approaching wall of gray mist.

"You always have to have everything worked out ahead of time, don't you," he said. "You can never just look at what you've got in the present and let the future take care of itself."

A shudder went through her body as a cold gust of wind whipped by them.

"Aside from the arguments of science, Katherine, I love you."

It was as if an unseen hand suddenly drew a curtain across the sky: the mist came rolling in across the escarpment, blotting out the fading sunlight. Then from far off, muffled by the wind and the mist, came the sound of the bell in the Marktplatz tower, tolling the four o'clock hour.

"We should go on, David," she said. "It's going to rain." Without waiting for his reply, she freed herself from his arm and turned back toward the escarpment.

By the time he retrieved his knapsack from the rocks, she had vanished into the dense gray mist. "Katherine!" he called out and started after her, but the only response that came back was the echo of his own voice. He caught up with her at the center of the escarpment and grabbed hold of her arm. "Dammit, Katherine! You disobeyed your father once, and you can do it again."

She looked back, terror blazing in her eyes. "You don't understand my father, David!" she cried out over the wind. "He meant what he said last night! If I don't obey him this time and go back to Berlin, I will never be able to return home again!" With sudden and surprising force, she pulled free and turned away.

For a moment, in astonishment, he watched as she once again vanished into the thickening mist. Realizing that the time for arguments of logic and reason had run out, he thought to himself: If I let her go back to Berlin, I will lose her forever.

Again, this time through an impenetrable blanket of mist, he started after her, following the sound of her footsteps on the loose limestone rocks. "Katherine, wait!" he called out.

A single garbled word came back to him over the deafening rush of wind.

"If you leave Göttingen, Katherine, I'll follow you!" he called to her again, knowing that his voice was lost in the wind. "I'll give up everything! I love you!"

Thirty feet ahead, through a sudden break in the mist, he caught sight of her as she swung to the left. It took a moment for him to realize where they were. "No, Katherine!" he yelled. "Not that way!"

But she kept moving and stumbled over a loose rock, heading, not for the path back into the forest, but for the northern face of the cliff. He dropped his knapsack and began running.

She stumbled again, sending a small avalanche of loose rocks down the side of the escarpment.

He saw, through a fleeting break in the mist, that she was approaching the cliffside. "No, Katherine!" He bolted ahead, grabbed hold of her arm, and pulled her back against his body.

She turned with astonishment and looked up at his face. In the next instant, a break appeared in the mist. Reading the terror in his eyes, she looked back and saw that they were five feet from the edge of the cliff.

She gave a soft broken cry and closed her arms around his waist.

For a while, they went on holding each other, listening to the steady rush of wind over the cliffside.

"We're almost there," he said. "And from here, it's only a short walk through the woods."

She nodded, holding him tightly around the waist, then turned with him up the slope of the escarpment.

9

BY the time they reached the wooded crest of the hill, a steady rain had begun to fall, and they took shelter under the spreading branches of a spruce tree.

"That's the Gästehaus Bürgerbräu," David said, pointing off toward a grassy meadow beyond the trees.

The inn, a two story thatched-roofed Fachwerkhaus, stood nestled in the trees at the far side of the meadow. Smoke billowed from the big stone chimney, and lights burned in the ground-floor windows.

"We still have that damn field to cross," he said, "but we can wait here until the rain lets up."

He had worn only a lightweight tweed jacket. "You're drenched, David," said Katherine, and touched his arm. "If we make a dash for it, we'll have a nice warm fire."

"You're right." He put his arm around her shoulder. "We're only postponing the inevitable."

Together, holding hands, they left the shelter of the spruce tree and raced across the open rainswept meadow toward the inn's gabled front porch.

When they reached the wooden porch, Katherine looked back and saw that there was only one automobile, a new Mercedes Benz sedan, parked in the gravel drive fronting the inn. "We didn't plan for rain, David," she said. "Do you think we can get a ride back to town?"

"We're bound to. This is a main crossroad between Waake and Göttingen."

"But if we don't, we'll have to walk back to Göttingen in the rain."

"There's an old expression in English, Katherine—'You can only cross one bridge at a time.' " He let go of her shoulder and opened the front door. "For now, let's just get warm."

The immediate warmth of the small, quaintly furnished reception room was welcome. There was a coat tree made of deer horns by the door and a collection of whimsical cuckoo clocks on the pine-paneled wall of the staircase leading to the second floor. From the public room beyond the varnished reception desk came the sound of a woman's raucous laughter.

"Here, sweetheart," David said, placing his knapsack by the coat tree. "Give me your coat. You're soaking wet."

"I'm also freezing. I hope they have something hot to drink."

He chuckled and hung her coat on the tree. "I think we'll have a choice between schnaps and beer. The owners are Bavarian."

"Willkommen!" a deep voice boomed out. "Kommen Sie herein!"

Katherine stepped back as a huge bald-headed man wearing Lederhosen hurried in from the public room, laughing and rubbing his hands together. As a child, she had always found the boisterous beer-hall cheer of the Bavarians somehow disquieting.

"Welcome to the Gästehaus Bürgerbräu!" he exclaimed.

"Guten Abend, mein Herr," said David. He saw Katherine's dismay and smiled. "What we need first, I think, is a warm fire. We're soaked to the bone."

"Ah! So." The man's enthusiasm collapsed as he caught sight of David's knapsack on the floor. "You're students, I take it, from Göttingen."

"That's right. We were on a walk and we got caught in the rain, so we stopped by for some of your Bavarian schnaps."

The man's round plump face brightened. "Excellent! Then come in, please! Come in!" He waved for them to follow and turned back to the public room. "I'll give you a table by the fire and my wife, Frau Kehler, will bring you the best schnaps in all of Germany!"

David took her arm and they followed Herr Kehler into a large pine-paneled room furnished to resemble a Bavarian Bierkeller, with wooden tables and chairs and heavy old-fashioned brass lamp fixtures. The only other patrons in the room were two elderly couples having supper. A fire blazed in the big stone fireplace at the far end of the room.

"This way, mein Herr, this way!" Kehler indicated the table nearest the fireplace. "I'm going to give you the warmest table in the house!"

David ushered Katherine to the chair closest to the fire. "Sit here, and you'll be dry in no time."

"So, mein Herr, you walked up from Göttingen," Kehler said.

"That's right. We came up the mountain by way of the Göttingerwald."

"Of course, you know it's a twenty-kilometer walk back to Göttingen. So if this rain keeps up, you and your wife may need a room for the night."

It took a moment for Katherine to reflect on the meaning of the man's words. She looked up and said with panic, "We're not planning to stay for the night, Herr Kehler. We were hoping to get a ride back to Göttingen with one of your guests."

"Ah!" Kehler laughed. "Not tonight, I'm afraid. Our patrons over there are staying overnight, and we rarely have visitors from Göttingen during the rainy season."

"First, we'll have some schnaps," David said and took his chair. "Then we'll worry about . . . "

"And for food?" Kehler urged. "The Weisswürste and Knödel are excellent tonight!"

Katherine thought of the three hundred Marks she had with her. "Just the schnaps for now, thank you."

"Take your time, meine Frau," Kehler said. "The first schnaps is on the house!" he called back as he hurried off.

For a moment, there was only the crackling sound of the fire and quiet murmur of the old folks' voices. David took his cigarettes from his jacket pocket. "Like I said, this is a main crossroad between Waake and Göttingen."

She looked up at the window where the rain was making a soft patter against the glass. "We can't take rooms for the night, David," she said. "I've only got three hundred Marks with me."

"I meant what I said, Katherine." He lit his cigarette. "Tonight, we will cross one bridge at a time."

"All right," she sighed, "I'll try." She sat back and turned her thoughts to the delicious warmth of the fire. He was right, of course. She had always somehow missed the present, worrying about the past and the future.

"You were crazy to run off from me like that on the escarpment," he said. "You knew you couldn't see where you were going."

He sat back as the owner's wife, a plump little woman with an irascible Hausfrau's face, hurried up carrying a bottle of schnaps and two empty glasses.

"Here we are!" she said, thrusting the glasses before them on the table. "I can see this is exactly what you young people need—a bottle of good Bavarian schnaps. Helmut tells me you got caught in the storm."

"Yes," David said. "We were on a hike up from Göttingen."

"And we've got to get back tonight," Katherine said.

"In that case, you'll have to walk. No one uses this road at night when it storms." She poured David's glass. "You and your wife would be better off taking a room for the night."

"I never argue with my wife," David smiled at Katherine.

"Suit yourselves." Frau Kehler placed the bottle on the table and turned away. "I'll leave the bottle with you. The first one's on the house. After that, it's fifty pfennigs a glass, and I'll ask you to keep count yourselves."

David sipped his schnaps, then said, quietly, "If you go back to Berlin, you know what's in store for you. And even if you did get back into the Institute, you'd have to start all over again—alone."

She took a sip from her glass and felt the sting of the schnaps in her throat. "I meant what I said, David. I will not disobey my father again." She sipped again, and again felt the sting in her throat. "I know he's foolish and he has terrible failings, but I love him."

"You don't love your father, Katherine, you need him. And love and need are not the same thing."

For a moment, she sat listening to the rain, thinking of David's offer to collaborate on his doctoral thesis. "And you?" she asked. "Is it really love or your need for my experiments that makes you want me to stay in Göttingen?"

The question both surprised and angered him. "You know the answer to that question, Katherine. You may not need me, Katherine, like you need your father," he said. "But the fact is, you love me."

She kept her eyes lowered and held her breath.

"I haven't ventured to say this before," he said, "but I want you to marry me."

The statement took her entirely by surprise, and when she looked up, the twilight in the window had faded to darkness and the only thing she could now see in the glass was the reflection of her own astonished face and the rainwater streaming down the glass.

"I can't marry you, David," she said helplessly.

He reached across the table and took her hand. "I love you, Katherine," he went on, "and I want to share my life with you. I also meant what I said—if you leave Göttingen and go back to Berlin, I'll give up my studies and follow you there. I'm not afraid of your father; and whether you do it here or in Berlin, you're going to have to make a choice between the two of us."

She thought with panic: I can't do that, I can't make that kind of choice. To slow down the pace of the conversation, she said, "But David, you and I have only known each other for five weeks!"

He said nothing.

She lowered her eyes and said, still stalling for time, "Frau Kehler is right. No one is going to stop here in this rain."

"No, they're not, so we'll have to stay the night. I'll ask how much the rooms are," he said, and got up.

When he had gone, she took another sip of schnaps. She thought of his astonishing proposition: I want you to marry me.

She reached again for her glass.

The schnaps went down, burning, leaving a bittersweet aftertaste in her mouth.

She took the bottle and refilled her glass.

David's words beat against her mind like the rain against the window: I'm not afraid of your father; and whether you do it here or in Berlin, you're going to have to make a choice.

He was right, of course. She could not love one without losing the other.

David came up and looked down at her. "The cheapest rooms they have are five hundred."

"In that case, I'll have to borrow two hundred."

"But that's silly. We're adults, and we can share a room."

The thought of sharing a room with him for the night, the intimacy of it, shocked and silenced her.

"Look," he said impatiently, "there'll be blankets, and I can make a bed for myself on the floor."

The heat she felt in her cheeks, she realized, was not from the nearby fire. "If we take a room together, David, how will we register?" she asked.

He finished the schnaps in his glass. "I've done that already. I signed the register as Herr and Frau David Linz." He grinned. "Are you ready?"

She hesitated, slowly drinking the rest of the schnaps in her glass, thinking to herself of the long night that was ahead of them.

"You'll be perfectly safe, Katherine," he said. "Trust me."

As she got up, she suddenly felt dizzy.

"Are you all right?" he asked.

"Yes, I'm fine. I had a second schnaps while you were gone."

He smiled and took her arm. "Only the first one was free."

As they crossed the public room together, she reached up and quickly tidied the loose strands of wet hair still clinging to her face.

Frau Kehler was busy with a dustcloth in the reception room. "Ah! There you are!" she exclaimed, stuffing the cloth into her apron pocket. "Your husband asked for a room with a view, Frau Linz, so we gave you number six." She took a key from the board behind the reception desk and turned toward the staircase. "Now, if you'll follow me, I'll take you up and we'll see if everything is to your liking."

Your husband . . . Frau Linz. The phrases, Katherine realized, were familiar to her, for she had said them to herself during the last week.

David gathered his knapsack from the floor and her jacket from the coat tree. "After you, Frau Linz," he said, with a gallant and playful gesture.

They followed Frau Kehler down a narrow hallway dimly illuminated by three small brass wall fixtures. She stopped at the end of the hall and opened the door.

"The bed, I assure you, is one of our best." Frau Kehler pointed with pride at a plain pine-framed double bed covered with a flowery cotton eiderdown.

Aside from a single straight-back chair and a wooden night table by the bed, the only other furniture in the room was a large maple armoire against the wall. "It's lovely," Katherine said.

Frau Kehler handed David the key and hurried to the door. "The faucet for water and the toilets are at the end of the hall. Showers, of course, are not included in the price of the room. There's a face towel on the nightstand . . . "

"Thank you, Frau Kehler," David interrupted.

At the door, she turned back. "If you should need them, Frau Linz, there are extra blankets in the bottom of the cupboard. Gute Nacht."

"Gute Nacht, Frau Kehler."

When the door closed, David turned the key in the lock, and for a moment there was only the soft patter of rain against the window.

"Are you hungry?" he asked.

"Yes. But I can wait till morning."

He switched off the bright overhead light, then went to the table and turned on the small bedside lamp. "I don't think the Kehlers realize that you're married to a Jew."

"Even if they did, what difference would it make?"

He looked back and smiled. "For one thing, a long night walking in the rain. There was one of those little Hakenkreuz flags hanging in the reception room. Herr Kehler is probably a member of that new Bavarian political party."

She thought of the Nazi newspaper she had seen in her father's study at home, and the mindless hatred she had witnessed in Berlin since the end of the war. "I know what goes on in Berlin, David," she said. "But do people mistreat you in a town like Göttingen?"

"Sometimes." He unsnapped the clasps on his knapsack. "But university towns are better than the cities."

In the softer light of the bedside lamp she caught sight of a faint cluster of lights in the darkness beyond the window. She went to the window and looked out. From here, there was a view of the valley, and far off in the darkness, like a tiny diadem of stars, were the clustered lights of Göttingen. Until now, she had never stopped to think what it would be like to be married to a man who lived every day of his life in the shadow of ignorance and hatred. She thought of her father's prediction that Adolf Hitler and the Nazi Party would one day come to power in Germany, and a feeling of fear came over her. Resting her forehead against the windowpane, she peered out at the impenetrable darkness beyond the rain-blurred glass.

Behind her, there was the sound of the armoire door opening and closing.

She thought again of the impossible choice she would have to make when she returned to Göttingen. Up to now, she had lived her life in the shadow of her father, trying to win his recognition and approval, but in David she had found something far more precious than respect or admiration, though their feelings for each other included both of these emotions.

Closing her eyes, she wondered if she would ever be able to find another love like his.

"Here," he said. "It's not Weisswürste, but at least it's something."

She opened her eyes and saw in the glass that he was holding two apples in his hand. "I'd rather have one of Frau Reichshauer's apples than the Kehlers' Bavarian Weisswürste," she said, and turned from the window.

"So would I." He dropped one of the apples on the bed, then came to her and lay the other apple gently in her hand.

"Thank you."

"You're welcome." He pointed at the narrow space on the floor between the bed and the wall. "There it is," he said. "A perfectly comfortable bed, just like I told you."

He had taken a blanket and a pillow from the armoire and had made what looked like an alpine hiker's sleeping doss on the floor beside the bed. "You'll be miserable down there," she said.

"Nonsense! Look how it works!" He knelt down to demonstrate his accomplishment with the blanket.

Touched by his clumsy effort to reassure her of his comfort, she watched for a moment as he rearranged the blanket, then turned back to the window.

His words that afternoon came back to her: I'll give up everything! I love you!

She had known from the very beginning that he desired her, and she had felt the same force inside herself from that very first day at Welch-zeckhaus.

He came up behind her and stood looking out the window. "I really don't mind sleeping on the floor," he said. "It's only for a night. I meant what I said, Katherine. You're perfectly safe with me."

Once again, she felt awakening inside herself the desire she had so far kept in check.

She thought: If I do this, if I give in to this desire, I will never be able to go back to Berlin.

"The choice you have to make will be hard, I know," he said, "but together we can both have the best of both worlds—careers and each other."

She thought of the impossible dream they both shared—of one day discovering the light at the center of this dark universe—and of the success that could be theirs together.

She stepped back slowly until she came to rest against his body. "I don't want you to sleep on the floor, David," she said.

Behind her, the sound of his breath suddenly stopped.

She felt in the pit of her stomach a sudden and curious feeling of release: as if a hand that had been holding her all her life had suddenly let go.

She turned to face him. "I want us to sleep together," she said.

He went on staring at her with confusion and astonishment.

"I said I want us to sleep together, David," she repeated, softly.

In amazement, like a bewildered child, he stepped back and stumbled over his knapsack on the floor. "I didn't know," he said. "I didn't expect you to . . ."

She took his apple from the bed and dropped it with hers into the knapsack. Then she went to the table and turned out the bedside lamp. "We'll eat the apples later," she said.

He stood motionless in the darkness, watching as she began to unbutton her blouse.

Is it fear he feels, she wondered, or desire . . . or perhaps, like me, both.

Over the patter of the rain against the window came the sound of his quickening breath as he, too, began to undress.

When she was naked, she drew back the eiderdown and lowered herself into the bed. The cold rough cotton sheets sent a shiver through her body. She closed her eyes and held her breath. She had always imagined that the act of sex would be something solemn, like a ritual, but this seemed somehow ordinary, even commonplace.

Saying nothing, he lowered himself onto the bed beside her and drew the covers over him.

She could feel the warmth of his body in the small space between them. He reached up and touched her face with his fingertips. "I love you, Katherine," he whispered.

He moved his fingers over her face; then slowly, gently, down her neck and over her shoulder, until his hand came to rest on her naked breast. She closed her eyes and swallowed, relishing the feelings that suddenly came over her.

For one brief moment, before he closed the space between them, she thought of the boundary she had irrevocably crossed and what she had given up forever.

Lying back, she welcomed the luxury of her new-found freedom—the slow gentle touch of his mouth on her breasts. She ran her fingers through his hair, thinking only of his hands and mouth moving over the length of her body.

Slowly and gently, making no effort to rush the pleasure of his exploration, he let his mouth travel across her shoulder and neck until his lips came to rest against her own.

It was as if they were speaking a language she had known all her life, but had never known she knew. She closed her eyes, welcoming the caress of his tongue against her own, and ran her open hands down his naked back.

He squirmed and made a soft noise of pleasure, shifting his weight over her body. She could feel the rapid beat of his heart against her breast and the growing fullness of his erection against her belly.

A passion she had never known was awakening inside her—and the force of it took her breath away.

He rose up and held himself suspended above her on his outstretched arms. "I love you," he murmured, "and if you leave, I will follow you. I will not let go of you."

She caught her breath, startled by the sharp pain that went through her body as he entered her. But the pain passed as quickly as it had come, leaving in its wake the exaltation of a pleasure she had never imagined was possible. She reached up, took hold of his head with both hands, and this time gave herself up entirely to the wonderful feeling of his touch.

10

IT was three thirty-two when David looked up at the clock on his bedroom bureau. "Damn!" he said, and leapt up from his desk. Today was the day Katherine was due to present her paper at the seminar, and he had promised to meet her at the Geismar Tor at three thirty.

Grabbing his briefcase, he left his room and hurried down to the ground-floor hallway.

"David, wait!" Frau Reichshauer came hurrying after him as he started out the front door of Welchzeckhaus. He kept moving, and she caught up with him in the street. "This arrived in the afternoon post," she said, handing him a large foreign-looking envelope.

From the envelope's stamp, he knew at once that it was from his father in America. "Thank God," he said. "I was beginning to wonder if my cable to America ever arrived." Setting his briefcase on the cobblestones, he quickly opened the envelope.

"It's from your father, isn't it?" Frau Reichshauer asked.

"Yes." He had almost given up hope of receiving any reply.

He took his father's one-page letter from the envelope and opened it. "Good God!" he exclaimed. "He sent the money—in cash!"

"I knew you were wrong to doubt your father, David," Frau Reichshauer said, watching him count the hundred dollar bills. "I told you he would send the money."

"Look at this!" he said. "It's a thousand American dollars! That's two hundred more than I asked for!"

"I'm not surprised, David. From what you've told me about your father, I never doubted his generosity."

Thumbing through the bills, he did a quick mental calculation. "You realize what this means, don't you?" he said. "Given the current rate of exchange, there's enough money here to support Katherine and me for an entire year."

She took his free hand. "You're lucky to have a man like Jacob for a father, David. Katherine isn't so fortunate."

"You're right. Katherine isn't so lucky," he said, thinking of the anxiety she had suffered over her father. The day after their hike to the Gästehaus Bürgerbräu, she had written him to say that she would not return to Berlin. For the last month, certain that he would carry out his vow to disown her, she had waited with dread for yet another phone call from Berlin, but so far there had been no response to her letter.

He looked at his watch. "You must forgive me, Frau Reichshauer," he said. "It's twenty minutes to four, and I was supposed to meet Katherine at three thirty. We have a four o'clock seminar."

"Ah! Then you'd better go. We can always talk about your plans for the future later," she said.

"By the way!" Frau Reichshauer called after him as he started off down the Lange Geismarstrasse. "Tell Katherine that supper will be at seven tonight, instead of six! We're going to have a little celebration, so for once I want you to be on time!"

"We'll be there at seven sharp! I promise!" He waved and picked up speed, thinking of the tacit encouragement that Frau Reichshauer had given him and Katherine during the last month. Though neither one of them had spoken about the affair they were having, it was obvious that the old woman knew that everything between them had changed, and that they were now sleeping together every night in Katherine's room.

As he turned south down the Kurze Geismarstrasse, he quickly read his father's letter.

Dear Son,

After a year of silence, I was surprised to receive your cable. As I told you in my letter of a year ago, I would be glad to help you in any way I can. I know that the deutsche mark has fallen drastically in the last few months, and I'm therefore sending you a little extra. The money is a gift, son, not loan, and I don't want you to think of returning it.

It's pointless, I know, to ask you once again to come back to America.

But in the year you have been in Germany I have read about the things that are happening there, and I am now deeply concerned for your safety.

I pray, as always, that you will put your trust in God and not in earthly powers.

                                                    Your loving father,

                                                    Jacob

Frau Reichshauer is right, he thought. I'm very lucky indeed to have a man like Jacob for my father.

He returned the letter to the envelope and looked again at his watch. He picked up speed, thinking of Katherine's excitement last night when she announced at supper that she would present her paper on spectral light emissions at today's seminar. In the month since she had made her choice to stay on in Göttingen, she had not only discovered the power of love in her life, she had also found in herself a new sense of confidence in her work.

As he left Göttingen's quiet residential section and entered the busy commercial district, the sound of a marching band came toward him from the direction of the Bürgerstrasse. There was the thump of a bass drum, the tinkle of a Glockenspiel, and the familiar off-key blare of cornets.

Ahead, where the Kurze Geismarstrasse met the town's Wall Promenade, he could see people hurrying south down the sidewalk toward the Bürgerstrasse.

The band's spirited marching song puzzled him. Today, November 18, was not, he was sure, one of the town's official holidays.

As he crossed the busy street, he caught sight of Katherine pacing back and forth under the medieval stone Geismar tower. She wore the fashionable blue dress she had bought in the Kurze Geismarstrasse in September, and her long blonde hair was tied back with a bright yellow scarf.

He smiled to himself, realizing that she had dressed in her best clothes.

"I'm sorry, sweetheart," he said, as he overtook her under the tower. "I was studying at home, and I forgot the hour."

"You're impossible, David." She stopped pacing and looked up at the clock in the tower.

"We're not late yet," he said. "It's a quarter to four, and the Institute's only a ten-minute walk from here."

"I'm supposed to lead the meeting today," she said with exasperation.

He said, realizing they were on the verge of their first argument, "Then let's not stand here arguing. If we cut across the park to the Bürgerstrasse, we can be there in plenty of time."

As they started across the Kurze Geismarstrasse toward the wooded Geismar park, there was a sudden gust of cold November wind. He put his arm around her shoulder and drew her close to him. "You should have worn a coat, sweetheart," he said. "It's supposed to turn cold today."

"I never worry about the cold, David." She shifted the briefcase she was carrying to her right hand. "I'm a Berliner."

He waited until they had turned down the park's gravel path, then said, "By the way, I have a surprise for you."

"A surprise?"

"This came in the afternoon post." As he handed her the envelope, he saw a flash of hope blaze in her eyes. "It's from my father in America," he added.

Watching her remove the money from the envelope, he thought again of the anxiety she had suffered during the last month, waiting for her father's response to her letter.

She came to a halt under one of the park's ancient lime trees. "David!" she exclaimed, "this is a thousand American dollars!"

"That's right. It's two hundred more than I asked for."

Her anger vanished as quickly as it had appeared. She said, staring with wonder at the crisp green bills, "I don't know what to say! I've never seen so much money!"

"Neither have I. With the money I have left from my Rockefeller grant, it will be enough to support the two of us for the rest of the year."

She lifted his hand from her shoulder and kissed his fingers. "This is going to solve all our problems, David. We'll be able to pay our expenses and live on together at Welchzeckhaus."

"That's true. And if the deutsche mark keeps falling, it will only mean that our dollars will rise in value."

She looked up as the sound of another rousing marching song came toward them through the trees. "Funny," she said. "I didn't know today was a holiday."

"It's not. But in a small town like this, any excuse will do for a parade."

"We'd better hurry," she said. "If there's a crowd on the Bürgerstrasse, we'll be late for the seminar."

As they turned south toward the Institute, she replaced the money in the envelope and began reading his father's letter.

He watched the changing expression on her face, thinking of the plans for the future they had made during the last month: their wedding during the Christmas holidays and their honeymoon at the Zugspitze in the Bavarian alps. Last night, they had sat up until the small hours, talking of their dream of collaborating as a research team.

He looked up at the brightly colored autumn leaves overhead, thinking of the wonderful future that lay ahead of them. In the last month, they had found in each other a completely new kind of human chemistry: a sense of peace and contentment that neither one of them had ever dreamed was possible. It was as if the two of them had been on long and lonely voyages and had finally come to rest in each other's arms.

"Frau Reichshauer is right, David," she said. "You were wrong to doubt your father. He obviously loves you very much."

He heard the note of grief in her voice and closed his arm around her shoulder.

This, he thought, is the only thing that stands in the way of our complete happiness: her refusal to once and for all let go of her father.

"I know it's hard, sweetheart," he said, "but you can't go on waiting like this. It's possible, after all, that you may never hear from your father."

"It's Papa's silence that hurts, David," she said. "It would have been better if he had simply disowned me."

Caught by a sudden gust of wind, a dead leaf broke from one of the limbs overhead and blew past David's face. "You've got to stop living in the past, Katherine," he said. "We have all the money we need now, and we have a wonderful future to look forward to."

"You're right. Papa must know by now that we're more than just friends, and it's pointless to keep hoping for the impossible."

They walked in silence for a moment, listening to the marching song in the distance.

"By the way," she said, "I have some good news for you, as well. On the way out of class this morning, I ran into Professor Born and he's given me permission to collaborate on your doctoral thesis."

It was his turn to come to a halt. "Then he approves of your barium experiments?" he asked with amazement.

"Yes. And he's glad that we'll be working together."

When they reached the south side of the park, the sidewalks lining the Bürgerstrasse were crowded with local townspeople. For a moment, they stood at the edge of the crowd, watching as the band, a motley group of uniformed locals, came toward them down the avenue. The music, David realized—if you could call it that—was the same rousing German marching song they had heard last week at the sausage fair in the Marktplatz. Behind the band came a phalanx of young men carrying hand-painted placards.

"We've got to find a way to cross the street," Katherine said.

"Then let's go on. We can try crossing at the intersection of the Nikolaistrasse."

As they turned west along the wooded edge of the park, a hand came out of the crowd to thrust a newspaper at her.

When she looked to see who had handed her the newspaper, she recognized at once the tough clean-shaven face of the young blond boy who regularly sold copies of the *Völkischer Beobachter* in Göttingen's railway station.

The glaring headline across the paper's front page read: RAUS MIT DEN JUDEN!

She started to drop the paper on the sidewalk, but David reached out and took it from her.

"I've seen this before," he said. "It's the new Nazi newspaper."

"Never mind. It's nothing but a silly propaganda sheet."

Suddenly, as the marching song rose to its climax with an off-key screech from the cornets and a honk from the bouncing tuba, she caught sight of the painted words on one of the placards behind the band: Der Deutsche Kampfbund von Göttingen.

The German Fighting Union, she remembered with a feeling of uneasiness, was one of the new patriotic leagues that had sprouted up all across Germany since the end of the war.

When they reached the intersection of the Nikolaistrasse, David drew up behind the crowd gathered at the corner. "At this rate," he exclaimed, "we'll never get to the seminar on time!"

The band had meanwhile come alongside them: older Göttingers, Katherine saw—veterans of the Great War wearing odd bits and pieces of their military uniforms. And behind the band, marching four abreast beneath a placard inscribed with the letters N.S.D.A.P. Deutscher Kampfbund, came the Göttingen Fighting Union: some fifty young men, most of them wearing the now familiar brown uniform of the new National Socialist Workers' Party's militant storm troopers.

She caught her breath as another placard turned in the wind, reflecting the afternoon sunlight: a large printed photograph of the fierce mustachioed face of Adolf Hitler, the party's outspoken leader. Until now, Katherine had always thought that the Nazis were a small group of rabble-rousing Bavarians. She had never imagined that the party would find a following in Germany.

In the next moment, as the Kampfbund started across the intersection, there was a boom from the bass drum and a crash of cymbals, as the band broke into a somber rendition of the German national anthem, giving the stirring melody the sound of a death dirge. The effect of the music on the crowd assembled at the streetcorner—the breathless silence and the looks of fervent expectation—was instantaneous.

"This is ridiculous!" David said. "You'd think that people in a university town like Göttingen would know better than to involve themselves with the bloody Nazis!" He held up the copy of the *Völkischer Beobachter*. "This is nothing but a lot of mindless anti-Semitic trash."

Nearby, an elderly couple turned to look at them. The man, Katherine saw, wore an armband emblazoned with the Nazi Hakenkreuz.

"David," she said, softly.

Katherine saw that two young men on their right wearing brown storm trooper uniforms had turned to stare at them. One of them bent toward the other, said something, and made an obscene gesture in her direction.

Glancing up at David's dark semitic-looking face, she realized what the gesture referred to and felt a sudden wave of anger sweep over her.

Until now, the only anti-Semitism she had experienced in David's presence had been with her father at Welchzeckhaus.

With a feeling of defiant protectiveness, she took hold of David's arm. "We can try crossing at the Bunsenstrasse."

As they turned together down the sidewalk, the words his father had written in his letter suddenly came back to her: In the year you have been in Germany I have read about the things that are happening there, and I am now deeply concerned for your safety.

11

FOR a moment, Katherine stood at the door to Frau Reichshauer's study, trying to decide whether or not to knock. After all, she could be only imagining things. Still, it was pointless to go on pretending that nothing was wrong, it had already been over ten days.

She needed to talk to someone with experience in these matters, and other than David, Frau Reichshauer was the only person in Göttingen she could trust.

Summoning her courage, praying that no one was in the study, she gave a soft knock.

"Come in!" Frau Reichshauer called with impatience.

She went in, thinking to herself how ignorant she was of the more practical matters of life.

Frau Reichshauer sat behind her desk at the far end of the room, with stacks of papers piled high around her.

"Ah! Come in, Katherine," she said. "I was going through the household accounts, trying to balance them before the year is out."

"I can come back later, if you're busy," Katherine said, stepping back to the door.

"No, no! I've almost finished and I need a break." Frau Reichshauer motioned to the sofa on the far side of the room. "Sit down, my dear, and Fräulein Weber will bring some tea."

As Katherine closed the door and went to the sofa, she remembered the afternoon she arrived at Welchzeckhaus. It was only three months ago, but it seemed as if a lifetime had gone by.

"You look worried, Katherine," Frau Reichshauer said as she left her desk and went to the bell rope next to the fireplace. "Is something wrong?"

"I don't know . . . I'm not sure . . . But I need to talk to someone."

Frau Reichshauer pulled the bell rope, then came and seated herself in the armchair next to the sofa. "I'm your friend, my dear," she said, "and you can tell me anything."

Katherine looked around the cluttered room, wondering where she could begin. In the six weeks since she and David first began their affair, they had made no secret of the love they felt for one another, but they had kept silent about the fact that they were sleeping together. "I don't know what to say," she said. "It's difficult for me to talk about these things."

"Does it have something to do with you and David?" Frau Reichshauer asked.

"Yes."

"With something private and personal?"

"Yes."

"You have nothing to fear from me, Katherine. I'm an old woman, and very little still surprises me."

When she turned to look at Frau Reichshauer, there was a knowing expression of compassion in her dark eyes. "You know everything about

David and me, don't you?" she said. "You know that we've been sleeping together."

"Yes, Katherine. I've known for almost six weeks that you and David are lovers. I knew it after you stayed the night together at the Gästehaus Bürgerbräu."

"But you said nothing."

"Of course not. It is not my place to say anything."

"It was not David's idea to keep our relationship a secret," Katherine said. "It was mine. I was brought up to believe that sex was something that took place in secret between married people, and it was something my parents never dared talk about."

"I understand, my dear. I was myself brought up in the strictest of homes."

"I forced David to keep everything a secret between us because we're not married and I thought you would not approve."

Frau Reichshauer sighed and shook her head. "Then you have forgotten everything, Katherine," she said. "The day you arrived at Welchzeckhaus I made it clear that I had no rules governing the private behavior of my boarders. As I told you and your parents, I believe that young people should be taught to make choices for themselves . . . and that they must take responsibility for the consequences of their choices."

Katherine thought of the choice she had made that night at the Gästehaus Bürgerbräu and the unforeseen consequences she now faced. "I came to Göttingen to be a scientist, Frau Reichshauer, nothing more than that," she said with misery. "I never dreamed I would meet a man like David, or that I would fall in love and have to make compromises with my career."

"You must tell me what you're afraid of, Katherine," said Frau Reichshauer. "I want to help you."

"I first became aware of it about ten days ago," she said, "when I realized that I had missed my period." She looked away, realizing she had never once in her life spoken so plainly of such matters.

"Go on," said Frau Reichshauer.

"At first, I thought it was only a natural delay," she said, feeling suddenly liberated by the truth. "Then the days went by, and I knew that something dreadful was happening, something neither David nor I had planned for."

"In other words, you're afraid that you are pregnant."

She turned back to find that Frau Reichshauer was smiling at her. "Yes."

"Have you said anything to David?"

"No. I've said nothing to anyone." The panic she had kept in check for the last week suddenly came rushing up. "In the past, we've talked about these things—about marriage and a family—but it was always something we were going to have in the future." Like water through a broken dam, the words came rushing out. "We've planned to get married during the Christmas holidays, when our classes are finished and we have time for ourselves. I know he wants to have a child, but not now, not while he's working for his doctoral degree."

The door opened and Fräulein Weber came in, carrying a tray with a teapot and a single cup and saucer. "Ah," she said. "I see there are two of you."

"Yes, Magda," said Frau Reichshauer. "So if you will fetch another cup and saucer, I will pour Katherine a nice cup of tea."

"Certainly, gnädige Frau." Sensing the tension between them, Fräulein Weber kept her eyes lowered, placed the tray on the table, and quickly left the room.

"Aside from your fears for David, you're also afraid of your father, aren't you?" Frau Reichshauer asked.

"Yes. If he has hesitated up till now, this will be reason enough for him to disown me."

Frau Reichshauer left the armchair and joined her on the sofa. "Listen to me, Katherine, for I will not say this again. You may have come to Göttingen to be only a scientist, but that has all changed now. You met and fell in love with David, and you were forced to make a choice between him and your father. You made your choice, and now you must accept the consequences."

"But I have accepted the consequences."

"That's not true, Katherine. You have physically separated yourself from your father, but you are still loyal to him in your heart. And if you don't cut the ties that bind you to him once and for all, you will end up destroying your marriage."

"It's the child I'm concerned about, Frau Reichshauer." The panic broke free and she began to cry, softly. "This is Germany, and if I'm pregnant, it will be our child who will suffer the consequences."

"I take it you have not seen a doctor."

"No. I kept hoping that I had made a mistake."

"The first thing we will do, Katherine, is pay a call on Dr. Felsberg, my family physician."

"If I'm right and I'm pregnant," she said, "it will change everything.

I will not only have to postpone my studies, I will also have to stop work on David's doctoral thesis." Remembering what he had once said about the best of both worlds, she covered her face with her hands and began to weep, helplessly. "This is not what we planned for, Frau Reichshauer! This is not the dream we dreamed for ourselves!"

"We must all learn to accept what we cannot change, Katherine." She reached out and took her in her arms. "And you must realize that love alone makes everything possible."

12

"KATHERINE, wake up," David said, his voice closer this time.

She opened her eyes and saw in the darkness a blinding white light.

"Sweetheart, are you okay?" He reached up and touched her forehead.

It was the full moon, she realized, shining down through the oriel window above her bed. "Yes," she breathed with relief. "I was dreaming."

He sat up and rested on his elbow. "You're beginning to worry me, Katherine," he said, stroking her face with his fingertips. "This is the second night in a row you've had a bad dream."

"It's nothing." She moved closer to him under the eiderdown. "I'm tired, that's all."

"This time, you called out your father's name."

"It was a dream about Papa. I dreamed that he came back to Welch-zeckhaus." She looked up, realizing that there was a cigarette burning in the ashtray on the bedside table behind David. "You were awake, weren't you?" she said.

"Yes. I woke up about a half hour ago." He ran the back of his hand along her face, touching the sweat that was there. "I was lying here thinking about the holidays. If we have the wedding ceremony on the twenty-third, we can leave for our honeymoon on the twenty-fourth and spend Christmas eve at the Zugspitze."

She thought of her visit that afternoon to Dr. Felsberg and the test results he would have for her on Monday. "Yes," she said. "I'd like that."

"Classes end this Friday. I've already asked Frau Reichshauer to be a witness for the wedding, and tomorrow I'll ask Professor Born to do the same. We'll have the ceremony on Sunday and leave for Bavaria on Monday."

She looked away at the full moon in the window. "The trouble is, David, I'm behind with my chemistry experiments, and I don't think I should leave town until next Tuesday."

"But that's Christmas day."

"I know. But I want to finish my experiments before we leave for Bavaria." She turned to face David, then said softly, "I was thinking about your doctoral exams. If you can go on working like you are . . . I mean, if nothing comes along to slow you down . . . you could be ready to take the exams next April."

He thought of her old habit of avoidance and postponement. Whatever was troubling her, she had been holding it inside for over a week now. "I'm in no hurry," he said. "We have two, maybe three more years here in Göttingen."

A sudden gust of wind rattled the loose pane in the leaded window. "I've been thinking about all the plans we've made," she said, "and I can't promise I'll be able to finish the barium graphite experiment by spring."

He recalled the curious looks Katherine and Frau Reichshauer had exchanged that night at supper: as if the two women were keeping a secret between them. It had something, he was sure, to do with the money Katherine had asked for that morning.

For a while, she went on staring fixedly at the moon in the leaded glass window. Then she said in a voice dragged down by misery, "This last month has been so perfect, David . . . I mean our work together at the Institute, and our plans for getting married during the holidays." She turned her head away on the pillow. "It was foolish of us to make so many plans."

He took his hand from her face and gently rested it on her shoulder. "I want you to tell me what's troubling you, Katherine," he said.

The wind rattled the windowpane again. She said nothing.

He thought of the weeks she had waited for some response from her father. "Is it your father?" he asked. "Have you heard something from Berlin?"

"No." She shook her head. "It's not my father. I've heard nothing from Berlin."

He could hear her panic in the rapid rise and fall of her breath. He let go of her shoulder and began gently moving his fingers up and down the side of her neck. Where he had failed with reason in the past, he had always succeeded with gentle affection. "We made a pact, Katherine, back in October," he said. "It was right after you wrote to your father and told him you were not going back to Berlin. I remember the night very clearly. We made love, and afterward we made a promise." He ran the tip of his index finger along her chinbone. "We promised that, no matter what, we would never again keep secrets from each other."

When she turned her head on the pillow, the moonlight caught the tears in her eyes. Still, she said nothing.

He kept moving his fingers gently over her neck. "If you won't tell me what's bothering you, how can I help you?"

"We had everything planned so perfectly, David."

The panic in her voice was contagious. He caught the tears with his finger as they ran down the side of her face. "What is it, Katherine? Tell me!"

For a moment, there was only the steady rattling noise of the windowpane. He held his breath, waiting for her to speak again.

"This afternoon, I went to Frau Reichshauer's doctor and he ran a test . . ." She reached up and took hold of his hand. "Ich glaube, dass ich schwanger bin," she said, softly.

Schwanger: the German word sounded somehow abstract. He tried to formulate a single logical thought, but his mind was empty.

"I won't know for sure until next Monday," she said, "but Dr. Felsberg thinks the test will be positive."

Pregnant. As he said the English word to himself, it was as if he had been suddenly lifted to a great height: a feeling of dizziness came over him. "You're going to have a baby?" he asked.

The words spilled out with all the air in her lungs. "I'm not sure, David, but I think so."

"Why didn't you say something?"

She turned her face away again. "I was afraid to tell you."

He took her by the chin and turned her face back to his. "What do you mean, you were afraid to tell me?"

She closed her eyes to hide from the moon's bright light. "This wasn't what we planned for, David," she said. "We always talked about having a child later, after we were married and had finished our doctorates."

It was true: in the weeks since they had become lovers, they had talked about marriage and children as if they were part of some reward they would one day have for present fidelities. "I want to have a child with you," he said. "But I thought we would have to wait. I thought you wanted to have a career first."

She opened her eyes. "That was what I wanted when I came here, David, but then I fell in love with you."

It was as if something inside himself, the two essential halves that had always been divided, had suddenly and miraculously come together. Saying nothing, he kissed her gently then closed her up in his arms. It seemed as if he could go on holding her like this for a lifetime.

She lowered her head into the pillow. "I feel so ashamed," she said.

He knew at once where her thoughts were running. "You have nothing to be ashamed of, Katherine. We love each other, and we will now make everything right by getting married."

"But it's not something we're doing now with freedom," she said. "We have no choice."

"Freedom or not, I made my choice months ago."

She reached up and touched his lips with her finger. "And I made my choice that night at the Gästehaus Bürgerbräu."

"And now, thank God, you can't change your mind." He grinned and kissed the end of her nose. "You're pregnant."

"I wouldn't, in any case."

Whether it was only the cloud that suddenly passed across the moon or the shadow of her fear, he couldn't tell, but her face suddenly darkened. He thought of her father's silence and the threat that had hung over her for over a month. "You're worried about what your father will do, aren't you?" he said.

"We're not married, David, and Papa is an old-fashioned man."

"Old-fashioned or not, there's nothing your father can do, Katherine. He must know by now that I love you, and all he can do is accept, for once, what he cannot change."

"He may know that I love you, David, but he doesn't yet know that I'm pregnant or that I'm going to marry you."

"Then you must write him again and tell him the news."

She looked up as the cloud passed, flooding her face with moonlight. "Yes," she said, "I'll do that."

He watched in silence as the tears broke from her eyes and ran down the sides of her face. "But you'd like to have his blessing, wouldn't you?" he said.

"He won't give it, David, you know that." She looked away. "Nor will your father. For the same reason."

"But there's a difference, Katherine. My father and I have an ocean between us, and the best I can do is write and ask him for his blessing. With your father, we can go to Berlin and ask him."

She shook her head. "It's impossible. He'll refuse."

"If he does, then at least you'll know that you did everything you could."

13

A HEAVY snow had begun to fall as the train crossed the river Elbe, and by the time David and Katherine reached Berlin five inches of fresh white powder had fallen on the city. Uncertain if they would remain overnight or take the midnight train back to Göttingen, they checked their one suitcase at the station's Gepäckaufbewahrungsstelle and hurried out to the crowded entrance to hail a taxi for the four-mile ride to Grünewald.

The sight of Berlin that night filled Katherine with a painful nostalgia. It was all so familiar. The Zoologischer Garten opposite the station and the busy avenues converging on the ancient Kaiser-Wilhelm-Gedächt-niskirche were magically lit for the night, and the crowd of pedestrians hurrying along the broad shop-lined Kurfürstendamm seemed to be moving with a single joyful purpose. It was the Christmas Eve Kurfürsten-damm she remembered from her childhood.

As the taxi passed the glittering façade of the Theater des Westens, David reached over in the darkness and took her hand. "You must try to relax," he said. "You have nothing to fear."

She smiled and looked away. "I can't help what I feel."

Saying nothing, he locked his fingers around hers and they drove the rest of the way down the Kurfürstendamm in silence.

"So this is where you spent your childhood," David said as they turned from the broad, well-lighted Bismarck-platz into Grünewald's quiet residential Königsallee.

"Yes. We moved to Grünewald in 1902, the year Papa became a major in the Prussian Army." She let go of his hand, opened her purse, and began fussing nervously with the two small gift-wrapped Christmas presents she had bought for her parents. "Papa believed that the Kaiser's second Reich was invincible," she added. "And he bought the house because he thought he would one day become a general."

"Then came the Great War."

"Yes. And the great defeat at Versailles."

They sat in silence as the taxi wound its way through Grünewald's magically wooded white landscape of spacious lawns and Jugendstil brick homes. On either side of the street was a dense forest of tall oak, birch, and pine trees.

As they passed the intersection of the Herbert Strasse, Katherine closed her purse and sat forward. "Go slow, driver," she said. "Number seventeen is the second driveway on the left."

"Ja, ja, gnädige Frau. I know all the houses on the Königsallee."

As the taxi slowed to make the turn between the two large stone columns at the foot of the drive, David took hold of her hand again. "Remember," he said. "When the time comes, I want to be the one to tell your father about the child."

"Yes. I promise." As the driver started up the long gravel driveway, Katherine's heart began to race. Through the birch and pine trees she could see lights burning in all the ground-floor windows of the two-story redbrick house.

"If your father agrees to give you his blessing, we'll stay and visit," David said. "If there's any trouble, we'll say goodnight and leave."

As they came out of the trees into the gravel turnabout on the western side of the house, Katherine saw that a single light burned on the second floor in her parents' bedroom window. As always, at this hour on Christmas Eve, even during the last two desperate years when there was little money for luxuries, they would be upstairs dressing for Frau Eichenwald's supper of roast goose, champagne, and Schokoladentorte. "Stop here, please," she said to the driver. "The front walk is between those two hedges."

David handed the driver ten one-hundred-Mark banknotes. "We agreed on a fare of seven hundred," he said, "but it's Christmas, so keep the change."

"Danke schön, mein Herr!"

"Bitte schön." David opened the door and helped Katherine out.

As the taxi pulled away, she looked off toward the two-story brick garage near the rear of the house and saw, to her relief, that the windows in Müller's second-floor apartment were dark.

"I can see why you've been homesick," said David, as he took her arm to guide her along the snow-banked walk leading to the front entrance. "It's beautiful here."

She could also see that her parents did not anticipate visitors that evening. The snow had not been swept from the front walk and porch lights had not been turned on. "It looks more welcoming in spring," she said.

As they reached the front door, David let go of her arm. "I meant what I said, Katherine. You have nothing to fear."

She pulled the bell cord. "My parents will be upstairs dressing for supper, but Frau Leinfelder, the housekeeper, will answer."

The porch lights came on as the front door swung open. Dressed, as always, in an ankle-length black skirt and white apron, with a starched white cap tied around the crown of her braided white hair, the tiny woman stepped back into the darkened foyer with a look of open-mouthed astonishment.

"Greta," Katherine murmured. "Fröhliche Weihnachten."

"Fräulein Katherine," Frau Leinfelder replied, her voice filled with surprise.

"I've come to see Mama and Papa, Greta," Katherine said evenly.

Hesitating, the old woman glanced at David. "Then don't just stand there, child," she said, and swung the door open. "Come in."

Katherine took David's arm. "This is Frau Leinfelder, David," she said, leading him into the small marble-floored foyer. "And this, Greta, is David Linz. He's my friend and colleague in Göttingen."

"Guten Abend, Herr Linz." The old woman gave a nervous curtsy and quickly closed the front door.

"Guten Abend, Frau Leinfelder," David nodded politely. "Fröhliche Weihnachten."

"Fröhliche Weihnachten, mein Herr."

When he turned around, David found that Katherine had left the foyer and was standing in the center of a long, softly lighted hallway, looking up toward the landing of a carpeted staircase leading to the second floor. The hallway was furnished with traditional Gründerjahre furniture, a large ornately carved oak table and two massive Victorian armchairs. Above the table was a nineteenth-century oil painting depicting a classical Roman battle scene.

"Here, child. Give me your coat," Frau Leinfelder said, hurrying toward Katherine in the hallway. "Your mother and father are upstairs dressing for Christmas supper, and Frau Eichenwald is in the kitchen preparing the goose. Müller has the night off." She threw David a look of despair as she took the coat. "You should have warned your parents you were coming, Fräulein," she said. "They don't expect you."

"We plan to visit only for a while, then take a taxi back into the city."
She caught David's eye and smiled.

"I see." Frau Leinfelder came forward to take his coat. "I take it you're
Fräulein Katherine's friend from America," she said, masking her trepi-
dation with her musical Rhenish accent.

"Yes."

With their coats over her arm, the old woman turned toward a door
leading off the hallway. "Your parents will be down in a few minutes,
Fräulein," she said. "While you're waiting, you must come into the parlor
and see the Tannenbaum."

Suddenly, before she could open the door, a woman's voice called
from upstairs, "Is that you, Greta?"

"Yes, gnädige Frau." As Katherine's mother rounded the staircase landing, hurriedly tying the belt of a long green velvet dressing gown, the
old woman gave Katherine a look of despair and hurried off down the
hallway.

Frau von Steiner came to an abrupt halt at the top of the stairs.

"Ja, Mutti," said Katherine. "Da bin ich."

For a moment, Frau von Steiner stood looking down at the two of
them in the hallway below. Then she reached out and caught hold of
the staircase bannister. "Oh, Katherine," she said softly, and, gripping
the bannister for support, started down.

Katherine met her at the foot of the stairs. "Fröhlichen Weihnachten,
Mutti," she said, and lifted her arms.

Murmuring inaudible German phrases, the two women embraced.

After a moment, Frau von Steiner drew back. "Dear God, child!" she
exclaimed, observing Katherine's new short-skirted dress. "Look how
you've changed!"

"If I've changed, Mutti," Katherine smiled, "it's because of David."

Frau von Steiner looked up and relaxed her grip on Katherine's arms.
"Oh, Katherine," she murmured, "you should have warned me."

"Good evening, Frau von Steiner," David said, and took a step forward.
"Please forgive the intrusion. It was my idea to arrive unannounced, not
Katherine's."

"I see." She reached up to finger the lapel of her dressing gown. "Then
you came up together from Göttingen," she said, directing her words
absently to the space between them.

"Yes. We took the morning train up, and we'll take the twelve thirty
train back tonight."

"We wanted to see you and Papa, Mutti," Katherine said, helplessly. "It's Christmas."

Upstairs, a door closed in a distant part of the house. The apprehension in Frau von Steiner's pale blue eyes gave way to terror. She turned quickly to the open parlor door. "You must come with me, both of you," she said. "We must talk before your father comes down."

David took Katherine's arm and they followed her mother into a large room decorated, like the hallway, with ornate and massive Gründerjahre furniture. A fire burned in a rough-stone fireplace in the opposite wall, and next to the fireplace stood a Christmas tree.

"Please close the door. We haven't much time."

As David stepped back to close the door, Katherine continued across the room toward the Christmas tree, a tall Bavarian spruce decorated with traditional strings of red berries, old-fashioned handmade ornaments, and tiny unlit candles.

"Now tell me why you and Katherine have come here, Herr Linz."

"Please, Mutti," Katherine pleaded, "we've just arrived!"

"I want to know now, Katherine, before Papa comes down!"

The sudden anger in her mother's voice silenced Katherine. It was all happening too fast for her. "I think you already know why we've come, Frau von Steiner," David said. "Katherine and I are going to be married, and we've come to ask for your and Major von Steiner's blessings."

"Dear God, Katherine, have you lost your mind?" Frau von Steiner took hold of the nearby armchair to support herself. "You've known from the beginning what your father thinks of your relationship with Herr Linz, and what you're asking is impossible."

"What you mean is that I cannot marry a Jew."

"Yes," Frau von Steiner sighed.

"It's wrong of Papa to blame all our ills on the Jews, Mutti. And besides, David is an American."

"You are wasting your time, Katherine. You knew when you came here that Papa would refuse to give you his blessing."

"If he doesn't, then at least he will know that I cared enough to ask."

Another door closed, this time on the ground floor.

Realizing that Katherine's strategy was not going to work, David took a step forward. "The fact is, Frau von Steiner, Katherine and I love each other. And love makes everything else—even your husband's anti-Semitism—meaningless."

"Not only that," Katherine hurried on, "David and I have a future we can share together; and unlike you, I won't have to give up my career for my marriage. We're both scientists, and my success will be his as well."

Frau von Steiner let go of the armchair. "It would seem you are using love as an excuse for ambition."

"You told me to follow my dream, Mutti," Katherine said. "And I think that I'm lucky to have found someone to follow it with me."

For a moment, as if sharing something private and secret between them, the two women stared at one another in silence.

"Listen to me, both of you," Frau von Steiner said, and began pacing back and forth in front of the fireplace. "What you've come here to ask of the major is impossible. Believe me, Herr Linz, his hatred of the Jews has nothing to do with you personally."

From the look that Katherine gave him, David could tell that she was thinking of their child. "Katherine and I will be married, Frau von Steiner," he said, "with or without the major's blessing."

"Then you will marry without it."

Katherine turned back to the Christmas tree. "I'm sorry, Mutti," she said, "but we have no choice."

Frau von Steiner's blue eyes suddenly widened with a look of fear. "If your love of Katherine is real, Herr Linz, it will endure the postponement of your marriage plans."

He wondered if he should tell her about the child now, or wait until the major arrived. "There are two things that will never change, Frau von Steiner," he said. "The fact that I love Katherine, and the fact that I am a Jew."

"If you and Katherine do this—if you ask the major for his blessing tonight—you will force him to do what he has so far hesitated to do. He will disown Katherine."

From behind David came the soft click of the door latch turning.

Katherine left the Christmas tree and came forward. "Fröhliche Weihnachten, Papa."

When the major spoke, it was not the bullying voice David remembered that afternoon in Frau Reichshauer's parlor, but the calm and resolute voice of a man who was sure of his advantage. "So," he said. "Frau Leinfelder told me you had come."

David turned. Instead of the braided and bemedaled uniform of the Kaiser's General Staff, the major wore a simple black dinner jacket with his Iron Cross First Class suspended on a ribbon beneath his wing-tipped collar. In his right hand he carried a thin leather folio of papers. "Herr Major von Steiner," he said, and bowed politely.

It was then that he saw the tiny emblem pinned to the major's lapel: a circular metal pin with a black Nazi Hakenkreuz in the center. Katherine had once spoken of his interest in the National Socialist German Workers' Party, but she had never dreamed that he would join the Party.

Standing in the open door, with his left hand resting on its brass lever, the major's only response was to stare at him with dignified contempt. "We will not pretend that you are welcome in this house, Herr Linz." The major closed the door and came forward. "You knew before you came that you are not."

"Please, Papa," Katherine pleaded. "It's Christmas, and we came to talk to you."

The major turned to his wife. "Did you know about this, Elizabeth?" he asked. "Did you know they were coming?"

"No, Eric." She lowered her eyes. "I knew nothing."

He turned to Katherine. "I told you in October that you would not be welcome in this house if you disobeyed me. Why have you come here with this man?"

David stepped in before she could answer. "It was my idea to come here, Herr Major von Steiner, not Katherine's. I've already explained the purpose of our visit to Frau von Steiner, but I will explain it again to you."

"David—" Katherine motioned for him to wait.

It's too late, he thought, for polite civilities. "Katherine and I came here tonight from Göttingen, Herr Major, to tell you and Frau von Steiner that we are going to be married. We came to ask for your blessing."

For a moment, the major went on staring at the leather folio in his right hand. Then a faint quiver ran through the corner of his mouth, the only sign so far of any feeling beyond that of contempt. He looked at his watch and said, quietly, to Frau von Steiner, "It's six forty-seven, my dear, and supper will be served at precisely seven. I want you to go upstairs and finish dressing while I conclude my business with Katherine and Herr Linz. Thirteen minutes, I think, will suffice."

Frau von Steiner started forward. "Eric, I beg of you."

"Enough, Elizabeth! Do as I say!"

The explosion of rage, like an artillery blast, brought her to a halt.

He said, resuming his tone of icy self-assurance, "When you've dressed, my dear, please join me in the dining room."

"Yes," she said vaguely to herself. "I'll dress and we'll have Christmas supper." It was as if the major had suddenly touched the lever on a mechanical doll. Katherine watched as her mother obediently left the room, closing the door softly behind her.

When she had gone, her father turned to David. "Before I give you and Katherine my decision, Herr Linz," he said, "I would like to ask a few personal questions."

The tone was familiar to Katherine. It was the calm reasonable tone he had always used when he was bent on trapping one of his subordinates in a lie.

"Ask whatever you wish, Herr Major," David said.

"You may sit down, if you like."

"I prefer to stand, thank you."

Katherine opened her purse and took out the two small presents she had brought for her parents—a crotcheted handkerchief for her mother and a silver pipe spoon for her father.

"Tell me, Herr Linz, when did you come to Germany?" her father asked.

"A year and a half ago."

"And you came here for what purpose?"

"To study physics at the University of Göttingen."

"I see." Her father opened the leather folio. "And you are at work on your doctorate in theoretical physics at Göttingen?"

"Yes. On the theory of the atomic electron structure."

"Whatever." Her father gestured dismissively. "In any case, I'm told that you have great ambitions as a scientist."

"I believe there's a great future in atomic science, Herr Major," he said.

"I'm also told that you plan to remain here in Germany after you finish your studies at Göttingen, Herr Linz."

David caught Katherine's eye and smiled. "It's Katherine's and my dream one day to work as a research team at the Kaiser-Wilhelm Institute here in Berlin."

"Indeed." The major turned a page in the folio. "In the meantime, I'm told that your doctoral thesis at Göttingen is related to the experimental work my daughter did here, at the University of Berlin."

"Yes," David said. "That's correct."

"And you've told me yourself that you knew of Katherine's experimental work before she arrived in Göttingen."

"Yes."

Katherine held her breath, wondering where her father was leading David.

"So you knew before she came to Göttingen that her experimental contribution to your theoretical dissertation would be essential to its success," he said.

"Yes. I told her that the very first day I met her."

"And is it true that you offered to promote her standing as a student at the Second Physics Institute in exchange for her collaboration on your thesis?"

"No!" David flared. "That isn't true!"

"For instance," her father went on, turning another page in the folio. "I see here that you arranged Katherine's invitation to the Institute's seminar on matter back in October. Then, in November, she began to collaborate with you on your doctoral thesis. The fact is, Herr Linz, you have used my daughter's need for recognition and her talents as a scientist for your own ambitious ends."

"That isn't true. I have done as much for Katherine as she has done for me."

Her father turned another page in the folio. "I'm sorry, but that is not what these documents seem to suggest."

As Katherine stood up and turned to face her father, a pain, like a sharp stab of a knife, streaked through her neck. "Documents, Papa?" she asked. "What documents?"

"I have letters here, Katherine, describing Herr Linz's ambitious plans for you dating back to September," he replied.

She thought of the months she had spent at the University of Berlin being watched by her fellow students. "Letters from whom?" she demanded.

He ignored the question and said to David, "I have a letter dated September 10, which states that you approached the Institute's director, Professor Max Born, regarding Katherine's collaboration on your thesis in July, before she arrived in Göttingen."

The color, she saw, had drained from David's face. She took two steps forward and said in a voice she had never dared to use with her father, "I asked you a question, Papa. Letters from whom?"

When her father looked up, the hint of fear in his eyes was only momentary. "I warned you before you went to Göttingen that the men you would meet there were not like the young men you had known here in Berlin," he said. "The fact is, Katherine, you have been used by Herr Linz since you arrived in Göttingen."

She took a step forward. "The letters you have there, Papa, they were sent to you by Herr Hugenholtz, the university Chancellor, weren't they?" she said.

"The letters I have here should come as no surprise, Katherine," he said. "I warned you that I would rely on Chancellor Hugenholtz's opinion of your behavior before you arrived in Göttingen."

"The truth is, Papa, it is you, not David, who has used me. Otto Hugenholtz is a friend of your commander, General von Seckt, and you were hoping to promote your career through his friendship."

He closed the folio. "It would have been far better if you had come back to Berlin, rather than stay on with Herr Linz at Welchzeckhaus."

"Better for whom, Papa? You or me? You see, David," she said, "I am not the only one with ambitions to succeed. Since the war, Papa has always dreamed of becoming a colonel in Seckt's Reichswehr."

Shaken loose by the truth, her father's anger broke to the surface. "You are a fool, Katherine, to think that you can safely marry a man like Herr Linz! This is Germany, you are a German, and he is a Jew!"

She went to David and took his hand. "Whether we are Jews or Germans makes no difference, Papa. David and I love each other, and that's enough."

Her father's face, when he turned back, was the color of parchment. "Don't you see what's happening in Germany?" he exclaimed. "That it's the Jews and the communists who are responsible for everything we have suffered since the end of the war? You are an Aryan and a Christian, Katherine, and if you marry a Jew you will make yourself an enemy of the people, and they will take their revenge. And you, Linz, if you remain here and marry a Christian, the German people will destroy you. If you and Katherine marry it will be your children who will pay the price for your stupidity."

David pointed to the emblem her father wore pinned to his lapel. "I see, Herr Major, that you have joined the Nazi Party since we last met," he said.

"Germany is on the verge of a revolution, Herr Linz, and the National Socialist German Workers' Party will be the answer to everything."

"Oh, Papa . . ." A feeling of sadness flooded over Katherine, dragging her heart down like a stone.

"My membership in the Party should come as no surprise, Katherine," her father said. "I told you last year that Germany's future now lies with Adolf Hitler and his party."

Remembering how she had promised that David would be the one to tell her parents about the child, Katherine closed her fingers around his hand.

His response was immediate. "Katherine and I are going to be married, Herr Major, with or without your blessing," he said in a calm voice. "Not only do we love each other, but Katherine is now pregnant with our child."

The folio slipped and fell from her father's hand, spilling its pages across the floor. For a moment, as if hearing nothing David had said, he stood staring vacantly into space. Then he said, quietly, "In that case, you give me no choice." Leaving the folio and the letters where they had fallen, he walked with stiff military dignity across the room and opened the door. "If what Herr Linz says is true, Katherine," he said, without turning, "then you have brought a curse on yourself, on your family, and on your child. As it is, I cannot break the ties of kinship and blood that bind you to this family, but I can break the ties of knowledge and fellowship. You will therefore leave this house tonight and never return." Without looking back, he went out and closed the door behind him.

In silence, gripping each other's hand, Katherine and David stood gazing at the papers strewn across the floor: handwritten letters bearing the University of Göttingen's formal letterhead.

"Forgive me," David said. "It was my mistake to insist on coming here."

"No. I'm glad that we came and told Papa the truth, face-to-face."

The grandfather clock in the hallway outside began to chime the seven o'clock hour. "We'd better go now," he said. "If we hurry, we can make the eight forty train back to Göttingen."

At the door, she glanced back at the Christmas tree with its collection of childhood ornaments which she would never see again. "Yes, let's go," she said.

As they turned toward the foyer, Frau Leinfelder hurried down the hallway with their coats. "Oh, Fräulein Katherine!" she exclaimed. "The major tells me that you and Herr Linz are leaving."

"Yes, Greta," she said, and came to a halt just inside the foyer.

Dressed in a black leather topcoat and high black leather boots, Ernst Müller stood in the shadows at the corner of the small room, pulling at the fingers of his left glove. "Guten Abend, Fräulein von Steiner," he said and smiled.

She took hold of David's arm as he joined them in the foyer. "Guten Abend, Müller."

"I was out when you arrived," he said, pulling at the fingers of his right glove, "but I gather you and Herr Linz have come for only a short visit."

She ignored him, took her coat from Frau Leinfelder, and said, "Would you be kind enough to call a taxi, Greta? Herr Linz and I have a train to catch."

"Yes, Fräulein, of course," Frau Leinfelder said, throwing Müller a warning look as she handed David his coat.

"Tell the driver the train leaves the Zoo-Bahnhof at eight forty and we'll wait for him at the front gate."

"Yes, Fräulein. I understand." Frau Leinfelder left the foyer and hurried off down the hallway.

Upstairs, in a far part of the house, a door slammed.

Removing his topcoat, Müller chuckled. "It was brave of you to come here tonight, Fräulein Katherine. I wish I'd been here when you arrived." He was dressed in the now familiar uniform of the Nazi Freikorps: a brown shirt with a black leather shoulder strap and brown woolen trousers.

"Katherine," David said in English, "let's go."

As he took her arm and opened the front door, her mother called from the top of the stairs, "Katherine! Wait!" Grasping the bannister with one hand, carrying an envelope in the other, she hurried down the steps. When she reached the foyer, she drew up, startled by the sight of Müller. "Müller!" she exclaimed. "What are you doing here?"

"The back way was muddy, Frau Major," he replied, flustered. "I thought I would—"

"I've told you before," she broke in angrily, "you are not to enter this house through the front door!"

"Yes, Frau Major." He started into the hallway.

"Not that way!" she shouted. "Go back out and come in through the back door!"

Her mother's unexpected anger astonished Katherine. She stepped back as Müller, hurrying out the door, threw her a look of hatred.

As a gust of cold wind blew through the foyer, her mother reached out and pushed the door closed. "Oh, Katherine," she said. "Why didn't you write and tell me?"

"I wanted to, Mutti, but there wasn't time."

"If I had only known, I could have helped you. But Papa has now forbidden it."

"I know, Mutti, and I understand."

"When is the baby due?"

"Next August. At the end of August."

"Have you seen a doctor?"

"Yes. I have a good doctor in Göttingen, and everything is fine."

Her mother turned to David and held out the envelope she was carrying. "I've been saving this for Katherine," she said. "It isn't much, but it will help when the baby comes."

He took the envelope and opened it. "I'm sorry, Frau von Steiner," he said. "We cannot accept the major's money."

"It isn't the major's money, Herr Linz. It's what's left of my own father's money. I want you to take it and promise me that Katherine will have the child in a good hospital, with good doctors."

"Thank you, Frau von Steiner." He placed the envelope in his pocket. "I can promise you that Katherine and the baby will have everything."

She reached out and took hold of David's hand. "Up to now, I have called you Herr Linz," she said. "But after this, I will call you David and you will call me Elizabeth."

"Yes," he smiled. "I'd like that."

"Tell me, do you really love Katherine?" she asked.

"Yes. With all my heart."

"That, David, is the most important thing. Not your scientific dreams or your ambitions. In the years to come, the love you and Katherine have for each other will be the most important thing for you and your children."

"Yes."

She let go of his hand and reached up gently to take hold of his face. "Whatever you do, you must rid yourself of any shame you may feel at being Jewish, David." She drew his head down and kissed him on the forehead. "If you don't, the world will use it to destroy you."

"I understand."

"We must go, Mutti," Katherine said, "or we'll miss our train." She opened her arms to meet her mother's silent embrace. For a moment, knowing she was about to let go of everything of value from her childhood, she closed her eyes and relished, for the last time, the feeling of her mother's soft, old-fashioned lace collar against her face.

As David opened the front door, another gust of cold wind blew through the foyer.

"One last thing, David," her mother said, as she followed them out onto the front porch. "Between now and August, if anything goes wrong, you must promise to call me at once. I will come."

"Yes. I promise," he said, guiding her down the icy steps. "But Katherine is in good hands, and nothing will go wrong."

As they hurried along the walk toward the driveway, Katherine looked back to see that her mother had come to the edge of the steps and stood silhouetted against the front-porch lights, watching them. At that moment, as she lifted her hand to wave, a wind suddenly swept up the hill through the trees, enveloping her in a blinding swirl of powdery snow.

TWO

14

"LINZ!" a voice called out from the direction of the soccer field.

Jacob drew up and looked off through the dense birch grove. In the deepening twilight, he could make out the figures of six boys coming toward him through the trees. They were dressed in brown Hitlerjugend uniforms, with swastika armbands around their shirtsleeves.

He started to turn away, but another voice called, "Don't go, Linz! We want to talk to you!"

He recognized the voice at once. It was Helmut Ziegler's, a fellow second-year student at the Bismarck Akademie.

He kept silent and scanned the faces of the other five boys. They were also students at the Bismarck. There was Hans Thuring and Fritz Weber and Heinrich Bernstorff, all three third-year students at the Akademie, and Karl Heydrich, a first-year student whose father was Reinhardt Heydrich, the head of Hitler's dreaded Sicherheitsdienst.

They came up and formed a circle around him.

"You know that Jews are forbidden to make use of public parks, Linz," said Bernstorff. "So what are you doing here?"

The question took Jacob by surprise. He and Bernstorff had worked together last year in the school's physics lab, and there had never been any hint of anti-Semitism. "I was on my way home," he said, "and Schmargendorf Park is a shortcut."

"That's not true, Linz." Ziegler stepped forward. The tallest of the six boys, he wore the emblem and the leather shoulder straps of a Hitlerjugend group leader. "We saw you playing soccer in the park."

"You weren't the only one breaking the law," Thuring said. "Your team mates were also Jewish. Soccer is a German game, Linz," Ziegler said, "and Jews like you have no business playing it."

Jacob glanced around at the five mute faces. "Soccer is an English game," he said, "and everyone has the right to play it."

"You forget, Ziegler," Fritz Weber stepped in. "Linz isn't just any ordinary Jew. His father is an American citizen, and he thinks that exempts him from the Nürnberg Laws."

"Not only that," said Bernstorff. "His parents are scientists at the Kaiser-Wilhelm Institute, and that makes him a privileged Jew."

"And what's more," Ziegler added, "his grandfather is Colonel Eric von Steiner, the head of the Army's Heereswaffenamt."

"You're right, Helmut," Weber laughed. "Having a Wehrmacht colonel for a grandfather makes all the difference in the world."

"That's not true," Jacob protested. "I scarcely ever see the man. And besides . . ." He left off, realizing that it was not worth trying to explain the hostile relationship he had with his grandfather Eric. For though he and his parents had lived in Berlin for six years, he had only visited his grandparents twice.

"Jacob is a Jewish name," Thuring said. "You couldn't have gotten that from your grandfather."

"It was my other grandfather's name. He's dead now, but he was an American."

"He was a Jew, Linz, just like you," said Ziegler, "and we don't need any Jewish pigs like you living in Berlin."

Jewish pigs like you: the phrase rang in his ears like a curse. "You're wrong, Ziegler," he said. "My father may be a Jew, but I'm an Aryan . . ." Again, he left off, realizing that it was useless trying to defend himself. Although Germans considered him a Jew, his mother was an Ayran and he was therefore, according to Jewish law, also an Aryan.

Ziegler said, inching forward, "Perhaps we should teach Linz a lesson."

"You're right," Weber laughed. "One that he will not easily forget."

Seeing the circle close around him, Jacob took a step backward.

"Remember this," Ziegler said. "The next time you and your Jewish friends come here to play ball, we'll be waiting."

"We don't want Jewish swine like you polluting our public parks," said Bernstorff.

With that, Ziegler doubled up his fist and savagely struck Jacob in the stomach.

The blow sent him reeling back against the two boys behind him. He felt their hands close around his arms.

"Pig Jew!" someone shouted and struck him in the face.

Jacob looked up at the darkening sky, trying to focus his vision, but the limbs of the trees above him were spinning in a circle.

"His mother sleeps with a Jew," someone said. "She should be forced to leave Germany."

"You're right," Ziegler said. "Aryans who fornicate with Jews should be driven from the country." Again, he doubled his fist and struck Jacob squarely in the stomach.

This time, the force of the blow knocked the air from his lungs. As he bent forward, gasping for air, he felt Weber's and Thuring's grips relax around his arms. He thought to himself: It's now or never.

"Linz thinks he's a privileged Jew because he's first in his class," someone said.

For a moment, waiting for the pain to pass, Jacob went on fighting to get his breath. The pain in his head and stomach was excruciating, but he only had a second to make his move. As he lifted himself, he jerked his arms free, then turned and began running.

Dodging his way through the dense birch trees, Jacob rounded a small marshy pond, heading toward the southeast corner of the park. Behind him there were angry shouts and the sound of rapid footsteps in the dry leaves.

He looked around, wondering if he should try to double back to the soccer field and warn his friends, but there was no way to go back without being caught again.

Jacob picked up speed, cursing himself for his stupidity, for it was he who had persuaded his Jewish friends to meet in the park after school for a game of soccer. He had known they were risking arrest, but he had never dreamed that students from the Bismarck would pass that way.

As he reached the edge of the park, he stopped and looked back. Though the woods behind him were now shrouded in deep blue twilight, he could see that Ziegler and his friends were no longer following him.

He stood for a moment, breathing in the cool autumn air, thinking of the mindless hatred he had witnessed since he and his parents had moved to Berlin. Though this was the first time he had been attacked by students from the Bismarck, it was by no means his first encounter with anti-Semitism. It was everywhere and twice in the last two weeks he had fought with the boys from Berlin-Dahlem's Hitler Youth gang. Yesterday, on his way home from school, he had watched the Gestapo drag an old Jew from his watch repair shop in the Kantstrasse.

Aryans who fornicate with Jews should be driven from the country:

Ziegler's words came back, this time igniting his anger. Though his mother had been the one who had wanted to stay on in Germany so she and his father could finish their research at the Kaiser-Wilhelm Institute, it was she who had finally become fearful of the Nazis. It had happened two weeks ago, when the government suddenly, and without warning, announced that Jews would now be forced to carry identification papers marked with an indelible *J*. There had been additions to the Nürnberg Laws in the past, but this one had been like an awakening for his mother. Arguing that it was no longer safe for them to stay in Germany, and that they had nothing more to gain from their research at the Kaiser-Wilhelm Institute, she had convinced his father to submit their resignations and leave the country. They could move to France as they had planned, she had argued, and would be able to find positions at the Joliot-Curie Radium Institute in Paris, where they could continue their research of the atom's nucleus—a search they had begun eighteen years before, when they were students at Göttingen.

They had set the date of the departure for December first, provided they could sell the house by then.

As Jacob started across the busy Forckenbeckstrasse, the bell in the nearby post office tower began to toll the six o'clock hour. If he hurried, he could be home in time to take a bath and change his clothes before his parents arrived at seven.

At the corner of the Wiesbadenerstrasse, he passed a Jewish-owned shop selling second-hand clothes. The shop was still in business, but someone had painted the words "Macht Deutschland Judenfrei" across its window.

He hurried on, thinking to himself of the foolish choices his parents had made. In the spring of 1932, after working for eleven years as a research team at the Second Physics Institute in Göttingen, they had been offered positions at Berlin's Kaiser-Wilhelm Institute, and that summer, on the eve of his eleventh birthday, they had left Göttingen and moved to Berlin. For his parents, the move to Berlin had been the fulfillment of a dream they had shared since their student days in Göttingen: to work as a research team at the famed Kaiser-Wilhelm Institute. But for him the move to the capital had been the beginning of a nightmare. Hitler had come to power the following year, the Nürnberg Laws had been passed in '35, and he had found himself subject to all the government's anti-Semitic restrictions. Even so, his parents were determined to realize their dream and, like so many other Germans, they had refused to believe that they had anything to fear from the Nazis.

It was his mother, more than his father, who had always dreamed of making a great scientific discovery; of one day finding a way to harness the atom's enormous nuclear energies. It would be a discovery, she had once said, that would force the world of German physics—a world dominated by men—to recognize her as a scientist. But over the years, whenever she talked about discoveries and recognition, he and his father had always known that it was her father's recognition that she really longed for.

As he turned south down the crowded Mecklenburgische Strasse, he suddenly realized that people were staring at him. Glancing at his face in a shop window, he saw that his right cheek was covered with blood.

He looked away and thought with anger of the taunting remark Bernstorff had made about his grandfather: that having a Wehrmacht colonel for a grandfather made him one of Berlin's privileged Jews.

Bernstorff was wrong, of course, for having a Wehrmacht colonel for a grandfather had only brought grief to his family. In '32, when he and his parents moved to Berlin, his mother had finally succeeded in bridging the gulf that had separated her from her father. Reluctantly, at the insistence of his grandmother, his grandfather had broken his eleven-year silence and had come to accept what he could not change. But it was only a partial surrender, for being a dedicated Nazi, with ambitions to make a name for himself in the Party, he had refused to acknowledge either Jacob's or Jacob's father's presence in Berlin; and other than his mother's monthly visits to her parents' home in Grünewald, there had been virtually no communication between the families for six long years.

It was dark when Jacob reached Berlin-Dahlem and turned down the quiet residential Lentzeallee. Fifth from the corner, their two-bedroom cottage was only distinguishable from the other whitewashed stuccoed cottages by the massive oak tree that stood in the front yard.

To his surprise, there was a light burning in the parlor window, which meant that his parents had returned home early that night from the Institute.

"Scheisse," he said aloud to himself. He would now have to explain everything to his parents.

As he pushed open the gate and hurried up to the front porch, he thought again of the predicament he had left his friends in. But at least there were twelve of them and only six Hitlerjugend boys. Finding the front door unlatched, he quietly let himself into the parlor.

From the kitchen came the smell of frying sausages and the sound of his parents' voices. "The fact is, Katherine," his father said, "if you could solve your radium-separation problem in the next two weeks, we could have everything finished before we leave." They were talking, he could tell, about his mother's recent uranium-bombardment experiments.

As he started toward the hallway door, he looked at his face in the mirror above the sofa. The blood on his cheek had dried, and there was a long ugly gash below his right eye.

"Jacob, is that you?" his father called from the kitchen.

"Yes, Papa. It's me," he said, and continued on to the hallway door. If he could at least wash the blood from his face before his parents saw him, he could avoid an ugly scene.

His father came into the room as he reached the door. "You're late tonight, son," he said. "Where were you?"

He wanted to say that they were early for a change, but he said instead, "I'm late, Papa, because I met some friends after school for a game of soccer."

"We came home early tonight, son, because we have some good news for you. We sold the house today."

As Jacob turned around, a look of shock came over his father's face. "My God, son! Your face! What happened?"

"It's nothing. I got into a fight, that's all."

"What do you mean you got into a fight! A fight with whom?"

"With some boys from the Akademie."

His mother came to the kitchen door. "Jacob!" she said with shock. "Your face!"

"It's nothing," he said. "Just a cut on my cheek."

As she started toward him, he turned down the hallway, wanting to escape his mother's solicitude.

"Come back here, Jacob!" his father called to him. "I want to talk to you."

"It wasn't my fault, Mother," he said. "I was on my way home and they attacked me."

"But why would they do that? I thought the boys from the Bismarck were your friends."

"I met some friends after school for a game of soccer," he said. "There's no place to play soccer, so we went to the soccer field in Schmargendorf."

"In other words," his father stepped in, "you went to a public park."

"We had no choice, Papa. You can't play soccer in the streets."

His father said, exchanging a worried look with his mother, "And your friends, I take it, were also Jewish."

"Yes, Papa."

His mother sighed with exasperation. "Why do you insist on making trouble for yourself. You know that it's against the Nürnburg Laws for Jews to use public parks."

"I don't give a damn about Hitler's Nürnberg laws," he said. He looked away. "And besides, I'm not really a Jew."

Katherine touched the wound on his face. "We've been through this a hundred times, Jacob. You may not be a Jew to Jews, but you're a Jew to other Germans, and you're subject to the Nürnberg Laws."

"Unjust laws are not really laws," he said, "and there's no reason I have to obey them."

His father came up and stopped beside his mother. "You still haven't explained why the boys from the Akademie attacked you, son."

He suddenly felt a lump rising in his throat. "The boys from the Bismarck are members of a Hitler Youth gang, Papa. When the game was over and I left the park, they were waiting for me in the woods near the soccer field."

There was a moment of shocked silence. "This is the third time in two weeks that you've had a fight with Hitler Youth gangs!" David said. "This is Germany, not France, and you could be arrested for entering a public park and sent to prison without a trial."

"Oh, Jacob," his mother said, wiping the blood from his face. "Why do you take risks like this? You know that there are police and Gestapo everywhere, and Jews are being arrested every day for no reason at all."

"If we had left Germany when the Nürnberg Laws were passed," he said, "none of this would be happening."

It's true, Katherine thought and looked away. It was she, not David, who had insisted on postponing their departure. They had come closer to an experimental breakthrough at the Kaiser-Wilhelm, and until two weeks ago, when the government passed the Jewish identification law, there had seemed to be no real danger from the Nazis. "You're right, of course, Jacob," she said. "We should have left Germany when Hitler came to power."

"What's done is done, son," his father said. "But if you can stay out of trouble for three more weeks, we'll be in France by the first of December."

As Jacob turned to his father, his anger increased. "I hate Berlin, I hate Germany, and I don't want to stay here for three more weeks."

The venom in the boy's voice startled David, and he looked at Katherine in alarm. "That's a lot of hate, son, for one person to feel," he said.

"There're a lot of Germans, and they're all Nazis."

"That's not true, Jacob," Katherine said. "There are many Germans who aren't Nazis."

The boy turned his back to them and took a book from the nearby bookshelf. "You're wrong, Mother," he said, thumbing through the pages. "No one in Berlin ever says or does anything against the Nazis. And when the führer goes by in the street, everyone salutes. I've seen them."

"They do that, Jacob, because they're afraid," she said.

"Hatred is a terrible thing," David continued. "If you let hatred take hold of you, you'll end up no different from Hitler and the Nazis."

For a moment, the boy went on leafing through the book's pages. Then he said, quietly, "Grandpapa Eric is a Nazi."

The remark silenced both of them.

With a sinking feeling of grief, Katherine thought to herself of the hatred that had divided her family for eighteen long years. Though she had made peace with her father when they moved to Berlin, he had refused to end the war he had waged with David since the day they met in Göttingen. But worse than the hatred that had torn their two families apart was David's refusal in the last few weeks, as the Nazi wall of repression closed around them, to allow her to seek her father's protection for their son.

"Yes, Jacob," she said, finally. "Grandpapa Eric is a Nazi."

"And you hate him, don't you, Papa," the boy said.

It was both a challenge, David realized, and a trap. He said, watching the blood drain from Katherine's face, "It's not that I hate Grandfather Eric, Jacob. I don't hate the man, I only hate what he believes in." He heard the false ring in his voice and added, quickly, "Actually, I pity Grandfather Eric."

Tears broke from the boy's eyes as he thrust the book back into the shelf. "I don't pity him, I hate him. He has hated the two of us from the very beginning. I've lived all my life in the shadow of his hatred, Papa. He's not going to change, and I want to forget him."

The truth of the boy's words cut through Katherine's heart like a knife. She put her hand gently on his shoulder. "You must not be afraid, sweetheart," she said. "We'll leave Germany as soon as we can."

"Your mother's right, son," David said. "We've sold the house, we've submitted our resignations from the Institute, and there's nothing now to keep us here."

Katherine said, looking at David for assurance, "There's an express train to France every afternoon at four and, if your father agrees, we'll change our plans and leave for Paris at once."

"I do agree," David said. "We can leave, if you want, by the end of the week."

The boy turned with wide-eyed surprise. "Do you mean it, Papa?" he asked.

"Yes, son. All we need to do is obtain our French visas and buy railroad tickets. Tomorrow, you can take the day off from school and we'll go and arrange everything."

Katherine stepped forward and grasped the boy by the shoulders. "Just think, sweetheart," she said. "By next Sunday, you'll be walking on the Left Bank, eating roasted chestnuts by the Seine."

"Is that a promise, Mother?" he asked.

"Yes, Jacob. That's a promise."

15

IT was 4:35 when Katherine finished sorting through the lab reports in her office filing cabinet and began gathering up the papers on her desk. They had planned to leave for Paris on Friday, but on Tuesday, when they went to the French Embassy to arrange for their entrance visas, they had been told, much to Jacob's disappointment, that there had been a sudden rush for French visas in the last two weeks, and it would take a week for the Embassy to process their applications.

She had spent the afternoon choosing the lab reports she would take with her to Paris, and as she placed the small stack of reports in her briefcase, there was a knock on the door. "Come in!" she called.

Konrad Bukowski, her colleague from the chemistry department, was standing in the door, holding a yellow lab file in his hands. "Thank God you're still here, Katherine," he said. "I need to talk to you."

"I can't talk now, Konrad," she said. "I have to be home to meet Jacob at five."

Clutching the file, he came into the room and closed the door. "I'm sorry, Katherine, but we have to talk about this now." He held up the file. "I've just finished the chemical analysis of the material you gave me this morning, and the results are quite amazing."

"Konrad, David and I have to be home when Jacob gets back from school. He had a big scare on Monday, and we don't want . . ." She stopped abruptly, seeing the look of fear in her colleague's eyes. In the five years she had worked with Bukowski at the Kaiser-Wilhelm, she had come to have a deep respect for his scientific opinions. A graduate of the University of Warsaw and a brilliant radiochemist, he had joined the Institute's chemistry staff in 1933, the year after she and David moved to Berlin, and since then he had carried out the chemical analyses of all her transuranic experiments.

The day before Bukowski had mistakenly reached for the wrong bottle and had used palladium as a chemical carrier, instead of the barium she had requested. Later, when he discovered his mistake and told her of the chemical results—that a small fraction of radioactive palladium had precipitated out with the non-radioactive carrier—she had berated him not only for using the wrong carrier, but also for misanalyzing the results. It was impossible, she had pointed out, that she could have produced radioactive palladium, an element with an atomic number of only 46, from uranium 238, an element with twice the atomic number. Then this morning, determined to complete her uranium experiments before the week was out, she had bombarded a second sample of uranium and had asked him to repeat his analysis, this time using the correct chemical carrier.

"I ran the analysis on your second batch of material, but I didn't use barium as a carrier. I repeated the procedure using the palladium again."

"You did what?"

"I was puzzled by what happened yesterday, so I decided to repeat the procedure using palladium sulfide again. I was right the first time, Katherine. Atoms of radioactive palladium came off with the palladium sulfide precipitate."

For a moment, she stared at the lab report on her desk and said nothing. Last night, when she told David about the mistake Bukowski had made with his chemical carrier, he had jokingly remarked that it would have gone off like a bombshell if their chemistry colleague had been right about the presence of radioactive palladium in precipitate.

"You realize, of course, that what you're saying is impossible," she said. "To bombard uranium and produce palladium would go against all the accepted laws of physics."

"It's all there in the report, Katherine. I was right the first time. You produced atoms of radiopalladium with your uranium bombardment."

She put her coat on and went back to her desk. Back in September, when Otto Hahn, the director of the Kaiser-Wilhelm Institute, approached her with the seemingly insoluble chemical problem of the new "radium" isotope that he and Fritz Strassmann had produced with their chemical irradiations of uranium, she had offered to investigate the problem using the Institute's Van de Graaf accelerator. Knowing that she would need a chemical analysis of the various by-products she produced from her uranium bombardments, she had asked Bukowski to work with her on the experiment.

"Otto Hahn and Fritz Strassmann have analyzed the results of their uranium irradiations countless times, Konrad," she said, "and they're convinced that it's radium they've been producing."

"Radium was an understandable choice," he said. "They've been looking for an element near uranium on the periodic table, and they chose radium because it's chemically identical to barium."

"I assume you're going to tell me that it was actually radioactive barium they've been producing all along," she said as she took the report from her desk.

"Why not? If you produced radiopalladium with an atomic number of 46, why couldn't they do the same with barium, with an atomic number of 56?"

The thought of it—that Hahn and Strassmann here in Berlin, and Curie and Savitch in Paris, could have been wrong all this time about the nature of the new transuranic elements they had been producing; and that they had simply been generating isotopes of already known elements on the periodic table—astonished her.

"My procedure was exact, Katherine," he said. "During the second analysis I put the precipitate under a Geiger counter and clocked the beta emissions. The activity in the crystals showed a half-life of five and a half hours, the same as radioactive palladium. It's all described in the report."

She thought of the years she and David had spent trying to unlock the door into the atom's nucleus: twelve years at the Second Physics Institute in Göttingen and six years at Kaiser-Wilhelm in Berlin. After all the risks they had taken, the thought that they might now, on the eve of their departure from Germany, and by a simple fortuitous accident, have found the answer to the question that had plagued them for eighteen years, made her suddenly want to laugh.

"Tell me, Konrad," she said, "who else has seen this report?"

"Only my assistant Kurt Waldhardt. We only finished it half an hour ago."

"I see." She closed the report and added it to the reports in her briefcase. Kurt Waldhardt was among the half dozen scientists who had come to the Kaiser-Wilhelm six months ago, following the Austrian Anschluss and the government's dismissal of all the Austrian Jews from the Kaiser-Wilhelm. Like the others, he was an ardent member of the Nazi Party. "In any case," she said, "for the time being I would appreciate it if you didn't say anything about your radiopalladium confirmation to anyone. Including Hahn and Strassmann."

He smiled. "As you wish, Katherine."

She said, glancing with panic at the clock on her desk, "You must forgive me, Konrad. I'm late."

"By the way," Bukowski followed her into the second-floor hallway, "I assume you've told David about my carrier mistake."

"Yes. I told him last night." She turned down the hallway, heading for David's office.

"And he had no theoretical explanation for the radiopalladium I found?"

"No. None. He said it was impossible."

As they reached David's office door, Bukowski took hold of her arm. "One more thing, Katherine," he said. "Whatever explanation David comes up with after he reads the report, I hope it won't change your minds about leaving Germany."

She knew what he was thinking. Aside from her father, who had been warning her for six years to leave Germany, Bukowski had been the one scientist at the Kaiser-Wilhelm who, from the very beginning, had seen and understood the Nazi threat, and as far back as 1935, when the Nürnberg Laws were first promulgated, he had been urging them to leave the country, insisting that it would be Jacob, a German Jew, who would feel the backlash of Nazi repression. In the five years she had known him, he had never spoken openly about his hatred of the Nazis, but she and David were convinced that he was secretly involved in one of Berlin's anti-Nazi movements.

"David and I may be ambitious," she said, "but we're not fools. Even if you're right about the radiopalladium, it will change nothing. We're leaving for Paris a week from Thursday."

"Good." He let go of her arm. "Then you'll have nothing to fear."

"David will read the report tonight, Konrad, and we'll talk tomorrow."

"Fine, fine." He waved and turned back down the hallway. "I'll stop by your office in the morning."

Tucking her papers under her arm, she tapped once on the door and opened it before David could answer. Already wearing his topcoat, he sat at his desk, reading a newspaper. "Sorry I'm late, sweetheart," she said. "I got trapped by Konrad Bukowski."

He tossed the newspaper on the desk and looked at his watch. "Never mind. If we leave now, we can still make it by five."

As he got up and began collecting his papers from the desk, her eye came to rest on the newspaper's front page headline: COMMUNIST JEW MURDERS GERMAN EMBASSY SECRETARY IN PARIS. The date on the paper was November 8—that afternoon's edition of the *Deutsche Allgemeine Zeitung*.

"My God, David, what's happened?" she asked, pointing to the newspaper.

"A bloody catastrophe. The *Zeitung* says that one of the secretaries of the German Embassy in Paris was murdered yesterday by a German Jewish refugee."

She went to the desk and quickly read the article's opening line: "From Paris comes the report that the third secretary of the German Embassy, Ernst von Rath, was yesterday shot down in cold blood by a German Jewish refugee . . ."

"A German government official murdered by a German Jew," David said. "This is exactly the kind of incident the government has been looking for."

"But that's ridiculous. The murder happened in Paris."

"Even so, Jews are being blamed for it, and the government is openly calling for revenge." He put the papers in his open briefcase. "We're smart to be leaving Berlin," he said. "If I'm right, there's going to be a big Nazi crackdown."

"We would have been smarter to have left a month ago," she said, "before the rush for French visas began."

"You've got to stop blaming yourself for the delay with the visas, Katherine. We've done everything we can to leave as soon as possible."

She folded the newspaper and tucked it under her arm. "By the way, Bukowski ran an analysis of the material I gave him this morning, and he says he was right the first time."

David looked up with surprise. "What do you mean he was right the first time?"

"I mean he repeated yesterday's procedure and used palladium sulfide again. He says that atoms of radioactive palladium came off with the sulfide precipitate."

She set her briefcase on the desk and took out Bukowski's lab report.

"This is the chemistry report on his second analysis, David," she said. "You can read it for yourself."

He took the report and opened it.

"It's four fifty," she said, "we're going to be late if we don't hurry."

For a moment, he scanned the three-page report and said nothing. When he spoke again, there was a note of nervous excitement in his voice. "Did Bukowski mention finding any other elements besides palladium in his analysis?"

"No. Nothing."

"Good. Then we're at least one step ahead of Hahn and Strassmann."

"I don't understand."

"This morning, I did some calculations on the figures you gave me last night." He closed the report and handed it to her. "It's a matter of simple arithmetic, Katherine. The uranium you began with has an atomic number of 92. If you produced palladium with an atomic number of 46, it would leave you with exactly the same number of protons unaccounted for."

She said, wondering where he was leading, "In other words, there would be two chemically identical radioactive palladium atoms in the precipitate."

"Exactly. Which would explain why Hahn and Strassmann have been unable to separate the radioactive barium from their barium carrier."

"You mean they've been producing atoms of radioactive barium all along?"

"That's right. Barium has a atomic number of 56, and it would be interesting to see if their by-products contained atoms of, say, krypton gas, with an atomic number of 36."

She kept silent, trying to work out the implications of his astonishing statement.

"If I'm right, Katherine," he said, "when you bombarded the uranium, the nucleus must have absorbed one of the neutrons."

"But that's impossible," she said. "The neutron only has the energy of a few electron volts."

"Impossible or not, a neutron must have penetrated the nuclear barrier and split the entire nucleus into a spectrum of different lighter elements— palladium, barium, and krypton."

She stared at the thin handwritten report in her hands, feeling her heart begin to race. "But that would break all the laws of physics, David," she said.

"As Jacob would say, erroneous laws are not really laws at all," he laughed. He took his briefcase from the desk and turned out the desklamp, leaving only the light from the hallway. "If what I think is true, Katherine, it's been happening all along. Ever since 1932, when everyone began bombarding uranium with neutrons. It's against all the accepted laws, I know, but what you've done is split the uranium atom."

An old and familiar feeling came over her: a feeling of vertigo that momentarily blurred her vision and made her dizzy. She held her breath, thinking of the fruitless years she had spent fighting for recognition as a female scientist, and of the tremendous prize that was now within their reach.

David looked again at his watch. "We'd better go, sweetheart. We're ten minutes late, and Jacob will be waiting."

16

WHEN they pulled out of the Kaiser-Wilhelm's gravel parking lot, the sun had just set, leaving only a pale amber ribbon of light behind the silhouette of Berlin-Dahlem's wooded horizon.

David looked at Katherine, who sat silently holding the copy of the *Deutsche Allgemeine Zeitung* in her lap. He knew, without asking, where her thoughts were running. "It's ironic, isn't it, that this should happen just as we're about to leave Berlin," he said.

"Yes." She folded the newspaper and looked out at the fading autumn light. "If it had happened two months ago, I could have done all the experimental verifications, you could have written your theoretical paper, and we could have had something ready for publication when we got to Paris."

As he made a quick right turn into the deserted Arnim Allee, he thought to himself of the years they had spent working to reach this moment. "You can do the experiments in Paris," he said.

"Paris will be too late, David. By the time we arrange positions at the Radium Institute, Hahn and Strassmann will have solved their radium problem and worked out the meaning of the uranium split."

He thought of the dreams that had brought them together as students in Göttingen. "Do you remember our first afternoon in the Ratskeller in Göttingen?" he asked.

She looked at him with surprise. "Yes. I remember asking you what was the most wonderful thing you imagined yourself accomplishing as a physicist."

"That's right." She looked out at the slow-moving rush hour traffic. "I had had too much to drink, and I told you all my childhood dreams."

"You said you had always dreamed that you would find wonderful uses for the energy that was locked inside the atom's nucleus . . . the power, you said, to light whole cities and to drive ships across the seas."

"I was a starry-eyed schoolgirl, David, and I knew nothing about the real world of science."

He reached over and took her hand. "The fact is, Katherine, I think you have done exactly what you dreamed of doing."

She sighed, softly. "What I've done is only a beginning, David. At best, all we know is that I've split the uranium atom."

"It seems so unfair," he said. "You've spent the best part of your life hoping for such a discovery, and you deserve this kind of success."

"There's nothing to be done, David. We have only eight days left in Berlin."

He looked at his watch, then swung north up the Engler Allee, heading for home. "How long would it take you to complete the necessary experiments?"

"I'm not sure. Aside from the palladium, Bukowski has never identified any other lighter element in the by-products of my uranium bombardments. If I was going to prove anything at all, I would have to start all over again, from the very beginnning."

"But how long do you think the experiments would take?" he persisted.

She sat forward as he sped up to pass a slow-moving truck. "If we could stay on safely for a while," she said. "I think I could finish everything by Christmas."

During the last year, as the government began tightening the Nürnberg laws, she had several times spoken of using her father's influence with the government if ever the need arose. "If you're going to ask me if you can speak to your father about arranging some kind of protection for Jacob, Katherine, the answer is no."

"I'm not asking for anything, David." She reached over and touched his hand. "But Papa has contacts at the Reichschancellery, and he could make everything possible for us."

He heard the note of appeal in her voice and wished he hadn't mentioned it. "I've already told you that I will never ask for anything from your father. Besides, there's going to be another Nazi crackdown, and we've made a promise to Jacob."

"You're right, of course." She looked down at the ugly headline glaring up at her from the newspaper in her lap: JEW MURDERS EMBASSY SECRETARY. "This man who murdered the embassy secretary, David, who was he?" she asked.

"A fellow by the name of Grynszpan. Herschel Grynszpan."

"The paper says he's a communist."

"Nonsense. You know as well as I do that to the Germans every Jew is a communist."

"It's ridiculous, David, for the government to blame the Jews here for what a madman did in Paris," she said.

He sighed. "The madman, Katherine, is a seventeen-year-old boy."

It was 5:25 when they turned into the narrow tree-lined Lentzeallee. Theirs was the only house on the street with no lights burning in the windows.

"Jacob's not here," Katherine said with alarm.

"Relax. He probably stopped off to visit one of his friends."

"But he promised to come straight home from school, David."

"If he's not home by six, we'll . . ." He turned off the motor and the headlights.

"We'll do what?" she asked. "Call the police?"

"We'll take the car and go look for him." He looked out at the darkened house. Sheltered from the corner streetlamp by the spreading limbs of its huge oak tree, the house was scarcely visible in the darkness.

"There's something wrong, David, I can feel it." She left the newspaper in the seat and quickly got out.

He took his briefcase and joined her on the sidewalk. The wooden gate had been left open, and as he started down the brick walk to the front porch—it took a few seconds for his eyes to adjust to the darkness— he caught sight of a figure sitting on the steps.

"Jacob?" he said.

There was no reply.

Katherine caught up and took his arm. "Jacob, is that you?" she asked.

"Ja, Mutti. It's me," the boy replied, his voice breaking midword.

As they started forward, David saw that the boy was sitting on the top step, with his arms dangling below his knees. He had taken off his school jacket, and his tie hung loose from the open collar of his white shirt. "Are you okay, son?" he asked.

"Ja, Papa. I'm fine."

"But why are you sitting here in the dark?" Katherine asked.

"I don't know. I just felt like it."

When they reached the steps, David saw to his relief that there were no new marks on the boy's face. His right eye was still dark and swollen and he wore the bandage Katherine had taped to his cheek, but there was no evidence of new injuries. "Is something wrong, son?" he asked.

"Wrong, Papa? What do you mean?"

The light from the window of the neighboring house reflected the moisture in the boy's pale blue eyes. "You know what I mean," he said, wondering if he had been crying. "Did you have trouble again with the Hitlerjugend?"

"No. You and Mother weren't here when I got home, so I decided to sit out here and wait for you on the front porch."

Katherine let go of David's arm. "I'm sorry, Jacob. It's my fault that we're late."

"It doesn't matter." The boy shrugged. "I just got home myself."

She looked up at the darkened front windows. "But why didn't you go inside?"

"I did go in. I put my books inside and came back out."

"Let's all go in, son," David said. "It's cold out here." As he started up the steps, he caught sight of what appeared to be a small pile of whittled woodchips on the step under the boy's feet. He continued on to the door. "You say you just got home?" he asked.

The boy got up. "Ja, Papa. A few minutes ago."

The ease with which he lied shocked David. "The reason we're late, son, is because Dr. Bukowski wanted to give your mother his chemistry report on the uranium bombardment she did this morning," David said as he fumbled for the parlor lightswitch. "He ran a second analysis this afternoon, and it turns out he was right the first time."

The boy came into the room, followed by Katherine. A head taller than his mother, and bigger than most boys his age, he had inherited something from each of them: from Katherine, his fair skin, his stubborn, chiseled chinbone, and his pale blue eyes; and from David, his height, his curly coal-black hair, and his name—after his grandfather Jacob, who had died a month before he was born in August of '21.

"But you said last night that Bukowski had made a mistake in his procedure," the boy said to his mother, "and that he had used palladium instead of barium for a carrier."

"That's right. And today he decided to use it a second time."

"It doesn't make any sense, son," David said, "but it seems that atoms of radioactive palladium came off with the palladium sulfide. And if my hunch is right, your mother has done something quite astonishing. She has split the uranium atom."

A look of shock came over the boy's face. "Split the uranium atom? But that's impossible."

"At this point, Jacob, Papa's idea is only a hypothesis," Katherine said. "Aside from the palladium, we have no experimental evidence to prove anything."

The boy thrust his hands into his pockets and began pacing back and forth between the bookcase and the sofa. "But if you did" he said, "if you had the evidence to prove that you split the uranium atom, it would be a great discovery, wouldn't it?"

"Yes, Jacob," she said, "it would be a very great discovery."

"But the experiments to prove it would take weeks to perform, wouldn't they?"

David said, reading the boy's look of apprehension, "You have nothing to fear, son. One way or the other, we are leaving for Paris a week from tomorrow."

"Papa's right," Katherine added. "The results of experiments will change nothing."

"I see you've brought a lot of books home tonight, son," David said to change the subject.

"That's right." The boy stopped pacing and went to the armchair. "I have a lot of books at school, and I need to pack them for Paris."

They watched in silence as the boy, looking preoccupied with some inner distress, began stacking the books in his arm.

"Why don't you leave the books there for now," David said, "and tell us what happened?"

"What do you mean, what happened?"

"You know what I mean. You've been crying."

The boy looked away. "There was some trouble at school," he said. "It's nothing."

"You've had another fight, haven't you?"

"No." He turned away. "I don't want to talk about it. We're leaving and it doesn't matter."

As the boy started down the hall, David saw Jacob's fishing knife in his back pocket. He thought of the whittled woodchips on the front step and the lie he had told him. "Stop right there, young man," he said.

The boy came to a halt in the darkened hallway.

"Come back here, Jacob," he said. "I want to talk to you."

"These books are heavy, Papa, and I can't stand here all night holding them." Without waiting for a response, he moved off down the hallway toward his bedroom.

"Jacob!" With a sudden rush of anger, David started after him.

"No, sweetheart, wait." Katherine intercepted him at the door. "Something terrible has happened, I know it, and if you go to him in anger, you'll get nowhere."

He took a deep breath. "You're right, as always," he said. Leaving her in the living room, he turned down the short hallway toward his son's bedroom at the back of the house. The door was closed and, for a moment, he stood listening to the clatter of the boy stacking books. Then he tapped on the door and said quietly, "Jacob?"

There was no reply, but the noise stopped.

He opened the door. "Is it okay if we talk, son?" he asked.

"All right, but I have work to do."

David left the door open and crossed to the bed. "We can't take a lot with us, son," he said, "so you're going to have to choose your books carefully." The boy's back pocket, he saw, was now empty.

"I know, Papa," he said. "I'm taking only the ones I won't be able to find in Paris."

It had been different with his own father, he remembered, for the quickest road into Jacob's confidence had always been science. "When we get to Paris, the first thing we'll do is file an admissions application at the Polytechnique," he said. "That's the best school for science in France."

"I know things are different in France," he said. "But will they object to my being a Jew?"

"No, Jacob."

"For once, I want to be like the other boys in school," he said. "I want to speak only French and I want to make lots of new friends."

"You will, Jacob."

The boy left off stacking his books and looked up. "I think you're wrong about Mother's uranium discovery," he said. "It's going to change everything."

"What do you mean, change everything?"

"If she has really split the uranium atom, she will want to stay on and verify her discovery."

"That's nonsense, Jacob. It's not even a theory, only an idea. And your mother would never dream of staying on only to verify an idea."

"You're wrong, Papa." The boy's blue eyes—Katherine's eyes—widened with fear. "If she's split the uranium atom, then she's found the answer to all of the questions you and she have been asking for the last eighteen years."

"It was your mother's idea to leave Germany in the first place, and she would never do anything that would risk your safety."

The boy went back to sorting his books, slowly and thoughtfully this time. "She's waited all her life for this kind of discovery. If she lets it pass by, she may never have another chance."

It's true, David thought. If she let this opportunity slip through her fingers, it would never come again.

"If you're right about what she has done," the boy said, "it could bring you both a Nobel Prize, couldn't it?"

"Yes. I suppose it could."

"If you think about it, splitting the atom would be for physics like Copernicus discovering that the earth is not the center of the universe."

"Yes. I guess it would."

The boy reached for one of his books on the floor. "I'm telling you this, Papa, because no matter what Mother says or does, I don't want to stay on in Germany any longer."

"Your mother and I have made a promise, son; one way or another we are leaving for Paris a week from tomorrow."

"It's a mistake, Papa, for us to stay here even that long." He thrust the book into the box. "Something terrible is going to happen before the week is out."

Seeing the opening he had been looking for, David sat down on the boy's bed. "All right, Jacob," he said, "do you want to tell me what happened at school today?"

"It doesn't matter now what happened. School for me at the Bismarck is finished."

"I want you to tell me what happened today, Jacob," David said firmly.

Still, the boy said nothing.

Behind David there was a soft rustle of paper, and when he looked around, Katherine was standing in the open doorway. In one hand she held Jacob's school jacket, and in the other hand a thin onionskin envelope. Her face looked deathly white.

"This was on the living room floor under your jacket, Jacob," she said, and held up the envelope. "Why didn't you tell us?"

"What difference does it make?" the boy said, without looking up from his book. "We're leaving Berlin, anyway."

Katherine came into the room and handed the envelope to David. "This is addressed to you. There's a letter inside from Ernst Humboldt."

Ernst Humboldt was the director of the Bismarck Akademie, and the envelope bore the school's official title, Deutsche Bismarck Akademie.

As he removed the thin, onionskin page, Katherine said, "You mustn't let this upset you, Jacob. You're the best student in your class, and all this ugly hatred cannot change that fact."

Herr Doktor David Linz, the letter began. The name had been spelled Lenz, crossed out, and corrected by hand. The letter stated in brisk, formal language that Jacob had been dismissed from the Deutsche Bismarck Akademie and his name removed from the list of the Akademie's students. The dismissal was effective today, November 8, 1938.

From the floor across the room came the sound of a suppressed whimper, and when David looked up, Jacob had slumped forward with his face buried in his hands.

"Oh, sweetheart." Katherine went to boy and knelt down beside him on the floor. "What are you so afraid of? There is nothing on earth that can stop us from leaving Germany."

"You're wrong, Mother. Humboldt called me to his office this afternoon and warned me to leave Germany at once." The book slid from his lap and fell to the floor. "He said that the government was planning to revenge the murder in Paris, and that a roundup of Jews would begin on Friday."

"But that's just two days away!"

"I'm so afraid, Mother." With a sob that seemed to spill from his soul, the boy buried his face against Katherine's breast. "If Humboldt is right, I could be arrested before the week is out."

She closed him up in her arms and turned to David. "This has gone far enough," she said. "You must let me go to my father and ask for his protection."

He hesitated, wondering if he was making a terrible mistake.

"For God's sake, David!" she cried. "It's only for nine days!"

"All right," he said, and sighed. "I guess we have no choice."

17

IT was almost nine o'clock when Katherine turned up the winding driveway to her parents' house in Grünewald. Ahead, through the dense grove of linden trees, she could see lights burning in the ground-floor windows of the parlor and her father's study, but the rest of the house was dark.

She turned off her headlights and sat for a moment, wondering how she would be able to persuade her father to give Jacob his protection for their last week in Germany. In all the years she had lived in Berlin, she had never dared to ask for either his help or protection, and she was afraid that he would now refuse.

But she had no choice. The papers that morning had been filled with articles calling on the government to take immediate retaliation for the murder in Paris and, as Jacob had said the night before, there had been talk that afternoon at the lab that a mass arrest of Jews would take place within the next two days.

She took her purse from the seat, got out, and hurried down the walkway to the front porch.

When she reached the porch, she found that the front door had been left unlocked. She let herself in and continued through the darkened foyer into the hallway. Aside from the light falling through the open parlor door and a light burning on the table opposite her father's study, the hallway was dark.

"Is that you, Katherine?" her mother called as she started past the parlor.

She drew up as Elizabeth hurried into the hallway. Wearing her old gray velvet dressing gown, with her long ash blonde hair hanging loose about her shoulders, she looked older that night than her fifty-seven years. "Thank God you're here," she said. "You're half an hour late, and I was beginning to worry."

"I took David and Jacob to a movie at the Ufa Palast, and on the way back I got caught in traffic on the Kurfürstendamm."

Her mother came forward, tightening the sash on her dressing gown. "I heard Papa talking earlier about a demonstration tonight," she said, "and I almost telephoned to tell you to stay home."

"A demonstration? What kind of demonstration?"

"I don't know. He didn't say."

"Where is Papa?"

"He's waiting for you in his study."

As they turned together down the hallway, Katherine thought of the telephone conversation she had had that morning with her mother, asking her to arrange the appointment with her father. "Did you tell Papa the reason for my visit tonight?" she asked.

"No, Katherine. I told him about Jacob's expulsion from the Akademie, but I said nothing about the purpose of your visit."

"He can't refuse to help me, Mutti. It's only for one week."

"It isn't a question of time. After what's happened in Paris, Papa can only follow the government's orders."

"But he must help me!" she exclaimed. "Jacob is his grandson!"

"I hope he can. But there are things happening here that frighten me, and I think that time may have already run out for you."

The curse her father had pronounced on her that fateful Christmas Eve eighteen years before came back to her: that if she, an Aryan and a Christian should marry a Jew and remain in Germany, it would be their child who would pay the price.

"I've told you, Mutti, we're leaving just as soon as we can."

Her mother reached out and took hold of her hands. "I will miss you, but I know you are doing the right thing. Paris is a beautiful city, and you and David and Jacob will be able to make a whole new life for yourselves there."

She thought with grief of the discovery she and David had made and the success that could have been theirs. "You're right, Mutti. And best of all, Jacob will be free for the first time in his life."

Her mother stepped back as the grandfather clock down the hallway began to chime the nine o'clock hour. "Do you think you could bring Jacob to see me before you leave?" she asked. "I want to say goodbye."

"Of course." She lifted her mother's hands and kissed her fingers. "I'll speak to Jacob."

She let go of her mother's hands and, as her mother hurried away down the hallway, she went to the study door and knocked softly.

"Come in!" her father called.

Dressed in his green silk smoking jacket, he was pacing behind his desk, smoking a cigarette.

"You're late," he said, before she could speak.

"I'm sorry, Papa. I was delayed by traffic in the West End."

"You have no business being out alone tonight," he said. "There was talk this afternoon of a demonstration to be held in the West End tonight."

"What do you mean, a demonstration?" she asked.

"I'm not sure. All I know is the government is planning some kind of anti-Jewish rally to protest the murder in Paris." He waved impatiently. "Come in and close the door, Katherine."

She obeyed, and when she turned from the door he had seated himself in his leather armchair behind the desk.

As she crossed the room to his desk, she looked around at the mementos displayed on the wall behind his desk: the autographed photograph of the führer above his armchair, the framed letter of commendation he had received last year from Reichsminister Göring, and the photographs of himself in the company of various Nazi luminaries: the accumulated evidence, she realized, of his long and misguided ambition to rise within the ranks of Hitler's Nazi Wehrmacht.

"I take it Mother has told you about Jacob's expulsion from the Akademie," she said.

"Yes. There has been a change of government policy toward the Jews, Katherine, and henceforth only Aryans will be allowed to attend Germany's schools."

"That was a stupid thing for the government to do," she said. "Some of the most brilliant students in Germany are Jews."

"Is that why you've come here—to complain about Jacob's expulsion from the Bismarck?"

"No, Papa. We're leaving next Thursday, and Jacob's expulsion doesn't matter now."

He sat back and drew on his cigarette. "Then why are you here?" he asked.

She hesitated, trying to recall the arguments she had devised to win his protection for Jacob, but her mind had gone blank. "Yesterday, Ernst Humboldt, the director of the Akademie, called Jacob to his office and said that a mass arrest of Jews would take place in the next two days."

"I know nothing about plans for a mass arrest, Katherine," he said, "but I do know that the government is planning to take action against the Jews."

"That's why I'm here, Papa," she said. "I want to ask a favor of you."

"A favor? What kind of favor?"

"I have never asked you to involve yourself with either David or Jacob," she said. "But I'm worried about Jacob's safety, Papa, and I've come to ask for your protection during the week left to us in Germany."

He sat forward and dropped his burning cigarette in the ashtray on his desk. "Have you told David why you've come here tonight?" he asked.

"Yes. He's as worried as I am about Jacob, and he's willing to admit that he needs your help."

Her father looked away and said nothing.

"I'm not asking for much," she went on. "All I want is some kind of assurance—a letter, perhaps, from one of your friends at the Reichs-chancellery."

"And from whom do you suggest I obtain such a document?" he asked.

"I don't know, Papa," she replied. "From Hitler, if necessary."

"I'm sorry, but what you're asking is impossible." He sat forward and rapped his finger against the newspaper. "If you wanted my protection, you should have come to me when there was still some chance for leniency, Katherine."

"You've got to help me, Papa," she said. "Whether you like it or not, Jacob is your grandson."

"Everything has changed in the last twenty-four hours, Katherine, and there's nothing I can do now to protect him. I warned you when the Nürnberg Laws were first passed that you should leave Germany, but you and David refused to heed my advice. Then I warned you again last March, after the Austrian Anschluss, that it was no longer safe for Jacob to go on living here, but still you refused to take me seriously."

Realizing that he was about to launch into the same lecture he had given her countless times in the last six years, she turned away and walked to the window at the far side of the room. "I know what you're going to tell me, Papa," she said, "and I don't want to hear it again."

"You'll hear it whether you want to or not," he said. "I warned you back in 1920 that you would bring disaster upon yourself and your family if you married a Jew and continued to live in Germany. And I warned you again the following year, when you gave birth to Jacob, that you could not safely raise a Jewish child in Germany. And now you come here asking me to save you from a disaster for which you alone are responsible."

She drew up at the window and looked out at the impenetrable curtain of fog hanging over the darkened garden. "Maybe it was wrong of us to stay on, Papa, but we thought that the anti-Semitism would go no further than the Nürnberg Laws."

"And you wanted to work together at the Kaiser-Wilhelm."

"Yes."

For a moment, there was only silence from the desk behind her. Then, when he spoke again, it was in a voice weighed down with resignation. "You are indeed a fool, Katherine. You aspire to professional greatness, but you have failed in the most fundamental of your human responsibilities. I mean, as a wife and mother."

She watched her breath condense on the windowpane and said nothing.

"Your greatest weakness has always been your ambition," he said. "This overreaching need of yours to prove yourself as a scientist."

She thought of his own ambition to rise to the rank of general in Hitler's army. "If I am cursed with ambition, Papa, it's you I have to thank for it."

He went on, relentlessly. "As a child, you always imagined that you had to be like a son to me, instead of a daughter, to gain my respect and admiration. So you chose to pursue a lofty and difficult profession, one that you knew I could not hope to understand."

"That's not true, Papa," she said. "I have always wanted scientific knowledge for itself."

He gave a heavy sigh, then said, "You and David have spent seventeen years gambling your son's life for scientific success, Katherine, but you have found only failure."

Failure: the word came back like an echo from her childhood. "You are wrong, Papa," she said before she could weigh her words. "David and I have succeeded beyond our wildest dreams." She reached up and gripped the window frame with both hands, wondering if she dared speak about what was, so far, unproven. "We have found the answer to the question we've been asking for eighteen years. We have unlocked the door into the atom's nucleus . . ." She left off, searching for words to describe the meaning of their amazing discovery. Knowing his predilection for the practical, she continued, "If David's theory is correct, Papa, we have stumbled on a new and powerful form of energy—the same energy that makes the sun shine."

In the silence that followed she sensed, for once, the beginnings of an acknowledgment from her father. "The energy locked inside the nucleus of the uranium atom will be the most powerful form of energy the world has ever known, Papa." She knew that she was venturing into the realm of pure speculation, but the temptation to win a victory over her father's lifelong skepticism was irresistible. "And if we are right about the future," she went on, knowing that she had no scientific evidence to prove what she was saying, "the day will come when science will be able to harness this miraculous new energy. It will be energy enough to light whole cities, Papa; and enough," she added, thinking again of his own ambitions, "to drive ships across the seas . . ." She left off and let go of the window frame, realizing how preposterous her words sounded.

Suddenly, the vanity of her boast seemed childish and stupid, and to avoid looking at the reflection of her face in the windowpane she closed her eyes.

The silence behind her seemed to stretch for an eternity.

"I take it you and David have proof of this remarkable discovery," her father said.

She opened her eyes, realizing that he had left his desk and was now standing directly behind her. A feeling of panic came over her. "No, Papa," she said. "I ran the experiment only two days ago, and it will take time to verify the evidence we have found."

"How much time?" he asked.

"More experiments have to be done," she replied, stumbling to retreat. "Six weeks, at least, maybe two months. I'm not sure."

"Then you plan to verify your discovery in Paris," he said, moving closer to her.

She suddenly felt as if she had wandered to the edge of a precipice. "Before we can do anything, we first have to arrange positions at the Joliot-Curie Radium Institute."

"But if what you say about this new form of energy is true, Katherine, you and David are on the brink of a very great discovery."

"By the time David and I get to Paris, it will be too late for us to document what we have done. There are scientists at the Kaiser-Wilhelm who are at work on similar uranium experiments, and they will soon make the same discovery."

"I know nothing about atomic physics, Katherine, but are you absolutely certain about the existence of this new atomic energy?"

"We're as certain as the experimental evidence allows us to be."

"And you think it could have practical uses in the future?"

She heard the wonder in his voice and thought of the years she had spent waiting for some sign of recognition. "Yes, it's possible."

The sigh behind her was like an admission of surrender. "I've always thought that this passion of yours for scientific knowledge was only a childish dream," he said. "When you were a little girl, you used to stand here at this same window and tell me all the scientific names of the trees and plants you saw out in the garden. I thought you had only memorized them to win my approval, and I pretended to be impressed."

"But you were right," she said. "I did memorize them to win your approval."

He moved still closer. "You'd like to stay on at the Kaiser-Wilhelm and verify this discovery of yours, wouldn't you?" he asked.

"It isn't a question of what I'd like, Papa. David and Jacob are my first responsibilities, and it's no longer safe for Jacob to stay in Germany."

"But if the threat to the boy's safety could be removed. If, for instance, he could be temporarily exempted from the Nürnberg Laws, there would be no reason for you leave Germany."

"Jacob has been repeatedly attacked by Hitler Youth gangs," she said with anger, "and it isn't just a question of the Nürnberg Laws."

"If he was under the government's protection, Katherine, you'd have nothing to worry about."

She watched her breath blur the reflection of her face in the glass, wondering at her capacity to go on dreaming. "We can't stay here," she said. "It's impossible."

"But if what you've said about the future uses of this new energy is true, Katherine, nothing would be impossible."

"It will be many years before any use can be made of our discovery, Papa," she said.

His hands came to rest on her shoulders. "As you said, I have friends with connections inside the Reichschancellery, and if the government thought that there could be some benefits from your discovery, almost anything could be arranged."

She thought at once of the fear she and David had always had that the Nazis might make use of their work at the Institute. She hesitated, wondering if she was opening a Pandora's box that could never be closed. "Before I could agree to stay on in Berlin, Papa, I would first have to speak to David and Jacob."

"Of course. But surely they understand what this discovery could mean to you."

Again, she hesitated, thinking to herself that she had never before compromised her loyalty to her family. But this was the chance of a lifetime, and if she let it pass by, it might never come again. "If David and Jacob agree to stay," she said, "we would have to have everything in writing."

"I understand." Slowly and gently he turned her to face him. "Of course, I can promise nothing, Katherine, but I have a meeting scheduled with General Halder tomorrow. I will tell him about your wonderful discovery, and I will speak to him about arranging protection for your family."

"The protection must be guaranteed at the highest level, Papa," she said, "and we must be able to leave when our work is finished."

"Of course." As her father drew her forward, she looked up with astonishment, unable to remember when he had last embraced her.

18

IT was 10:25, and Katherine was half an hour late, when she reached the West End and saw the medieval Gedächtniskirche tower amid the glittering lights of the Kurfürstendamm. A crowd of homeward bound theatergoers had just spilled into the street from the nearby Theater am Kurfürstendamm. She braked and slowed as she crossed the intersection of the Uhlandstrasse. On the opposite corner the crowd of young men she had passed two hours before had swollen in size, and among them were now some dozen older men dressed in the familiar uniform of the Nazi storm troopers.

Recalling her father's warning about the anti-Jewish demonstration that night, she pressed down on the accelerator and swung out into the Kurfürstendamm's faster eastbound traffic.

A block ahead, another group of storm troopers was milling about near the entrance to the popular Kakadu nightclub, but the sidewalk in front of the club, where crowds of young people usually gathered at this hour, was otherwise deserted.

Vaguely aware of the tension in the air, she moved on, thinking with excitement of the offer her father had made that night. The question was how and when she should tell David and Jacob of the offer.

Keeping pace with the traffic, she turned into the colorful neonlit Breitscheidplatz and drew up under the glittering marquee of the huge Ufa Palast theater.

As he had promised, David was there—pacing the sidewalk in front of the box office—but there was no sign of Jacob.

"Where is Jacob?" she called through the passenger window as he hurried forward.

"Buying pretzels." He pointed down the sidewalk where the boy was handing money to an old man selling hot pretzels from a portable vendor's stand.

"Here, sweetheart, you drive." Leaving the motor running, she quickly moved to the passenger side.

"Come on, son, let's go!" David called in English as he rounded the car to the driver's side.

Watching the boy leave the vendor and make a dash toward the car, Katherine wondered if David had seen the group of six men standing under the nearby streetlight. Two of them wore brown storm troopers' shirts, and two others were dressed in black Schutzstaffel uniforms. One of the six, a middle-aged man who was carrying what looked like a wooden truncheon, turned and said something to Jacob as he passed.

"How did the meeting go?" David asked as he got in.

"It went well," she replied, wondering how she would convince them to accept her father's astonishing offer. She had gone to him to ask for only a few days of protection, but she had come away with the possibility of weeks of protection. "Papa has a meeting tomorrow with his commander, General Halder," she said, "and he promised to ask Halder for a letter of temporary immunity for Jacob."

David turned to her with surprise. "I'm amazed. This is the first time in six years your father has ever offered to help the boy."

She wanted to say that it was the first time he had ever allowed her to ask for her father's help, but she said, instead, "This is the first time Jacob has ever been in any real danger, David, and Papa was glad that I asked for his help."

Carrying his bag of roasted pretzels, Jacob got into the back seat. "Those guys over there under the lamp," he said, breathless from his run, "one of them called me a bloody Jew when I passed. He said I had no business being out in the streets tonight."

Thrusting the car into gear, David pulled out into the traffic circling the Gedächtniskirche tower. "Never mind, son," he said.

Katherine thought again of her father's warning about the anti-Jewish demonstration. "Papa's right, Jacob," she said. "Those fellows wander the streets here in the West End every night."

"Something's going on, I can tell," the boy said. "There were storm troopers outside Ufa Palast when we left the movie."

She remembered the crowd of storm troopers she had passed at the corner of the Uhlandstrasse. "I'm sure there's nothing to worry about, Jacob," she said. "We'll be home in twenty minutes."

As David turned west down the Kurfürstendamm, Katherine looked out anxiously at the pedestrians hurrying along the brightly lit street. "I spoke to Grandpapa Eric, Jacob," she said, "and he's promised to ask for a letter of temporary immunity for you."

"You mean he actually offered to help me?"

"Yes. He's going to speak to General Halder at the Reichschancellery tomorrow."

The boy took a bite from a pretzel. "That's a first," he said. "He's never offered to help me before."

She hesitated, thinking of the dazzling prize that was now within their reach. It would be difficult, but if she could convince David and Jacob that all the dangers to the boy's safety could be removed, she might be able to persuade them to postpone their departure.

"So tell me about the movie, sweetheart," she said, playing for time. "Did you like it?"

"Yes. I especially liked the chase scene at the end, when Tom Mix and the good guys chased the bad guys into the canyon where the Indians were waiting—the part where the Indians finally got their revenge."

At the word revenge, David glanced at Katherine. "I liked the part where Tom Mix fell in love with the judge's daughter," he said, and braked for the slow-moving traffic.

"That was okay, Papa, but I hated the judge. He was the one who forced the Indians to leave their land, and everyone cheered when the Indians finally killed him."

The note of relish Katherine heard in the boy's voice startled her. She thought with sadness of the attacks he had suffered in recent weeks by the Hitler Youth gangs and the bitterness that had taken root in his heart. "It would be wonderful, Jacob, if life were as simple as they make it in the Hollywood movies," she said. "We'd have a perfect world if the 'good guys,' as you call them, always won in the end."

"Maybe it's like that in America," he said. "Maybe Americans are different from Germans."

David glanced again at Katherine. "Except in Hollywood, Americans are no different from Germans. People are the same all over the world."

"I don't believe it, Papa. In America they don't have any Nürnberg Laws, and they don't hate people for being Jews." The boy bit again into his pretzel. "Besides, if people are the same all over the world, why are we bothering to leave Germany and move to France?"

"You're right there, Jacob," David said. "France will be quite different from Germany. And when we get there on Friday, you're going to see for once what it means to be free."

The crowd from the Theater am Kurfürstendamm had dispersed, Katherine saw, but the group of young storm troopers had grown.

"What the hell's going on?" David said, and quickly applied his brakes.

In the next instant, Katherine felt herself being thrust foward against the dashboard; and when she looked up, the car directly in front of them had come to a halt in the center of the intersection.

"Oh my God," David murmured.

She saw what he was staring at: four older men, rough-looking veterans of the Sturmabteilung, had just rounded the corner and were moving down the sidewalk toward the crowd, which had turned to wait for them. Scanning the signs above the windows, the men came to a halt in front of a shop displaying expensive jewelry. Brandishing the wooden truncheon he was carrying, the largest of the four older men angrily shouted something at the waiting crowd of brown-shirted youths. Like soldiers galvanized by a superior's military order, the younger storm troopers came to immediate attention. Turning to the nearest shop window, the man paused to gather his strength, then lifted his truncheon and swung it savagely against the window's plate glass.

"That's old Anton Kapensky's jewelry shop," Katherine said with astonishment.

Jacob sat forward. "Don't you understand anything, Mother?" he asked. "Anton Kapensky is a rich Russian Jew."

As the crowd of young storm troopers came to life, another shop window shattered.

Suddenly, halfway down the Uhlandstrasse, a bright yellow flame shot into the air.

"They're setting fire to the synagogue," David said.

For one paralyzing moment, as she watched the flames rise above the surrounding rooftops, it seemed to Katherine that the entire city of Berlin had come to a complete halt. "For God's sake, David," she whispered, "let's get out of here."

19

"Ah! Katherine!" Her father turned from the window where he had been standing. "I was beginning to wonder if you would come."

For a moment, startled by his cheerful greeting, she stood in the open office doorway.

"I'm sorry to be so late, Papa," she said, "but I was not at home when your secretary phoned."

"Not to worry, my dear," he said, rounding the desk to his leather armchair. "Please come sit down. We have a lot to talk about."

It had been years since she visited his offices at the Heereswaffenamt, and she had forgotten how luxuriously he had furnished the room. Illuminated by three tall windows overlooking Unter den Linden, the huge wood-paneled room resembled the office of a Wehrmacht fieldmarshal. There was a carved mahogany desk under the far window and a gilt-framed portrait of the führer on the wall above the bookcase.

As she crossed to the upholstered chair in front of the desk, she recalled the offer he had made two nights ago and the shameful chances she had taken with Jacob's safety.

"First of all, Katherine, I apologize for calling you here on a Saturday. But everything seems to have happened all at once. Since this morning, in fact," he added, and smiled.

"Before you say anything, Papa, there's something you should know. Things have changed since I last saw you, and I've decided to leave Germany on Thursday, as planned."

His smile vanished. "You should have told me this before I involved myself with the problem of Jacob's safety."

"There has been a mass arrest of Jews all over Germany, and we've been living in fear night and day. You knew when we met last Wednesday that Hitler's storm troopers were planning to attack the Jews, didn't you?"

"No, Katherine. I knew only that they were going to burn the synagogues. Nothing else."

"You should have warned me that David and Jacob were in danger, Papa. We were on the Kurfürstendamm when the attack started, and they could have been injured or arrested."

"But I couldn't warn you. I was sworn to secrecy."

She sat back, appalled by his loyalty to the Party. "In any case, the roundup of Jews is still going on, and we're leaving the country as soon as our French visas come through."

"I think it's a mistake for you to leave Germany at this point, Katherine. I promised to help you, and I have."

She watched as he opened his desk drawer, thinking to herself of the endless lectures he had given her on the dangers of remaining in Germany.

He took out one of his gray office files. "Last Wednesday, when you came to me and told me about the discovery you had made at the Kaiser-Wilhelm, I promised to do what I could to arrange for Jacob's protection during the time it would take you to complete the experimental verification of your discovery."

"I didn't come to you that night to ask for weeks of protection, Papa," she said. "I came to ask for only one."

"The next morning I met with General Halder at the Army High Command, and during the meeting the subject of Germany's industrial capabilities came up. That, of course, was the opportunity I had been looking for. I told Halder about the uranium discovery you had made at the Kaiser-Wilhelm, and I repeated what you had said about the possible practical uses of atomic energy."

"A lot of what I told you last Wednesday was only speculation, Papa," Katherine interrupted. "It's true, there's an immense amount of energy locked inside the uranium atom, but we have no scientific evidence that it will ever be accessible."

"Nonetheless, the general was very interested in what I told him. Especially the industrial uses of this new atomic energy."

"But you don't understand," she said. "At this point, it's foolish to even think about such things. Even if I could experimentally prove that atomic energy exists, there are immense obstacles to our ever gaining access to it. It was wrong of me to tell you about our discovery, Papa," she said. "David would be horrified to know that I even mentioned it."

Her father looked up with surprise. "Are you saying that David knows nothing about the offer I made to you?"

"It was pointless for me to tell him. After seeing what happened on the Night of Broken Glass, I decided we had to leave Germany as soon as possible."

"Be that as it may," he went on, "I described to Halder the experiments you would have to do to verify your discovery. I also told him that you were married to a Jew, that you had a seventeen-year-old son, and that you were afraid to stay in Germany and complete your experiments." He sat forward and opened the file. "At first, the general said there was nothing he could do to help you and your family. With the Nürnberg

Laws, the government's Jewish policy has changed, and no exceptions can be made now. Then, at the end of the meeting, he called me aside and told me he would think the matter over and get back to me." He rummaged among the papers in the file and took out a single page. "Then this morning, quite unexpectedly, I received a summons to appear before Fieldmarshal Wilhelm Keitel at the Reichschancellery. Keitel, as you know, is the new Chief of Army High Command, and his proximity to the führer is well known." He cleared his throat, then said, "My meeting with the fieldmarshal was quite astonishing, Katherine. Halder, it seems, had spoken to him about your experiments; and he, in turn, spoke to the führer." He placed the paper on the desk in front of her. "This is a letter that Fieldmarshal Keitel gave me, Katherine. In essence, it says that the government is prepared to give you and your family full protection and immunity from the Nürnberg Laws during the time it will take for you to complete your experimental work at the Kaiser-Wilhelm."

She stared with amazement at the official-looking document. "This makes no sense, Papa," she said. "What could Halder and Keitel hope to gain from such an offer? Surely they realize it will be years before any practical use can be made of our discovery."

"It's a question of Germany's scientific reputation, Katherine. A discovery like this, even if it has no immediate practical benefits, could bring great honor to the Reich."

"We can't stay in Germany any longer, Papa," she said. "Jacob has been living in constant fear of arrest for the last two days, and now he refuses to even leave the house."

"I told the fieldmarshal about your fears for Jacob's safety, Katherine, and he assured me that with the government's protection no harm could come to the boy."

"It's not just a question of Jacob's safety, Papa. We've made him a promise that we will be in Paris by next Friday."

"Perhaps it would help if I spoke to the boy and explained the government's offer."

She thought of his refusal to accept Jacob as his grandson. "It's pointless for us to talk like this," she said. "We've submitted our resignations from the Kaiser-Wilhelm, and they've been accepted."

"I mentioned that to the fieldmarshal, and he assured me that your resignations could be rescinded. Not only that, Jacob could be reinstated at the Bismarck Akademie."

"I'm telling you, Papa, this is a waste of time. Jacob would never agree to return to the Akademie."

The colonel considered her statement, then said, changing his tactic, "Aside from your country's honor, a discovery like this would also bring honor to the von Steiner family."

She looked at him with astonishment, remembering the years she had spent waiting for him to acknowledge her talent as a scientist.

"Furthermore," he added, "it will bring you what you have wanted all your life—the recognition of your fellow scientists."

Like the strategist he was, he aimed his attack at the places where he knew she was most vulnerable. "I'm sorry, Papa," she said, "but the price I would have to pay for recognition would be too high."

He sighed with exasperation. "But I've told you, Fieldmarshal Keitel has personally promised to ensure Jacob's safety, and with his protection nothing can possibly happen to your family."

She shook her head. "I don't trust Fieldmarshal Keitel's promises. You know as well as I do that he would break any promise if it pleased the führer."

"You don't understand what I'm saying. The führer himself has expressed interest in your uranium discovery, Katherine; it's very important to me that you stay and finish your experiments."

She lowered her eyes, knowing that he was tempting her with the one reward she had waited for all her life—his respect and admiration.

He read her thoughts and said, "If you have done what David says you have done, it could even mean promotion for me, perhaps, to the rank of general."

She hesitated, knowing that her power to reason was beginning to evaporate and that she would have to rely on her intuition. Her intuition told her to refuse.

He leaned forward, smiling, and pushed the letter toward her across the desk. "You have nothing to fear, Katherine," he said. "The promises in this letter come from the very highest levels."

She stared at the letter's printed heading—Deutsches Reichskanzleigericht—waiting for her racing heartbeat to subside.

"Aside from assuring Jacob's safety," he said, "the letter also promises that you and your family will be given safe passage from Germany when you are ready to leave the country."

She took the letter from the desk and read the date typed under the government's Seal of State: 12 November, 1938. And scrawled below the typewritten letter was the signature:

Fieldmarshal Wilhelm Keitel

When she looked up, her father was smiling at her with pride. "It's addressed to you personally, Katherine, and the fieldmarshal mentions me by name."

She said, knowing that he was opening a door for her that she would never be able to close, "I will agree to stay on and finish my experiments, Papa, but only if David and Jacob will agree to postpone our departure."

"That's fair enough," he said.

She placed the letter in her purse. "I will speak to them tonight and let you know by tomorrow."

"Excellent." He closed the file on his desk. "I'm sure they will see it's the right choice."

She looked at her watch. "It's three thirty, and I've promised to be home by four."

"Oh. One more thing, Katherine," he said, as she stood up. "Fieldmarshal Keitel asked me to provide him with some documentary evidence of your discovery."

She stepped back with surprise. "What kind of documentary evidence?"

"Something written that describes the nature of this new atomic energy."

"It's too soon for us to have any written evidence of our discovery, Papa. I've only just begun the experiments."

"I'm not asking for much. Just a scientific explanation of your work for the fieldmarshal."

"The only thing I have is a chemical analysis of my uranium bombardments."

"What about your laboratory notes? Surely you have something that discusses the practical meaning of your discovery."

She thought of the paper David had begun last Wednesday. "David is writing a theoretical description of my uranium split," she said, "but it's only in the early stages."

"A theoretical description, Katherine, is exactly what I need."

She said, remembering David's adamant refusal to involve himself with the Nazi scientists at the Institute, "What you're asking is impossible, Papa. David would never consent to my giving his research to Fieldmarshal Keitel. He doesn't trust the government."

Her father lit a cigarette, then said, "But why would he have to know about it? You could make a copy of his paper and give it to me in private."

She watched in disbelief as he drew impassively on his cigarette. Until now, she had never known how strong his loyalties to the Nazis were.

"I know what I'm asking is repugnant to you, Katherine," he said, "but neither one of us has a choice in the matter. The fieldmarshal was adamant about my providing him with written evidence of your discovery."

She recalled the choice she had been forced to make between David and her father as a student in Göttingen.

"Besides," the colonel added, "it's a small price to pay for the chance to win a Nobel Prize."

A sense of fear suddenly brought back the memory of the nightmare that had plagued her as a child, in which she stood at the edge of a precipitous chasm, looking out into an immense and impenetrable darkness. She wanted to run from the room, but knew that it was already too late; she had gone too far to turn back. She looked away and said, quietly, "I will give you a copy of David's paper, Papa, but only on the condition that he is told nothing about it."

He nodded and drew again on his cigarette.

20

KATHERINE had planned to tell David and Jacob about the visit to her father that night over supper, but they had spent the entire meal talking about what the Nazis had done, and she could not bring herself to speak about another postponement of their departure. The news David had heard from their friend Konrad Bukowski had horrified her: across Germany, one hundred synagogues had been burned, eight hundred Jewish shops had been destroyed, and two hundred private homes set on fire. She had not wanted to believe him, but he had insisted that Bukowski was right, and that 20,000 Jews had been arrested so far.

She finished washing the dishes, then went to the window to close the curtains. Snow had begun to fall after supper and, for a moment, she stood looking out at the deserted street, wondering how she could persuade David that it was now safe for them to remain in Germany.

"Come here, Katherine," he said. "There's something I want to show you."

Closing the curtain, she took the envelope with the letter her father had given her from her purse on the kitchen table and joined him in the parlor.

"I've done some new calculations on your uranium split," he said, "and if I'm right, we're dealing with much more energy than I thought we were."

As he began turning the pages of his notebook, she recognized his notes for a theoretical paper on her uranium experiments. "You mean, of course, nuclear energy," she said.

"Yes. If I'm right, the single neutron you released with your uranium bombardment would have struck and split another uranium atom, and that neutron would, in turn, have struck and split still another."

She stared at his neat handwriting, trying to work out the implications of his statement. "You're saying that a neutron from one uranium split could set off a chain reaction with other neutrons."

"Exactly." He pointed to one of his mathematical formulas. "So far, I've only worked out the rough mathematics of my theory, but if I'm right, the energy released from such a reaction would be a billion times greater than the energy from just one atomic split."

She suddenly remembered the promise she had made to turn over his theoretical work to her father. She looked away, wondering if she had made a terrible mistake.

"Is something wrong?" he asked.

"What do you mean, wrong?"

"I don't know. You've been distracted all evening."

Realizing that it was now or never, she turned and sat down beside him on the couch. "I don't know how to tell you this, David," she said, "but I have a confession to make."

"Go on," he said, seeing her hesitate.

"Last Wednesday night, when I went to see Papa, I didn't tell you everything that happened."

As she told of her visit with her father and his initial refusal of protection for Jacob, David closed his notebook and stared up absently at the ceiling.

"It was the same lecture he has given me a hundred times in the past," she said. "He accused me again of staying too long in Germany and of gambling with Jacob's safety for the sake of ambition." Again, she hesitated, searching for words to describe what she had said to her father that night. "I know it was foolish of me, David," she said, "but I told him he was wrong and that we had succeeded beyond our wildest dreams."

He looked at her with amazement. "You mean, you told him about your uranium split?" He shook his head and sighed. "That was a foolish thing to do, Katherine."

"Foolish or not, I've lived with his contempt for so long that I had to tell him what we had done."

"But you know as well as I do that it's purely speculation, and it will be years before any use can be made of our discovery."

"I explained that to him, David, but he was nonetheless impressed."

He looked down at the envelope she was turning nervously in her hand. "What are you trying to tell me, Katherine?" he asked.

"I went to Papa to ask for a week of protection, but when I told him that it would take at least six weeks to verify our discovery, and that I could not possibly finish the experiments before we left for Paris, he offered to speak to General Halder, the Army Chief of Staff, and ask for a letter of extended immunity for Jacob."

For a moment, David focused on the notebook in his hands. Then he said, quietly, "Did you know this when you picked us up at the theater on Wednesday?"

"Yes. I had planned to tell you and Jacob on the way home, but with everything that was happening I decided it was best to leave Germany as we had planned."

"Then why are you telling me this now?" he asked.

"Things have changed, David," she said. "This afternoon, quite unexpectedly, I received a phone call from Papa's secretary at the Heereswaffenamt . . ."

As she told of her meeting that afternoon with her father and the summons he had received to appear before Fieldmarshal Keitel at the Reichschancellery, David thought of the years she had waited for some sign of recognition from her father.

"It seems Halder had spoken to Fieldmarshal Keitel about our uranium discovery." She took the letter her father had given her from its envelope. "The fieldmarshal is interested in our work, David, and he ordered Papa to give me this letter."

She handed him the letter, and as he read it she watched the changing expression on his face—astonishment, then disbelief, and then fear.

"I take it you want to stay and finish your uranium experiments," he said.

"Now that we have Fieldmarshal Keitel's promise of protection for Jacob, there's no reason for us to leave Berlin."

"Why would Keitel offer us temporary immunity from the Nürnberg Laws unless he expected something in return?"

"I questioned Papa about his interest and he assured me that Keitel knew that it would be years before any use could be made of atomic energy, and by then the entire world would know about it. The field-marshal's only interest, he told me, was the honor and recognition that would come to Germany from such a discovery."

He folded the letter and handed it to her. "Be that as it may, we've made a promise to Jacob."

"But if we explain that no harm can possibly come to him," she said, "what objections can he have to staying on for a while? This could mean a Nobel Prize for us, David."

For a moment, David looked up at the tiny spider-shaped crack in the ceiling above him, thinking to himself of the love and the loyalty that had bound them together for eighteen years. Never once, in all the years of their marriage, had she ever placed her career before her responsibilities to her family.

"All right," he said. "I will agree to stay on, but only on certain conditions. First, we must have Jacob's consent. Second, I must have everything in writing."

"I'm sure that can be arranged," she said.

"Third, the government must agree to respect the absolute privacy of my research; and when the time comes for us to leave Germany, they must agree to let me take my scientific papers, all of them, with us. Untouched and unexamined."

Katherine thought again, this time with panic, of the promise she had made to her father.

"I will speak to Papa, David," she said.

David put down his notebook and got up. "And I'll go talk to Jacob."

When he entered the boy's room, Jacob was standing at the window, looking out at the fresh white snow.

Joining the boy at the window, he said, "I've always liked Berlin when it snows, everything is clean and white and silent."

"Yes, but that's only an illusion. Underneath, it's still the same."

"I know you're so afraid, son," David said. "But this afternoon, your grandfather had a government letter issued, giving you immunity from the Nürnberg Laws and Fieldmarshal Keitel's promise of protection."

"Why do I need a letter of immunity, Papa," Jacob said, turning from the window. "You promised we would leave Germany by the end of this week."

"I know we made a promise, son, but it's not fair for you to hold us to it. We were leaving because we were concerned about your safety, but all that has now changed."

The boy left the window and sat down by his father on the bed. "Do you remember what Mother said the night I was expelled from the Bismarck?" he asked. "She said that nothing on earth could stop us from leaving Germany."

"You have nothing to fear now," David said. "You can go back to the Bismarck, if you want to, and you can even play ball in the park."

"You've always said that promises are sacred, Papa, but that was obviously a lie."

"Your mother has given you her word that no harm will come to you."

"It isn't Mother that I don't trust," he said, "it's Grandpapa Eric. He would never have gotten a letter of immunity for me unless he expected something in return."

David had thought of that as well. He wanted to agree, but he said, repeating Katherine's explanation, "Your mother asked your grandfather that same question, Jacob, and he assured her that Keitel was only interested in the honor our discovery would bring to Germany."

Jacob was silent.

David moved closer and put his arm around the boy's shoulder. "Your mother has worked all her life to be recognized. This could be the most important scientific discovery of the twentieth century, son, and she deserves the success."

The boy considered his statement, then said, "All right. I will stay until Christmas, but I think you and Mother are making a terrible mistake, one that you will both live to regret."

21

As David and Jacob turned the corner into the busy Forckenbeckstrasse, Jacob pointed to an open space in the dense grove of pine and birch trees at the southeast corner of Schmargendorf public park. "The soccer field's over there, Papa," he said, "just beyond those trees."

David walked in silence for a moment, thinking of the distance that had grown between himself and his son during these last months. It was only in the last ten days, after the government agreed to his demands for privacy and he started working at home, that he began to have firsthand experience of his son's private life.

Jacob slowed his pace and looked off anxiously through the trees. The snow that had fallen the second week of November had melted, but the cold winter wind it had brought with it was still blowing.

As they approached the soccer field, Jacob looked back over his shoulder. "Papa, I think it was a mistake for us to come here this afternoon."

"A mistake? Why?"

"That fellow in the black overcoat I pointed out, the one we passed when we left the house, he's following us."

David started to turn around, but the boy caught his arm. "Don't look back, Papa. I know I'm right because I've seen that same man before. He was waiting outside the house yesterday morning, when Mother left for the Institute."

David looked away, pretending to survey the façade of the newly built Schmargendorf Sports-Halle. So far, he had said nothing to anyone about his suspicions, but twice in the last week he had observed the same car, a black two-door Mercedes sedan, parked down the street from their house. "I'll tell you what," he said. "Let's take a taxi over to Charlottenburg and have an ice cream at Bulendorf's."

The boy looked up with surprise. "But I thought you promised to meet Dr. Bukowski here at two thirty."

"I did, but Bukowski and I can meet somewhere else another time." David glanced at his watch, thinking to himself of Bukowski's puzzling telephone call that morning, asking if they could meet that afternoon. It was Sunday, Katherine had gone to visit her parents, and he had planned to take a walk with Jacob to the park in Schmargendorf.

"I don't understand," Jacob said. "Why does Bukowski want to meet you like this, in secret?"

"I don't know, son. All he said was that he wanted to meet me away from home; he couldn't explain his reasons on the telephone."

There was a sudden shout as the soccer field came into view beyond the trees. Some fifteen boys of varying ages had just started down the field, racing after a tall lanky boy who was gracefully guiding the soccer ball with both feet toward a goalpost. David recognized a few of the boys and said, motioning toward the field, "I guess we'll have to forget the ice cream. It looks like your friends are here, after all."

Jacob came to an abrupt halt. "I don't understand. They said they weren't going to meet again in public."

Seeing the look of fear on the boy's face, David reached up and put his arm around his shoulder. "Well, obviously they changed their minds," he said, and laughed.

Jacob glanced back again down the sidewalk. "It's stupid of them to come here and play ball. The Gestapo is everywhere now."

As the tall lanky boy passed under the goalpost with the ball, a cheer went up from the team that had made the goal.

For a moment, they watched in silence as the two teams turned back toward the center of the field.

"It looks to me like one team needs another player," David said. "They're playing with uneven numbers."

Jacob turned to him with surprise. "You've forbidden me to play ball in public parks."

"You were better off when you fought for your rights."

Again, Jacob glanced at the man in the black overcoat, who had stopped to watch the ballgame. "I don't dare go out there, Papa," he said. "Our friend is watching us."

"So what? You have the government's letter of immunity, and there's nothing he can do to you." David pointed toward an empty park bench further down the sidewalk. "Look, while I'm waiting for Dr. Bukowski, I'll sit on that bench over there and watch."

The boy fingered the buttons on his coat, hesitating. "You don't understand," he said. "They don't expect me."

"What do you mean, they don't expect you?"

"Just that. I told them I was leaving Berlin, and now they think I'm in Paris."

David let go of Jacob's shoulder and said, quietly, "Take off your coat and go play. They'll be glad to see you."

The boy hesitated, then, saying nothing, he removed his coat, handed it to him, and walked off toward the center of the field where the two teams were lining up for the next play. At first, no one seemed aware of his presence. Then suddenly, as he drew up and thrust his hands into his pockets, the boys of both teams turned to stare at him. For a moment, no one moved. Then the lanky boy who had just made the goal came forward, stopped a few feet away, and said something. Jacob went on staring at the ground and shook his head. The boy looked back at the team behind him, said something, and two of the players left the formation and came forward. There was an exchange of greetings, then the tall boy stepped forward and shook Jacob's hand. The handshake was repeated with the other two boys, then the three of them joined the waiting members of the uneven team.

From the corner of his eye David caught sight of a figure moving toward him down the sidewalk, and when he turned he recognized Konrad Bukowski. He was dressed, as usual, in an English mackintosh, with a long wool scarf wrapped around his neck and a wide-brimmed hat pulled down over his abundant black hair. As he reached the edge of the pine grove, he paused and looked back in the direction from which he had come, then hurried on, nervously scanning the passing pedestrians on the opposite sidewalk.

As he approached the park bench, David looked back to see that the man in the black overcoat had seated himself on a bench some thirty feet down the sidewalk and was now reading a newspaper.

Winded from his fast walk, Bukowski came up and sat down beside him. "We might as well have met in front of the Gestapo's offices on the Bendlerstrasse," he said and caught his breath.

"It's the best I could do, Konrad. When you phoned, I was on my way to the park with Jacob."

Bukowski struck a match to light his cigarette. "I saw Katherine at the lab yesterday, and she seemed excited about her new experiments."

"She's running four bombardments a day, and she hopes to be finished by the second week of December."

"As you know, I think your decision to stay was a mistake, Linz. It would have been better if you had moved to Paris as you had planned."

"Katherine and I have been waiting for this kind of breakthrough for eighteen years, Konrad; we would have been fools to let it pass."

They watched in silence as a small rugged-looking boy with dark curly hair began maneuvering the ball toward the goalpost. Along with two of his teammates, Jacob raced forward to overtake him.

Bukowski drew nervously on his cigarette. "They tell me you and Katherine have made arrangements with the government to grant Jacob temporary immunity from the Nürnberg Laws."

David looked up with surprise. Other than Katherine's father and a handful of government people, no one had been told of Jacob's letter of immunity. "How did you know?" he asked.

Bukowski drew again on his cigarette. "They also tell me that it was the government that gave you permission to work on the theoretical side of Katherine's experiments at home."

David's surprise gave way to astonishment. He had said nothing to anyone about his arrangements with government. "They?" he asked. "Who are they?"

Bukowski ignored the question and went on, "I have it from reliable sources that the government has also agreed to let you remove all your research papers from the country when you leave. And that they will not ask to examine them."

"Tell me how you know these things, Konrad," David said.

Bukowski leaned forward, resting his elbows on his knees, and watched the game in silence. "I assume you know that I'm involved in anti-Nazi activities here in Berlin," he said.

"Yes. I've known it for some time."

"As a matter of fact, I belong to a secret political organization, and we have a contact inside the Wehrmacht at the Army's Weapons Department."

An icy chill ran down David's neck. For the first time, he turned to look at Bukowski. The man had not shaved for at least two days, and there was a look of fearful exhaustion in his dark eyes. "What do you mean, a contact at the Army's Weapons Department?" he asked.

"I'll come to that in a minute, David, but first tell me this. When did you remove your files from the Kaiser-Wilhlem?"

"I brought them home ten days ago," he said, "the day the government agreed to let me carry out my research in private."

"And since then, where have they been kept?"

"In my study, locked in a metal filing cabinet."

Bukowski looked away nervously at the man seated on the next park bench. "I couldn't tell you this on the telephone, Linz," he said, "but you're being watched by the Gestapo. In fact, you've been watched and followed ever since Katherine arranged for Jacob's immunity with her father."

David thought again of the car he had seen parked outside the house during the last week. "I know I'm being followed, Konrad, but I can't understand why."

Bukowski shook his head and sighed. "Either you're a fool, Linz, or you're blind."

"What do you mean by that?"

"I've been carrying out the chemical analysis of Katherine's bombardment experiments, and if I'm right about this new atomic energy it could have military applications."

"Why do you say that?"

"I've analyzed the nuclear reactions of the elements she's produced, and in the right combination I think you could create a tremendous nuclear explosion."

David thought of the paper he had written last week describing a uranium chain reaction in which he had mentioned the possibility of an explosive reaction. "A nuclear explosion of uranium might be theoreti-cally possible, Konrad, but the experimental obstacles would be insur-mountable."

Bukowski sat forward. "I will tell you something, Linz, because you're my friend and I trust you. The contact I spoke about inside the Army is a Wehrmacht officer assigned to the office of Colonel Eric von Steiner at the Heereswafenamt. Last week, he informed the organization I belong to that he had come across copies of some 'unusual-looking scientific papers,' as he called them, in Colonel von Steiner's files at the Heer-eswaffenamt. He was asked to supply us with photographs of the papers."

Scientific papers, files at the Heereswaffenamt: unable to keep up with the thoughts that were running through his mind, David watched in silence as Jacob took the center position on the field, preparing to run the ball for his team.

"That was on Wednesday," Bukowski went on, "then two days later, on Friday, Kurt Waldhardt, my assistant at the Institute, was summoned to meet with Colonel von Steiner at the Heereswaffenamt. Waldhardt, as you know, is an outspoken Nazi."

"Are you saying that Waldhardt met with von Steiner to discuss our work?" David asked.

"I don't know what was discussed, David. All I know is that Waldhardt is a brilliant radiochemist, that he's familiar with the chemistry of Kath-erine's uranium experiments, and that Colonel von Steiner is head of the Army's Weapons Department."

Bukowski looked off again toward the man seated on the next park bench. "As you know, David, I have never read anything you have written on the subject of Katherine's recent uranium experiments. But yesterday, when I saw the photographs of the paper from Colonel von Steiner's files, I recognized some of your theoretical ideas."

"It's impossible," David said. "I've removed all my research from the Institute, and the only people, besides myself, who have access to my filing cabinet are Katherine and Jacob . . ."

He left off as he caught sight of a movement in the trees at the far western end of the playing field: three boys emerging from the pine grove at the edge of the field, heading toward the goalpost. They were dressed in the familiar Hitlerjugend uniform.

The thought taking shape in his mind seemed suddenly irrelevant to him.

Behind the three boys, one by one, some dozen other boys wearing the same uniform began to emerge from the trees.

At that same moment, the ball was passed to Jacob. The boy caught it with his right foot, then stumbled as he turned west and saw the Hitlerjugend converging on the goalpost. Quickly regaining his balance, he began maneuvering the ball with both feet toward the goalpost.

"We don't know for sure if the papers in von Steiner's files are yours, David," Bukowski said.

A feeling of astonishment came over David as he watched Jacob race with all his might toward the boys gathering around the goalpost.

Speechless, trying to recall the few sentences he had written about an explosive chain reaction, David watched as Jacob slowed his pace.

"I'm not accusing anyone," Bukowski said, "I'm only telling you what our organization has found in Colonel von Steiner's files at the Heereswaffenamt."

Seeing that four of the opposite team members now blocked his way, Jacob hesitated, took aim, then slammed the ball forward. It shot between the four boys, passed through the center of the goalpost, and came to rest some five feet from the line of Hitlerjugend boys assembled on the edge of the field.

A cheer went up from the boys of both teams.

David lifted his chin, feeling as if a hand had suddenly gripped his neck. "This organization you belong to," he said. "What kind of organization is it?"

Out on the field, the three boys who had greeted Jacob when he arrived grouped around and began hugging and jostling him.

Bukowski took another long drag on his cigarette. "First, Linz, I want to know how far I can trust you," he said.

Trust: the word suddenly sounded obscene to David. "What do you mean, how far you can trust me?"

"Just that. Can I trust you with my life?"

"You're my friend, Konrad," he said.

At that moment, both soccer teams stopped moving and turned to stare at the Hitlerjugend boys waiting behind the goalpost.

Their hesitation seemed to grip Bukowski. He drew again on his cigarette, then said, quietly, "I'm a member of the German Communist Party, David. Our organization is called the Rote Kapelle."

It took an eternity, it seemed, for David to grasp the meaning of his friend's astonishing announcement. He had read articles in the newspapers about the German Communist Party, but all he know of the Rote Kapelle was that it was the last remaining underground anti-Nazi organization in Germany, and that its members were being hunted night and day by the Gestapo.

"I didn't know," he said.

He sat back and watched as Jacob, followed by the members of both teams, began slowly walking toward the Hitlerjugend waiting behind the goalpost.

Bukowski blew cigarette smoke into the cold winter air. "If I'm right," he said, "Katherine has been collaborating with her father, and she has turned over your uranium research to the Heereswaffenamt."

"That's impossible," David said. "I've been married to Katherine for seventeen years, and I know her as well as I know myself. She would never betray me."

David thought back to Göttingen and the choice she had been forced to make between him and her father. The one weak link in the long chain of their marital loyalties had always been her need for her father's approval. He held his breath and went on watching as Jacob motioned for his teammates to stay behind, then moved on by himself.

As Jacob reached the scrimmage line, the fifteen Hitlerjugend boys closed ranks in an open semicircle around the soccer ball.

The feeling of helplessness that came over David was like a weight pressing down upon him. "You've come here to ask me to identify the papers, haven't you?" he said.

"Yes."

David watched in silence as Jacob calmly walked toward the ball.

"Understand," said Bukowski, "if you agree to meet with the Rote Kapelle and identify the papers we've obtained from the Heereswaffenamt, you will be bound by our rules of strict secrecy."

When the boy reached the center of the circle, he bent down with deliberate slowness and retrieved the ball from the ground. Saying nothing, holding the ball with both hands, he turned around and started back toward his waiting friends.

"You will have to swear," Bukowski went on, "at the risk of your own life, to say nothing of what you see or hear to anyone—including Katherine."

The look of courageous defiance David saw in his son's adolescent face suddenly filled him with shame. As an American, he had never, until now, allowed himself to become involved in the politics of Nazi Germany.

Shifting back and forth on their feet, with their hands angrily thrust into their pockets, the fifteen Hitlerjugend boys watched in malevolent silence as Jacob continued walking toward his teammates.

David thought to himself of the price the boy had paid for his and Katherine's ambitions, of the hatred and the intolerance he had endured. He said, quietly, "When does the Rote Kapelle want to meet with me?"

"Our next meeting will be tomorrow afternoon."

Remembering the words Jacob had said the morning he agreed to stay on in Germany—that he would live to regret his decision—David looked off toward the man seated on the next park bench. "All right," he said.

22

"I'M proud of you, Jacob, that was very brave," Katherine said. "And after you took the ball back, did the Hitlerjugend try to stop your game?"

"No. They were outnumbered, so they just stood around waiting for the game to end."

She watched as the boy helped himself to still another piece of the chicken David had prepared that night. To her surprise, she had returned home from her visit to her parents a little after six to find that he had made supper for them: a feeble attempt, he had explained, to make an American meal.

"And this time," she said, "when you left the field, did they try to attack you?"

"No. This time Papa was with me and they didn't dare."

"That's nonsense, Jacob," David said. "They didn't attack you because they knew you and your friends would fight for your right to play soccer." He hesitated, then added, "What you proved to everyone today is that it takes courage to stand up for what you know is right."

Katherine stared in bewilderment at the food on her plate: the half-baked chicken, the over-boiled green peas, and the soupy mashed potatoes. It was obvious that the remark was directed at her.

"Papa's right, Jacob," she said. "What you did today was very brave; I wish I had been there with you."

The boy glanced at his father. "But you weren't," he said. "You were with Grandpapa Eric."

Katherine took up her knife and fork and sliced a small bite from her untouched chicken. She had noticed that David seemed preoccupied the moment she entered the house that night. When she tried to question him about his walk to Schmargendorf with Jacob, his thoughts seemed a million miles away.

"Tell me, Jacob," she said to fill the silence, "were there other people at the park to watch the game?"

David caught the boy's eye before he could speak. "No," he said. "I was there alone."

"That's right," Jacob agreed, a little too quickly. "Papa sat by himself and watched the game from a park bench." He glanced between the two of them, then added, "After that, we took a taxi to Bulendorf's and had an Italienisches Eis."

"I see." Katherine wondered why the boy seemed anxious. She was sure that he was as puzzled by David's strange behavior as she was, for twice during the meal she had caught him staring with confusion at his father.

"I do wish I had been there with you, Jacob," she said.

Again, David looked up. "Yes," he said, "it's a shame you weren't with us. After our ice at Bulendorf's we took a taxi back to Dahlem and spent the afternoon window-shopping in the Königin-Luise-Strasse."

"That's right," said Jacob. "There's a Jewish-owned butcher shop in the Königin-Luise-Strasse, and when we passed it Papa decided to cook supper tonight." He speared his chicken leg with his fork and held it up. "It's the American way of cooking it."

"It's delicious, David," Katherine said.

"It really doesn't taste as good as I remember it tasting," he said, "but I had a yearning this afternoon for something American." He gave a soft sigh and went back to toying with his food.

It's pointless, Katherine thought, to try to break through his wall of isolation. Angrily, she broke a piece of bread from the loaf of rye he had bought and began buttering it.

"Is something wrong?" David asked.

She stopped buttering the bread and looked up. "Wrong?" she countered.

"You seem worried about something."

She went back to buttering the bread. "Funny," she said. "I was going to say the same thing about you."

"You're right, sweetheart. I'm sorry." He put his fork and knife down on his plate. "I know I've been acting strangely since you got home, but it's just that I'm worried about all this progress we've been making with our research."

"That's odd," she said. "Last week you were worried about our lack of progress."

"I know. But that was before I began work on my theory of a uranium chain reaction, and now things have changed."

"Changed?"

"Two weeks ago, when I began writing the paper, I told you that my theory was nothing more than a mathematical abstraction. Now, I'm not so sure."

"What do you mean, you're not so sure?"

"This afternoon, when I got home from our walk, I did some more calculations on your uranium split, and it looks like a uranium chain reaction could actually be generated in the laboratory."

"So far, all we've been able to produce in the laboratory are single, isolated atomic splits," she said.

"But that's because you've only used microscopic amounts of uranium. Given enough concentrated uranium, I think you would see a different reaction."

She bit into her bread, wondering where he was leading her. "What are you trying to tell me, David?" she asked.

"I'm telling you that we've been wrong about the nature of our uranium discovery," he said. "And if my calculations are right, we are dealing with much more energy than we thought we were."

She stared at her plate, trying to work out the implications of his statement.

"But what worries me more than anything," he said, "is that a chain reaction of uranium would release its energy in a tremendous explosion. The equivalent, I think, of several thousand tons of TNT."

She caught her breath, remembering the meeting she had had last week with her father and the papers she had given him. "There's not a shred of experimental evidence to support such a theory." She looked up. "And as you've always said, theory without experiment is meaningless."

He replaced his knife and fork on the plate, and said nothing.

Feeling her heart begin to race, she went on. "We've talked about this before. It will be years before any practical use can be made of atomic energy."

"We were wrong," he said. "There are scientific and industrial obstacles that stand in the way, but with enough money and the proper kind of research a powerful bomb could be built with uranium, a nuclear bomb of unimaginable destructiveness."

"To build a bomb from uranium would be impossible, David. The amount of uranium you would need would be enormous, and there isn't enough raw uranium ore in Europe, let alone Germany, to even think of making military weapons."

"That's not true," he said. "Outside the Belgian Congo, the biggest uranium mines in the world are the Czechoslovakian Joachimsthal mines in Bohemia. Hitler has already occupied both Slovakia and the Czech Sudentenland, and he's got his eye on the rest of Czechoslovakia. You'll see, in the next six months, with the help of the English and the French, he will add Bohemia and Moravia to the Reich; and when he does that, the Czech Joachimsthal uranium mines will be his."

It seemed as though his words had come from someone else's mouth. He had never concerned himself with the machinery of Hitler's diplomatic maneuvers in Czechoslovakia, or spoken of German politics with any passion.

She thought again, this time with panic, of the paper she had turned over to her father last week at the Heereswaffenamt. He had insisted that it was the evidence he needed to justify the government's financing her research, and believing that the research David had been doing at home was only theoretical speculation, she had told herself that it would do no harm to cooperate with her father. "What is it you're trying to say, David?" she asked.

He caught Jacob's eye across the table. "I'm saying that the theoretical research I've been doing could prove very dangerous, if it falls into the wrong hands."

She held her breath, wondering if he was speaking of the paper she had given her father. When she looked up, Jacob was staring at her with an expression of questioning uncertainty.

A sudden impulse to escape from the table came over her. "It's getting late and I'm tired," she said. "Are you two finished?"

"Yes." Jacob returned his knife and fork to his plate.

"So am I," David said, pushing his plate away.

Katherine got up, gathered the plates from the table, and went to the kitchen sink.

"By the way," David said, as she placed the dishes in the sink and turned on the faucet, "I may be imagining things, but when I came home this afternoon, I looked in my filing cabinet and found that some of my papers were not in their proper places. My paper on nuclear chain reactions, for instance. It had been taken out of the cabinet and returned to the wrong file."

She felt the blood suddenly drain from her face. It's impossible, she thought. She had taken every precaution when she photographed the paper to return it to its proper file. Hurrying to fill the accusing silence, Katherine said. "It's possible I'm at fault, sweetheart. I reread your paper on chain reactions last week, and I could have returned it to the wrong file."

He lit a cigarette and said nothing.

She stared down at the water rising in the sink, wondering if she was only imagining things. She had told herself that it could do no harm to give her father the paper, that the source of David's research would remain a secret between them.

"I haven't thought about it until now," David said. "But we sometimes go out during the day and we leave the house unlocked. In the future, I think it would be wise if we kept the house locked at all times. There've been a lot of strange-looking people in our neighborhood since the Night of Broken Glass."

Jacob caught his father's eye again. "For one thing, there's been a strange-looking car parked down the street during the last week."

Katherine said, feeling as if the walls of a trap were closing around her, "That's true. I've seen the car—a Mercedes—parked at the corner when I went to work. And I think Papa is right. We should keep the house locked at all times."

"It's a pity that we have to live in an atmosphere of suspicion and fear," David said, "but no one, not even our neighbors, can be trusted."

Katherine turned off the faucet and looked down at her face reflected in the water, suddenly remembering the words her father had said when she pleaded for his protection: You are indeed a fool, Katherine. You aspire to professional greatness, but you have failed in the most fundamental of human responsibilities. I mean, as a wife and mother.

23

HIS father's instructions for his afternoon study period had been clear: I want you to sit at your desk and read Professor Heisenberg's paper. When I return from the library, we'll take a walk together and talk about it.

Jacob closed the periodical his father had given him and tossed it on the desk. It was obvious, when his father announced that morning that he would spend the afternoon doing research at the library, that he was lying. Soon after his mother had left for the lab, he had overheard him talking on the telephone in the living room: a brief conversation about a meeting he would attend that afternoon at one o'clock. Unobserved, Jacob had watched from the hallway as his father wrote the address on the back of an envelope. Then after he left the house, he had found the envelope wadded up in the wastebasket next to the telephone.

He took the envelope and looked at the address his father had written: 387 Schönherrstrasse, Mahlsdorf-Nord. Mahlsdorf-Nord was a working-class district on the east side of Berlin he had never visited.

Last night, he had stayed up until the small hours of the morning trying to understand his parents' strange behavior at supper: his father's suspicious interrogation of his mother and his mother's nervous defensiveness. The pieces of the puzzle did not fit together, but he was sure that today's meeting had something to do with the meeting his father had had yesterday with Dr. Bukowski, and he was also sure that his father's suspicions of his mother had something to do with the research papers that had been misfiled.

It was like looking for the missing term in a mathematical equation, but he was certain that the answer to all his questions would be found in Mahlsdorf-Nord. The bus ride from Dahlem to the east side of Berlin would take at least forty-five minutes, but if he hurried he could be there by one o'clock.

Moving quickly, he got up and put on the most nondescript clothes he could find: a short brown wool jacket and a dark blue cap.

Jacob went to his father's study, opened the bottom drawer of his desk, and took out the Berlin street and bus directory.

The clock on his father's desk read 12:14, which meant that he had exactly sixteen minutes to reach the Kurfürstendamm for the twelve thirty bus to the West End.

He smiled to himself as he hurried into the living room: If nothing else was certain in Berlin, at least you could count on the führer's public buses to run on time.

Outside, he saw to his relief that the street was deserted in both directions. He locked the front door, then turned north, heading toward the Kurfürstendamm.

Fifteen minutes later, certain that he had not been followed, he boarded the twelve thirty eastbound Kurfürstendamm bus and took a seat in the back of the vehicle. Of the five passengers who had boarded the bus with him, only one even remotely resembled a Gestapo agent: a thin middle-aged man in a nondescript tweed topcoat and black hat.

It was 12:45 when Jacob left the Kurfürstendamm bus at the Breit-scheidplatz. Looking back to see if anyone had followed him from the bus, he caught sight of the man further down the crowded sidewalk. Increasing his speed, he quickly rounded the Gedächtniskirche tower, crossed the busy Budapester Strasse, and hurried through the gates leading into the wooded Tiergarten. In spite of the cold November wind, the park's winding paths were crowded with strolling Berliners. Crossing the Landwehrkanal, he looked back to find the man nowhere in sight.

Five minutes later, when he boarded another eastbound bus at the Friedrichstrasse, less than a block from Hitler's granite-faced Reichs-chancellery, he was all but certain that no one was following him.

It was ten minutes after one when he left the bus at the Hörnower-strasse, Mahlsdorf-Nord's main thoroughfare, and turned north between the district's dismal four- and five-story turn-of-the-century redbrick apartment buildings.

Passing a group of elderly women chatting in front of a small shop whose front door and window had been boarded up, he hesitated a moment to read the words that had been painted in black letters across the boards: MACHT BERLIN JUDENFREI.

Continuing up the street, he came to the Schönherrstrasse. Jacob followed the ascending street numbers to his destination, the fourth build-ing from the corner. Except for four small boys playing ball at the far end of the block, the street was deserted. Glancing back again to see if he had been followed, he turned down the street and walked past number 387: a four-story brick tenement with concrete steps leading up to the front door.

Maybe I've come all this way for nothing, he thought, staring up at the building's empty windows. Maybe Papa went to the library, after all.

Halfway down the the block he stopped for a moment to watch the boys as they happily played soccer with a small black rubber ball. Recalling that he and his Jewish friends had always played soccer with a leather ball, he wondered at the irony of their fortune.

The boys here may be poor, he thought to himself, but at least they're free.

He looked at his watch and saw that it was already 1:35. He would wait five more minutes at the far end of the street, then return home. When he looked up, he noticed a man standing on the southeast corner of Am Lupinenfeldstrasse, lighting a cigarette. Dressed in a short gray jacket, with a black billed cap pulled down over his eyes, he was not, Jacob thought, anyone he had seen earlier.

He hesitated, feeling conspicuous and out of place. Then suddenly, the boys' little black ball came rolling toward him across the brick pavement. Turning away, he reached down and caught the ball with both hands. The gesture took only a second; but when he looked up, the man on the corner had vanished and the four boys had drawn back to the far side of the street, where they stood watching and waiting to see what he would do with their ball.

The suspicion he saw in their eyes was familiar.

With a reassuring smile, he tossed the ball to the smallest of the boys.

Surprised, the boy caught the ball; then with looks of relief, he and his friends went back to their soccer game.

As he turned away from the boys, another man rounded the corner. Dressed in an English mackintosh and black felt hat, with a plaid wool scarf drawn up around his chin, he looked out of place in their dismal surroundings. Quickly crossing the street, the man hurried up the steps of the tenement building at number 387. But it was not until he opened the door and turned around to look down the street that Jacob recognized the anxious face of Dr. Konrad Bukowski.

24

"TAKE your time, Comrade Linz," the man named Karl said. "It's important that you make no mistake."

Playing for time, David slowly examined the photographs spread across the table in front of him. There was no mistake. The papers the Rote Kapelle had photographed at the Heereswaffenamt were his. A bead of sweat broke on his forehead and ran down the side of his face.

"The paper, as you see, is unsigned, Doktor Linz," the woman named Frieda said. "So we must rely entirely on your word."

A cold draught suddenly moved through the room, stirring the dense cigarette smoke above the parlor table.

David sat back and looked at the two men who sat across from him at the table. Karl, a heavy-set man in his late sixties, had the rough look of a German factory worker. And next to him, looking like a banker in his dark blue suit, was a tall thin man named Helmut.

"These are photographs of my theoretical papers," David said.

The light from the overhead fixture caught the lenses of Helmut's horn-rimmed spectacles, momentarily concealing his penetrating gray eyes. "Are you absolutely certain?" he asked.

"Yes. There is no mistake."

Frieda lit another cigarette and threw the burning match into the ashtray on the table. "When did you write this paper, Doktor Linz?" she asked.

"I began the paper on November 12, two days after it became clear that my wife had split the uranium atom, and I finished it a week later, on November 19."

She drew on her cigarette and said, letting the smoke curl up her pale angular face, "Then you wrote most of the paper after you began working in private, after the government gave you permission to continue your theoretical research at home."

He looked down at the incriminating photographs on the table, wondering how much Konrad Bukowski had told the Rote Kapelle of the arrangements he and Katherine had made with the government. "Yes," he said, "that's correct," and glanced at the empty chair on his left. When Bukowski telephoned that morning with instructions, he had assumed that he would be present at the meeting.

Karl reached out and took a photograph from the table. "The part of your paper that interests us, Doktor Linz, is what you wrote about an explosive uranium chain reaction. Can you describe what you meant?"

He thought of Bukowski's warning yesterday about the military use of their uranium discovery. "The few sentences I wrote about an explosive chain reaction were pure speculation," he said, "and there was no mention of any military applications."

The man caught Frieda's eye and smiled, patiently. "We are not scientists, Doktor Linz," he said, "so we do not understand your mathematical abstractions. Even so, at the end of your paper you made a statement about an explosive release of atomic energy, and we would like to know what you meant."

"I meant exactly what I said—that it's theoretically possible that a neutron chain reaction could result in an explosive release of atomic energy," he said. "I did not bother to elaborate because the paper was never meant for publication."

"Nonetheless," said Frieda, turning her cigarette between her fingers, "your paper somehow found its way into the files of the German Army's

Weapons Department, and it has aroused the interest of the Nazi military authorities."

As he opened his mouth to speak, there was soft knock at the apartment door. Frieda stubbed out her cigarette, quickly rose, and went to the door. A few words were spoken—the same passwords they had exchanged when he arrived—then the door was unbolted.

"Thank God you're safe," Frieda said as Bukowski hurried into the room. "We were worried."

"I was late making contact with Comrade Lothar. I came as soon as I could." As she rebolted the door, he removed his mackintosh and hat, threw them on a chair, and looked nervously around the room.

"Come," Frieda said. "We haven't much time left."

With a silent nod in David's direction, Bukowski took the chair next to him.

"You said nothing in your paper about the military use of atomic energy, Herr Doktor," said Karl, "but could it be inferred from what you wrote that a uranium bomb was possible?"

He remembered his warning last night about the military use of atomic energy and Katherine's refusal to believe that a nuclear bomb was possible. "It's possible." He glanced at Bukowski. "But to make that kind of leap would require firsthand knowledge of the physics of uranium disintegration."

"So," Frieda said, "someone with knowledge of your uranium discovery has turned over your research."

Lamely, taking pains to avoid eye contact with Bukowski, he said, "I cannot explain how my research found its way to the Army's Heereswaffenamt."

"By the way, Doktor Linz," Helmut said, "now that you are working at home, where do you keep your research papers?"

"I keep everything locked in a metal filing cabinet in my study."

"I see. And who, besides you, has access to your filing cabinet?"

David took a deep breath, feeling as if he would suffocate in the airless room. "There are only two people with access to my files," he said. "My wife, Katherine, and my son, Jacob."

"And your wife, Katherine, is responsible for the experimental side of your uranium research, is she not?" Karl asked.

"That's right. It was through her experiments with uranium bombardment that we made our discovery."

Again, Frieda stubbed out her half-smoked cigarette in the ashtray on the table. "We've been told that your wife is German, Herr Linz. Is that correct."

"Yes. She was born here in Berlin."

"And her name before she was married was von Steiner, was it not?"

He knew at once where her questions were leading. "Yes," he said, "and her father, as you know, is Colonel Eric von Steiner, the director of the Army's Heereswaffenamt." He sat back and looked around, reading the resolute expressions on all four faces. "I know what you're thinking," he said, "and you are wrong. My wife is incapable of collaborating with the Nazis."

"The evidence we have," Bukowski spoke for the first time, "speaks for itself, David. Katherine has firsthand knowledge of your uranium discovery, and she has access to your files."

"I've told you, Konrad, I don't know how Colonel von Steiner came to possess my research papers," he said, "but Katherine would never betray me to her father."

"We know the colonel arranged a letter of immunity for Jacob, David, and Fieldmarshal Keitel would hardly make an exception to the Nürnberg Laws without a promise of something in return."

A sudden impulse to escape from the apartment came over David. "Katherine would never make such a compromise." He turned with panic to Bukowski. "Konrad," he said, "you have worked with Katherine for five years, and you have seen how she has suffered as the wife of a Jew here in Germany. Not only that," David said with vehemence, letting his anger break free, "you know very well that she has opposed her father's membership in the Nazi Party from the very beginning, and she hates everything he stands for . . ." His voice broke and fell away in the accusing silence around the table.

Bukowski reached into his suitcoat pocket and took out a long gray envelope. "What you say is true, David," he said, placing the envelope on the table. "I have known Katherine as a friend and colleague for five years, and I have no doubts about her hatred of the Nazis. But I also have no doubt of her overwhelming ambition to succeed as a scientist."

David opened his mouth to speak, but the familiar inscription printed across the top of the envelope silenced him:

Oberkommando der Wehrmacht
Heereswaffenamt

"The fact is, Doktor Linz," Frieda said, "the Rote Kapelle has very good reasons for asking you to come here and identify your research papers." She opened the file folder on the table and took out another group of photographs. "Last Tuesday, following the discovery of your papers, our contact at the Heereswaffenamt informed us of a secret conference that was held on November 26 in the office of Colonel von Steiner at the Heereswaffenamt. Present at the meeting were two other ranking Wehrmacht officers—Fieldmarshal Wilhelm Keitel, Chief of Armed Forces High Command, and General Franz Halder, the Wehrmacht's Chief of Staff."

Bukowski stepped in. "Also present at the meeting was Kurt Waldhardt, my assistant in the chemistry lab."

At the mention of Waldhardt's name, David felt a chill run down his neck.

Frieda said, thumbing through the photographs, "The purpose of the conference was to discuss the possible military uses of your uranium discovery, Doktor Linz, and I have here photographs of the minutes from the conference." She removed one of the photographs and returned the others to the folder. "Basing his opinion on the evidence of your theoretical paper, Waldhardt informed the generals that the new atomic energy, and I quote, 'will most certainly prove to be of crucial military importance to Germany's future. And though the scientific evidence we have so far obtained is incomplete, the German Army can look forward to the development of a powerful and unprecedented new military weapon.' "

As she rummaged among the photos in the folder, Bukowski took the Heereswaffenamt envelope from the table and opened it.

"It was at the end of his speech to the generals that Colonel von Steiner finally disclosed his plans for the Heereswaffenamt's development of an atomic military weapon," Frieda said, removing a second photo. "Reminding the generals of the führer's plans for German Lebensraum, he made the following recommendation, and I quote, 'It has taken the German Nation nineteen long years to recover from the crushing humiliation we suffered at Versailles in 1919, and it is the führer's vowed resolution that Germany will redeem both the honor and the power that were taken from her at the end of the Great War. Therefore, gentlemen, in the light of the führer's October 21st directive ordering the liquidation of Czechoslovakia, and his recent November 24th directive ordering preparations for the occupation of Polish Danzig, it is my urgent recommendation that the Heereswaffenamt department of the Oberkommando der Wehrmacht be given complete administrative control of the Kaiser-Wilhelm Institute, and that immediate steps be taken to ensure the speedy development of a German uranium bomb . . ."

Bukowski took a single sheet of gray letter paper from the envelope and placed it on the table. "I met with our contact at the Heereswaffenamt an hour ago," he said, scanning the faces around the table, "and I have here a copy of Eric von Steiner's order for the Heereswaffenamt's takeover of the Kaiser-Wilhelm. It was issued last night and signed by Fieldmarshal Keitel."

25

As David rounded the landing and started down to the tenement's first floor, the impulse to escape came back again. "It's crazy to think you can do anything to stop von Steiner's takeover of the Kaiser-Wilhelm, Konrad," he said. "Security is going to be doubled, and the Institute will be watched night and day."

As they left the building, Bukowski took hold of his arm and drew him to a halt. "The decision has already been made, David. It won't be long before Hahn and Strassmann work out the meaning of their barium separations, and the Rote Kapelle must now take steps to stop all further uranium research at the Institute. If necessary, we will destroy the laboratories and the building housing the Van de Graaf accelerator." He let go of his arm, and they continued down to the sidewalk in silence.

"I will come to your next meeting," David said, "but I will not participate in any scheme to destroy the Kaiser-Wilhelm."

"Fair enough," said Bukowski. "We will meet at a new location tomorrow afternoon, and between now and then I will contact you by telephone and give you directions."

"It will have to be in the morning, when Katherine is at the lab."

"I'm sorry you had to learn about it this way, David. I know how much you love her."

"I still don't believe that she gave my papers to her father," David said.

When they reached the sidewalk, Bukowski stopped and scanned the street in both directions. Aside from the young boys playing soccer, the Schönherrstrasse was deserted. "Did you follow my instructions coming here?" he asked.

"Yes. I'm absolutely sure no one followed me."

"Tomorrow, you must obey my instructions to the letter. The Gestapo keeps watch over your movements around the city, and the members of the Rote Kapelle are at the top of their most-wanted list. You must say nothing to anyone about what you have seen and heard today, including Jacob."

"I understand."

"Good." With a wave, Bukowski left him standing on the sidewalk and hurried across the street.

Not daring to take the same route, David turned north up the Schönherrstrasse.

As he approached the boys, they left off with their soccer game and stood watching him with suspicion. At that moment, he caught sight of a figure in the darkened doorway of a building across the street: a figure he immediately recognized, even before Jacob left the doorway and stepped out into the light.

As the boy came toward him across the street, the only thought he could summon to his mind was the sheer impossibility of his presence here, on this remote street, at the far eastern end of Berlin.

When the boy reached the sidewalk curb, he stopped. The fear David saw in his son's blue eyes was contagious. "What are you doing here?" he asked.

"I knew you weren't going to the library, so I decided to follow you."

Saying nothing, trying to escape the terror that was now closing in on him, he left the sidewalk and crossed the Schönherrstrasse.

Jacob followed, keeping two steps behind.

"I overheard your conversation on the telephone this morning, Papa, and I saw you write the address on an envelope."

He said, turning east into the narrow Strindbergstrasse, "It was wrong of you to come here, Jacob. You could have been followed by the Gestapo."

"But I wasn't followed, Papa. I changed buses and I watched everyone around me."

David looked around at the deserted tenement buildings, wondering how he could escape answering the boy's questions.

"You lied to me, Papa, and I want to know what's happening."

Knowing that one fact would lead to another, David kept moving and said nothing.

"It was your friend Dr. Bukowski who telephoned this morning, wasn't it?" the boy asked.

"How do you know that, son?"

"I was waiting in the street when Dr. Bukowski arrived. This is the second time in two days that you and Bukowski have met in secret, Papa."

"It was nothing," David said. "A meeting of some scientist friends of mine."

"They why did you lie to me and say you were going to the university library?"

His son's logic, as always, was impeccable. He knew that Jacob would go on asking questions until he learned the whole, terrible truth.

"The meeting you went to was dangerous, Papa, wasn't it?" Jacob asked.

"Yes, it was very dangerous."

"It was Dr. Bukowski who asked you to attend the meeting, and it has something to do with Mother, doesn't it? With Mother and Grandpapa Eric and your research paper on uranium chain reactions."

The terror David had kept at bay suddenly broke over him like a wave. Seeing that the crowded Hörnowerstrasse, the only refuge left to him, was but a few yards away, he picked up speed and left his son behind.

The boy overtook him as he made a right turn into the dense pedestrian traffic. "For God's sake, Papa, I have a right to know the truth!" he shouted. "She's my mother!"

The desperation David heard in his son's voice brought him to an abrupt halt. He stood for a moment, watching the faces of the people coming toward them up the street, wondering to himself how he could begin to defend Katherine in the face of such damning evidence. He reached out, put his arm around the boy's shoulder, and said, quietly, "All right, son. I will tell you everything."

26

KATHERINE pulled alongside the curb in front of the house and looked down the street in both directions. The old Citroën she had seen parked at the corner two hours ago was gone and the street was now deserted.

She turned off the motor and sat for a moment, trying to sort out the puzzling events of the last two days. Last evening, she had returned from the lab at five o'clock to find a note from David saying that he and Jacob had gone to a movie at the Ufa Palast and that she should not wait up for them. When they returned well after midnight she was horrified to find that David's suspiciousness had spread, like a contagious disease, to Jacob. She had lain awake the rest of the night, feeling as if she had gone to bed with a total stranger. This morning, when she left for work, the tension in the house had been like an electric current, and she had spent a distracted hour at the lab, trying to decide if she should return home and break the silence that was strangling her family.

Wondering how she would explain her foolish collaboration with her father, she left the car and hurried up to the front porch.

"Katherine!" David looked up with surprise as she entered the parlor. "I thought you were at the lab!"

He was dressed, she saw, in his brown tweed suit and blue topcoat. "I was," she said, "but there's something wrong, David, and I think we should talk about it."

He considered her statement for a moment, then said, "I wish you had said something at breakfast this morning, Katherine. Jacob and I have an appointment at ten thirty."

"An appointment?" she asked.

"Yes." He turned toward the mirror over the sofa and began nervously adjusting his tie. "We're supposed to meet Konrad Bukowski for coffee."

She thought of Bukowski's strange behavior during the last week. This morning, when she visited the chemistry lab to collect the report on yesterday's uranium bombardments, he had treated her like a stranger. "That's odd," she said. "I saw Konrad not an hour ago, and he said nothing about meeting you and Jacob."

"I hope he hasn't forgotten." David gave a nervous laugh. "I've been having trouble with my paper on uranium disintegration, and I phoned him this morning to ask him if he could meet with me."

"You could always phone and leave a message saying you'll be late," she pleaded.

"I can't be late, Katherine." He opened the briefcase and began nervously rummaging among the papers inside. "The meeting was my idea, and Konrad would be furious if I kept him waiting."

There were footsteps behind her, and when she turned around Jacob was standing in the hallway door, staring at her in wide-eyed surprise. Like his father, he was dressed in his heavy winter coat, with a long wool scarf tied around his neck.

He glanced between the two of them with confusion. "I thought you had gone to the lab," he said.

"Your mother wants to have a talk, son," David said. "But I told her we have an appointment with Dr. Bukowski at the Gute Stube coffee bar."

Jacob left the door and came into the room. "That's right," he said, hurrying to confirm what his father had said. "And Papa's letting me tag along."

Bewildered, Katherine turned away and set her purse down on the table. It was obvious that they were both lying. How could she say what she had come to say when they were determined to leave.

"We'd better go, son," David said, closing his briefcase. "It's almost ten o'clock and we have a half-hour's bus ride to the West End."

Katherine said, trying to fill the silence as she followed Jacob and David to the front door, "If you think you're going to be late, perhaps you should take the car."

"No, you'll need it to go back to the lab."

At the gate, David turned back and said, "What time do you think you'll be home from the lab?"

"I'm scheduled to do an experiment at three," she said, "but I should be home by five."

"Good. Then we can talk this evening."

Wondering at the strange look of sadness she had seen in David's eyes, Katherine went to the top step of the porch and watched as the two of them walked down the street.

A block away, at the intersection of the Gregor Mendel Strasse, they made a left, instead of a right turn, heading in the opposite direction from the Kurfürstendamm.

For a moment, feeling as if she were now trapped in a labyrinth, she tried to imagine where they could be going, but the only thing that came to mind were the foolish hopes she had had for a Nobel Prize and the promise she had broken.

Realizing that she would only find the answer to her question by learning their real destination, she left the porch and started after them.

At the corner of the Gregor Mendel Strasse, she paused and waited until there was a safe distance between them. Then, without noticing the two-door black Mercedes that had just swung around the corner from the Breitenbachplatz a block away, she turned south in the direction of Zehlendorf.

27

THAT afternoon, shortly after four o'clock, Jacob answered a knock at the front door.

It took a moment for him to recognize the face behind the heavy wool scarf. "Dr. Bukowski!" Startled by the man's unexpected appearance, he let go of the door and stepped back. He and his father had seen Bukowski that morning at the Rote Kapelle meeting in Zehlendorf, but there was no mention of his visiting them that afternoon.

"Is your father in?" Bukowski asked.

"Yes. He's working in his study."

Glancing back nervously over his shoulder, Bukowski quickly came in and closed the door behind him. "Don't just stand there, Jacob," he said, removing the wide-brimmed hat he was wearing. "I need to speak to your father at once."

Jacob hesitated, remembering Bukowski's anger that morning when he arrived with his father at the meeting. "I know it was wrong of me to come to the meeting this morning," he said, "but I found out about Papa's involvement with the Rote Kapelle, and I forced him to take me along."

"That isn't why I've come, Jacob." Bukowski looked at his watch. "Go get your father, we haven't much time."

Before Jacob could respond, David appeared at the hallway door. "Konrad!" he exclaimed. "This is an unexpected surprise!"

"Something disastrous has happened, David," he said.

David closed the book he was carrying and came into the room. "I don't understand. I thought we were forbidden to meet like this."

"It makes no difference now. The Rote Kapelle's plans have changed." Bukowski loosened the scarf around his neck. "It's now five minutes after four, and my orders are to see that you and Jacob get to the Bahnhof Zoo in time to catch the five-o'clock train to Paris."

David looked at Jacob with amazement. "The five-o'clock train to Paris? What are you talking about?"

"As you Americans say, David, 'The game is up.' The Gestapo knows everything—the names of our Rote Kapelle comrades and where they live—everything."

David read the look of shock in his son's eyes. He had warned the boy that they would be risking arrest if they met with the Rote Kapelle. "For God's sake, Konrad," he exclaimed, "tell me what's happened!"

Bukowski began pacing back and forth, nervously turning his hat in his hands. "I'll explain everything, David, but first you should know about the message that was delivered this morning to Colonel von Steiner at Heereswaffenamt. It was from the office of Heinrich Himmler, the head of the Gestapo." He stopped pacing and took a pack of cigarettes from his pocket. "The message was delivered at eleven thirty, but the colonel was absent, and it was intercepted by our contact at the Heereswaffenamt, who telephoned the head of the Rote Kapelle." He paused and nervously lit his cigarette. "Himmler's message informed the colonel that warrants will be issued this afternoon for the arrest of all the members of the Rote Kapelle. The arrests are scheduled to begin at precisely five o'clock," he said, "and your names are on the list."

David's mouth had gone dry. He swallowed. "But Jacob and I are not members of the Rote Kapelle," he said.

"You and Jacob were present at this morning's meeting."

David said, trying to avoid his son's horrified gaze, "Are you telling me that the Gestapo followed us to the meeting?"

Bukowski stopped pacing. "The security chief informed von Steiner that it was through the colonel's daughter that the Gestapo was finally able to identify all the members of the organization. Apparently, Katherine followed you to the meeting in Zehlendorf this morning and she, in turn, was followed by the Gestapo."

Jacob's face, David saw, had gone deathly white.

"What you're saying makes no sense, Dr. Bukowski," said Jacob. "Mother came home from the lab this morning and wanted to have a talk with Papa and me. She was very upset."

"Jacob's right," David said. "She kept saying that she had something important to tell us."

"And did you have a talk with her?" Bukowski asked.

"No. It was almost ten o'clock, and I told her we were meeting you for coffee at ten thirty."

"I see." Bukowski began pacing again. "Then that would explain how she followed you to Zehlendorf."

"You're being absurd, Konrad. Katherine may have followed us to the meeting in Zehlendorf, but she would never betray anyone to the Gestapo."

"Our contact at the Heereswaffenamt read the entire message to me on the telephone, David," said Bukowski. "At the end of it, the security chief congratulated the colonel on both his and his daughter's loyalty to the Reich."

"I don't give a damn what the security chief's message said, Bukowski," David said. "Katherine would never betray us."

Bukowski went to the parlor window and cautiously looked out. "In any case, whether it was Katherine or someone else who betrayed you and the Rote Kapelle to the Gestapo no longer matters. The fact is, the Gestapo will issue warrants for your and Jacob's arrests at five o'clock. You have exactly fifty minutes to get to the Bahnhof Zoo."

The man's equanimity was like a catalyst to the anger that had slowly welled up in David. He threw the book savagely against the parlor wall. "You don't know Katherine like I do!" he shouted. "She's incapable of doing what you say she's done . . . we will not leave Berlin without her."

"You have no choice, David," said Bukowski. "It's possible that Katherine is innocent, but you don't have time now to prove it."

"You're wrong," David said, and started toward the telephone. "I'll telephone her at the lab, and she will explain everything."

Bukowski left the window and intercepted him as he lifted the receiver. "No, David, you can't telephone Katherine. There are too many lives at stake."

For a moment, he held the receiver to his ear, searching his mind for some alternative. A feeling of hopelessness came over him. It seemed that he had spent the last eighteen years of his life racing to reach this one moment, that the years had simply run down like a clock and he was now left with only a few miserable minutes of life.

Bukowski took an envelope from his topcoat pocket and handed it to him. "Here," he said, "take this."

David returned the receiver to the hook and took the envelope. "What is it?"

"I was ordered to give you all the money I could find. It isn't much, but five hundred Marks should get you across the border into France."

Into France. The realization of what he was being asked to do finally dawned on David. He wanted suddenly to laugh.

Bukowski turned away and stubbed out his cigarette in the ashtray on the table. "When the authorities learn that you and Jacob have left Berlin, they will probably suspect that you are heading for France," he said. "Unfortunately, the five o'clock to Paris is not an express. It will stop four times before it crosses the frontier at Saarbrücken. There's the possibility that the train will be searched at any of the four stations where you'll stop—at Potsdam, at Magdeburg, at Düsseldorf, or at Saarbrücken—but that's a chance you'll have to take."

"Do you really expect me to leave Berlin without Katherine, Konrad?" David asked.

"Yes, my friend. I'm afraid you have no choice."

As Jacob turned to face him, tears broke from his eyes and ran down his face. "I'm afraid, Papa," he said.

Bukowski looked again at his watch. "It's now four twenty-one and the Gestapo, as usual, will be quite punctual. The warrants will be issued in exactly thirty-nine minutes; and being both a Jew and a German citizen, your son will be the first to be arrested."

David said, stalling for time, "Why are you doing this, Konrad? You should have left Berlin by now."

"I'm a Pole, David, not an American, and I might be able to get as far as Eberswalde, but no further. But you, at least, have a chance. You're an American citizen, and Jacob will be traveling with documents of immunity signed by Fieldmarshal Keitel himself."

Again, Bukowski looked at his watch. "It's now four twenty-two, David, so make up your mind. If we rush you can still make the five o'clock to Paris."

Walking mechanically, David left the telephone table and went to Jacob across the room, and gently put his arm around the boy's shoulder. "We have no choice."

28

FOR a moment, Katherine stood in the doorway, wondering at the eerie silence in the house.

"David?" she called, "Jacob?" But the only sound she heard was the steady tick of the clock on the parlor mantelpiece.

Shifting her grocery sack to her left hand, she came into the room and closed the front door.

That's odd, she thought, remembering David's promise that morning to be at home when she returned from the lab at five.

She went to the kitchen and set her grocery sack on the table. The dirty breakfast dishes were still stacked in the sink. For a moment, she stood at the kitchen table, listening to the soft tap of water dripping from the faucet.

She thought of the silence that had hung like a cloud over the house for the last two days. But this was not the same kind of silence. This was the silence of absence, the silence you heard in a house that had been abandoned—total and absolute.

With a feeling of uneasiness, thinking of her trip that morning to Zehlendorf, she took off her coat and went to the bedroom to hang it up.

She stopped abruptly as she entered the bedroom. The drawers of David's clothes bureau were open and there were clothes all over the floor.

With a sudden feeling of panic, she turned and raced down the hallway to Jacob's bedroom. The bureau drawers gaped open and his clothes were strewn across the floor.

For a moment, she stood clutching the door handle, trying to catch her breath. She left the boy's room and hurried back down the hallway to David's study. She went to the desk, turned on the lamp, and saw that the drawer—except for a single German passport, a French and a German travel visa, and single railway ticket—was empty. She opened the passport and saw that it was hers . . . as were the travel visas and the railway ticket.

Again, feeling her heart begin to race, she searched her mind, trying to find a single thread that would connect the events of the last two days— the single missing fact that would explain her husband's and son's sudden departure.

It's impossible, she thought. Nothing I have done would warrant their leaving Berlin without me.

Suddenly, the telephone began to ring.

Feeling a wave of hope rise in her breast, she returned her passport and visas and railway ticket to the drawer and hurried into the living room.

"Hello!" she said.

"Katherine," her father said. "I've been trying to reach you for an hour."

"I just got home."

"Something dreadful has happened, Katherine, and I need to see you at once."

"They've gone, Papa . . ." Her voice began to shake uncontrollably. "David and Jacob have left Berlin."

"Calm down, Katherine," he said, "and listen to me. I received a telephone call an hour ago from my secretary at the Heereswaffenamt.

There isn't time for me to explain everything on the telephone, but the Gestapo has issued warrants for David and Jacob's arrest."

"What do you mean, warrants for their arrest!" she shouted.

"I'll explain everything when you get here, Katherine. I want you to bring your passport and travel visas and come to the house at once. It's five fifteen, and a warrant for your own arrest will be issued in fifteen minutes."

There was a clicking noise as the line disconnected.

For a moment, she stood listening to the monotonous dial tone, thinking to herself of the wreckage she had made of her life.

29

THE snow that had begun to fall when they crossed the Rhine at Mainz had hidden the ugly ragged hills of the industrial Saar Valley under a fresh white blanket. David looked out at the familiar landscape, thinking of the years that had passed since he had travelled from Berlin to Paris. Through the transparent reflection of his face in the window, lights came toward him out of the darkness.

Jacob shifted anxiously on the seat opposite him. "Is this Saarbrücken, Papa?" he asked in English.

"Yes, son. I think so."

The boy looked at his watch. "They must have telegraphed ahead by now," he said. "It's eleven thirty-five."

"Not necessarily." David sat forward. "Saarbrücken is only one of a hundred frontier towns and we passed through Düsseldorf without any incident." He gave the boy an encouraging smile and sat back. Although they had seen two suspicious-looking men moving up and down the platform when the train stopped at Düsseldorf, there had been no official search of the second-class carriages.

On the seat next to Jacob, Herr Siedmacher suddenly stirred, murmured an incoherent phrase in German, then dropped off to sleep again with his chin resting on his chest. Before the train left the station, Siedmacher, a talkative glove salesman from Nürnberg, who prided himself on his modest command of English, had made it clear that he was both a successful German businessman and a card-carrying member of the

Nazi Party. Since then, David and Jacob had been forced to play the charade of being two American tourists, father and son, en route from Berlin to Paris after a two-week holiday in Hitler's amazing Third Reich.

Unable to restrain himself, the boy sat forward and said in a sudden misery of fear, "What if Dr. Bukowski was right, Papa? What if she did follow us to the meeting in Zehlendorf?"

David glanced at the old woman on the seat beside him. Though her eyes were closed, it was obvious she was awake and listening. He leaned foward and took the boy's hand. "Listen to me, son," he said under the monotonous racket of the carriage wheels. "Bukowski is wrong about your mother, I'm sure of it. She may have followed us to the meeting, but she would never wilfully betray anyone to the Gestapo."

"She betrayed you once, Papa. She gave your research to Grandpapa Eric, and then he ordered the takeover of the Kaiser-Wilhelm."

David sat back, thinking once again of the terrible price he and Katherine had paid for their dream of success. In the distance, the lights of Saarbrücken's industrial outskirts came into view between the surrounding buildings. The dismal landscape—the uniform council houses with their identical slate roofs and smoking chimney pots—was the same as he remembered it that night, years ago, when he passed through Saarbrücken on his way to the university in Göttingen. But he had changed. The twenty-one-year-old student who had passed through Saarbrücken that night, filled with innocent and idealistic dreams of conquering the world of physics, was not the disillusioned forty-year-old atomic physicist—the desperately uncertain husband, the frightened father—who was now fleeing Hitler's Nazi Germany.

The brakes screeched, the train lurched across a siding, and Herr Siedmacher awakened with a start. "Ach! What is it?" he called out. Caught between the twilight of his comfortable sleep and the sudden reality of his surroundings, he looked around with bewildered surprise. "Wo sind wir?" he asked.

"Saarbrücken," the old woman muttered, and reached down to retrieve her small suitcase from under the seat.

As the rails opened out into the station train yard, Siedmacher quickly got to his feet and reached up to retrieve his suit jacket, his topcoat, and his black leather traveling case from the overhead rack. Looking down, he caught sight of Jacob nervously feeling in his jacket pocket for his passport and travel visa. He drew the case from the rack and chuckled softly to himself.

As the train rolled into the station's steel enclosure, belching steam and rocking gently, David and Jacob turned to survey the crowd lined along the platform. The uniformed frontier police were there, stationed every thirty yards down the platform. David noticed two men wearing the Gestapo soft-brimmed hat and belted topcoat.

There was another screech of brakes, then a blast of hissing steam as the train came to a halt. In an instant, as if on cue, the passengers rose and spilled out noisily into the aisle.

Siedmacher adjusted his topcoat lapel and pushed his way past the elderly woman into the aisle. Reaching back for his travel case in the seat, he gave Jacob a meaningful smile. "Machen Sie es gut in Amerika, Junge," he said, and hurried off down the aisle.

"Blödes Nazischwein," the old woman muttered to herself as she struggled off with her suitcase.

Jacob kept his gaze lowered until the seats around them had emptied. When he looked up, there was an expression of hopeless resignation in his dark eyes. "They're here," he said. "I saw them."

"Yes, son. I know." The departing passengers were moving toward the forward end of the carriage. He looked back and saw that the corridor leading to the rear of the carriage was deserted. "Listen to me, son," he said. "You have a couple of minutes before the police come on board. I want you to leave this car by the rear door and continue on until you reach the third-class carriages. There'll be doors on both sides of the cars that you can use. Get out on the side opposite the platform, and follow the tracks away from the station." He looked up as the last of the departing passengers left the carriage. "Don't say anything, Jacob," he said. "Just get up and go. You haven't much time."

The boy turned away and looked out at the station platform. "If I do what you want me to do, Papa," he said with infuriating deliberation, "if I leave the train and get away, where will I go? Back to Berlin?"

"You're within a mile of the French border. You can head north and cross the frontier near Saarlouis."

"But Papa, if they arrest you now and I'm not with you, they will know that I'm in the vicinity."

"You can go to another German town. You can wait there until it's safe to cross into France."

Tears spilled down the boy's face. "No, Papa," he sighed. "It's impossible. I may speak like a German, but I look like a Jew."

"Reisepässe!" a voice called out from the far end of the carriage.

David looked back as an elderly frontier guard entered, followed by two heavy-set men, one a head taller than the other, wearing soft-brimmed black hats and black belted topcoats.

"Reisepass, bitte," the old man said impatiently to the passengers in the first seat.

David watched the people passing by on the platform, passengers arriving and passengers departing, astonished to think of the distance he had traveled since he arrived here in Germany.

"Reisepass, bitte." The voice was closer, seven or eight seats away.

He closed his eyes and, for one brief moment, reached back in his mind for some logical and reasonable explanation for the mess he had made of his life. The dreams—the ambitions—that had brought him to Germany were not enough to explain why he had stayed so long.

"Reisepass, bitte, mein Herr." The voice, David realized, was directly beside him.

As he opened his eyes, he suddenly realized that the explanation was lost to him now, along with Katherine, in the terrible chaos of his heart.

"Mein Herr," the voice commanded, "Zeigen Sie mir Ihren Reisepass!"

David obeyed, and when he took his passport from his breast pocket and handed it to the conductor, he saw that Jacob was staring fixedly at the floor between them. The look of hopeless resignation on the boy's face was like a confession of guilt.

Dwarfed by the two bullfaced men standing on either side of him, the frontier official scrutinized his passport. "Your German travel visa," he said in English.

David handed him the visa.

Without bothering to inspect the passport or the visa, the old man turned and handed both documents to the agent on his left, a sullen-faced man with a square, hard-boned jaw and a thin, carefully trimmed, brown moustache.

"Reisepass und Visum, Junge," the frontier official said to Jacob in a voice that seemed weary of this familiar routine.

The boy's effort to appear relaxed, as he fumbled in his jacket pocket, was useless; for when he handed the documents, his hand shook uncontrollably and his passport slipped from his fingers and fell to the floor.

It fell open, David saw, to the page that had always angered and shamed the boy: the page indelibly stamped with the large yellow J.

"Sorry," the boy said, and quickly retrieved the passport.

With maddening deliberation, the agent scrutinized both the passport and the German visa, comparing the face in the passport photograph with Jacob's face. Then he handed all four documents to his shorter and younger companion, a blond-haired fellow with watery blue eyes and a disarmingly boyish face.

It was he who finally spoke. "You will get up," he said in stilted English, "take your coats and the suitcase, and come with us."

Obediently, with a feeling of weariness, David got to his feet. "Do what he says, son," he said.

Jacob shook his head and remained in his seat. "They can't force us to leave the train, Papa," he said. "We have letters of immunity signed by Fieldmarshal Wilhelm Keitel, letters authorized by the führer himself."

The boy's words brought a smile to the blond agent's face. "Your letters of immunity are no longer valid," he said. "You are both under arrest. Warrants for your arrests have been signed by Reichsführer Heinrich Himmler."

"On what charges?" the boy demanded. "We have a right to know the charges."

"Right?" the dark-haired agent laughed. "This is Germany, Junge. You are both Jews, and you have no rights."

David's anger snapped like a string. "Jew or not, I am an American citizen!" he shouted.

The passengers in the forward part of the carriage turned to stare at them with astonishment.

The blond agent drew back his topcoat to display the pistol that was strapped to his chest. "You will take your luggage and come with us!" he barked. "Now!"

"It's no use, Papa," the boy said, and reached up to remove their one suitcase from the rack.

The two agents stepped back. "Dahin!" the younger man said, pointing to the forward end of the car.

As David and Jacob walked obediently down the aisle, followed by the two agents, there were knowing, but disinterested, looks from the other passengers.

When they left the carriage, except for the uniformed conductors stationed alongside the carriages, the platform was deserted.

David circled Jacob's shoulder with his free right arm and drew the boy close to him. "Don't be afraid, son," he said in English.

"Schnell! Mach schon!" The older agent gave the boy's arm a shove to hurry him on.

"Hier! Rechts!" the blond agent pointed toward the glass and steel archway leading into the station.

As they left the platform, David looked back and saw the beam of the engine's headlamp stretching off into the darkness. Suddenly he realized how close they had come to the French frontier—to freedom. As close, he thought to himself, as Katherine and I came to success.

A half dozen people were milling about the vaulted station lobby when they entered. A young couple with a child stopped to stare in their direction, but quickly turned away when they recognized the Gestapo.

"Geht da rüber!" The blond agent motioned to a nondescript door halfway between the station's newsstand and a sign, Gepäckaufbewahrungstelle, painted on the wall above the cloakroom.

When they reached the door, the young agent said, "You will leave the suitcase here," and pointed peremptorily to the floor.

Jacob obeyed, and the door was unlocked and opened. They followed the agent into a long dimly lit room with bare white plastered walls and a rough concrete floor. A single window with metal bars looked out onto the brightly lit station platform. The only light in the room was a naked bulb hanging from a frayed electrical cord. Crude wooden benches stood against all four walls.

"You will wait here until orders come from Berlin," the older agent announced from the door.

From the platform came another blast of steam, and a voice somewhere shouted, "Fünf Minuten!"

"Look," David said, "I'm an American citizen, I am traveling to Paris with my son, and we have a train to catch . . ."

The young agent had returned to the door and closed it before David could finish the sentence.

"You're wasting your breath, Papa," Jacob said as the key turned in the lock.

When David turned toward his son, he realized they were not alone in the room. Seated in the shadows on a bench at the far end of the room was an elderly couple. The woman wore a white peasant's scarf around her head; and the man, a black brimmed hat, which sat on the top of his ancient head like a statement of defiance. Hanging on the wall above them was an old-fasioned metal clock; and beneath the clock, suspended from a nail, a gilt-framed portrait of the führer.

"There's no point in just standing there, Papa," Jacob said. "Come sit with me."

He sat down next to Jacob on the crude bench. On the wall above the führer's gloating portrait, the clock's minute hand jumped to 11:56. Looking up at the crumbling plaster ceiling, he remembered the nights he had spent with Katherine in Göttingen, staring up at the cracks in their bedroom ceiling. If he had known where it would all lead . . .

He looked down at the floor and silently cursed himself for his blind stupidity; and for the weakness of his own heart.

"Where will they take us, Papa?" the boy asked.

"I don't know, son," he replied. But he did know. He had heard Konrad Bukowski talk of the detention camps that they were building in the newly occupied territories of the Reich. Jews like themselves were being taken to a camp called Dachau near München.

There was another blast of steam, and the old man suddenly looked up. In the light from the bulb overhead, David saw the sad frightened face of an old East Prussian orthodox Jew.

At the far end of the room, a key turned in the lock.

The door swung open and a man stepped into the room—one he did not recognize—carrying their passports and travel visas in his hand. "I regret to inform you, Herr Linz, that an unfortunate mistake has been made," he said in perfect English. "Orders have come from Berlin stating that you and your son will be allowed to reboard the train and cross the frontier into France." Clearing his throat, he looked back at the train through the window. "But I'm afraid you will have to hurry."

For a moment, neither David nor Jacob moved.

"I repeat, Herr Linz, unless you have decided to postpone your departure from Germany, you will have to hurry!"

In the next instant, David and Jacob were on their feet. As he passed the elderly couple, David looked back and read the smile on the old man's face: a smile of relief and encouragement.

"Your passports and visas." The man smiled politely and handed the documents to David.

As they reached the platform, there was another loud blast of steam. The train, David saw, was already in motion.

The boy looked back. "The suitcase, Papa!"

"Forget the suitcase, son!" David shouted, remembering again all the research he had left behind in Berlin for the Germans. "Take the first door you can!"

As he and Jacob ran up the platform alongside the train, a first-class carriage rolled by. Another carriage, with its rear door open, came alongside. Grasping the metal handle, Jacob swung himself up and through the carriage door, turned, and held out his hand. "Here! Grab hold!" he shouted.

The train lurched and picked up momentum. Realizing that he had only seconds left before the carriage came to the end of the platform, David reached out and grabbed the boy's hand.

In the next instant, with amazing strength, Jacob pulled him into the safety of the carriage's enclosure.

In the sudden darkness, over the clatter of the wheels, the boy called out, "Papa!" and drew him away from the open door. The carriage rocked across a siding. Reaching out to brace himself against the metal wall, David met, instead, the boy's open arms. For awhile, in the shared exhilaration of their unexpected freedom, they held each other in the rocking darkness.

This time, Jacob led the way, and when they entered the carriage they had occupied from Berlin, there were looks of surprise from the passengers they had passed only fifteen minutes before.

"Votre passeport, Madame," a man's voice came toward them from the forward end of the car.

David looked up and the boy turned around. This time, the frontier official standing in the aisle wore a deep blue uniform with red and white piping on his sleeves and lapels.

The boy was smiling when he turned back. "He spoke French, Papa."

"Yes, we're in France now."

David took the passports and visas from his pocket and handed Jacob his own.

"I won't be needing the German visa anymore, will I, Papa?" he asked.

"No, son. Not anymore," David replied, and thought of the terrible uncertainty he was carrying with him to France: the question of Katherine's innocence.

When they reached their seats, Jacob stood up and pulled down the carriage window. The blast of cold wind that swept over them brought with it a flurry of snow. Balancing his shoulder against the window, he began to tear the visa into small pieces.

Smiling to himself, Jacob reached through the window and opened his hand. In an instant, as if whipped away into nothingness, the paper fragments fluttered by and vanished into the darkness behind them.

THREE

30

As David hurried up the staircase to the Radium Institute's fourth floor, the familiar laughter and joking calls of scientists and technicians bidding each other good day floated up from the second floor laboratories.

Once outside, however, their laughter would be silenced by an eerie calm. The city had been like this since last Friday, when its inhabitants awakened to the news of Hitler's lightning invasion of Poland—a curious feeling of tranquility filled the air, as if the French, remembering the nightmare of the last German war, had somehow quietly withdrawn from reality. Though it was Sunday, he and many of the Institute's scientists had come to work, seeking distraction from the suspense of France and England's undeclared war.

Wondering at the summons he had received from Frédéric Joliot, the Institute's director, David turned down the corridor and hurried to Joliot's office.

"Come in!" Joliot replied in English to his knock.

When he entered the ornately furnished office, the Institute's director was pacing back and forth in front of the window. A world-renowned physicist, Joliot had also married into France's most distinguished family of scientists. Handsomely dressed as always, he wore a white labcoat and white trousers, with a green silk cravat carefully knotted at his neck. "Ah! Dr. Linz!" he exclaimed. "So you got my message."

"Yes. I was on my way home when Kowarski stopped me in the hall."

"Forgive me for calling you here at this hour," he said, motioning for him to come forward, "but this is a matter of some urgency."

David closed the door and walked across the huge room to the director's Victorian desk. The effect of the room's furnishings—the red damask walls, the collection of scientific awards and prizes, and the gallery of family portraits—was intimidating. Marie and Pierre Curie, the famous mother and father of Joliet's wife, Irene, hung on one wall; the less famous uncle Jacques on another; and suspended from a silk rope above the desk was an oil portrait of Frédéric and Irène, wearing their French Légion d'honneur ribbons. Glancing across the room, he observed that the private door connecting Joliet's office with his wife's had been left ajar.

"Tell me, Dr. Linz, are you and Kowarski making any progress with your experimental separation of uranium?"

Considering the urgency of Joliot's summons, the question puzzled David. He and his colleague Lew Kowarski had begun work on the experimental separation of U235 from its parent U238 last month, soon after it became clear that it was the rare U235 isotope that was responsible for the neutron chain reaction in what was now being called atomic fission. "I've worked out the theoretical problems of uranium separation," he said, "but Kowarski is having trouble with his experiments. Apparently, there are only microscopic amounts of U235 present in natural U238. Why do you ask?"

"I'll come to that in a moment," Joliot said, motioning for him to be seated.

As David sat down, a faint shimmering light suddenly illuminated the office window.

Startled, Joliot turned toward the big leaded-glass window. "I'm not one to believe in omens," he said, "but my wife tells me there's a storm blowing in from the east—a sign that there will be war."

David smiled to himself, remembering Katherine's fear of electrical storms. "My wife Katherine was a strong believer in nature's omens," he said. He looked up at the window as another bolt of distant lightning illuminated the sky, thinking to himself of the months he and Jacob had spent waiting for Katherine to join them. He had begun his search for her in December, soon after their arrival in Paris, but in the nine months that had gone by he had learned nothing.

"Tell me, Dr. Linz, have you had any news of your wife's whereabouts?"

"No. None," he sighed. "I've written twenty-six friends and colleagues in Berlin asking about her, but not one of them has bothered to reply."

"It's possible, of course, that your letters have all been confiscated," said Joliot. "After all, you are wanted for treason in Germany."

"I've also made inquiries through friends and colleagues here in Paris, and no one has been able to learn anything."

Joliot sat forward and opened his desk drawer. "As you know, we've heard nothing about the research being done in Germany since the publication of Hahn's and Strassmann's article back in February." As the thunder faintly reverberated through the room, he reached into the desk drawer and took out what looked like a foreign scientific journal. "The reason I've called you here, Dr. Linz, is because this morning I received the July issue of the German journal *Naturwissenschaften*, and there's an article inside dealing with atomic fission."

David shifted nervously in his chair, remembering the paper on chain reactions he had written last November, the paper Katherine had turned over to her father at the Heereswaffenamt.

"As it is," Joliot went on, "I can only conclude from reading the paper that the Germans have made real progress with the theory of uranium fission."

"Are you going to tell me that the paper deals with the theory of uranium chain reaction?" David asked.

"Yes, it gives a detailed theoretical description of the chain reactive release of neutrons in uranium fission. But even more alarming, it mentions the possibility of an explosive release of energy from such a reaction."

"I see." David sat back as a ragged bolt of lightning, closer this time, streaked across the eastern sky.

"Tell me, Dr. Linz," said Joliot, "does the name Kurt Waldhardt mean anything to you?"

Waldhardt: the name startled him. "Yes," he said. "Kurt Waldhardt is a radiochemist at the Kaiser-Wilhelm Institute. He was an assistant to my friend Konrad Bukowski, and he worked on the chemical analysis of my wife's uranium experiments."

Joliot began turning the pages of the journal. "Correct me if I'm wrong, Dr. Linz," he said, "but I vaguely remember your telling me at our first meeting back in January that you had written a paper on uranium chain reactions before you left Berlin."

"That's correct." David's mouth had gone dry, and he swallowed.

"And you left the paper behind in Berlin with all your fission research, did you not?"

David hesitated, thinking to himself of that first meeting with Frédéric and Irène, when he approached the famous couple for a research position at the Radium Institute. He had described in detail his and Katherine's uranium discovery at Kaiser-Wilhelm, but, unwilling to accuse her of collaborating with the Nazis, he had said nothing about her giving his papers to her father.

"Yes," he said. "In retrospect, I probably should have destroyed all my research papers, but everything happened so fast that there wasn't time." He watched as Joliot went on turning the pages of the journal. "Why do you ask?"

"It strikes me as odd that a radiochemist would publish a paper on the physics of chain reactions," said Joliot.

David looked away as another distant bolt of lightning illuminated the sky. "Kurt Waldhardt is a brilliant chemist, but he would not be able to solve, let alone understand, the physical problems of uranium chain reactions."

"It's unthinkable that any respectable scientist would publish another man's work," said Joliot, "but perhaps you should have a look at Wald-hardt's article." He pushed the journal across the desk and sat back.

David lifted the journal and read the title of Waldhardt's article—Die Physik der Kettenreaktion vom Uranatom.

With a sinking feeling he said, "Waldhardt did not write this paper. It's a copy of the paper I left behind in Berlin."

"Are you absolutely certain?" Joliot asked.

"Yes, absolutely."

"Then it appears that your research papers were confiscated—unless your wife allowed Waldbordt to publish your work."

In the months he had been waiting for Katherine's arrival in Paris, David had always explained her absence by the fact that as a valuable scientist she could have been detained by the Nazis. But he had never spoken about her betrayal or revealed the identity of her father.

A feeling of terrible weariness came over David. "It's possible, but Katherine would never consent to work for the Nazis."

The director pushed his chair back and stood up. "Whether or not your wife has collaborated with the Nazis makes little difference now, Dr. Linz. The fact is, with the publication of your chain reaction paper, we can assume that the Germans are at work on the development of a uranium bomb."

31

A THUNDERSTORM was rolling in from the east, but nothing could dampen Jacob's feeling of elation. He wanted to shout the news he had just heard on the radio at the Rue de Rennes corner newsstand: the French and the English had finally declared war on Germany!

Now, within sight of the Joliot-Curie Radium Institute, he slowed his pace. There were lights still burning in the windows on all four floors. He had promised to meet his father at the Institute at five thirty, but he had hung around the newsstand until a quarter of six, listening to President Daladier's patriotic speech in defense of France's declaration of war.

Like his father, he had both wanted and dreaded a French declaration of war; wanted it because there would otherwise be no end to Hitler's voracious appetite for German Lebensraum, dreaded it because war would mean an end to any further contact with Germany. And assuming that his father was right, and his mother had been detained against her will in Germany, an end to any hope of a reunion here in Paris.

He wondered where his mother had been when Hitler addressed the nation on the radio and told the German people that there would be yet another Great War. Perhaps she was now at her parents' home in Grünewald, listening to her father extol the führer's courageous patriotism; or maybe she was at home in Berlin-Dahlem, looking back with remorse on the choice she had made.

As he reached the corner, the Radium Institute's big wooden front door opened and his father stepped out into the street.

"Papa!" Jacob called.

His father lifted his head, took one hand from a pocket, and made a gesture, a vague greeting, in the air. Then he turned and came toward him.

"Hello, son," he said, but kept walking.

Jacob kept pace, following him down the hill toward the Boulevard St. Germain and the river. "Are you okay?" he asked.

His father took a deep breath and shook his head. "I'm fine."

For a moment, they walked together in silence.

"Did you hear the news?"

"Have the French and English declared war?"

"Yes. The English did it at noon, but the French waited until five o'clock. There've been speeches on the radio, Daladier here in Paris and Hitler in Berlin, each blaming the other."

As his father swung right onto the Rue Mouffetard, lightning broke over the rooftops behind them. He looked up and said, absently, "In a way, I'm relieved. At least we can stop looking back and start looking forward."

He meant, of course, the long months they had spent waiting for news of his mother's whereabouts. "But, we don't know if she's still in Germany."

"Don't be foolish, son," David said. "Your mother knew that we would wait for her in Paris. If she's alive, she's living in Berlin."

The statement startled Jacob. Up to now, his father had always been the one who had found excuses to justify his mother's absence.

David looked up again as lightning flooded the sky behind them. "In any case, son," he said, "the time has come for us to make some plans for the future."

"What do you mean, plans for the future?"

"Now that the war has finally come, I think we should talk about leaving France. I think it would be best if we left Europe altogether and moved to America."

Jacob dropped behind and let his father continue ahead. It was not the startling announcement, but the eerie tone of his father's voice that suddenly frightened him. "You're moving too fast, Papa," he said. "We've been at war with Germany for exactly one hour, it's too soon to make any plans for the future."

His father stopped and looked around as he reached the huge prison-like Faculté des Sciences, but said nothing. Jacob saw that his unblinking gaze was fixed on the lights at the western end of the Isle St. Louis in the distance—the island where he always went on Sunday afternoons to fish and enjoy the peaceful solitude of Paris's "l'heure bleue."

"Do you remember Kurt Waldhardt, who worked in the chemistry department at the Kaiser-Wilhelm?" David asked.

"Yes. He was Dr. Bukowski's assistant."

"I thought we had seen the last of Waldhardt when we left Berlin, but it seems he has reappeared." David's voice began to shake, but he went on. "Professor Joliot called me to his office to show me an article by Kurt Waldhardt, an article dealing with the physics of uranium chain reactions."

Jacob stopped, remembering the paper his mother had turned over to her father at the Heereswaffenamt.

They had reached the north side of the Faculté des Sciences building. "The paper Waldhardt published was the one I left behind in Berlin," his father said, then covered his face with his left arm, and began to cry.

Jacob kept his distance and watched, both amazed and frightened, for he had never seen his father cry before. He wept without shame, letting go of all the pain, the grief, the frustration, and—Jacob was sure—all the hope that he had clung to for the last nine months.

After a few moments, he wiped his face with the back of his hand and took a deep breath.

Jacob spoke first. "Waldhardt could have obtained a copy from Grandpapa Eric, or the Nazis could have simply confiscated your files."

As if anticipating another flash of lightning, his father looked up at the sky; and when it came, he spoke. "We've got to stop denying the truth, son. We've been here for nine months; your mother would have found some way to notify us."

"All you know for sure is that Dr. Waldhardt plagiarized your paper and published it," Jacob said.

"Your mother betrayed me once, and there was nothing to stop her from doing it again," David said and began to walk away.

His father stopped for a moment at the intersection of the Boulevard St. Germain and the Quai St. Bernard. Then he started across the busy boulevard, heading toward the Pont Sully. He walked like a man in a trance, oblivious of the traffic around him.

Ahead, like a many-faceted jewel in the middle of the river, lay the Ile St. Louis; and beyond that, the bright lights of the Right Bank and the dark fortress walls of the Bastille.

Jacob followed, hating the feelings that were pulling him apart inside. Until now, he had thought that once he could say with certainty that his mother had stayed behind in Berlin, that she had wilfully chosen to betray them, he would be free to turn his back on her. He had always thought— he had always been taught—that knowledge brought freedom.

As he reached the bridge, lightning struck again, illuminating, ahead of him, the figure of his father.

He hurried, wanting to outrun the inexorable force that seemed to be pulling at him from behind. He looked out over the balustrade of the bridge and saw, in a momentary flash of lightning, the Seine, rolling silently. Staring into the water, he felt overwhelmed by a tide of grief and loss, and love.

When Jacob reached his father, he said, without waiting to get his breath, "If you leave Paris, I will not go with you. This is the only place where Mother knows to find us."

"We stayed on too long in Berlin," his father said. "And look what that led to."

"But you can't leave now, Papa. The war is going to be fought here, not in America, and you can help the French create a nuclear bomb and defeat the Nazis."

His father leaned forward and looked down at the river below them. "If your mother is still in Berlin," he said, "then I would only be helping the French to build a weapon to destroy her."

"Being in America will change nothing, Papa."

"Perhaps not. But there will be an ocean, at least, between us."

"You did that once before, too," Jacob said. "You left your father in America and came to Germany."

David looked away as lightning illuminated his son's face. "I've been here long enough, son," he said. "I'm an American, and I want to go home."

"But I'm a German, Papa—thanks to Mother. And thanks to you, I'm also a Jew, and I want to stay in France and fight the Nazis." Either it was the sudden bolt of lightning or his words, but Jacob saw a shudder run through his father's body.

"I'm tired, son," he said. "I want to rest now." He turned away and slowly walked in the direction of the Right Bank.

Jacob stood watching, knowing that it was not rest that his father wanted, but escape. He caught up with his father as he passed the midway point on the bridge. "What happened to us in Germany is a fact, Papa," he said, "and it won't do any good trying to run away from it!"

His father came to sudden halt. "You've been in Paris for nine months, son, but so far you've done nothing with yourself. You've been living in the past, and it's time you started thinking about the future." He began walking again, absorbed in his own thoughts.

Jacob caught up and kept pace beside him. "There's a bookstore on the Left Bank, and they want to hire someone who can read French, English, and German. I could get a job selling books."

"I would rather see you go back to school."

"There's only one good school for science in Paris, Papa, and they have refused to accept me."

His father kept walking and said nothing.

This time, the lightning and the thunder brought a gust of wind and a few feathery drops of rain. "We can't go on walking like this," Jacob said. "It's going to rain."

Jacob took hold of his father's arm. "We'll turn back and go home."

32

"LET'S turn here!" David shouted over the noise of the rain. "It's shorter!"

As he turned the corner into the narrow Rue du Bac, his shoulder collided with a figure in the darkness.

"Merde!" a woman's voice murmured. There was the sound of something striking the pavement and the noise of scattering papers. "You've made me drop all my lecture notes—everything!"

She was dressed in a gray suit and wore her long dark hair tied in a knot at the back of her head. Though she was smaller and younger-looking, her resemblance to Katherine startled him. "Forgive me," he said. "I shouldn't have been in such a hurry." He knelt down beside her in the darkness and began gathering her papers from the wet pavement.

For reasons he could not define, Jacob found himself unwilling to join them.

Suddenly, his father laughed. "This can't all be lecture notes," he said.

"It's lecture notes and tomorrow's speech on Soviet economics," she said and then she laughed too. "Forget it. This is ridiculous!" she said.

In the momentary silence Jacob took a few cautious steps forward. He could make out the faint outline of their bodies. They were kneeling on the pavement, close to one another, each holding a handful of papers.

"I managed to find a few," his father said.

Jacob held his breath. For one brief moment, when she reached for the papers, their fingers touched.

"Are you a teacher?"

"Yes. I teach economics at the Sorbonne. I've just finished for the day and I'm on my way home."

"It's not safe on the Left Bank at night," he said. "Perhaps you will let us walk you the rest of the way home."

She quickly stood up. "Thank you, Monsieur, but my apartment is only a short distance and I can make it quite safely from here." Clutching her papers to her breast, she hurried off into the darkness. At the corner of the Rue de l'Université the woman stopped and scanned the deserted street in both directions. The man's touch had frightened her. This is silly, she said to herself, childish. But she realized why she had been frightened. His touch had brought back the feeling of another man's touch: that of Henri Bouget, whose hands had held hers the afternoon he pleaded with her to remain with him in Rheims, give up her scholarship to the Sorbonne, and marry him—the last time a man had held her in his arms.

As she crossed the Rue de Lille, the Pont Royal came into view at the end of the block. She had told Henri the first time they met that she had long ago made her choice for the future. She had made it at the age of twelve, during the Great War, when she realized what kind of life was in store for her as the daughter of a French coal miner. And at eighteen, the day the facist German storm troopers murdered her father, she had committed herself completely and irrevocably to the Communist revolution.

Voices came toward her from the darkness behind her. She stopped at the riverside and looked off toward the darkened steeple of Notre Dame. She could still feel the warmth of the American's touch on her hand. It had brought back everything: the memory of that last afternoon with Henri, the feeling of his desperate embrace, and the look of defeat in his childlike brown eyes.

Until last February, the night of her thirty-fifth birthday, she had never once stopped to look back, to regret.

When she turned her head, she saw the American standing beside her. "You mustn't blame yourself for the papers, Monsieur," she said. "It was an accident." The boy, she saw, had lingered behind and was watching her from the shadows of a doorway.

In the lamplight David saw that the hair she had so carefully tied into a chignon had come entirely undone and now fell around her face in long, haphazard strands. "If I hadn't been in such a rush," he said, "it wouldn't have happened." He noticed the long slender hands clutching the chaos of papers to her breast. "Where do you live?" he asked. "We'll walk you the rest of the way home."

She glanced at the boy behind him. "There's really no need. I live nearby—on the Ile St. Louis."

"I see you didn't bring a raincoat, either."

"No. When I came to work this morning, the sun was shining."

The lamplight had caught her profile. The shape of her nose, the upturned angle of her chin, brought to mind the memory of another rainy night: that night in the mountains above Göttingen, when he and Katherine first made love. "Come," he said and stepped forward. "We'll walk you down to the Pont Sully."

"I would be grateful, Monsieur," the woman said, then added, "Forgive me, but I must ask your name."

"Linz. David Linz. And this is my son Jacob."

A feeling of disappointment came over her. "I see," she said, then hurried to cover the evidence of it in her voice. "Bon soir, Jacob!" she exclaimed with forced brightness.

The boy stepped out of the shadow of the doorway. At the first sight of his face in the light she was struck by his great, though unfinished, beauty: a beauty he had inherited not from his father, she realized, but from his mother. "Bon soir, Mademoiselle," he nodded. His voice, though still unsettled, had the same deep and commanding resonance as his father's.

"What a fine young man," she said to fill the silence.

The obvious difference in the two men's accents puzzled her. "Are you both Americans?" she asked David.

"I'm an American. Jacob is German."

"I was born in Germany—in Göttingen," the boy announced. "But we moved to Berlin when I was eleven."

"I see," she said. But in fact, what she saw was the strange furtive look he exchanged with his father, a look that told of some painful secret shared between them. "We'd better hurry. It's going to rain again," she said, and turned down the sidewalk toward the Rue des Ecoles.

David joined her, but the boy remained several paces behind. "Jacob and I have a small garret apartment on the Rue de Buci," he announced after a moment.

"That's quite close to the Ile St. Louis."

"A nine-and-a-half-minute walk, to be exact. I've timed it," he said, then added, "On Sundays I sometimes go fishing off the Pont Sully end of the Ile St. Louis."

"What a coincidence," she said, pleased by the thought that suddenly came to her. "I often spend Sunday afternoons reading in the park at the end of the quai. Perhaps I've seen you there. I live only a block away— on the Rue Bretonvilliers."

"Well, since we're neighbors, I should know your name."

"My name is Aloise Frégand," she replied.

All at once, a brilliant flash of lightning illuminated the entire street, followed by a deafening boom of thunder. Then the sky opened up and, like a force held in check too long, the rain came back in a deluge. Clutching her papers, she quickened her pace.

"Here!" Linz called out.

His jacket was around her shoulders before she could stop him. "No, monsieur! You mustn't!" she exclaimed, reaching up to remove it.

"Keep it," he laughed, adjusting the jacket around her shoulders. "I don't mind the rain!"

The Ile St. Louis was still two blocks away. She tried to hurry, but the memory of Henri Bouget came back, with a feeling of terrible emptiness. She was deeply affected, she realized, by Linz's manly solicitude. To fill the silence, she said, "What kind of work do you do, monsieur?"

"I'm an atomic scientist," he replied, "and I work at the Joliot-Curie Radium Institute."

"That's interesting," she said. "I was at the Radium Institute last week when Professor Joliot gave a lecture on the new atomic energy they discovered in Germany."

"As a matter of fact, my wife and I were at the Kaiser-Wilhelm Institute in Berlin when the uranium atom was first fissioned."

As lightning flooded the street, Aloise saw, for the second time, the evidence of some terrible loss in his face.

Slowing his pace, Jacob dropped back and watched his father trying to walk in step with the professor.

"Actually, Dr. Linz, the Joliot-Curies are close friends of mine. I've known Frédéric since I served as a Communist Party deputy to Parliament, and he was a member of the Party's Central Committee here in Paris."

"I'm not a member of the Party myself," David said, "but I was briefly involved with the German Communist Party in Berlin."

Aloise drew his jacket close around her shoulders. "Tell me, Dr. Linz," she said, "now that France is at war with Germany, do you plan to go on working here in Paris?"

David walked in silence for a moment, then said, "I don't know yet. My wife was supposed to join us in Paris, but she's been detained in Berlin by the authorities. We may have to wait for her in America."

He reached down and fingered the rolled-up copy of *Naturwissenschaften* he was carrying in his jacket pocket. "There are other problems, as well," he said. "For one thing, Jacob is finding it difficult to go to school here. He tried to enroll in the Lycée Polytechnique, but he's a German citizen and they refused to accept him."

"As a matter of fact, I am one of the directors of the Lycée Polytechnique. I can't promise anything, but I owe you a favor and I would be glad to speak to the other directors about making an exception to the rules."

"That would be terrific," David said. "I would appreciate any help you could give us.

"By the way," he added, "you must call me David. That's my first name."

"And you must call me Aloise."

"Aloise. C'est jolie—Aloise."

"Merci." She smiled up at him.

When they reached the street corner, Jacob watched as she took his father's arm for support, then gave a laugh and leapt the pool of rainwater swirling in the gutter.

Midway across the street, his father looked back. "Come, Jacob! It's going to rain again!"

"I'm coming, Papa," he replied in English, but remained behind. When he looked up, his father had placed his left arm around the professor's shoulder.

33

FOR the third time in the last half hour, Aloise Frégand returned to the window of her Ile St. Louis apartment and looked out across the Seine. It had taken forever, it seemed, for "l'heure bleue," as Linz called it, to come that afternoon, but across the river the hazy September sun had just touched the rooftops of the buildings along the Quai St. Michel. She smiled to herself. In all the years she had lived in her apartment overlooking the Left Bank, she had always looked forward to the sun coming up, never to the sun going down.

Remembering that she had told Linz she spent Sunday afternoons reading in the public park at the end of the Quai de Bethune, she took a book from one of the cases in the living room. Then on the way down to the ground floor, she remembered that she had forgotten to lock the door.

I must be losing my mind, she thought. But she had been like this for a week—since the night she met David.

As she left the apartment building she glanced down at the book she had grabbed from the shelf: an old leatherbound copy of Baudelaire's *Les Fleurs du Mal*. Had she stopped to reflect on what she was doing, it was not the title she would have chosen for this, her second meeting with the American physicist.

On the other hand, she had no illusions about what to expect from the meeting. Linz had made it clear that he was undecided about remaining in Paris. She had lived quite successfully as a single woman for many years, and had no desire now to involve herself with a married man.

By the time she reached the overhead span of the Pont Sully, twilight had settled over the little wooded park at the end of the quai. How like me, she thought, and picked up speed. Having postponed her appearance for the climax of "l'heure bleue," she had now waited too long and the romantic blue light over the city had faded.

As she passed under the span of the Pont Sully and came out into the tiny triangular park at the end of the quai, she wondered if she should turn back and forget the announcement she had come to make. On Tuesday, following France's declaration of war, she had met with the other directors of the Lycée Polytechnique to discuss what policies the school would follow during the war. Reminding her colleagues of a precedent set during the Great War, she had persuaded them to once again open the school's doors to worthy foreigners for the duration of the war.

She spotted the handsome American scientist: seated on the low stone wall at the pointed end of the quai, holding a bamboo fishing pole between his knees. She drew up alongside the wrought iron fence and watched as he recast his fishing line, wondering what had possessed her to involve herself with a man like David Linz. Not only was he married, he was also quite deeply in love with his wife. She had sensed that right off, when he told her that he and his son had been waiting for nine months for the woman to join them in Paris.

Last Monday morning, on the pretext of talking about France's declaration of war, she had telephoned her friend Frédéric Joliot and had mentioned in passing that she had met one of his colleagues the night before. Joliot had gone on to talk of the man's German background: how he and his scientist wife had worked as a research team at the Kaiser-Wilhelm Institute in Berlin; how they had been the first to fission the uranium atom; and how Linz and his son, being Jews, had fled Berlin without her.

As Aloise approached the point-end of the quai, one of the old regular fishermen recognized her and waved as she passed by. "Bonsoir, Madame."

"Bonsoir, Monsieur," she said, absently.

At the sound of her voice, Linz turned around with a look of surprise.

"Aloise!" he called and waved. "So you decided to join me for my famous Sunday afternoon 'l'heure bleue,' " Linz said, when she reached the end of the quai.

She held up the copy of Baudelaire. "I was reading in the park, and I remembered that you come here to fish on Sundays."

He laughed. "I'm about to catch a very big carp. Come sit and watch," he said.

Cautiously, she took a seat on the wall a few feet away from him. She waited until he recast his line upstream, then said, "I didn't know if we would meet again."

He watched in silence as his fishing line came drifting toward them on the river's current.

"Have you caught anything?" she asked.

He turned to face her and smiled. "Of course not. Nobody ever catches anything in the Seine."

"Then why do you bother to fish?"

"I don't know. I guess I like the impossible odds."

"I wouldn't be much good at this," she said. "I don't like to gamble."

Linz turned away and sat looking up river toward the Pont d'Austerlitz. "The real reason I come here is to sit and listen to the water and watch the boats go by," he said. "And for a while, at least, I don't have to think about the future."

She waited until his fishing line drifted past them, then said, "So you still haven't made your mind up about going back to America."

"No, but I'm an American and America is not at war with Germany."

"But if all communications between France and Germany are broken, how will your wife know you've gone to America?"

He sighed. "I have my son to think about."

"But your son seems to want to stay here," she said.

Linz shook his head. "You don't understand the problem I'm having. Jacob is gifted, but he has done nothing with himself since we came to Paris. In America, he would at least be able to get a good education."

She wondered if she was making a terrible mistake by involving herself with this man. It had taken fifteen years to put all the pieces of her life into place, and she could not afford to make mistakes now.

"Last Sunday, I told you that I would try to help Jacob obtain admission into the Lycée Polytechnique. On Tuesday, I met with the directors of the Lycée, and I convinced them to suspend the rule forbidding the admission of foreigners for the duration of the war. If Jacob wants to submit his application again, I'm sure he will be accepted."

Though Linz's face was almost invisible in the fading twilight, she could read the astonishment in his dark eyes. He turned and said, "You're amazing, do you know that?"

"Why?"

"You scarcely know me or Jacob, and yet you go out of your way to help us."

She smiled. "I made a promise, and promises have to be kept."

He looked away and said nothing. His gaze, she saw, was directed up river toward the Pont d'Austerlitz, where the hooded green and red guide lights of a river barge had just come into view.

"I'm afraid I haven't told you the whole truth about myself, Aloise," he said.

"What do you mean, the whole truth?"

"The story I told you about my wife being detained in Berlin wasn't true," he said. "The truth is, I really don't know what the truth is. All I know for sure is that my son and I were forced to leave Germany overnight, that my wife stayed behind, and that we have been waiting nine months for news of her whereabouts."

She looked at him with amazement. "You have no idea where your wife is?"

"I don't know for sure, but all the evidence I've been able to find points to the fact that she is still in Berlin."

"And you've made inquiries about her?"

"Yes, endless inquiries, but I no longer have any friends or contacts in Berlin, and all my letters have gone unanswered."

Aloise hesitated, wondering again if she were making a mistake. "I don't know what happened to you and your family in Germany, David," she said. "But I have contacts at the Russian Embassy in Berlin, I would be glad to help you if I could."

He sat up and looked at her with surprise. "Do you think it's possible, with the war on?"

"The Soviet Union maintains close diplomatic ties with Germany, David. I could make inquiries through the Foreign Office in Moscow."

My God, he thought, do I dare? In the nine months he had been in Paris, he had not spoken of Katherine's suspected collaboration with the Nazis with anyone.

"You can trust me," she said.

It was as if she had said a magic password and a door had opened. The worlds flowed out like a confession he had long ago prepared: the story of his and Katherine's years of research, their discovery on the eve of their departure from Germany, and their reckless decision to stay on so Katherine could experimentally verify their discovery.

Feeling as if he had suddenly let go of a terrible weight that he had been carrying inside him for nine long months, he told of Katherine's lifelong need for her father's respect and admiration, her collaboration with her father and the Nazi Heereswaffenamt, and that he and Jacob were forced to leave without her. It seemed to him as if he was telling a story that he had only imagined for even now he could not believe that he had lived through those last weeks in Berlin.

Aloise turned to watch the barge coming toward them down the river, its dull red and green guide lights swinging back and forth like a warning in the darkness. "But you don't believe that Katherine has stayed behind in Berlin to collaborate with the Nazis, do you?" she asked.

He turned to look at her in the falling darkness, and the moonlight from behind them caught the tears streaming down his face. "I don't know what to believe."

She wanted suddenly to leave her place on the wall and go to him, but the hopeless grief she heard in his voice prevented her. "If your wife has done what they say she has done, then you will have to force yourself to let go of her."

She waited until the throbbing noise of the barge's engine died away before she spoke again. "But if you go to America, she may never find you, and you'll never know the truth."

He sighed and looked down at the black water rolling by under their feet. "I think this will be a long war," he said, "and I'd rather sit it out in America not knowing about Katherine, than stay here in France wondering if we are now enemies at war."

"We'd better go now," she said after a few moments, "it's already dark."

"You're right." He lifted his line from the water and swung his legs around. "I told Jacob that I would take him to the new American film at the Odéon. He was supposed to meet me here at five thirty."

As he wound his fishing line around the pole, she tucked her book under her arm and lowered herself from the wall. "Tell me, David," she said, "when did you and Katherine marry?"

"In December of '20."

"I remember 1920 very well," she said. "But it was in 1922 that I myself almost married."

"But you didn't," he said, securing the hook around the pole.

"No, I didn't. I was living with my mother in Liège, studying at the university during the day and working in a textile factory at night. I had a chance to study economics at the Sorbonne—to make a future for myself—so I left Liège and came to Paris."

"And you've never looked back?"

"No," she lied. "Never."

As she started back along the quai, he came up beside her. "I've told you the truth, Aloise. Now it's your turn. Who was this fellow you left behind in Liège?"

She had never once, in seventeen years, spoken of her love for Henri. "His name was Bouget . . . Henri Bouget. I met him when I went to work at the textile factory in Liège. It was through Henri that I attended my first meeting of the French Communist Party, and he arranged my membership in his Party cell at the factory. In March of '22, a week before he asked me to marry him, I was given a government grant to study economics at the Sorbonne."

"Then you were eighteen when you came here to study."

"Yes."

Aloise went on, thinking to herself that she had never said such things to anyone before. "For me, the choice between Liège and Paris was a choice between freedom and reliving my parents' lives all over again. Before the Great War, my father was a coal miner in the Ardennes, and my mother was an elementary school teacher. After the war, when the Germans defaulted on their reparation payments, my father was among the first French coal miners who were sent to occupy the Ruhr. He was murdered there in the spring of 1921 by storm troopers from Hitler's new National Socialist Party. That was my first brush with fascism. After that, my mother and I moved back to France . . . to Liège. Three months later, I met Henri Bouget."

She looked up at the full moon that was rising in the sky above the Pont Sully. "You were lucky, David. You and Katherine shared the same ambitions. I loved Henri, it's true, but he wanted me to give up my studies, have a family, and become a part-time elementary school teacher, like my mother. I wanted something quite different. I wanted to become a university professor and a leader of the Communist Party. Six months after I left Liège, my mother died of a heart attack, and I've never been back."

She left off, puzzled by the sight of five figures standing above them at the Pont Sully's stone balustrade.

In the next moment, she felt David's right arm come to rest on her shoulder: the same gesture he had made that night a week ago in the rain. As simple as it had seemed, it was a gesture she had not dared to reciprocate—a gesture that belonged to her youthful past. Now, she reached up and closed her fingers around his hand on her shoulder.

As they reached the bridge, she glanced up again at the five figures looking down at them from the balustrade. Though they were only silhouettes against the moonlight, one bore a striking resemblance to young Jacob.

34

As David and Aloise passed under the bridge, Jacob leaned out over the balustrade.

On Jacob's left, Hans Scheringer, an Austrian who had come to Paris following the Anschluss and the oldest member of their group, lit a cigarette and dropped the match over the side of the bridge. "You didn't tell us your father has a girlfriend, Jaco," he said.

"She's not his girlfriend, Hans. He met the woman only last Sunday."

"I don't understand you, Linz," said Vojtech Karmasin, the leader of La Cougoule. "You force us to come halfway across Paris so you can introduce us to your father, then you refuse to speak to him because he's with some woman."

"That's not the reason I didn't introduce you," Jacob said. "I changed my mind, that's all." Feeling trapped between his embarassment and the shock of his discovery, he stepped back from the balustrade. He should have forgotten about his promise to go to the movies with his father. He should have gone straight to the Caveaux des Oubliettes with his friends.

"That wasn't just any woman, Karmasin," Léon Baraduc, Karmasin's friend, said. "That was Aloise Frégand. She was the Left Bank's Communist deputy to Parliament during the Blum administration."

"Merde!" Karmasin laughed. "I didn't recognize the whore!"

Jacob kept his face averted and said nothing.

"If what you've told us about your mother is true, Linz," said Scheringer, "if she's being held under arrest in Berlin, then why shouldn't your old man have a girlfriend here in France?"

He said the only thing he could think of. "I told you, Hans, my father scarcely knows the woman. He met her by accident the night France declared war on Germany. This is the first time he's seen her since then."

Wanting to distance himself from Karmasin's mockery, he turned away

and started back along the bridge toward the Boulevard St. Germain and
the Left Bank. It's true, he thought. Papa has met Mademoiselle Frégand
only once before this. But during the last week he had spoken several
times about the chances of meeting her again.

"Come on, you guys," Baraduc said. "We promised Chvalkovsky and
Mazurkiewicz that we would meet them at the Caveaux at six, and it's
already six thirty."

As the group fell in behind him, Jacob suddenly wanted to run.

He had met Karmasin and his group five weeks ago, on one of his
visits to the Caveaux des Oubliettes, and had been immediately seduced
by the atmosphere of camaraderie that surrounded them. Made up of an
assortment of refugees from Hitler's Lebensraum in Eastern Europe, the
group had been drawn together by a shared sense of rejection and alien-
ation. Dominated by Karmasin, a tough bricklayer's son who had fled
Prague following the Nazi occupation of Czechoslovakia, "la bande,"
as they sometimes referred to themselves, shared a two-room flat on
the Latin Quarter's Rue de la Harpe. Alone and friendless since he
came to Paris, Jacob had wanted, more than anything, the luxury of
belonging.

When he reached the moonlit Quai de la Tournelle he stopped and
rummaged in his pockets for his cigarettes.

"Wait up, Jacob!" a woman's voice called out.

He stared across the Quai de la Tournelle, but in the blackout the
speeding automobile traffic was hard to pass through.

His friend caught up with him mid-street. "Why do you let Karmasin
and Baraduc get to you like that?" Sara asked.

He continued across the street, searching his pockets for his cigarettes.

Sara kept pace as he continued down the Boulevard St. Germain. He
had met her soon after he began hanging around Karmasin's group, and
as Jewish refugees from Germany, they had become close friends. Born
in the Rhineland, she had lost both her mother and father in the anti-
Semitic violence following the Nazi reoccupation of the region. Or-
phaned at the age of twelve, she had made her way to Paris, where she
met Karmasin on the streets of the Latin Quarter. Of La Cougoule's six
members, she was the only one he had come to trust, and in the five
weeks they had known each other he had ventured to tell her the real
story of his flight from Berlin.

"For God's sake, Jacob, don't you understand what's going on?" she
said. "The reason Karmasin treats you like that is because he's jealous of
you."

"Why would Karmasin be jealous of me?"

"First of all, he believes everything you told him about your background in Germany—that you were involved with the Rote Kapelle in Berlin and that you were part of a plot to burn down the Kaiser-Wilhelm."

"It was stupid of me to lie like that," he said. "I wanted Karmasin to accept me into the group, and I thought I had to impress him."

"I shouldn't tell you this, Jacob," she said, "but there was a meeting yesterday to vote on new members. When your name came up, Karmasin and Baraduc voted against you."

"On what grounds?" he asked.

"Karmasin said that you knew nothing about living off the streets, and Baraduc agreed."

The time had come, he realized, to tell his one La Cougoule friend what he had kept secret for a week. When they reached the corner of the Rue des Bernardins, he stopped and said, "I might as well tell you the truth. It no longer makes any difference whether they vote me into the group or not."

"But I thought you wanted to be a member of La Cougoule more than anything."

"Last Sunday, my father told me that he wants to leave France and return to the United States."

"But why?"

"Because he no longer believes my mother will join us here in Paris." He left the curb and quickly made his way through an opening in the traffic.

When Sara caught up with him and spoke again, there was anger in her voice. "Whether your mother ever joins you or not makes no difference, Jacob. You are a German and a Jew, and you have a responsibility to stay and fight the Nazis."

He thought of the change the French declaration of war had made in Sara. Content up to now with a life of aimless wandering, she had suddenly, overnight, found a sense of purpose. "If my father decides to leave Europe," he said, "I will have no choice but to go with him."

"Your father is also a Jew, Jacob. And he knows what the Nazis have in mind for Europe's Jews."

He said nothing and moved on, threading his way through the oncoming pedestrians in the moonlit darkness.

She kept silent until they reached the next street curb. "If I'm right about your father, Jacob," she said, "there may be a way for you to persuade him to stay on in France."

He scanned the heavy traffic crossing the Boulevard St. Germain, looking for an opening. "How?"

"Mademoiselle Frégand is an attractive woman; and your father, I think, is a lonely man."

It took a moment for him to realize what she was saying. "I told you, my father scarcely knows Mademoiselle Frégand," he said with shock. "He met her last Sunday, and they're practically strangers."

"Strangers or not, he's obviously interested. A few minutes ago, when they passed under the bridge, I saw him put his arm around her shoulder."

"So what?"

As he left the curb, she grabbed hold of his arm. "For God's sake, Jacob, don't be a fool. You can't expect your father to go on waiting for your mother forever."

He had thought the same thought a thousand times, but had never dared to voice it. "You don't know my father," he said. "No matter what, he still loves my mother very much."

"He may love her, but he has also lost her."

"That isn't true. And I don't think he believes it, either."

"Don't kid yourself, Jacob. If your father doesn't find someone else in France, he will find someone in America."

The thought of what she was suggesting appalled him. "You're saying that I should encourage my father to have an affair with Mademoiselle Frégand, aren't you?"

"I'm saying that I'm afraid of what the Nazis have in store for the Jews, Jacob," she said. "I'm saying that I need you, and I want you to do whatever you have to do in order to stay on in France."

In the five weeks they had known each other, he had never imagined that she felt anything more for him than a kinship of background and loyalties. He pulled his arm free and stepped back. "Wait here," he said with panic. "I need to buy a pack of cigarettes."

As he started toward the corner newsstand, she called after him, "It won't do any good moving to America, Jacob! You're a German, and the war will follow you there, too!"

He kept moving, thinking only of his need to put distance between himself and her words. The very thought of encouraging his father to fall in love with Mademoiselle Frégand was ludicrous! How could the girl know about the ties that still bound his father and mother irrevocably together.

When he turned from the kiosk, Karmasin, Baraduc, and Scheringer had joined Sara at the corner. The thought of drinking away the evening with them at the Caveaux des Oubliettes now seemed meaningless.

He turned in the opposite direction, heading toward the river and home.

35

''N o w we come to the conference held in Berlin on April 29," Frédéric Joliot said.

Seated on his right, David watched as the Institute's director turned another page of the German War Office document. It was the first official news they had seen of German fission research, and there was a palpable tension in the room.

Joliot looked up to scan the anxious faces of the Radium Institute's four research scientists. "Tell me, gentlemen," he said, "does anyone recognize the name Kurt Diebner?"

"I've never heard of him," replied Hans von Halban. The irascible Austrian physicist, the oldest of the group, took up his pencil and began tapping its eraser on the table.

"Aside from Werner Heisenberg, Otto Hahn, and Carl von Weizsäcker, I know none of the names you have mentioned," said Francis Perrin, the experimental physicist responsible for the Institute's critical mass experiments. "Of course," he added, glancing at David on his left, "being an Englishman, I've had no direct contact with the atomic scientists working in Germany."

"That's true of all of us, Frédéric," said Lew Kowarski. The big, red-headed Russian physicist caught David's eye from across the table.

David shifted nervously in his chair. It was pointless, he knew, to go on pretending ignorance. The names Joliot had so far identified from the War Office report read like a guidebook to his and Katherine's six years at the Kaiser-Wilhelm. "Yes," he said, "I know the name Kurt Diebner. He's a nuclear physicist who works for the Wehrmacht's ordnance department."

Von Halban, Perrin, and Kowarski were waiting, he knew, for him to elaborate. He reached for the crystal decanter in the center of the table and poured himself a glass of mineral water.

"In any case," Joliot went on, "Diebner called a conference at the Reich Ministry of Education on April 29, and a week later the government announced a ban on any further uranium exports from the confiscated Czech Joachimsthal uranium mines."

Watching Joliot turn another page, David wondered how he had come to obtain a copy of a War Office report marked Geheimn—Most Secret.

"Then in May," said Joliot, "Kurt Diebner was appointed head of the German War Office's new uranium weapon research department."

Joliot's words rang in David's ears like a gunshot. He took another quick swallow of water.

Von Halban stopped tapping his pencil eraser and looked up. "Then our suspicions have been right all along," he said, "and the Germans have been at work for months on an atom bomb."

"Yes," said Joliot. "So it would seem."

David's hand shook as he replaced his glass on the table. "I was not personally acquainted with Kurt Diebner," he said, "but when I left Berlin, he was in charge of the Army's weapons research program."

"And was your wife acquainted with this Diebner fellow, Dr. Linz?" Joliot asked.

He hesitated, wondering where Joliot was leading, then said, "My wife was acquainted with the man, but I was not. Her father was the military director of the Army weapons department, and she met Diebner once at his offices."

There was an exchange of questioning looks between von Halban, Perrin, and Kowarski.

Joliot ignored the exchange and went on. "Following his appointment to the War Office, Diebner organized two secret, high-level scientific conferences in Berlin, the first on September 16 and the second on September 26. The conference on the 26th was the decisive one," he said, "and besides Diebner, there were four other scientists present at the meeting—Werner Heisenberg, Georg Joos, Paul Harteck, and Erich Bagge . . ."

David's hand shook as he reached for his glass and took another quick swallow of water. Joos, Harteck, and Bagge: all three men were experimental physicists at the Kaiser-Wilhelm.

"The discussion at the September 26th conference centered around the possibility of harnessing atomic energy for military purposes," said Joliot. "It was decided that all German nuclear fission research would henceforth be conducted under the supervision of Kurt Diebner's new War Office department. Heisenberg would direct the theoretical research,

Bagge would establish the feasibility of using heavy water to build a nuclear power reactor, and Harteck would look for efficient ways to separate fissionable U235 from ordinary U238 . . ."

Aware that von Halban, Perrin, and Kowarski were staring at him, David replaced the glass on the table and drew his shaking hands out of sight.

Joliet turned to the last page of his report. "Our colleagues in Germany have made a decision which will alter the course of all further uranium research here in France, in England, and in America. On September 26, it was also decided that the German War Office, under the supervision of the Wehrmacht's Army Weapons Department, would take complete control of the Kaiser-Wilhelm Institute and all future uranium research would be directed toward the production of a workable atom bomb."

There was an electrifying moment of silence, followed by an exchange of murmurs around the table.

Joliot removed two pages from the report, and went on. "I have here, gentlemen, a list of the names of all the scientists currently employed throughout Germany on the production of a Nazi atom bomb," he said. "Aside from those mentioned in the War Office report, there are some two dozen other scientists secretly at work on the project."

As Joliot placed the pages on the table, David saw that list, unlike the pages of the report, had been typed on ordinary French onionskin paper, the kind sold in every Parisian stationery shop. "If you don't mind, Professor," he said, "I'd like to see the list, if I may."

"Certainly." Joliot gave David a knowing smile as he handed the pages.

As David started down the two columns of typed names, Joliot sat forward. "The implications of this report, gentlemen, are obvious," he said. "We must now begin to look at the political ramifications of our discoveries . . ."

Only half listening to Joliot's description of the unprecedented nuclear arms race that was now underway between the Allied democracies and Nazi Germany, David raced down the alphabetical list of German names.

Carl Gerlach, he remembered, was a name Katherine had mentioned in passing once or twice.

Dreading what he would find when he reached the L's, David slowly read through the H's, the I's, and the K's.

Langsdorf, Wolfgang; Lederer, Kurt; Lerner, Friedrich . . .

He stopped when he reached the name Albert Lessing. It was a name he remembered from his student days in Göttingen.

"As you know, gentlemen, the European supplies of heavy water are very small," said Joliot. "As a result, the German chemical cartel I.G. Farben has offered to purchase the Norwegian firm Norsk Hydro's entire stock of heavy water . . ."

A bead of sweat broke on David's forehead and ran down his cheek. Making no move to wipe it away, he let his eye continue down the list: Löffler, Luettwitz, and Lutze . . . He wanted suddenly to laugh. Never had he imagined that the evidence of Katherine's innocence would be delivered like this, in the form of a stolen document from Hitler's own War Office.

He turned to the second page and let his eye run down the names beginning with M.

Joliot said with satisfaction, "Tomorrow, I will meet with the French Minister of Armaments and discuss the government's financial involvement in a counteroffer to purchase Norsk Hydro's entire stock of heavy water."

He skipped to the names at the end of the second column—Thiel, Udet, Ulm, Vermehren, von Weizsäcker—then came to a dead halt at the fourth name from the bottom: von Steiner, Katherine. He stared at the name, but it looked alien to him on the page: a name, it seemed, that belonged to a total stranger.

He read the name again, but he had believed in her innocence for so long that he could not accept what his eyes told him was true. In all the months he had been searching for evidence of her guilt or her innocence he had never imagined that she would abandon his name, the name she had built her career on, and go back to her family's—her father's— name. It was like a rejection of everything they had shared: their love, their marriage, their family, and even their dreams of success. It was a name, he realized, that no one in the room had ever heard of.

He placed the typed pages on the table and said, "Forgive me, gentlemen. I'm sorry, but I must say goodnight." As he pushed his chair back and got up, a feeling of nausea came over him.

Joliot looked up, startled. "Is something wrong, Dr. Linz?"

He stepped back from the conference table and gripped the back of his chair for support. "I'm not feeling well," he said. "I just need some fresh air, that's all."

As he reached the door, Joliot said, "Are there any questions?"

"About this document you have, Professor," said von Halban. "I'm curious to know how you came to possess a copy of a classified German War Office report."

David stopped with his hand on the doorknob.

"It was delivered to me yesterday at the Russian Embassy," he heard Joliot say.

"By whom?" Kowarski asked.

"I cannot give names," said Joliot, "but Irène and I are fortunate to have a friend here in Paris with diplomatic connections in Moscow. Are there any other questions, gentlemen?"

David suddenly remembered Aloise's words that night on the Quai de Bethune: I don't know what happened to you and your family in Germany, David, but I have contacts at the Russian Embassy in Berlin, and I would be glad to help you if I could.

As he left the conference room and turned down the corridor, he suddenly wondered why Aloise had said nothing to him about the documents. A single light burned in the empty stairwell. He turned down the steps, thinking with amazement of his own self-deluding capacity for hope. For ten long months, he had clung to nothing more than a tenuous thread of hope. He had always imagined that he would react to the news of Katherine's presence in Berlin with righteous anger. He only felt tired, empty, and now finally and irrevocably alone.

When he left the building and turned down the Rue Pierre Curie, an icy wind was blowing up from the river. It's beginning all over again, he thought: another long, cold Paris winter.

Suddenly, the realization came to him: he had gone through the entire day without remembering that this was his forty-first birthday! A few days ago at supper, Jacob had spoken about celebrating his birthday together, but he had since forgotten it. What I am today, he thought with anguish, is a middle-aged man who lives in the past, a modestly successful atomic scientist with only a long and uncertain war to look forward to.

He had forgotten to wear a coat that morning, but it was not the wind that sent a chill through his body. As he picked up speed, he recalled Joliot's words a few minutes ago: Irène and I are fortunate to have a friend here in Paris with diplomatic connections in Moscow.

It was true for him, as well. He was fortunate to have a friend like Aloise Frégand. Asking nothing in return, she had encouraged and supported both him and Jacob from the very first day they had met. And though Jacob had continued to resent her presence in their lives, adamantly refusing to take advantage of the opening she had given him at the Lycée Polytechnique, she had remained a steadfast friend, filling up the emptiness of his life in Paris.

He stopped for a moment at the corner of the Rue St. Victor, thinking again of her puzzling silence last night at supper. If she was indeed the one who had supplied Joliot with the German Office documents, it was strange that she had said nothing about the list of German scientists. Aside from Jacob, she was the only person in Paris who knew the whole story of Katherine's betrayal and she had promised to do everything in her power to help him find her.

It makes no sense, he said to himself. She either knew that Katherine von Steiner was my wife, or she did not. And in either case, why would she keep the news of the report from me?

He looked at his watch. It was 6:05—time enough for him to visit Aloise at her apartment and still be home by seven.

An old woman was selling cut flowers at the corner of the Quai de Montebello. Feeling uneasy about his unexpected appearance, he stopped and bought a large bouquet of white chrysanthemums.

It was 6:18 when he arrived at Aloise's apartment building. Climbing the steps two at a time, he hurried up to the fourth floor and came to a breathless halt at Aloise's door. He shifted the bouquet to his left hand and knocked.

36

"DAVID!" Aloise's bright green eyes widened with shock as she opened the door and stepped back. Fresh from her bath, wearing a dressing gown, she looked much younger than her thirty-six years.

He stepped away from the door in embarrassment. "I'm sorry," he said. "I should have telephoned."

She seemed confused by the flowers in his hand. "No, no . . . it's all right. Come in, please."

"Maybe I should come back another time," he said.

"No, no!" She motioned him inside. "You must forgive my appearance, though. I've just finished my bath."

As he entered the living room, he held out the chrysanthemums. "I thought you might like these," he said. "They're the last of the season."

She closed the door and took the bouquet. "They're lovely, David. Thank you."

"Look," he said in English, "if you're busy, I'll come back another time."

"No, I'm not busy at all." She started past him, carrying the flowers like an unexpected prize. "First, I'll put these in water, then I'll make you a drink."

As he watched her hurry across the living room toward the kitchen door, he suddenly wondered if she already knew why he had come. "Actually, I could use a drink," he called after her.

From the kitchen came the noise of cabinets opening and closing. "Please make yourself comfortable," she said. "I'll only be a moment."

He looked around, startled by the changes she had made in the living room's decor since he last visited the apartment two days ago. Two new crystal lamps burned at either end of a plush new velvet sofa; and instead of the usual clutter of textbooks around the room, her huge collection of books was now housed in wooden shelves along the walls. The speed with which she'd made her domestic rearrangement amazed him. The dining table in the alcove at the far end of the room, which she had always used as a worktable, had been cleared of its books and papers. The only thing she had failed to change in the two rooms, he saw, was the improvised blackout curtain he had hung for her over the dining alcove window.

On the coffee table was a new silver cigarette lighter and a silver bowl filled with cigarettes. Wondering why she had redecorated the entire apartment, he went to the table and took a cigarette from the bowl and lit it. It was an American Lucky Strike, he saw—his favorite brand.

When she came into the room, carrying the chrysanthemums in a ceramic Chinese vase, he saw that she had made a hurried attempt to arrange her long dark hair. "I'm sorry if I seemed taken aback when you arrived," she said, placing the vase on the coffee table. "I wasn't expecting visitors."

"I see you've made a few changes," he said.

"Yes. I thought it was time for a change." She went to the bookcase where the liquor bottles and glasses were now neatly arranged on one of the shelves. "If you live alone as I do, you tend to let domestic things slide."

He thought of the order Katherine had always managed to keep in their home in Berlin-Dahlem and the bachelor chaos of his and Jacob's apartment here in Paris. "You don't have to live alone to let domestic things slide."

As he watched her pour two highballs of Scotch, he realized that his taste in drinks had become predictable to her.

"So how is Jacob doing?" she asked.

"Not good. He still refuses to submit his application to the Polytechnique, and he still spends his time wandering around the Latin Quarter with those La Cougoule friends of his."

"I think he resents my presence in your life," she said.

"Nonsense," he lied. "He's been like that since we came to Paris." He looked at his watch; it was 6:27. "By the way," he said, wondering how he could phrase the question he had come to ask, "I've just come from a conference with Joliot at the lab, and there's finally been some news about the work the Germans are doing at the Kaiser-Wilhelm."

He waited until she shot an inch of soda into each glass, then said, "The reason he called the conference, Aloise, was because he has a friend here with connections in Moscow who turned over some German War Office documents to him."

There was a rattle of glass as she returned the siphon bottle to the shelf. He drew on his cigarette, watching the movement of her eyes as she came toward him with the drinks. "It was you, wasn't it, who gave him the documents?"

She handed him his drink, then said, quietly, "Yes. How did you know?"

"I remembered you telling me that you had contacts, and that you would be glad to help me if you could."

She took a quick sip from her glass. "The report was sent to me by a friend at the Soviet Foreign Office in Moscow, David. I wrote to him at Joliot's in September and asked him to find out what he could about the fission research the Germans were doing. He made inquiries through the Soviet Embassy in Berlin and came up with a German War Office report on the Army's secret atom bomb project." She turned away, set her glass on the coffee table, and took a cigarette from the dish. "The package was sent to me at the Soviet Embassy here in Paris, David, and it also contained a list of all the German scientists involved on the project."

He watched as she took the silver lighter from the table and nervously lit her own cigarette. "I take it, you know that my wife's name is on the list of scientists employed at the Kaiser-Wilhelm," he said.

"Yes, David." She looked away and blew a jet of smoke into the air. "I'm sorry."

"But how did you know that her name before she married was von Steiner?" he asked.

She looked up with surprise. "You told me, David, don't you remember?" she said.

"No. I don't."

"Yes. You told me that her father was Colonel Eric von Steiner, and I recognized the name at once."

"I see." He drew on his cigarette. "Then you knew last night that Katherine's name was on the list when we met for supper."

"Yes."

"Why didn't you tell me?"

"I wanted to, but I was afraid." She turned away and began pacing back and forth. "David," she said, "you've talked of little but Katherine for the last six weeks, and I didn't think you really wanted to know the truth."

He took a swallow of Scotch. "You're right. I've been telling myself that there was always room for hope."

"I should never have given those documents to Joliot," she said.

For a moment, he watched the changing expression on her face, then he said, "There are some things I don't understand about the documents themselves, Aloise. The War Office report was a photographed copy of the original, but the list of scientists' names was typed on ordinary French paper."

She stopped at the coffee table and took another sip from her drink. "The list of names the Embassy gave me was handwritten on the back of a letter to the Ambassador. I had the list typed before I gave it to him." She set the glass back down on the table. "Of course, if you want to see the original list, I can always speak to the Ambassador and ask him to show it to you."

"Funny," he smiled. "It never occurred to me that you might be in contact with the Russian Embassy here in Paris."

For a moment, she considered how much she should tell him. "I teach economics at the Sorbonne, David, because I need the money," she said. "But my real work in Paris is for the Russian Communist Party. It's not something I like to talk about, but I represent the Soviet Commissar of Information here in France."

He shook his head and laughed. "Are you telling me that you're a Russian spy, Aloise?" he asked.

"I'm merely telling you that I work for Soviet Intelligence, nothing more." Seeing that her dressing gown had parted, she reached up and quickly drew the gown closed.

An old familiar feeling suddenly stirred in David's body. He took a long slow drink, thinking again of the words Aloise had said that night on the Quai de Bethune. "I remember something you once told me," he said. "It was the night you came to me on the quai while I was fishing—the night we met for the second time and I told you the truth about Katherine." He drew again on his cigarette. "I remember your exact words, Aloise. You said, 'If your wife has done what they say she has done, then you will have to force yourself to let go of her.' "

She stopped pacing and looked at him. "I said something to that effect, but it's one thing to know that your wife is still working at the Kaiser-Wilhelm, David, and quite another to let go of her."

The statement silenced him. He set his glass down on the coffee table and looked at his watch. It was now 6:40; he would have to leave in five minutes if he wanted to be home by seven.

"I once told you, didn't I, about my father," he said. "How he hated the fact that I wanted to become a scientist, instead of an orthodox rabbi."

"Yes."

He stubbed out his cigarette in the ashtray, then walked slowly toward the darkened dining alcove at the far end of the room. "When I left America and moved to Germany, my father gave me the present of a fountain pen. I didn't know it at the time, but he wrote a letter and put it inside the pen's case."

When he reached the alcove, he drew back the makeshift blackout curtain from the window and looked out across the river at the Left Bank's skyline darkly outlined against the moonless sky.

"I didn't discover the letter until I had been in Göttingen for a year," he said. "But when I finally read it there was one thing my father wrote that I have never forgotten. He said, 'Gifted scientist that you are, you will one day find yourself at the end of your powers to reason. Hopefully, you will then realize with humility that the answers to all the ultimate human questions can only be found in the darkness of blind faith.' "

As he looked out at the city's wartime darkness, the emptiness he had left behind in the street came back, dragging like a stone at his soul. Then suddenly, far off in the direction of the Mont de Paris, in defiance of the blackout, a tiny light went on in one of the Latin Quarter's mansard rooftop windows.

He went on. "When I left Berlin and came to Paris with Jacob, I had reached the end of my scientific quest. Katherine and I had fissioned the atom. But then, where scientific knowledge had ended, human ignorance began. When I came here, I didn't know if Katherine had betrayed me, or if she had stayed behind in Berlin to collaborate with her father." He closed his eyes and lowered his forehead against the windowpane. "I've been living on blind faith for the last ten months, Aloise. But that's all over now, and the truth is quite simple. If Katherine is still at the Kaiser-Wilhelm, then she has done what they say she has done, and I want to let go of her."

When he opened his eyes and lifted his face from the windowpane, he saw in the glass that she was standing behind him in darkness. "What I had with Katherine is finished," he said, "and I can't go on living in the past. Do you understand what I'm saying?"

He wondered, suddenly, if the desire he felt for her body would ever replace his need for Katherine's love. Lowering the blackout curtain across the window, he turned to face her. "I want to be free now to make a life for myself," he said.

She must have sensed what he was thinking, for she took a step backward. "I'm thirty-six years old, David, and I'm no longer a young woman." She reached out and nervously took a gift-wrapped box from the dining room table.

He pointed to the box. "What's that?"

"A birthday present." She looked away with embarrassment. "I didn't know you would come tonight," she said. "I was going to give it to you tomorrow."

"But how did you know it was my birthday?"

"I figured it out. At supper last night you mentioned that you were about to become a middle-aged bachelor, and then later you said that you and Jacob were going to spend tonight together."

He glanced again at his watch, but it was too dark to read the minute hand. "Neither one of us is young, Aloise," he said, "so it's got to be now or never."

"But I don't know if I will ever be able to . . ." She left the sentence unfinished and took another step backward as he moved toward her in the darkness.

It was as if he was reaching out for something that he knew in his heart he had lost forever. As he took hold of her shoulders and drew her forward in an embrace, the momentary resistance he felt in her body was merely the hesitation of a second thought.

"David," she murmured, and closed her eyes, for the familiar pleasure that he suddenly awakened in her body was, she realized, like a flame that had been burning inside her for eighteen years, a flame that had never gone out. She lifted her arms and drew them around his shoulders.

It seemed to David that the months of longing and frustration had suddenly and miraculously ended. The desire he had all but forgotten came rolling up from far down inside him like a wave.

Saying nothing, holding her close to him, he led her into the bedroom. When he drew her bathrobe over her shoulders and let it slip behind her to the floor, she made no move to resist.

Slowly, like a man long used to the art of love-making, he inched his mouth over her naked body, then pulled her on to the bed.

She closed her eyes and gave herself up to the exquisite pleasure of his body, for she already knew, before he lifted himself and entered her, that he had opened a door that she would never be able to close again.

37

JACOB reached for the bottle of Scotch whiskey on the kitchen table and poured himself another glass. He had never liked the bitter taste of his father's favorite liquor, but there was nothing else in the apartment to drink.

As he raised the glass to his mouth, his eye went back to the clock above the sink: 9:34. By now, it was obvious that his father would not be home that night to celebrate his birthday. Given his distracted state of mind of late, it was quite possible that he had gone through the entire day without remembering the dreaded occasion.

He stared at the chocolate birthday cake he had had specially made for the occasion. He had even found American birthday candles in a novelty shop on the Boulevard St. Michel.

He would give his father until 9:45, then he would leave and go look for his La Cougoule friends. At this hour on Friday nights he could always find them at the Caveaux des Oubliettes near the Place St. Michel, and if he hurried there would be time to order one drink before the curfew hour at ten. If he was lucky, Sara would be there.

He took another swallow of whiskey. Maybe his father had not forgotten his birthday, at all. Maybe he had decided to spend the evening with Aloise. The thought of it sickened him.

He sat back, his vision swimming from the liquor. In retrospect, he should have known that it would only be a matter of time before Aloise and his father became lovers. What had amazed him in these last six weeks was his father's trusting belief that she wanted nothing more from him than an innocent friendship. He had seen it that night in the dark tunnel, when they groped around in the darkness for her papers—that his father was like a moth blindly flying toward Frégand's consuming flame.

He finished off the whiskey in his glass and got up. He left the birthday cake on the table, turned out the kitchen light, and hurried to his room. He had to get out, breathe some fresh air, and look for his friends. He took his jacket from the wooden clothes cupboard and stuffed the thirty francs he had saved from his part-time job at the bookstore into his pocket. For a moment, waiting for the minute hand of his watch to reach the deadline he had set, he looked around at the shabby living room he and his father had shared for the last ten months. At first, their apartment had seemed like a refuge to him—a place of their own they could share, a home away from home—but he had come to hate their three miserably furnished rooms.

As he started out of the apartment, he caught sight of his father's telephone pad on the living room desk. Of course, he could easily solve the mystery of his whereabouts with a simple phonecall. Opening the pad to the F's, he quickly jotted Aloise's telephone number on the back of an envelope.

If he hurried, he could be at the Caveaux in four minutes and have a drink with Sara before closing time. The cold wind blowing up from the river whipped past him as he raced across the open space of the Place St. Michel. He wanted suddenly to let go of his anger and shout a curse to the empty darkness. For what frightened him was not the thought of his father celebrating his birthday with Aloise Frégand. It was the thought that he had finally turned his back on his mother.

He passed the ancient medieval walls of the church of St. Julien-le-Pauvre and drew up outside the Caveaux des Oubliettes' open door. From inside came the sound of the cabaret's small band and the voice of a female singer. As he pushed back the leather blackout curtain and went in, the young singer stepped forward on the small stage, lifted her arms, and bellowed out the climax of a popular French show tune. There was a burst of applause, then the pink and amber stage lights went out.

He continued into the long smoke-filled room, scanning the crowded tables, thinking to himself that he needed Sara tonight, more than he had ever needed her before. He drew up between the tables, feeling dizzy. There was no one in the entire cabaret that he recognized.

A waiter came toward him, carrying a tray laden with empty glasses. "I'm sorry, Monsieur," he said, "the Caveaux is no longer serving drinks. It's closing time," the waiter motioned to the door. "So I must ask you to leave."

The rage he had kept in check until now came welling up inside him. Reaching into his pocket, he pulled out his wad of franc notes. "I didn't come in here to drink, Mister!" he shouted in English, waving the notes in the waiter's face. "I came in to use your telephone!" Pocketing the notes, he continued on toward the door at the back of the room leading to the toilet and the telephone.

As usual, there was an old woman seated at the end of the hallway keeping guard over the Oubliettes' facilities. With drowsy indifference she watched him lift the telephone receiver from its hook and retrieve the envelope from his jacket pocket. There was only a single dim light burning in the hallway, and with his vision blurred by the whiskey, he could scarcely read the number he had written. As he began dialing the exchange, the door to the toilet opened and a woman wearing an expensive fur coat came out. Leaving the door ajar, she dropped a few centimes in the dish on the concierge's table and hurried by, checking her makeup in her compact mirror. The stench from the toilet brought back the feeling of nausea.

He went on dialing the number, wondering to himself what excuse he would use for a telephone call at this hour. From her table at the far end of the hallway, the old woman watched him with a look of exhausted but resolute indifference.

The line connected. "Allo?"

He heard the note of impatience in Aloise's voice and simultaneously, from somewhere in the apartment, came the sound of a phonograph record playing.

"Allo, Allo?" she repeated.

Then he recognized the music on the phonograph: Edith Piaf's plaintive voice singing his father's favorite French ballad, "Je ne regrette rien."

"Is something wrong?" he heard his father ask.

"Je ne sais pas," she replied. "Allo, Allo! Qui est là?" she demanded.

"It's nothing," she said, "they have the wrong number," and the line disconnected.

When he hung up the phone, he heard the old woman make a noise and tap the plate where she kept the payments for the telephone calls. He went down the hallway, dropped a five franc note in the plate, then hurried into the toilet and began vomiting the half-bottle of whiskey he had drunk.

38

WHEN David telephoned Aloise with the news of Jacob's arrest, her instructions were brief and simple: he was to leave the matter entirely in her hands and meet her outside the Foreign Ministry building at four o'clock.

He had left the Institute at three thirty, but it had taken twenty minutes to find a taxi, and it was almost four o'clock when his taxi reached the river and turned west along the Quai d'Orsay.

"We'll stop at the Ministry and pick up another passenger," he said to the driver, "then we'll go on to Fresne Prison."

"You're going out to Fresne, Monsieur?" the old man asked with surprise.

"Yes. My son was arrested this morning; he's being held there until we can arrange his release."

"Ah!" The old man sighed and shook his head. "Was he at that pro-war student demonstration outside the president's palace this morning?"

"Yes." David sat forward as the Foreign Ministry building came into view. "He believes all those stories we've been hearing of German troop movements on the Dutch border, and he thinks the government should mobilize the army."

"That's nonsense, Monsieur. We've had peace for over four months, and all this talk of a German invasion is nothing but idle speculation."

Dressed in her heavy winter coat and Russian sable hat, Aloise was pacing the sidewalk in front of the huge granite-faced Ministère des Affaires Etrangères building.

"Stop here," David said. "That's our other passenger."

As they pulled alongside the curb, Aloise waved and hurried forward.

A cold January wind was blowing across the river from the direction of the Tuileries, and when he opened the passenger door an icy gust caught her from behind.

"Thank God, David," she said. "I thought I would freeze to death."

He quickly closed the door as she took her place beside him on the passenger seat. "I'm sorry, sweetheart. I had trouble finding a taxi."

"Never mind. They've transferred Jacob from Fresne Prison to the local Préfecture de Police, and that's only a short drive from here." She leaned forward and said to the driver, "We're going to the Ile de la Cité Préfecture de Police, Monsieur."

"Oui, Mademoiselle."

Aloise sat back as the driver swung out into the westbound traffic. "It's all right," she said. "Everything has been arranged."

"What do you mean, everything has been arranged?"

"I've just come from a meeting with René Duclos, the new Deputy Foreign Minister, and he's agreed to intervene with the police on Jacob's behalf. He says he will speak to President Lebrun himself, and the charges against the boy will be dropped." She reached over and nervously took hold of his hand where it rested on his knee. "In the meantime, I have a letter to the Prefect of Police ordering his release."

The statement silenced David. He sat back, thinking to himself how, in all the months he had known Aloise, she had never ceased to amaze him. Even though the French Communist Party had been outlawed for six months, the doors of power had never been closed to her. "Do you really think they'll drop the charges?" he asked.

"Yes, David. But only on certain conditions."

As they approached the busy Gare d'Orléans, the cars ahead of them suddenly slowed. He waited until the driver's attention was occupied with the traffic, then said, quietly, "What conditions?"

"First, he must agree to give up all contact with his La Cougoule friends. Second, he must appear once a week at the Préfecture de Police and give an account of his activities. And third . . ." Hesitating, she turned away and looked out at the rush hour crowd hurrying into the Gare d'Orléans.

The nervous tremble in her voice puzzled him. "And third?" he asked.

"He must agree to place himself under my supervision and follow my instructions to the letter."

He said nothing, thinking to himself of Jacob's adamant refusal to accept Aloise's presence in their lives. In the last few months, his private resentment had taken the form of public rebellion. Two days ago, he had attended a public rally at Les Invalides to protest the government's refusal to mobilize the army, and this morning, according to the police, he and his La Cougoule friends had been among the hundred pro-war demonstrators outside the presidential palace.

"And if he refuses?" he said, finally.

"If he refuses, he will be charged as an enemy alien with sedition and committed to Fresne Prison for the duration of the war."

"You know as well as I do that Jacob will never agree to place himself under your supervision," he said.

"He has no choice, David. He's wanted for treason in Germany, and if he's in prison when the Nazis invade France, then they will send him back to Berlin."

"What do you mean, when the Nazis invade France?"

Seeing that the driver was eavesdropping on their conversation, she quickly lapsed into English. "Things are much worse than they've led us to believe, David. This afternoon, Duclos told me that the government now has clear evidence of Hitler's plans to launch an attack on France." She tightened her grip on his hand. "Three days ago, a German military plane en route to Cologne was forced to land in Belgium near the town of Mechelen-sur-Meuse. The plane was carrying a Luftwaffe staff officer, a Major Helmut Reinberger, and in his briefcase were the plans for Hitler's attack in the West. Apparently, Reinberger tried to burn the plans when the plane landed, but enough of the papers survived to prove that an all out attack on Holland, Belgium, and France has been planned for the seventeenth of January."

Suddenly from across the river, as if echoing her announcement, came the sound of Notre Dame's bells, tolling the vesper hour.

He had known for months, ever since the war began, that Hitler's Drôle de Guerre peace was an illusion, but he had never imagined that the attack would come so soon. "And what is the government doing about these plans?" he asked.

"Nothing. Believe it or not, Lebrun and Chamberlain are both interpreting the papers as a German 'plant.' But Duclos says they are real, David, and he's convinced that the Nazis will occupy Paris before spring is over."

David looked out across the river at the darkening façade of the Palais Royal, knowing before she spoke again what she was thinking. Twice in the last week she had tried to force him to talk about his plans for the future—where he would go if the Germans invaded France—but he had refused to make any long-range plans.

"We can't go on postponing our decision forever," she said. "If Duclos is right, the three of us are going to have to leave France."

"I've told you," he said, "I can't make plans without Jacob, and the boy refuses to talk to me about leaving France."

"I'm a member of the French Communist Party, you and Jacob are Jews, and you are both wanted in Germany for treason. If the Germans invade France we'll all have no choice."

He kept his gaze averted and said nothing.

"Duclos is an old friend of mine," she said. "He was a member of the

Communist Party when I was a deputy to Parliament, and I got him his first job with the Foreign Ministry. He knows I will have to leave Paris if the Germans invade France, and he told me that he could arrange a position for me at the French Embassy in London. The Communist Party is still legal in England, and with the contacts I have in Moscow I could be quite useful to the British Communist Party."

He sensed at once where she was leading. "Then by all means," he said, "you should accept his offer and go to England."

The nervous tremble in her voice came back. "I also spoke about you, David. I told him about the uranium fission work you're doing here at Joliot's Radium Institute, and he said that a similar position could be arranged for you at the Imperial College in London."

"You mean, with the British Tube Alloys project?"

"Yes. He told me that the British were making great progress on their atom bomb research and that they were looking for experienced physicists to join the project."

He kept silent until the taxi turned onto the Pont St. Michel, then said, "You know as well as I do that Jacob will never consent to our leaving France together."

"You could go to London first," she said, "and I could join you later."

He let go of her hand and sat forward. "Stop here, driver," he said. "We'll walk the rest of the way."

"But I can't stop in the middle of the bridge, Monsieur," the old man protested. "There's too much traffic."

"To hell with the traffic!" David shouted. "Do as I say!" He took his wallet from his pocket as the car pulled into the curb. "Here. Keep the change." He handed the driver a ten-franc note and quickly got out.

Aloise followed and caught up with him as he passed the midway point on the bridge. "I love you, David."

"Please try to be patient with me, Aloise," he said. "In time, the boy will accept you, and we'll be able to live together."

"But there isn't any time!"

A gust of icy wind came whipping over the bridge. Relenting, he took her by the shoulder and drew her close to him. "You've got to understand what Jacob's been through," he said. "I'm responsible for everything that's happened to him, and I cannot force him."

"I'm not a fool, David. I know that Jacob loves his mother. But we must—all of us—learn to compromise."

"I've done that once before," he said. "I forced the boy to compromise in Berlin, and I cannot do it again."

She slowed her pace and looked down river, where the soft reflection of the sunset was fading from the high Gothic towers of Notre Dame. "When I met you, David, I was prepared to go on living my life alone, but you came into my life and you changed everything."

He thought with horror of the responsibilities he had blindly taken on and the impossible choice he would have to make between the woman he had made his lover and the son he had failed.

As they came to the end of the bridge and turned down the Quai de Marché Neuf, heading toward the entrance to the huge barrack-like Préfecture building, the sun had nearly set.

"You told me that you wanted to forget the past and make a new life for yourself," she persisted. "You made love to me, and you opened a door which you can no longer close."

He drew up at the massive wooden door to the Préfecture. "I love you, Aloise. I'm doing everything in my power to keep us together. But my first responsibility is to Jacob."

When she turned to face him, there was a look of fierce determination in her bright green eyes. "I meant what I said, David. I love you, and I want to share my life with you. If you leave France and go back to America, I'll give up everything and follow you there. I don't give a damn what Jacob thinks of me, and whether you do it here or in America, you're going to have to make a choice between the two of us."

He stared at her with astonishment, remembering that he had said those same words to Katherine the afternoon he forced her to take a walk in the mountains above Göttingen, the night they first made love.

"I will not give up, David. You have changed my life forever, and I will not let you go."

He stepped forward and took her face in both hands. "If we can get the boy out of jail, I will speak to him about England. I can't promise anything, but I will try."

"That's all that I'm asking you to do, David, just try."

Except for the officer behind the desk at the far end of the marble-floored hall, the Préfecture's reception room was deserted.

Aloise stopped just inside the door, opened her purse, and removed an envelope. "Before I left the Ministry, Duclos told me to present his letter at the desk."

"You'll do better alone," he said. "I'll wait over there."

She smiled. "This won't take long, I'm sure."

As she continued across the hall toward the reception desk, he went to the only seat in the room, a long wooden bench, and sat down.

There was a brief exchange at the reception desk, then Aloise handed the envelope to the officer.

As David watched the man read the letter, it suddenly struck him that he had been in a similar place before: sitting on a similar wooden bench in a similar dismal public room. It was the night he and Jacob were detained at the railroad station in Saarbrücken: the night they waited as their fate was decided by the authorities in Berlin.

When the receptionist finished the letter, he got to his feet, said something to Aloise, bowed politely, and hurried off toward a small door at the back of the room. Pacing back and forth, Aloise took her cigarettes from her purse and lit one.

She turned and smiled at him across the hall. "It's all right," she said. "They expected us."

A moment later, Jacob appeared through the door, accompanied by the receptionist and a younger man wearing a billed police cap with elaborate gold braid. Taller and heavier than the two French gendarmes, he carried himself with an air of defiant self-confidence.

Motioning for David to wait, Aloise moved forward to meet the two officers approaching with Jacob. She said a few words to the younger officer, then took the boy's arm and drew him to the far side of the hall.

As she spoke, Jacob turned his back to her and looked up at the red, white, and blue French flag suspended from the opposite wall.

Unmoved by his defiance, Aloise went calmly on, gesturing emphatically with her cigarette, looking as if she was delivering a lecture to her students at the Sorbonne. When she finished, she dropped her cigarette on the marble floor, crushed it with her foot, then stepped back and waited.

For minutes, it seemed, the boy went on staring at the flag above him on the wall.

Aloise spoke again; and when he turned to reply, Jacob's gestures reminded David of Katherine: the way she always stabbed the air with her finger when she bartered for her way.

Aloise said something and took a step forward.

To David's astonishment, she held out her right hand and the boy shook it in a gesture of agreement.

Grasping his hand, she led him across the hall to the two police officers waiting at the desk.

It seemed as if the reconciliation David had thought was impossible had occurred. Unable to move, he could only watch Aloise as she spoke quietly with the young officer. Then she let go of the boy's hand and motioned toward an official-looking paper lying on the desk.

As Jacob bent to sign the paper, she left the desk and came toward him where she stood in front of the bench.

"Your son drives a hard bargain," she said.

"You mean, he agreed to the conditions?"

"Yes. But only on the condition that the authorities agree to release one of his La Cougoule friends, a Jewish girl by the name of Sara Bechtel."

"And you agreed?"

"It's not an unreasonable request, David," she said and smiled. "He says that he's in love with the girl."

39

AFTER the bitter winter that had just passed, one of the worst of the century, the Luxembourg Gardens were ablaze with bright spring flowers, the apple trees along the Rue de Médicis were in full blossom, and the small park in front of the Musée de Cluny was filled with the sweet smell of lilacs.

David stopped at the Place Maubert and bought the late afternoon edition of *Paris Soir*. The news of the Belgian surrender had come over the radio at 11:00 A.M., but it was only now, when he saw the newspaper's headline—LE ROI DE BELIGIQUE REND LES ARMES—that he realized the fate of France was already sealed.

He wondered if he should stop by the Rue de Seine bookstore, where Jacob worked, but it was already a quarter to five, and when Aloise had telephoned the Institute a half hour ago, insisting that she had some important news for him and needed to see him at once, he had promised to meet her at her apartment punctually at five.

In retrospect, the worst part of the long winter had been the waiting, for they had sensed in January, when Aloise learned of Hitler's plans to attack Holland and Belgium, that it would only be a matter of time before he repeated his Polish Blitzkrieg in France. True, the April attack on Denmark and Norway had taken them by surprise; but by the middle of May, when the Germans turned south and, overnight, occupied both Holland and Belgium, it was clear that it would only be a few weeks, at

most, before the Nazis reached the gates of Paris. Despite Aloise's efforts
to win Jacob's friendship, it was obvious that the boy would never consent
to her plan for their move to England. Following the Dutch surrender,
David had booked passage for Jacob and himself on an American ship
due to sail from Marseilles to New York on June 6. It was only then,
that Aloise had accepted the fact that they would be separated for the
duration of the war and took the job at the French Embassy in London.

David let himself in to Aloise's apartment and with his key still in the
lock, he came to an abrupt halt. Overnight, without warning, she had
removed almost all of the furniture from the living room. The only things
left were the sofa and, on the floor next to the sofa, a lamp. Everything
else was gone: the upholstered armchairs, the coffee table, the cherished
nineteenth-century French still life that had hung over the sofa, and even
the dining-room table, where only last night they had eaten supper together. The shelves along the walls, which had been filled with books,
were now completely empty.

He went to the bedroom and looked in. The bed was there, with the
rumpled bedclothes as they had left them, and so was the old antique
clothes bureau. But the rest of the furniture was gone. For one anxious
moment, until he saw that her clothes were still hanging in the bureau,
he wondered if she, too, had suddenly vanished.

To his relief, he found that the kitchen was as they had left it that
morning, with the unwashed pots and pans and dishes from last night
still stacked in the sink.

He looked at the clock over the stove and saw that it was four minutes
after five.

Odd, he thought. It was Aloise who had insisted on their meeting at
five.

To occupy the time he busied himself making a pot of coffee. He
thought again of the "important news" she had spoken about on the
telephone. It was somehow connected, he was sure, to the feeling of
preoccupation he had sensed in her during the last four days: a feeling
that some kind of silent battle was being waged within her.

He heard the sound of her key rattling in the lock. When he reached
the living room, she had just opened the door.

"David!" she said with surprise. "I didn't think you'd be here on time!"

"Actually, I was five minutes early," he said.

"I came as soon as I could," she said. "The students were in an uproar
over the news of Belgium's surrender, and I was held up after class."

Watching her remove her key from the lock, he saw that there were dark lines of exhaustion under her eyes that had not been there in the morning.

"I see you've made a few changes," he said as she stooped to retrieve her briefcase from the doorway.

"Yes, I've made changes. I should have mentioned it, but I had other things on my mind." As she came forward, she looked around as if seeing the empty room for the first time. "Last Friday I contacted a moving company and made arrangements for them to come and take everything away; I forgot that this was the day."

"Your timing was perfect—the Belgians have surrendered, and the Allies are trapped on the coast at Dunkirk."

"It's worse than you think, David. I spoke to René Duclos at the Foreign Ministry this morning, and he tells me that General Weygand's armies have been cut off in the north and there's nothing now to stop the Germans from turning south. Paris, he thinks, will be occupied within the next two weeks."

"But that isn't the reason you asked me to come here, is it?" he said.

She looked up. "Is that coffee I smell in the kitchen?" she asked.

He had forgotten about the coffee. "Yes. I was brewing a pot when you came in."

"It smells wonderful. I'd like some. If you'll sit down," she said, motioning to the sofa, "I'll pour us both a cup, and then we can talk."

As he watched her vanish into the kitchen, he remembered that night in November when, stalling for time, she vanished into the kitchen with the flowers he had brought her, the night they made love for the first time.

She came hurrying in, carrying two steaming cups of coffee.

"It looks like we have only the sofa left to sit on," she said, handing him a cup.

He smiled. "There's always the bed in the bedroom."

When she looked up, there was fear in her eyes. "The living room is better, David. We can talk here." As she seated herself, her cup rattled nervously in its saucer.

"So Duclos thinks the Nazis will be in Paris within the next two weeks," he said to fill the silence.

"Yes. He's been in touch with the Belgian Foreign Minister and he says the way south through the Somme is completely open." Her hand shook uncontrollably as she sipped her coffee.

"So what is this important news you have for me?" he asked.

She said, holding her cup with both hands, "First, I want you to know that what I will tell you must change nothing. The decision you've made to go to America is the right one, David. Jacob has suffered enough, and your first responsibility is to your son, not to me. Perhaps, in time, he will forget the nightmare he has left behind here in Europe, and the feelings of resentment he has toward me will change. And perhaps, God willing, the day will come when I can join you in America." For a moment, they sat in silence. "In the meantime," she said softly, "it's my turn to forget and let go. With no questions asked."

He sipped his coffee, thinking to himself that her words sounded curiously like a speech she had memorized for the occasion. "You're a strong woman, Aloise," he said, "and God willing, this war will be a short one."

"It's frightening, David, to think what Hitler has in store for us," she said. "I was ten when the last German war began, and I was fifteen when it ended. But if I'm right, the Kaiser's war was nothing in comparison to this one."

Sensing that she was about to tell him something he was wholly unprepared for, he anxiously took a sip from his cup.

"You remember the friend I told you about in Moscow," she said, "my friend at the Foreign Ministry who sent me the list of German scientists working at the Kaiser-Wilhelm?"

"Yes. What about him?"

"Four days ago, I received another letter from Moscow. This time, my friend wrote to explain why the German government has refused to answer questions about your wife's whereabouts." She reached down slowly and placed her cup on the floor beside her briefcase. "Last October, as you know, he made inquiries about Katherine through the Soviet Embassy in Berlin. In December, he made further inquiries to confirm she was at the Kaiser-Wilhelm and was told only that she was no longer working there." Again, she turned away and looked off absently at the alcove window.

"What are you trying to tell me, Aloise?"

"Two months ago, in March, my friend finally discovered the reason for the German government's silence about your wife. Last November, she suffered a mild case of radiation poison in her laboratory at the Kaiser-Wilhelm and was sent to a sanatorium outside Berlin." Her voice, like her hand, began to tremble uncontrollably. "She was confined there for four months, David, but her radiation poison was worse than they had thought . . ." She took a deep breath, then said, quietly, "She died at the sanatorium on the sixteenth of February."

The cup slipped from his hands and shattered on the floor. For a while, unable to summon even a single coherent thought, he sat staring at the pieces of broken china on the floor. "I don't believe your friend in Moscow," he said. "Katherine was always very careful with the radioactive materials she used."

Aloise bent down, opened her briefcase, and brought out a long white envelope. "I have the letter with me, David." She removed a single handwritten page from the envelope and handed it to him. "It's written in Russian, but you're welcome to take it and have it translated."

He took the letter and thrust it into his jacket pocket. "I still don't believe your friend, Aloise. There must be some mistake."

She removed a small photograph from the envelope. "There's no mistake, David," she said. "He also enclosed a photograph of Katherine's death certificate."

He took the photo and turned it to the light. Though the certificate was shrunken in size, he could read the printed words of its old German script: Frau Professor Doktor Katherine von Steiner, it said, had died of "natural causes" on February 16, 1940, at the German Army's military sanatorium in Blakenfelde.

He read the certificate twice, but the words meant nothing to him.

"I'm sure of it," he said hoarsely. "They've made a mistake." He reached down and began gathering the fragments of the shattered cup from the floor.

"Never mind, David," she said in English. "Leave it."

Holding five splintered pieces of china in his palm, he got up and walked across the room to the dining alcove window. The sun had dropped behind the rooftops to the west, and the cloudless spring sky had faded to a soft—and now infinitely empty—blue.

He thought of the months that had gone by, months that Jacob had spent waiting for his mother to join them here in Paris and never imagining that death could be the reason for her silence.

He went on staring at the fading light, waiting for the shock of Aloise's words to overtake him. But he had lived with the grief of Katherine's absence for so long that the knowledge of her death seemed like a blessing.

"I should have kept this to myself," he heard Aloise say.

He thought of that night in November, when he stood at this same window and prayed that he could find the strength to finally let go of Katherine.

He opened his hand and let the fragments of broken china fall to the floor. Then, with a boundless feeling of emptiness, he turned from the window. "It's finished, completely finished. I can rest now," he said, but the break in his voice betrayed his hopelessness.

This time, it was Aloise who opened her arms and came forward to embrace him. "Yes, my love," she whispered. "You can rest now."

40

"I SHOULD go now," Sara said, pacing back and forth in front of Jacob, who was sitting on the synagogue's front steps. "If I'm here when your father comes, it will only cause trouble."

"Don't be silly, Sara. It's Aloise, not Papa, who objects to my seeing you."

She stopped and looked down the busy Rue Notre Dame de Nazareth toward the traffic circling the Place de la République. "Even so, I'm not supposed to leave the Latin Quarter; and if the police find me here on the Right Bank, they'll arrest me again."

"Oh to hell with the police," he said with exasperation. "If they stop and question us, I'll tell them you're my lover. The French understand those kind of things."

"I'm not your lover, Jacob, I'm your friend. And it was wrong of you to make me come here with you."

"I'm sorry, Sara. I didn't mean that." He looked away, feeling tears well up in his eyes. "I asked you to come with me because I don't want to be alone today." Embarrassed, he leaned forward and buried his face in his arms. "You're the one friend I have here and I need you now, more than ever."

She came and sat down beside him on the steps and took hold of his arm. "I know what you're feeling, Jacob," she said. "This happened to me, too—with both my parents. At first, you feel like the world has stopped moving and that there's nothing left worth living for. But grief like this is a passing thing, it won't last forever."

It's true, he thought. The periodic waves of grief he had felt all morning were nothing like the grief he had felt last night, when he finally forced himself to accept his mother's death. At first, when his father came home and told him what Aloise had learned from her friend in Moscow, he had refused to believe that his mother was dead. But his father had shown him the Russian letter from her friend in Moscow and the photograph of his mother's German death certificate; faced with undeniable truth, he had no other choice but to believe.

He lifted his head from his arms. Still, it was not until the small hours of the morning that he finally realized that the long months of waiting were over, that his mother was gone forever, and that he would now have to let go of her.

"It's funny how the mind protects itself," he said. "I thought about my mother all night, and now it seems much easier, knowing that she's dead."

"Did you tell that to your father?"

"No. I must have fallen asleep and when I woke up, he was gone."

Sara turned around and looked up at the synagogue's bald granite façade. "Why did your father want to meet you here, Jacob?" she asked. "At a synagogue, of all places."

"I don't know. He left a note on the kitchen table telling me to meet him in front of the Beth El synagogue at noon. He didn't explain why."

"It seems odd," she said. "I didn't think he was religious."

"He's not. I don't think he's been in a synagogue since he lived in America."

"And what about you? Have you ever been in a synagogue?"

"Once. I visited one in Berlin the day after the Night of Broken Glass. It was our local temple in Berlin-Dahlem, and I went inside to see what the Nazis had done. It was terrible. They had burned everything, including the Torah scroll."

"If the Germans occupy Paris, Jacob, they will burn this synagogue, too," she said.

He thought of the warning Aloise had given his father yesterday following the news of Belgium's surrender. "Papa tells me that the French and Belgian and British armies have been surrounded in the Belgian town of Dunkirk, Sara, and there's nothing now to stop the Germans from turning south."

"Do you think he's right?"

"Yes. He got his information from Aloise, and she's always right about these things. In fact," he added, "she says it will only be a week or two before the Germans occupy Paris."

Sara let go of his arm. "What are you trying to tell me, Jacob?"

"I'm telling you that time is running out, Sara, and you've got to make some plans for the future."

"I've told you a thousand times," she said. "I ran in fear from the Nazis once, but I will not do it again. I've made a life for myself in Paris, and I will not leave."

"Don't be a fool," he said. "You're a Jew, like me, and if you're still here when the Germans arrive they will arrest you and send you back to Germany."

"If I'm here when the Germans arrive, I will leave the city and join the French underground. France is my home now, and I will stay and fight for her liberation."

"You're braver than I am," he said. "I just want to go away and leave the past behind."

She took his arm again. "To tell you the truth, Jacob, I think you're very lucky. Just think, in ten days you'll be on a ship in the middle of the Atlantic Ocean, bound for America."

"But I've told you, all that may change now."

She shook her head and sighed. "Do you really think your father will marry Aloise?"

"I don't know. We didn't talk about it last night, but there's nothing now to stop him from marrying her."

"Your father loved your mother very much, and I don't think he'd marry again so soon."

"It may be too soon for Papa, but not for Aloise. She's leaving for England in nine days, and she would do anything, I think, not to be separated from him."

"Do you think he really loves her?"

"He says he does, but it isn't the kind of love he had for my mother. It's more like a desperate kind of need, a need to fill the emptiness my mother left in his heart."

"Did he say anything last night about going to England?"

"No. But he talked about the atom bomb work the British are doing, and he said that he felt guilty going to a country where nothing is being done to counteract the Nazis' work on an atom bomb. He feels responsible for pointing out the potential application of the experimental work my mother was doing in Germany."

She let go of his arm and sat forward as a police car suddenly turned the corner.

She got up quickly and turned her back to the street as the police car approached the synagogue. "I'm going back to the Left Bank," she said nervously. "I'll see you later."

"All right, but where will I find you?"

"I'll be at the Caveaux at six o'clock." Without waiting for his reply, she hurried off down the sidewalk in the direction of the Place de la Republique.

As the police car came alongside the synagogue, it slowed and the two policemen in the front seat looked out at him with mild suspicion.

It's the same everywhere, he thought, remembering how the Gestapo had watched and followed him in Berlin. But here, at least, there was no law against Jews loitering outside a synagogue.

The car moved on and vanished around the next corner.

He looked at his watch. His father's note had said he would meet him at noon. He smiled to himself, remembering the joke his mother always made about his father—that in all the years of their marriage he had never been on time for anything.

When he looked up, his father was coming toward him, dressed in his best gray suit and carrying a brown paper bag under his left arm. Jacob stood up and watched as his father made his way through the passing cars. It was obvious from the haggard look on his face that he had not slept last night.

"Sorry I'm late, son. I had an errand to do on the Pont d'Orsay."

His father looked up at the synagogue's façade. "I guess you're wondering why I asked you to meet me here," he said.

"Yes, Papa," he smiled. "As a matter of fact, the question did cross my mind."

"Let's go in," he said, and put his arm around his shoulder. "I'll explain everything inside."

When they reached the synagogue's massive wooden door, Jacob found to his surprise that it opened quite easily. "I take it, you've been here before," he said.

"No. This is my first time."

The door opened into a large marble vestibule that was lit from above by a single window in the shape of a Star of David. A long wooden table sat next to the door leading into the temple.

"This won't take long," his father said. "It's something I want to do for your mother."

Jacob watched as his father opened the paper bag and took out a folded piece of soft white cloth.

"This is what they call a tallith, son," he said, "the shawl Jewish men wear during prayer. I bought it this morning at a shop on the Left Bank."

He unfolded the shawl, put it around his shoulders, and took out two small black caps from his jacket pocket. "This, you know, is a yarmulke," he said, "and I want you to put it on."

He did as he was told, wondering to himself at his father's new-found observance.

"As you know, son, I haven't been in a synagogue for over twenty-five years," his father said, folding the paper bag, "but what I've come here to do is important to me, and I've been planning it since last night." Placing the paper bag on the table, he turned toward the door leading into the sanctuary. "Let's go in now, and I'll explain everything."

Jacob said, making no move to follow, "Before we go in, I want you to answer one question."

His father stopped with his hand on the sanctuary door. "What's that?" he asked.

"I want to know what your plans are for Aloise?"

He let go of the door and turned to face him. "Once I've done this last thing for your mother, Jacob, my duty to her is finished. She will always be on my mind and I will always remember her with love, but I can no longer continue to devote my life to her. I loved her more than I will ever be able to love Aloise. But she's dead now, and the life we had together is finished."

"Then I take it, you plan to marry Aloise?"

"I haven't asked her yet, but there's no more time for postponement. This afternoon, after I've finished what I've come here to do, I will go to her and ask her to be my wife."

"Then we're going to England, after all."

"Yes. This morning, I cancelled our reservations on the boat to America and I booked passage for us on the same ship that Aloise is taking to England." For a moment, his father studied the expression on his face, waiting for some reaction, then he said, "I remember you once telling me that you would never accept Aloise as my lover as long as your mother was alive. Well, I'm not asking you to accept her as my lover, son, but you must now accept her as my wife."

He tried to think of something to say, but could only acknowledge his surrender with a nod.

"Let's go in, Jacob," his father said. "It's the Kaddish I've come here to recite."

The Kaddish, Jacob remembered, was the Jewish prayer for the dead. He joined his father, and together they went through the door into the synagogue's sanctuary.

"Wait here," his father said. "I'll find us copies of the Shabbat service."

Jacob surveyed the huge, silent room. It was arranged exactly like the temple sanctuary he had visited in Berlin: the same rectangular-shaped space in the center, surrounded on three sides by wooden stalls, with a wooden gallery on the second floor. In the dim light at the far side of the sanctuary, partly hidden behind an ornately carved wooden screen, he could make out the huge silver arc containing the synagogue's Torah scroll.

His father returned and handed him one of two leather-bound prayer books. "The Kaddish is at the end of the service, and you'll find it written in both Hebrew and French." He found the page he was looking for, then waited for Jacob to open his copy to the same page. "We'll stand together in the sanctuary to recite the prayer," he said, and continued down the aisle.

"You know I can't read Hebrew," Jacob whispered.

His father smiled. "I'm not much good at it myself," he said, "but I'm going to try." He pointed to the open space near the sanctuary's lectern. "You can stand there and follow me with the French translation."

When Jacob reached the place his father had indicated, he looked down at the prayer's French title printed on the page opposite the Hebrew transcription: Hymne à la Gloire.

For a moment, as his father stood gazing up at the small round window high above the sanctuary screen, the only sound in the room was the soft rise and fall of his breathing. After the merciless clamor of these last two days—the relentless news of war and death hammering at his ears—the palpable stillness of the huge sanctuary brought him a sudden and welcome feeling of peace. He closed his eyes, wanting the silence to go on forever.

Then from the center of the room came the strange unearthly sound of his father's voice, half chant, half recitation. "Yit ga dal . . . ve yit ka dash," he called out, plaintively. "She mei ra ba . . . be al ma di ve ra . . ."

Jacob opened his eyes and looked down at the words of his French translation: I sing hymns and compose songs because my soul longs for thee.

". . . Chi re u tei . . . ve harm lich mal chu tei," his father went on, lifting his voice higher.

My soul desires thy shelter, to know all thy mystery . . .

". . . Becha yei chon . . . u ve you mei chon . . . a ve cha yei de-chol . . . !"

Behind his father's Hebrew words, he heard what sounded like a cry of excruciating grief: When I speak of thy glory, my heart yearns after thy love . . .

"Beit baahala uvi . . ." His voice broke, but he forced himself to go on, ". . . yeman Kari vei meru!"

Hence I utter thy glories, and offer thee songs of love . . .

41

AS Jacob came out onto the ship's portside, the sun had just broken through the bank of gray morning mist lying low along the eastern horizon. A biting English Channel wind was blowing down from the North Sea, but it would be another warm, cloudless summer day.

Balancing himself against the ship's rolling pitch, he walked toward the forward end of the ship's small passenger deck. Last night, as they sailed past the U-boat infested coastline of Brittany and entered the waters of the English Channel, the sea had turned rough; but knowing that it might be the last time he saw France, he had gotten up a little after three A.M. to watch the distant lights of the coast pass by. For the rest of the night, unable to sleep for the thought of his father and Aloise together in the next cabin, he had lain awake, trying to imagine what kind of life was in store for them in England.

When he reached the forward end of the deck, he saw the ragged green coastline of England, stretching east and west as far as he could see. Directly ahead, massed along the entire eastern shoreline opposite the high Devonport peninsula, lay the cranes and warehouses and smoking chimneys of Plymouth, the island's most strategic southern port. Docked at the far end of the narrow sound he could make out the gray funnels of two British warships.

I'll bet they're all around here, he thought to himself as he looked back across the inscrutable expanse of white-capped channel waters to the east. Scores of Hitler's U-boats could be lurking under the surface, tracking the passage of their ship across the narrow channel. Aloise was a fool to think they could isolate themselves from Hitler's Nazi continent by crossing the English Channel. Last night at supper, she had cheerfully announced to the other six passengers—German Jewish refugees like himself—that they were now "safe from the reach of Hitler's Third Reich and could begin thinking about the future." She had obviously forgotten the news they had read in the French newspapers that morning: that the Germans were already halfway across Belgium and had broken through the British and French lines at Arras.

Suddenly, from the stern end of the passenger deck, came the sound of Aloise's laughter over the wind; and when he looked around, he saw his father, grinning like a lovesick bridegroom as he held her around the waist. He had been like this for the last seven days, since the afternoon of their hastily arranged wedding at the Place Vendôme Ministère de la Justice. That, too, had been organized by Aloise—with her High Court justice friend Médard performing the ceremony and his father's colleagues Frédéric and Irène Joliot-Curie standing as witnesses.

"Good morning, Jacob!" his father greeted him with forced cheer. "Did you sleep well?"

"I slept just fine, Papa," he said and turned away to survey the approaching harbor.

"Your father and I were awake all night," said Aloise, as she joined him at the railing. "It was a rough crossing."

"So this is Plymouth harbor," his father said, joining him on his left side. "It looks even bigger than I thought it would."

"Plymouth is England's most strategic southern port, Papa," Jacob said. "We're less than a hundred miles from Cherbourg."

"Actually, they say it's one of England's safest harbors," ventured Aloise. "It has the advantage of a narrow sound."

"Safe maybe from Admiral Raeder's U-boats," Jacob corrected. "But not from Goering's Luftwaffe."

His father leaned forward and rested his arms on the railing. "I just spoke to the captain, son," he said. "He tells us that the German passengers like yourself will have to go through a separate passport control when we dock. There's nothing to worry about, though. It's only a formality."

"When we dock, I'll give you a letter addressed to the frontier authorities from the Foreign Ministry in Paris," said Aloise. "It confirms your status as a trustworthy German refugee."

Amazing, he thought to himself. In the week since she began arranging their move to England, she had not left one stone unturned. First, she had pressed his father to cable Sir Henry Tizard, the Chairman of the Committee for the Scientific Study of Air Warfare, with an offer to work for the expanding British atom bomb project; then she had used her government contacts in Paris to arrange an interview for him with Sir

John Anderson, the Chairman of the British Scientific Advisory Committee of the War Cabinet. "You think of everything, Aloise, don't you?"
he said.

The deck suddenly pitched in the rolling swells. She took hold of the
rail with both hands to steady herself. "If I try to think of everything,
Jacob, it's because I want everything to be perfect for us."

"Aloise could be a big help to you here in England," his father said.
"She knows almost everyone in the academic world, and she could help
you get into an excellent school, if you let her."

He knew at once why they had left their cabin and joined him on the
deck. For the last seven days, they had gone out of their way to make
him feel a part of their marriage, as if they all belonged together, as if
they were a family. He kept silent and watched the ship's bow rise and
fall over the white-capped tidal waves rolling in across the harbor's narrow
sound.

"Have you had breakfast, son?" his father asked.

"No. They were serving coffee and toast when I came out, but I'm
not hungry."

"I'm starved myself," he said, glancing at Aloise. "I think I'll go back
to the galley and eat something."

"You go ahead, sweetheart," she said. "I'll stay here and keep watch
with Jacob."

"That's a great idea." He turned back down the deck. "But don't stay
too long, we've got bags to pack."

This, he realized, was the first time that he and Aloise had been alone
together since they left Paris.

For a moment, she too pretended to study the coastline. "When we
dock, we can look around the town and eat lunch, if you want. Our train
to London doesn't leave until two o'clock."

He gripped the railing, leaned back, and let his body rock with the
swaying motion of the deck.

"You'll like London," she said. "It's a quiet and friendly city. Very
different from Berlin or Paris."

He said nothing and went on watching the outer reaches of the harbor
close around them.

"Your father and I have decided to look for a flat in the Kensington
area of London," she said, looking off toward the high Devonport promontory. "If your father gets the job he's hoping for, Kensington will be
convenient to both the French Embassy and the Imperial College."

"That's great. Then you can both walk to work."

"We'll rent something with plenty of space," she said, "and you can come down from Cambridge on the weekends."

He turned to look at her. "What do you mean, come down from Cambridge on the weekends?"

"I haven't told you this, Jacob, but last week I submitted an application through the French Embassy for you to take the entrance exam to Cambridge University."

"But that's impossible," he said. "I didn't finish my studies at the Gymnasium in Berlin, and I never went to school in Paris."

She smiled. "That doesn't really matter, Jacob. If you can pass the entrance exam, they'll let you enroll in one of the university colleges. You've had a lot of excellent tutoring from your father, and all you will need, he thinks, is a week or two of intense review."

The ship pitched and he pulled himself up against the railing. "I know about the Cambridge entrance exams," he said, "I would never be able to prepare myself for them."

"Your father and I have talked this over, and when we get to London he's going to spend the next two weeks helping you. The exams will be held the last week of June, and he's convinced you will do very well on them."

"But that's only a month away, and a month of study will never be enough," he said. "I've forgotten all my literature and history."

"Your father wants this for you more than anything, Jacob. And if necessary, he will work with you night and day."

She was tempting him, he knew, with the one thing he most wanted in the world: the chance to prove himself as a scientist. He thought of the ambition that had driven his mother to destroy her marriage and their family, but he longed to succeed at all that she had wanted to, and no longer could.

Aloise went on, lifting her voice above the wind. "The weekened before the exams, your father will take you up to Cambridge himself. He wants you to meet some friends of his there. James Chadwick, for instance, the Cavandish Laboratory's director. And the Russian physicist, Peter Kapitza, and the famous Dr. George Thomson."

Chadwick, Kaptiza, and Thomson: he repeated the names to himself, all three of them Nobel Prize—winning vanguards of atomic physics.

"When we get to London, he also wants you to meet some of the scientists working on the British atom bomb project—Rudolf Peierls and Otto Frisch," she said, dangling the names before him like a temptation.

He looked off toward the isolated white lighthouse at the mouth of the harbor, knowing already the price he would have to pay for the chance to attend Cambridge.

"I know what you're thinking, Jacob," she said, "but there are no strings attached. All I want is your friendship."

Weighing his memory of the past against his hopes for the future, he watched the steady rise and fall of the ship's prow.

"But what I don't understand," he said, "is why you've waited until now to tell me."

She took hold of his hand on the railing. "I waited because I wanted Cambridge to be a surprise for you."

For one brief moment, he was tempted to ask if she had also planned the timely news of his mother's death. He looked down at her hand resting on his, at the little diamond wedding ring his father had given her.

Instead, he said again, "You think of everything, Aloise."

FOUR

42

"DAMN!" David said aloud to himself as he turned the corner at Queen's Gate. There wasn't a single bloody taxi to be had tonight in the whole of Kensington!

He looked at his watch: 7:18. He had promised Aloise that he would be on time for her speech to the Bloomsbury chapter of the British Communist Party, but Carter and Wiggins had delayed the critical mass experiment until five o'clock. He stopped when he reached the Queen's Tower and looked up and down the darkened street. There was nothing to be done. He would have to walk to the Party's headquarters on Baker Street.

Shifting his briefcase to his left hand, he headed toward Exhibition Road. It was another warm June night and the moon, for the third night in a row, hung like a lantern in the sky—another perfect night for a visit from Goering's Luftwaffe.

Perhaps Aloise is right, he thought, remembering what she had said last night at supper: that the empty skies over England these last few days were proof that Goering had transferred the entire Luftwaffe to Germany's eastern frontiers. There had recently been rumors of a massive Nazi military presence along the Polish and Balkan borders; and despite Moscow's assurances to the contrary, she was convinced that Hitler was about to launch his long-promised invasion of the Soviet Union. Determined to do what she could to reverse the British Communist Party's anti-war policy, she had prepared a speech for the meeting that night urging the party to support Churchill's recent offer of a British military alliance with the Soviet Union.

Rounding the corner onto Exhibition Road, he looked up at the empty sky overhead, wondering at the compromises he had made in the last year since he began working for the British Tube Alloys project. Last night, fearing the violent opposition she would face from the passivist members of the Party, Aloise had pleaded with him to break his long-standing rule and attend a Party meeting: "For moral support," she had said, "if nothing else."

He shook his head and sighed.

Last night, knowing that he was risking public exposure of his ties to Aloise's Soviet intelligence work here in England, he had agreed for the first time to attend a meeting of the British Communist Party.

As he passed the neo-Georgian building housing the College's School of Mines, a car turned the corner behind him. Sputtering noisily, it came up beside him and pulled into the curb.

"I say there, old man!" came a familiar voice from the darkness. "Long time no see!"

Startled, David turned to see Michael Rakovsky's smiling face in the open driver's window. "Hello, Mike," he said, nonplussed by his friend's unexpected appearance. In the last month, knowing that his fellow-American at the Tube Alloys project was working closely with the British government's secret MAUD Committee, he had gone out of his way to avoid him.

"If you're heading in the direction of Mayfair, David, I'd be glad to give you a lift," Rakovsky called out over the noisy sputter of his ancient Humber's engine.

Mayfair: the offer came to him like a reprieve. "As a matter of fact, I am heading to Mayfair," he said.

"Then get in, man!" Rakovsky laughed. "You shouldn't be walking the streets on a night like this, in any case."

David was halfway to the car's passenger door before he realized the laughable irony of his predicament: that he was on his way to a Communist Party meeting and Rakovsky, a second-generation American of Russian descent, was a fierce and outspoken anti-Communist.

"I'm on my way to Hyde Park Corner," Rakovsky said as he got in, "but I'd be glad to take you home."

David said, quickly thinking of a destination near Baker Street, "Actually, I'm meeting Aloise for a drink at the Cumberland Hotel. If you could swing by Marble Arch, I'd appreciate it."

Rakovsky shifted gears and swung back out into the street. "Marble Arch is fine. I have an eight-o'clock meeting with Thomson, Chadwick, and Cockcroft at Burlington House."

Burlington House, David recalled, was where the MAUD Committee held its weekly meetings, and the physicists were all members of the

Committee. Settling his briefcase on his lap, he recalled the night in early May when Rakovsky came to dinner: the night Aloise ventured to question him about his involvement with MAUD. That was the night she later came to him in his study and told him that the MAUD Committee's report on the practical feasibility of an atomic bomb would be key to her Soviet intelligence work here in England—that it would provide the proof Moscow was looking for that the bomb was really possible. That was the night he finally realized that he had made himself indispensable to Aloise's intelligence operation, and that he had gone too far with his "harmless" violations of the British Official Secrets Act to turn back.

Passing the Albert Hall's blacked-out façade, Rakovsky made a right turn into Kensington Road. "So you're meeting Aloise for a drink at the old Cumberland," he said.

"We thought we'd take a break tonight and go out for dinner. She has a new job at the embassy, and she's been working night and day."

"I hear she's taken over the French Embassy's intelligence department," said Rakovsky.

David shifted uncomfortably on the seat, wondering what else Rakovsky might have heard. "Is there anything going on in London you don't know, Mike?" he asked. "That was supposed to be a closely guarded secret."

Rakovsky laughed. "It's my job."

David looked off through the trees of Hyde Park at the moonlit surface of the park's Serpentine lake. It was back in March, he recalled, following the visit of James Conant, Roosevelt's representative from the National Defense Research Council, that he first became aware of Rakovsky's real job here in England. A physicist and a professional soldier with the rank of major, he had ostensibly been sent to England by the American Army's Corps of Engineers to act as a military advisor to the British Tube Alloys Project. But following Conant's return to America and Roosevelt's subsequent establishment of the powerful Office of Scientific Research and Development, word had leaked out at the Imperial College that Rakovsky had been sent to England by Roosevelt himself to keep the president informed about British progress with atomic bomb research. It was said that Roosevelt was playing a double game with the pacifist American Congress, and that he was planning to bring America into the war and take over the entire British atom bomb project.

"By the way," said Rakovsky, "how is young Jacob? I haven't seen him for months now."

"Jacob is fine. He likes Cambridge and he's working hard at his studies."

"I was talking to Mark Oliphant the other day, and he tells me that Jacob is making quite a name for himself at the Cavandish lab."

"That's right. He's offered to work as Oliphant's assistant at the lab."

Rakovsky slowed as they approached the blacked-out automobile traffic moving around Hyde Park Corner. "You're a lucky man, David," he said. "Sometimes I find myself thinking that my son, if he had lived, might have also wanted to be a scientist."

Though it had happened almost a quarter of a century ago, while he was fighting in Europe during the Great War, Rakovsky had never been able to free himself from the tragic memory of his wife and son. In 1917, following America's declaration of war on Germany, he had volunteered for the Army and had gone off to fight with the American infantry in France, leaving his pregnant wife behind in America. Two months after his arrival in Europe, he had learned that his wife had died giving birth to his son; and though his presence in America would have changed nothing, he had always blamed himself for their deaths.

"If there's one thing I've learned since Katherine's death, Mike," David said, "it's how pointless it is to go on speculating about what might have been. We have a war to fight for the future, and we can't afford to let ourselves live in the past."

Rakovsky kept silent until they passed Achilles Way and turned north up Park Lane. "Speaking of the past, David, I'd like to know if I've done something to offend you."

"What do you mean?"

"I have the impression that you've been avoiding me. When I stopped you last week in the hall and asked your advice on the MAUD Committee's critical-mass estimates, you told me the Committee's report was none of your business. You said you didn't want to talk about it and left me standing there like a fool."

"I'm not a member of the MAUD Committee, Mike, and you don't have government clearance to talk to me about the MAUD report. It's a violation of the Official Secrets Act."

"I wasn't asking you to talk about something you don't already know, David. I trust you, and I was asking your advice as a friend."

Ahead, the huge white façade of Marble Arch came into view. "I'm sorry if I seemed rude, Mike," David said, thinking with misery of his divided loyalties. "My department has been under a lot of pressure to finish the critical-mass experiments and, as of last week, we're two months behind."

"You guys aren't the only ones under pressure, David. As you know, the future of the British atomic bomb now rests on the government's response to the MAUD Committee's feasibility report, and without government financing the entire Tube Alloys project will have to be junked. It's a matter of politics and money. Before they invest any more money in the project, Churchill's War Office wants proof that the bomb is a practical possibility."

"So what's this advice you want from me, Mike?' David asked.

"I'd like to know your opinion of Rudolf Peierls' estimates of the U235 critical mass," replied Rakovsky. "In fact, I stopped by your office this afternoon to talk about it, but they said you were with Carter and Wiggins in the lab."

"They were running an experiment on my own calculations," David said. "It was a calculation I'd made in France, before we had any U235 to experiment with; but if I'm right, it will take roughly a pound of pure U235 to make a critical mass."

Rakovsky braked as they met the vortex of traffic circling Marble Arch. "That would be an important thing for the government to know," he said.

"So what do you want me to do?" David asked. "Write up a report on Carter's and Wiggins' experiment?"

"No. It's too late for that. The committee has drawn up its first draft of the report, and I'm on my way now to meet with Thomson, Cockcroft, and Chadwick to talk about the final draft. I want you to read the first draft and give me a brief written picture of your own critical-mass estimate."

"All right, Mike. I'll drop by your office tomorrow and take a look at the report."

Rakovsky drew up at the bus intersection of Oxford Street. "Thomson wants a final draft by the end of the week, so I'll need your opinion the first thing in the morning. You can read it at home overnight, write your opinion, and bring it to work in the morning."

David thought with panic of Aloise's relentless demands for a copy of Rakovsky's MAUD report, and wished he had refused his friend's offer of a ride, wondering to himself at the monstrous web of deceit he had woven over the last year. It had begun in innocence last September, a month after he began working for Tube Alloys, when Aloise announced that she had been approached by an agent of the NKVD here in London with the offer of a job for Soviet intelligence: "a job," she had said, "that your own work makes me uniquely qualified for." Pleading that this was the chance she had been looking for to establish her place in the Party, she had begged for some "scientific information" about the British atomic bomb project. Trusting that she would ask for nothing more, he had given her a copy of the U235 critical-mass estimates he had brought with him from Paris. Then four months later, at the end of December, when she told him of Moscow's offer of a promotion within the Party and tearfully pleaded for "just one more little gift," he had turned over copies of John Cockcroft's experimental work with uranium separations. But it was not until a month ago, when she began asking for a copy of the MAUD Committee's report, that he realized he had gone too far.

"I'd rather meet you early tomorrow morning and read the report at the college," he said.

"You're being paranoid, Linz." Opening the briefcase in the seat between them, Rakovsky took out a large manila envelope. "It's only five pages. You can read it when you get home from supper."

I can wait until Aloise goes to bed, David thought, and read it after she's asleep.

"All right, then," he said. "I'll return it with my written opinion in the morning." He opened the briefcase in his lap, tucked the envelope behind his papers, and then carefully fastened the latches.

"Tell Aloise that I've missed seeing her and we'll get together soon for dinner," said Rakovsky.

"Right. I'll do that." He opened the door and got out.

"Goodnight, David."

"Goodnight, Michael."

Rakovsky smiled up at him in the darkness. "And thanks for the favor."

"You're welcome." Closing the door, David rounded the car and hurried toward the hotel's front entrance. It was the endless little deceptions he had to act out every day to maintain appearances, both at work and at home, that exhausted and disgusted him. It was as if he had slowly, over the last eleven months, blindly wandered into a labyrinth from which he could not extricate himself.

He watched from the hotel's entrance foyer until Rakovsky's Humber disappeared down the street, then he went back out and joined the crowd of London's homeward-bound office workers hurrying along Oxford Street's darkened sidewalk.

It was an eight-minute walk from Marble Arch to the address Aloise had given him on Baker Street, and he was now ten minutes late. Blackout curtains were drawn across the windows of the four-story brownstone headquarters of the CPGB, and the building, like its neighbors, appeared deserted. He hurried up the front steps, rang the bell, and stepped back to look up at the sky overhead. There, connected to the ground by its unseen cable, was a gigantic barrage balloon, looking like a child's toy in the bright moonlight.

He thought of Jacob in the safety of unbombed Cambridge and wished that the boy would have the sense to stay away from London. But the first week of May, during one of his occasional overnight visits, he had met a girl, the pretty blond-haired daughter of a Soho pubkeeper, and had since returned each Friday night to spend the weekend.

Maggie Ryder: the name rang with her Cockney accent. He had met the girl two weeks ago, when Jacob brought her by the apartment to introduce her, and, despite Aloise's objections, David had found her charming. She was not, of course, the kind of girlfriend Aloise would have chosen for an ambitious young atomic physicist like Jacob, but she seemed an honest and trustworthy girl.

The door was opened by a young man with a scruffy brown beard wearing horn-rimmed glasses and a baggy tweed suit. "Yes?" he asked.

"Good evening. I'm David Linz. My wife Aloise has asked me to join her here for . . ."

"Right," the young man interrupted. "Comrade Linz is expecting you." He drew the door open and stepped back. "Come in, please, quickly."

As David entered the wood-paneled foyer, there was a garbled shout from the far end of the ground-floor hallway.

"Comrade Linz told us to expect you at seven twenty-five," said the young man, quickly closing the door behind him. "She was hoping you'd arrive in time for her speech."

"So was I, but I was delayed at work."

"I'm Aston," the young man said, eyeing him with suspicion.

"Nice to meet you, Aston."

Ignoring his proferred hand, the young man brushed past David into the hallway. "If you'll come this way, I'll take you in to the meeting room," he said as another furious shout erupted in the room at the end of the hallway.

"It sounds like my wife has finished her speech," said David, keeping pace down the musty smelling wood-paneled hallway.

The young man smiled back at him over his shoulder. "They thought she was going to speak on the subject of Churchill's wartime economics, but she talked about a military alliance between England and the Soviet Union."

"But you're wrong, Comrade Linz!" a voice in the meeting room shouted. "Stalin himself has publicly stated that there's no danger of a German invasion!"

"She's right, you know," David said. "If Hitler attacks Russia, the British Party is going to have to change its anti-war policy."

"We'll cross that bridge when we come to it." The young man drew up at the open meeting room door. "Now since you're not a member of the Party, sir," he said with contempt, "you'll have to sit apart from the group. Comrade Linz has put a chair for you in the back of the room."

"Thanks," David smiled. "I think I can find my way from here."

As he stepped through the door, pandemonium broke out in the crowded meeting room.

"It comes down to your opinion against Stalin's, Comrade Linz!" a man in a blue business suit shouted. "If you are right, then the Soviet Premier and the Politburo are wrong!"

"It's not a question of opinion, Comrade!" Aloise shot back. "It's a matter of military evidence, and you cannot . . . !" She left off as she caught sight of David standing at the door.

He nodded and smiled.

Wondering what excuse he could offer for his failure to appear on time, David turned away and began making his way through the crowd toward the one empty chair at the back of the room.

"The British Communist Party will not support Churchill's capitalist war with Nazi Germany!" someone else shouted.

When he reached the chair and turned around, David saw that Aloise had stepped back from the speaker's podium and was staring at him with disappointment. He had always been able to read the silent language of her bright green eyes.

As she went on staring at him, he felt a sinking feeling of guilt and thought of his promise last night to come and give her moral support. His reaction was immediate, like the reflex response of a muscle. He smiled again and mouthed the word "Maud'" to her.

She seemed not to understand.

He raised his briefcase and mouthed the word again, slowly this time, "MAUD!"

It took a moment for the realization to register. The grief gave way to a look of shocked surprise, then her eyes widened with amazement.

As he sat down and placed his briefcase on the floor, it came over him again: the gnawing feeling of helpless guilt at the thought of this, his third and worst betrayal.

At the forward end of the room a man he recognized as a former editor of the *Communist Daily Worker* stood up and called out in a challenging voice, "If these rumors of a Nazi invasion of Russia are true, Comrade Linz, then why has Stalin failed to mobilize his troops along the Polish and German borders?"

At that, another volley of angry shouts went up.

MAUD: it was as if he had said a magic word. Aloise stepped back to the podium and raised her hand to call for silence.

One by one, the shouts died away, then she lowered her hand. "Comrades," she said in a voice of calm self-assurance, "I would not presume to contradict the official statements from Moscow regarding the rumored threat of a Nazi invasion of the Soviet Union. I'm only asking you to consider the evidence for such an attack. Namely, the German occupation of Bulgaria, Rumania, and Hungary, and more recently, in April, the conquest of Greece and Yugoslavia. In the last three weeks there have been reports in the international press of a massive build-up of German forces in eastern Poland. Hitler, we are told, has moved a million Nazi troops into the occupied Balkan states." She stepped back and surveyed the hundred or so reluctant faces. "Given the evidence of Germany's new military presence along the Soviet Union's thousand-mile western frontiers, we can only draw the obvious conclusion. Believe me, the Russian premier must be well aware of the promises Hitler made in his Nazi manifesto, *Mein Kampf*, and he must have known the führer's plans for the total liquidation of Russia when he signed the Soviet-German Pact of Non-Aggression."

She continued in a fearless voice, "This is no time for the luxury of ideologies, Comrades. If Hitler is fool enough to attack the Soviet Union, its survival will depend on her military alliance with the capitalist Allies, England and Free France." She looked at David and smiled.

There was a moment of silence as she began gathering up the pages of her speech. A murmur rolled through the room, then the crowd broke into noisy, animated debate. Several people stood up preparing to leave.

Seeing that there would be no applause, David sat forward and began to clap, loudly. Here and there, a few people ventured to join him, but their applause was drowned out by the din of angry voices.

Aloise looked up and motioned for him to join her. Leaving her papers behind on the podium, ignoring the people who were waiting to speak to her, she started down the side of the room toward the door.

"You were great!" he exclaimed.

"I thought you weren't going to come," she said with reproach.

"Nonsense." He took hold of her arm. "I told you I would be here, but I was held up in the lab." He smiled. "I got a ride to Marble Arch with Mike Rakovsky. It was a stroke of luck, because he wanted to talk to me about the MAUD Committee's report."

He saw the excitement in her eyes. "Of course, it's only a first draft, and it will have to be rewritten," he added, attempting to retreat a little.

"I knew I could depend on you," she said, looking back at the arguing Party members who had followed them into the hallway.

"Do you know what this means, David? If scientists like Thomson and Chadwick and Cockcroft say that the bomb is possible, then Igor Kurchatov and his colleagues at the Lebedev in Moscow will have to listen!"

"It's one thing to know that the bomb is possible, Aloise, and quite another thing to make it a reality. I haven't read the report yet, but we already know that it's going to cost a bloody fortune. To start with, the uranium separation plant will cost in the neighborhood of five million pounds. And as you know, that's more than the British government can afford now."

The young man who had met him when he arrived suddenly appeared at the far end of the hallway. "It's getting late, Comrade Linz," he called to her, "and we still have the question period to finish."

"I'll see my husband to the door, Comrade, then I'll come and answer questions." She turned back to David and sighed. "I'm going to have to stay for a while, sweetheart. But there's no need for you to wait for me."

"You waited for me, so I'll wait for you." He looked at his watch. "Besides, it's almost nine o'clock, and I don't want you out in the streets alone at this hour."

"Don't be silly." She took his arm and turned down the hallway. "There's nothing to worry about. When we're finished, I'll get one of the men to find me a taxi."

"All right then," he said as they reached the foyer. "But only if you promise to take a taxi."

She squeezed his arm playfully. "I promise."

"How long will you be here?" he asked. "I'm going to stay up till you get in."

"No longer than an hour, I'm sure." She stepped forward and kissed him gently on the mouth. "And when I get home, we'll stay up and read the MAUD report together."

She read his look of guilt and smiled. "This is the last time, David. I promise."

He started to say, "What difference does one more betrayal make after so many others?" He chuckled, instead, and said, "I guess I'm what they call a fool for love."

"Fool or not, David, you have made my life perfect. And I love you for it."

"Remember, no longer than an hour." He turned to open the door. "By the way, Jacob telephoned from Cambridge this afternoon, and he's coming down again for the weekend."

"I wish he wouldn't," she said. "It's not good, his visiting every weekend."

He smiled. "But I thought you said that the skies over London are now clear."

"You know what I mean, David."

He said, opening the door, "She's a nice girl, Aloise. The boy is only twenty; this is a passing thing."

"Take a taxi home, darling," she said. "It's late and you're tired."

Leaving her to close the door after him, he called back over his shoulder, "Remember, just one hour!"

"I promise." She laughed and closed the door.

When he reached the curb he looked in both directions, but Baker Street was deserted. He would rather walk than spend the money on a taxi, and could take the scenic route through Portman Square, cut across Hyde Park, and take the back way home up Albion Street.

As he turned down Baker Street toward Portman Square, Aloise's words in the meeting room came to him. She was wrong, of course, about the life he had made for her here in England: it was anything but perfect.

43

FOUR minutes later, David stood at the corner of Seymour and Old Quebec Streets, listening with growing fear as the deafening wail of London's air raid sirens filled the air.

"Damn!" he cursed aloud and turned back down Seymour Street.

He stopped abruptly: Old Quebec Street, he realized, was halfway between Aloise at Party headquarters and the tube station at Marble Arch. For a moment, he stood listening for the familiar drone of aircraft engines from the direction of Southwark and the Thames. Even if he ran, he could never get to Baker Street in time. For Aloise, the closest shelter would be the tube station at Davies Street.

God, he thought, the stupid choices I make! I should have waited for her at the Party headquarters. With a feeling of weariness, he turned south toward Oxford Street. After a year of raids, he had lost count of the nights he had spent with Aloise, either at home or at the local Edgware Road tube station, holding her in his arms until the all clear signal sounded. He thought of her sitting out tonight's raid alone on Davies Street's crowded platform. It was not the bombs she feared so much, it was the thought of their being separated, of not knowing for hours if the other had survived.

He looked up at the moon shining down on London like a spotlight and smiled to himself. It's all a game of chance, he thought. And tonight, God has rolled His dice in the führer's favor.

As he hurried into the station's lobby, the elderly warden on duty at the door shook a scolding finger at him. "A few more minutes," he said, "and you'd be spendin' the night with the Luftwaffe!"

Picturing the suffocating enclosure awaiting him below, the frightened children crying all around him, David started down the long concrete staircase leading to the station's platform, taking the steps slowly, one at a time. The siren's unbroken wail came echoing after him down the white tiled walls.

Packed together like tinned herrings—standing, lying, and sitting— the crowd extended the entire length of the platform. Hoping to find an open space at the far end of the platform, he began maneuvering his way through the chance assortment of people from London's West End. Most of them had been caught unprepared. He passed an elderly couple wearing raincoats clutched around their faded pajamas; further along, a young soldier lay drunk in the arms of his embarrassed girlfriend.

As he approached a small open space at the rear end of the platform, a child's rubber ball came rolling toward him, heading precariously for the platform's edge. He caught the ball with his foot and shifted his briefcase to his left hand. Bending down to retrieve the ball, he caught sight of a small boy hurrying toward him with outstretched arms. The black curly hair and the chubby little face reminded him of Jacob as a child.

Squatting down, he held the ball out in his right hand and smiled. The boy hesitated, wondering if his offer was only a teasing game; then he came forward, seized the ball, and ran back to his mother.

Rising, David caught sight of a woman's face in the shadows some twenty feet away. Hemmed in by the crowd, she stood with her back to the platform wall. He started to turn away, then looked again. Her eyes, he saw, though obscured by the shadows, had suddenly widened with a look of shocked recognition.

He froze, half-standing, as a faint rumble rolled through the station's tunnel. He felt the blood suddenly drain from his face. In the next moment, the concrete floor reverberated under his feet.

Then he read the single silent word that formed on the woman's lips: "David."

For a moment, he stood still, feeling paralyzed between his past and the present. It's impossible, he thought to himself, staring vacantly at the woman. But the blonde hair, the delicately chiseled face, and the pale blue eyes were unmistakable. Then, like the rush of water from a broken dam, the undeniable truth flooded over him: Katherine.

He went on staring, unable to lift himself against the gravity pulling at his body. Shaped by the logic of probabilities, his mind could only formulate one single thought: the mathematical impossibility of this, her presence here in a city of three million people . . . in a foreign city five hundred miles from Berlin . . . in a country at war with her native Germany.

Nor could she herself move. Her head merely dropped back against the wall. The eyes remained fixed in shock, it seemed, for an eternity. As her mouth opened, he read in the movement of her face the kaleidoscope of her feelings: recognition gave way to astonishment, astonishment to disbelief, then disbelief to an explosion of joyful relief. But the relief was only momentary; as she lifted her head from the wall, he saw in her pale blue eyes a look of fear.

Again, the platform shook, and the boom of a distant explosion echoed from the walls.

As he rose up, she took a step forward into the light, and came up against the people in front of her. He could see that she was torn between the desire to come to him and a sudden impulse to escape. She wore her long blonde hair carelessly tied behind her head, her face was cadaverously thin, and her eyes, he thought, had the hollow look of a soul exhausted with suffering. She was beautiful—still.

Then like a sudden revelation, it came to him. The truth he had kept hidden from himself these last two years, the truth he had tried to deny and forget: that try as she might, Aloise had never even begun to fill the void Katherine's loss had left in his heart.

She thought with panic of the countless times she had imagined this very moment and the choice he would have to make between his over-whelming need to accuse her and his selfless will to forgive. It would be a choice, she had always known, between the love they had once shared and the hatred of what had driven them apart. She hesitated, wanting at the same time to escape and to remain. But she had lived alone too long with the misery of her betrayal not to risk both the strength of his love and the power of his forgiveness.

She pushed at the shoulder of the person in front of her, but a wall of people separated them.

"Please!" she called out, but the woman only glared at her with indignation.

Again, the platform trembled under her feet; and when she looked up, he was struggling toward her through the crowd, clutching a briefcase under his left arm. Still closer, a third explosion shook the station. The thought that death might separate them now—that she had lived for two years on the mere hope of this impossible moment and would now die without even the chance for his forgiveness—filled her with terror. "David, hilf mir!" she cried out in the waiting silence.

David tried to edge forward. At the sound of her German, the shock in the faces of the people around Katherine suddenly changed to menacing hostility.

Seized by an overwhelming desire to embrace and protect her, he shouted angrily, "Dammit! Let me through!" and managed to push the two men blocking his way aside.

An aftershock rolled through the tunnel, bringing with it a gust of wind.

Oblivious of the crowd, the bombs, and the dust falling around her, Katherine forced her way between the people blocking her path and moved forward to close the space between them.

Suddenly, under the force of a direct hit, the walls of the station shook violently. A cry went up as the platform seemed to heave. Knocked off balance by the lurching crowd, Katherine stumbled and fell. "David!" she called out, but her voice was lost in the rumble from above them and the cries of women and children.

He took a step forward, searching the turmoil of arms and heads. Through a haze of falling plaster dust, he caught sight of her as she struggled to stand among the press of panicked bodies. "Katherine!" he yelled out, forcing a path through the people between them.

From the longing she saw in his eyes as he came toward her, Katherine realized that her fears were unfounded. Weeping, half from the feeling of sudden release that came over her, half from joy, she rose to her feet and lifted her arms to meet him. "David!" she cried out as his arms opened to receive her. "Oh, God!" She closed her eyes, feeling herself being lifted bodily from the platform. "Oh, dear God, David . . . !" Over the cacophony of voices and the deafening boom of another direct hit, the words poured from her mouth, a garble of German and broken English, "Endlich! You are come! Das war ja eine Ewigkeit! . . ."   Before she could open her eyes, the crowd thrust the two of them backward against the wall. In the next instant, David's free right arm was around her waist, pulling her protectively to his side.

"We must get out of here," he said with panic, and began weaving a path for them through the terrified mob. As they reached the deserted space at the foot of the station staircase, another bomb detonated in the street above them. Without waiting, he started up the staircase, pulling her along by the hand.

She looked up at the pulsing reflection of fiery light at the top of the stairs. "No, David! We can't leave now!" she shouted, but her voice was lost under the bomb's thunderous echo. He continued up, pulling her by the hand, taking the steps two at a time.

When they reached the top of the staircase, he let go of her hand and leaned against the wall. "Let me get my breath," he said.

Katherine watched as he lowered his briefcase to the floor. It was not exhaustion, she realized, but the past that had overtaken him. From the open station door came the brilliant blazing light and the crash of falling debris. She touched his shoulder. "David! Please look at me!"

But he could only think of the terrifying realization that had come to him on the platform: if Katherine had not died in Germany, as he had been led to believe, then what of these last two years with Aloise?

Katherine gripped his arm and said, frantically, "I know what you're thinking, David, and it's true! I am responsible for everything that happened to us! I wanted success more than anything, and I betrayed both you and Jacob for it!"

He turned his face to the wall. "Then it's true, after all," he said. "You stayed behind and worked for your father."

"I was a fool, David! Papa wanted proof that we had succeeded. He wanted Hitler to promote him to the rank of general. He promised that no harm would come to you and Jacob if I helped him. I gave him what he wanted," she said. "The fission research we had done at the Kaiser-Wilhelm, your paper on chain reactions—everything."

He thought of the curse that had always hung over their marriage: her lifelong need for her father's recognition and approval. As he turned to face her, he saw in her pale blue eyes a mirror image of his own horror. He asked over the relentless wail of the air raid siren, "Are you telling me that you betrayed me and Jacob and the entire Rote Kapelle to the Gestapo?"

"No, David!" She grabbed hold of his shoulders. "I did not betray anyone to the Gestapo!" The words she had long ago prepared—the speech of self-defense she had repeated to herself a thousand times in the last two and a half years—suddenly evaporated. "Oh, David . . ." She began to weep. "I did not stay in Berlin. I left the same night you and Jacob did; I crossed the German border two hours after your train left Saarbrücken. I went to Holland and then came here, to England."

The bombs, David realized, had stopped falling. There was only the unbroken wail of the siren. He stepped back, trying to comprehend what she had said, but between the facts Aloise had gathered during those long months in Paris and the events she had just described, he couldn't make sense of her words.

"But you knew that Jacob and I would go to Paris," he said. "You knew where to look for us!"

Clinging to his shoulders, still weeping, she leaned forward and rested her forehead against his chest. "I couldn't come to Paris, David—not after I had destroyed everything we'd had together."

David suddenly recalled that afternoon in Paris a year and a half ago: the afternoon Joliot showed him the list of German scientists Aloise had obtained from Moscow.

He leaned back, watching the reflection of burning light rise and fall against the opposite wall, and thought to himself: if she left Berlin the same night that Jacob and I left, then . . .

Lifting her head, she looked up and said, "Jacob, where is he, David?"

"Here. Here in England. He is . . ." He left off, reading in her eyes the answer to the terrible question now widening in his mind. Like a chain reaction, one truth would lead to another, he realized, and speaking of Jacob would lead to Aloise.

"He is what?" she cried out. "Tell me!"

It was a desperate mother's cry of terror. "The boy is safe, Katherine," he said. "He's fine!"

"Is he here, David—in London?"

Praying she would not press for more, he lied and said, "Yes. He lives with me here in London."

"And you, David . . . ?" She started to touch his face as if seeing all that he had not revealed.

She could see, he knew, the wreckage of his last two years. Before her fingers could touch him, he reached up and took her head in his hands, drew her forward, and silenced her with a kiss.

Knowing that there was no need to ask for his forgiveness, Katherine relaxed into his arms, closed her eyes, and for one brief moment let herself succumb to the pleasure of his kiss, but the joy of it passed as quickly as it had come. In the feverish movement of his embrace, she suddenly sensed that something was wrong: that he was silently fighting feelings of desperation that went far beyond anything she could imagine. When he finally spoke, she heard the fall of defeat in his voice. "Katherine . . ."

With dread, she lowered her face against his neck and waited.

"I have made a life for myself here—" he left the sentence hanging as the cacophonous whine of an approaching fire truck filled the air. She started to look up, but he held her head fast against his neck. "No, Katherine! Please!" he exclaimed.

She thought of the two years she had spent wondering if she was beyond forgiveness. But the dread she now felt was worse than all her doubtful ignorance. "Tell me, David! I want to know!"

He dropped his head back against the wall and began to cry. "Don't ask me to explain . . . not here . . . not tonight."

It was the hopelessness she heard in his voice that horrified her. "Explain what?' She tried to imagine what he could not bring himself to explain. "For God's sake, tell me!"

"What I have done with my life," he replied, rocking his head back and forth against the wall. "I need time, Katherine. All I ask for is time, time to find the answers for you." He lifted his head and looked at her, searching her face for some sign of lingering trust. "Not long, a day or two at most. Will you do that?" he asked. "Will you give me time?"

She nodded.

"Where do you live?"

"In South Lambeth. On Clarence Street, just off Paradise Road. Number twenty-one."

"I will come to you. Wait for me, Katherine, I will come. I promise." He took her head in his hands again. "Can you still trust me?" he asked.

She stared at him, wondering how he could have conceivably failed her more than she had failed him. She took his hand and kissed it. Before she could speak again, he had withdrawn his hand, retrieved his briefcase from the floor, and turned away. She followed him a few paces, then stopped and watched as he raced out through the station entrance into the rain of falling fire.

44

ALOISE stopped pacing and lit another cigarette. It was 12:25. She had left Party headquarters two minutes after the air raid sirens sounded at 8:25; and despite the warden's order to take shelter, she had gotten as far as Edgware Road when the bombs began falling.

She went to the window and drew back the blackout curtain. Bayswater hadn't been damnged, but there were fires still burning in the vicinity of Park Lane and Marble Arch; and off to the southeast, in the direction of Buckingham Palace, you could see a brilliant orange glow.

Of course, it was possible that he had been caught by the bombs and unable to take shelter. The picture came back to her: David lying alone in a hospital somewhere, wounded. Or even more unthinkable, dead in some city morgue. She drew again anxiously on her cigarette. The worst part was not knowing, and not being able to find out. She had tried four times in the last hour to telephone the local hospital, but the Bayswater lines were still down.

She lowered the blackout curtain and turned from the window. His papers on the endtable next to the sofa were stacked in a loose haphazard pile, just as he had left them that morning. And next to the papers, like a terrifying reminder of his absence, was his half-empty cup of coffee.

She put her cigarette out in the ashtray on the coffee table and hurried into the kitchen. It was a habit with her now, making him a pot of hot tea before they went to bed—like the habit he had of making sure the apartment door was locked and the screen properly arranged in front of the fireplace.

She opened the cupboard and took out a tin of English Breakfat tea, his favorite.

These are the simple habits that you take for granted in a marriage, she thought, the habits that remain with you, one way or the other, for the rest of your life.

She left the unopened tin of tea on the counter, took the kettle from the stove, and went to the sink.

In the thirteen months they had been married, she had never allowed herself to imagine life without him, and the thought of making tea alone every night for the rest of her life filled her with horror.

But the horror was only momentary, for as she began filling the kettle, she heard the rattle of his key in the apartment's front door lock. She turned off the faucet and took a deep breath.

When she reached the living room, he was standing in the open doorway, with his briefcase clutched under his arm, trying to remove his key from the lock.

He said, as if in a daze, "I got as far as Oxford Street. I was in Oxford Street when the bombs started to fall."

There was a little rivulet of dried blood extending from his hairline to his chin—and a dark ugly bruise above his cheekbone. "My God, David!" She hurried across the room as he removed the key from the lock. "Sweetheart, what happened?!"

"I was between Old Quebec Street and Marble Arch. I was in the street when a building fell." He turned away and closed the door. "The whole thing came down."

"Your head! You've been hurt!" She reached up to touch his face.

He drew away. "No, don't. It still hurts."

"You have a deep cut on your head, David. You need a doctor."

"It looks worse than it is, and I don't need a doctor, Aloise. I'm fine."

She saw in his eyes the lingering aftermath of a terrible shock. "We should go to the hospital and have someone check you, sweetheart. You could have a concussion."

"Nonsense. It was just a grazing blow." As he moved past her into the living room, she detected a curious expression of questioning doubt behind the lingering shock in his eyes. "I went on to Marble Arch and spent the rest of the raid in the tube station," he said. "When I left at ten thirty, Bayswater Road was cordoned off and I couldn't get through. So I took a walk through Hyde Park."

"But David, darling, that was two hours ago."

"The station was crowded—I wanted to walk and get some fresh air."

She went to him and took the briefcase from his hand. "Come sit down, sweetheart. I'll get a wet towel to clean your face and some bandages for the cut."

He said, looking round at the furniture, as if seeing the room for the first time, "Right. I'll just sit here and rest on the sofa for a while."

As she set the briefcase on the coffee table, she remembered that he had been carrying the MAUD Committee's report during the raid. She watched as he took a cigarette from the coffee table and lit it. His thoughts, she could see, were a million miles away. There's something wrong, she thought with panic. He's not himself at all.

In the bathroom she took the first aid kit and a pair of scissors from the medicine cabinet, then she grabbed a clean white towel from the linen cupboard and turned on the hot water faucet. First, she would clean the blood from his face and bandage his wound, then she would make him a pot of hot tea.

Waiting for the water to heat, she felt again the questioning doubt she had seen in his eyes. For one brief moment, she had an unnerving premonition that he had witnessed something else besides a falling Oxford Street building.

When she returned to the living room with the hot towel, he was sitting on the sofa with a drink in his hand.

"I was going to make you a pot of hot tea, sweetheart," she said.

"Thanks. But I need a drink now, more than tea."

She saw that he had poured himself a full glass of whiskey. "Of course. I should have thought of that." She placed the first aid kit and the scissors on the coffee table and sat down beside him. He winced as she began sponging the dried blood from the wound.

"You should have come home as soon as the raid was over, David," she said. "A head wound is dangerous, David, it bleeds profusely."

He sipped his drink. "That's because the head is so close to the heart."

"This is all my fault, David," she said. "I should have let you stay at Party headquarters."

"You couldn't have known what the Germans had in store for us tonight."

She saw it again: a look of questioning doubt flashed across his dark brown eyes.

"By the way," he said, glancing at his briefcase on the coffee table, "I've been thinking about the report Rakovsky gave me tonight. It's only a first draft, so maybe I should wait and give you the final draft."

She dabbed the last of the blood from his cheek. "I know you think I've been making unreasonable demands on you, sweetheart," she said, refolding the towel. "But it's Moscow, not me, that's making the demands. Last week, Commissar Beria, the director of Soviet Intelligence in Moscow, sent a message to me through the chief of the NKVD here in London, asking about the MAUD Committee's report. The Kremlin, he says, won't give its approval for a Soviet atom bomb project until Stalin knows for sure that a bomb is possible."

She paused as David took another sip from his glass. "And you think that the MAUD report will change Stalin's mind?" he asked.

"Yes, David, I do. And I also think that the war will be decided by whoever has the first atom bomb. Not only that," she added, "the bomb will be the thing that will determine the balance of power in Europe after the war is over."

"I see." He sipped his drink again and looked away, thoughtfully.

"If this is a first draft, how long do you think it will take to finish the final draft?" she asked.

"Two weeks. Maybe three."

"The thing is," she said, "if Hitler goes ahead with his invasion of Russia, communications between London and Moscow may be cut off."

"But I thought you still had diplomatic contact with that Foreign Ministry friend of yours in Moscow."

"No, darling, I'm afraid not. My friend Kursinov died last year, and the only contact I have with Moscow is through the NKVD here in London."

"I see," he said, and sipped again at his drink.

She looked down at the towel and saw, mixed with the blood stains, a curious streak of darker red, not the bright color of the blood she had just wiped from his cheek, but the dull color of a woman's lipstick.

"I've cleaned your wound as best I can," she said. "Now, you'll need a bandage."

"We won't bother with the bandage, sweetheart." He finished off the whiskey in his glass. "Wounds like this heal faster if they're left exposed to the air."

"Yes. Perhaps you're right."

"It's getting late and I'm very tired." He set his empty glass on the coffee table.

"Yes, darling, a good night's sleep is what you need." She glanced down at the towel to see if she had only been imagining things, but the blood had already mingled with the stain. It could have been anything, she thought. Even paint.

"I'm going to the study to get some papers together for tomorrow's critical-mass experiment," he said, and got up. David took the briefcase from the coffee table and turned toward the door leading into the hallway. "We'll talk about Rakovsky's report in the morning, sweetheart," he said. "You may have to be satisfied with a rough draft."

"A draft will be better than nothing," she said, watching him vanish down the hallway.

When he reached his study, David turned on the light and placed his briefcase on the desk. From the kitchen he could hear Aloise running the water tap. Realizing that he would have to forget his promise to read Rakovsky's report overnight, he opened his briefcase and took out the five-page document.

Opening the desk drawer, he took out a small key and unlocked the filing cabinet's bottom drawer, where he kept his personal and private papers. As he tucked the report between the papers in the drawer, his eye came to rest on a file marked Personal at the back of the drawer.

It was the file containing the papers he had brought with him from Paris: a file he had stored away in the drawer a year ago, never thinking he would want to look at it again.

He took the tattered yellow folder from the drawer and opened it.

They're still here, he thought with relief: the envelope containing the handwritten Russian letter describing Katherine's death in the sanatorium outside Berlin; and tucked away behind the envelope, the little photograph Aloise had given him of Katherine's death certificate.

45

FOR the third time, David ran down the list of names posted on the wall next to the building's front door. She had said Clarence Street in South Lambeth, he was sure: number twenty-one, just off Paradise Road. But she was not listed among the building's dozen tenants. He went back out into the street and checked the number over the tenement's front door. London's industrial South Lambeth had been hard hit in the bomb raids, but the building, one of the few left standing in the street, was number 21.

Recalling how deafening the noise had been last night, as she told him the street number, he thought to himself, "Christ, if I've made a mistake . . ."

He looked up at the building's dingy redbrick façade. There were two apartments on each floor. He would begin on the first floor and work his way up. Hurrying back into the building, he entered the ground-floor hallway and knocked on the first door. There was no answer.

As he continued down the darkened hallway to the second apartment, a door slammed closed on the second floor. He went back to the foot of the staircase and looked up to see an elderly woman coming toward him down the steps, wheezing loudly. "Excuse me," he called up. "Do you have a tenant in this building by the name of Linz?"

The old woman paused and caught her breath. "Do I have what?" she yelled back.

"Do you have a tenant here by the name of Linz, Katherine Linz?"

She shook her head and continued down. "There's no one here by that name."

"What about von Steiner? Is there a Katherine von Steiner living here?"

"Never heard of that one, either."

He was sure she had not listened to the name. "The woman I'm looking for is in her late thirties," he said. "She has blonde hair. She's a foreigner."

Wheezing with asthma, the old lady drew up on the bottom step. "There's a blonde-haired foreign woman in the back flat on the fourth floor," she said, staring at the small white bandage Aloise had placed on his head that morning. "She's been here for two and a half years, but I still don't know her name. The neighbors say she's Polish, though," she added with a scowl.

Taking the steps three at a time, he started up the staircase. He had said nothing last night about the time of his visit, nor had she mentioned having a job during the day, and he now wondered if she would have waited the entire day for him. He had left home at seven that morning, debating whether or not he should go to his meeting with Rakovsky at the Imperial College or come straight here to South Lambeth. But fearing that he might arouse Aloise's suspicion, he had decided to postpone his visit until after work.

As he reached the fourth floor, he looked round at the newspapers and the bags of trash stacked in the stairwell, wondering what kind of life Katherine had made for herself here in London. Except for a faint shaft of sunlight falling through the grimy window at the front end of the building, there was no light in the narrow fourth-floor hallway.

He knocked twice, softly.

There was the sound of a chair being shifted in the apartment, then Katherine's anxious voice. "Who is it?" she asked.

"It's me," he replied. "David."

The latch turned at once, and as the door swung open she stepped back into the room. Saying nothing, gripping the door with both hands, she stared at him with wide-eyed wonder.

The exhaustion he had seen in her face last night was still there, but her hair was now tied into a neat bun at the back of her head and she looked for all the world like the Katherine he had left in Germany.

"David," she murmured.

Realizing that there was nothing he could say to express the joy of this, his greatest discovery, he went in and took her in his arms. He closed his eyes and held her with all his strength, wanting both to laugh and cry for the miracle of them here together in this remote South Lambeth flat.

"David," she murmured. ". . . *so lange her.*"

He drew her still closer and thought to himself: Yes, a lifetime. As he lowered his face into the crook of her neck, he suddenly remembered the last time he had had this same exquisite feeling of having come to rest. It was that stormy night at Welchzeckhaus in Göttingen, when they came together in the darkness of his room and embraced for the first time. In spite of everything, it seemed that nothing had changed. The body in his arms, though thinner and more fragile now, was the same body he had held and loved for years. In that moment, the full meaning of their miraculous reunion suddenly came to him—she had come back to him from the dead.

As if reading his mind, she said, softly, "I thought I had lost you forever."

Her words brought back the horror of his dilemma. He opened his eyes and wondered how he would find the words to tell her what he had made of his life since Berlin: of his bigamous marriage to Aloise and the unbridgeable abyss of compromising betrayals that now separated them.

She drew back and looked up at the bandage on his head. "You were hurt last night, David. What happened?"

"It's nothing," he said, "I was hit by a piece of falling masonry." He took her back into his arms. This time, holding her in the peaceful silence, he looked around the room for the first time.

She stepped back and looked up at him. "It's not much, David," she said, misreading his bewildered surprise. "But I've made it quite comfortable."

"Those curtains—" He smiled. "I remember how you made curtains like that for our apartment on the Gauss Strasse in Göttingen."

A familiar look of amusement filled her eyes. "They're the only kind of curtains I know how to make," she said.

He realized, suddenly, that there were no books in the room. "You've given up science, haven't you?"

She nodded. "Yes, David. My work was the cause of everything bad that has happened to us. I gave it up the night I left Berlin."

"You said last night that you left Berlin at the same time that Jacob and I left."

"Yes. That very same night."

For the thousandth time, he thought of the evidence that Aloise had given him to prove that Katherine had remained in Germany: the list of Kaiser-Wilhelm scientists her friend Kursinov had sent from Moscow and the German death certificate. "But I don't understand," he said, feeling the full force of the truth. "We had proof in Paris that you had stayed at the Kaiser-Wilhelm."

"No, David." She shook her head. "The afternoon the Gestapo issued the warrants for your and Jacob's arrest, I came home to find that you had gone. When Papa telephoned to tell me about the warrants, I knew at once that you had taken the afternoon train to Paris . . ." She left off and looked away, her gaze fixed on some distant and painful mental picture.

"Tell me everything that happened, Katherine," he said. "I want to know."

She took a deep breath, then went on, as if repeating the words she had spoken to herself over and over again. "I went to my parents' home to ask for my father's help. A warrant for my own arrest was to be issued that night, and he told me to leave Berlin." When she looked back at him, there was the horror of some remembered nightmare in her pale blue eyes. "I took his old Maybach and drove that night to the German frontier."

He thought of the long months he and Jacob had spent waiting for her in Paris. "You mean to Saarbrücken, to the French border?" he asked.

"No." She sighed. "I crossed the German frontier that night at Minden—into Holland. I took a boat two days later from Ostend to Dover and came here to England."

"But why to England, when you knew that we had gone to France?"

She took hold of his arms and began to cry. "I couldn't face you, David, not after what I had done in Germany."

"We waited . . . Jacob and I waited for you . . ." He left the sentence unfinished, not daring to tell her that he had finally stopped waiting.

Tears spilled from her eyes and ran down her face. "Where is he, David?" she pleaded. "Where is Jacob?"

"He's here with me in England," he said. "Studying at the university."

He had stayed awake last night, trying to assess the dangers that would follow if Aloise discovered Katherine's presence in England. "He's at Cambridge," he said.

"Cambridge?" Astonishment broke through the longing in her eyes. He looked away, wondering where to begin.

"Is there something wrong?" she asked, and let go of his arms.

"You wouldn't recognize him now. He weighs a hundred and eighty pounds and he's over six feet tall."

It was useless to pretend. She heard the ring of false enthusiasm in his voice. "He believes that I'm still in Germany, doesn't he?" she said, quietly.

Knowing that she had always been able to read the truth in his eyes, he looked away. "No, Katherine. He doesn't believe you're still in Germany."

"Those last days in Berlin were a nightmare," she went on. "I knew you were involved in something dangerous, and I wanted to stop what I had started. That last morning in Berlin, I followed you and Jacob to a building in Zehlendorf. I didn't know it at the time, but the Gestapo suspected that you were a member of the Rote Kapelle. They followed me that afternoon, and without knowing it, I led them to the Rote Kapelle's meeting place."

"You can't be blamed for that, Katherine. Everything happened so fast." He forced himself to look at her. "The afternoon we left, Konrad Bukowski came to the house and told us that warrants were being issued for our arrests and that we had only an hour to leave Berlin. We didn't believe him, but there wasn't time to find you, to prove that you were innocent."

She turned away and began to cry again, softly. "I went to Papa that afternoon and asked for his help. I knew that your train would cross into France at Saarbrücken, and that Papa was the only one who could arrange for your safe crossing into France . . ."

Saarbrücken: the name brought back the memory of that strange night, when the Gestapo detained them at the railway station for a half hour, then suddenly, and without explanation, announced that they could reboard the train.

"That night," she went on, "Papa gave me a letter of safe passage and ordered me to drive to the German frontier. When I refused to leave Berlin without him and Mama, he gave me a choice that he knew I could not refuse—he promised to use his authority to intervene with the Gestapo when your train stopped at Saarbrücken."

The missing piece in the puzzle of his and Jacob's escape from Germany fell into place. "Then it was your father who saved our lives that night," he said.

"Yes, David. And mine, too." She began walking slowly toward the open window. "I wrote to Papa and Mama when I got to London, but there was no answer. Then, a few months later, I received a letter from Greta, their housekeeper. She told me what had happened to them."

He watched as she drew back the white muslin curtain from the window, remembering the mindless hatred that had kept him and her father apart for twenty years.

"The day after I left Berlin, Papa and Mama were both arrested by the Gestapo on charges of high treason. Father thought that in the time it would take the authorities to trace your release back to him, he and Mama could escape. But Müller had seen me leave, and he reported Papa to the Gestapo. Two days later, Papa was shot before a military firing squad at Moabit Prison. Mama, Greta told me, had been sent to a German prison camp in Poland, but Greta didn't know which one."

He left the door and went to her at the window. "I'm sorry, Katherine," he said. "For once, it seems your father and I have something in common. Like him, when I see the disaster I've made of my life, it's too late."

She turned to face him, and said, "But it's not too late, David. We're together now and you have nothing to fear. Please, tell me everything."

Knowing the worst horror of all was yet to come, he took her by the shoulders and turned her to face him. "It began ten months after we arrived in Paris," he said. "The day France declared war on Germany."

46

FROM the nearby Lambeth docks came the plaintive moan of a ship's horn. Katherine opened her eyes. In the hour they had spent making love, a full moon had risen in the cloudless sky over London.

"So when did you and Aloise meet?" she asked.

"It was the third of September," David said, "the day France declared war on Germany." He stopped stroking her shoulder and lifted himself on his elbow. "We began as friends, Katherine, and we went on as friends until the middle of November."

"And then?"

"She knew that I had been writing letters to Germany, trying to find out what happened to you. In October, she wrote to a friend in Moscow, a member of the Foreign Ministry who had connections in Berlin, asking him to find out what he could about the German atomic bomb project at the Kaiser-Wilhelm. Five weeks later, the second week of November, she received a German War Office report on the progress of Hitler's atom bomb and a list of the German scientists working on the project at the Kaiser-Wilhelm. You were listed as Katherine von Steiner, and, at the time, it didn't occur to me that she would have added your name to the list."

"By then, I had been living in England for almost a year."

"I know," he sighed. "But that was the night I gave up waiting for you, and we became lovers."

It was amazing to think that she could still feel jealous after so many years. "And you were married the following June?"

"Yes. By then, Hitler's armies had turned south and we knew that it was only a matter of days before the Germans occupied Paris." Gently, he moved his hand down her neck until it came to rest on her breast. "It's funny how everything seems possible when you're caught up in a war. Ten days before Jacob and I were due to sail for America, Aloise received another letter from her friend in Moscow, and with it, a photograph of your German death certificate. It was then, on June the third, that we were married."

She looked away, thinking of the "disastrous mess," as he had called it, he had made of his and Jacob's lives. "It's pointless to dwell on the mistakes we've both made," she said. "If I had trusted in your forgiveness—if I had gone to France instead of England—none of this would have happened."

"You've got to stop blaming yourself for what happened in Paris, Katherine. I alone am responsible for Aloise."

A breeze stirred the muslin curtains over the window, shifting the moonlight's reflection on the ceiling. "Tell me the truth," she said. "Do you love her?"

"I was lonely when we met, Katherine, and I needed someone to fill up the emptiness I felt." He leaned down and kissed the bridge of her nose. "I thought I loved her, but love and need are not the same thing."

She thought of the lengths to which the woman had gone to marry David. "Do you really think that Aloise has been lying to you, that she changed the list of scientists and drew up a false death certificate?" she asked.

"She had the motive and the opportunity, and she could have easily had it forged."

"It seems astonishing that she would take such a risk."

"Jacob had refused to go to England, and the only way she could keep us together was to become my wife."

She thought of the year and a half the boy had spent waiting for her to join them in Paris. "Jacob must have hated me by then," she said, "more than anything."

"No, Katherine, he didn't hate you at all. In fact, it was not until Aloise produced your death certificate that he finally believed you had stayed behind in Germany."

Suddenly, far off across the Thames, the clock in Big Ben's tower began to toll the hour.

He stopped stroking her shoulder and sat up. "It's eight o'clock. I've got to go now. I've promised Aloise that I would be home by seven tonight, and she'll be waiting."

He waited until the bell finished tolling the hour, then swung his legs from the bed. "If I'm late, she always questions me about where I've been."

"In other words, you're married to a jealous woman."

"Yes." Feeling his way in the moonlit darkness, he went to the sofa where he had left his clothes and began dressing. "By the way," he said, "I spoke to Jacob this morning in Cambridge."

"David!" She sat up quickly. "Why didn't you tell me?"

"Because there was nothing to tell. He had read about last night's bomb raid in this morning's paper, and he telephoned to find out if I was all right."

"And you said nothing about last night?"

"I couldn't, Katherine. Not on the telephone." He bent down and quickly pulled up his trousers. "Aloise's real work is for Soviet intelligence, and if she learns that you are alive and living in London, it could prove very dangerous for all of us."

He had told her of his work for the British Tube Alloys project and of his knowledge of Aloise's espionage, but he said nothing about his position in her spy network. Nonetheless, Katherine understood. "In other words, you're saying that Aloise has used you in her espionage work here in England."

"Yes. It began innocently enough—but one thing led to another, and now . . ."

Katherine suddenly saw David's dilemma with blinding clarity. She left the bed and took her nightgown from the clothes cupboard. "What are we going to do?" she asked.

"I don't know. But for the time being, until I find a way out of this nightmare, we must say nothing to anyone, including Jacob, about your presence here in England."

She thought of the disastrous silence she had kept in Berlin. "I can't do that, David."

He took his jacket from the dining room chair. "We have no choice, Katherine."

When she lowered the blackout curtain over the window and turned on the bedside lamp, he was fully dressed. "Can you go to Scotland Yard, David, and tell them everything?"

"The only proof I have that Aloise is working for the Soviets," he said, "is my own espionage activities."

His uncharacteristic patience suddenly seemed like helpless impotence to her. "I'm frightened, David," she said, "and I want to see Jacob."

Saying nothing, he left the sofa and took her in his arms. "You must be patient, sweetheart. Until I can work out a plan to get the three of us safely out of England, we must go on as if nothing has changed. It will take a few days, but I will find a way to contact Jacob in Cambridge and tell him everything.

"Trust me," he said, softly.

It was a request that she knew she could not refuse. She nodded.

For a while, relishing the miracle of their reunion, they went on holding each other in the peaceful silence.

He stepped back and removed an envelope from the breast pocket. "These are the papers I told you about. I want you to keep them here with you until I know what to do with them."

"All right." She took the envelope and placed it on the table.

"It's almost eight fifteen," he said. "I've got to go."

She took his arm and walked him to the door. "Will you come tomorrow?" she asked.

"Yes. After work."

She reached up and grasped his face with both hands. "Whatever mistakes we've made, I have never stopped loving you, David," she said, and kissed him on the mouth.

He looked back and smiled as he opened the apartment door. "Our love is the one thing that neither of us ever lost."

47

JACOB stopped as he and Maggie reached the corner of Sussex Gardens and looked back down the Edgware Road. In the waning moonlight you could see where the bombs had fallen. Beyond Kendal Street, all the way past Marble Arch, the east side of Park Lane was a wasteland. "Papa and Aloise were damn lucky," he said. "Another three blocks and that would have been the end of Sussex Gardens."

"How did you learn about your father's accident?" Maggie asked. "Did Aloise telephone you in Cambridge?"

"No. I read about the raid in yesterday's morning paper, and I called Papa."

She looked down Sussex Gardens toward his father and stepmother's apartment building. "Maybe you're imagining things," she said. "Maybe he's perfectly all right."

"He didn't sound all right, Maggie. I know my father, and I could tell something was wrong. Besides, he said things that worry me." He shifted his overnight bag to his left hand and offered his arm. "Come on," he said. "It's almost eight thirty." As she took his arm and they turned down Sussex Gardens, he could sense her reluctance to go on. "I know you didn't want to come," he said. "But you're a nurse, Maggie, and if Papa's been injured, maybe you can persuade him to see a doctor."

"I'm not a nurse, Jacob, I'm only a student nurse. And I don't mind coming with you, but you should have warned me."

"I know. I'm sorry. I should have phoned you from Cambridge, but there wasn't time." He had raced to catch the express to London after his last class, and when he reached the station the train was already waiting. Of course, he could have phoned when he arrived in London, but it was already 7:35 when the train pulled into King's Cross, and he had taken the tube straight to her parents' pub in Soho.

"I don't understand," she said. "If you were worried about your father, then why did you wait to come down?"

"I waited because Papa asked me to. He thought there might be another bomb raid last night, and he didn't want me to come to London."

Just ahead, at the corner of Southwick Street, he saw that the four-story brownstone apartment building was completely untouched, just as his father had said it was.

With relief, he thought to himself: Maybe Maggie's right. Maybe I'm only imagining things.

As they reached the building and started up the steps to the front door, she stopped and ran her hands quickly through her long blonde hair. "I look like a charwoman," she said. "If I'd known we were going to visit your parents . . ."

"I think you're making too much of this business with my stepmother, Maggie," he interrupted. "Everything is going to be fine." Jacob opened the door and stepped back for Maggie to enter.

"Your stepmother doesn't like me, Jacob. That was clear the first time we met," she said. "The truth is, your stepmother doesn't approve of me. You're a student, with a great future ahead of you, and I'm a working-class Cockney who's never been beyond Blackheath."

Her honesty sometimes astonished him. "That's nonsense," he said. "It's you who's imagining things now, and besides, my father likes you and that's what counts."

"I'm not imagining things. Aloise has great plans for you." She gripped his arm as they started up to the second floor. "I haven't told you this, Jacob, but when I met your stepmother two weeks ago, she took me aside and questioned me about my politics. She was trying, I think, to find out if I knew she was a member of the Communist Party."

"I see," he said, smiling. Two weeks ago, he had told Maggie about Aloise's membership in the Party, but he had said nothing about her work for Soviet intelligence. "And did you tell her that you not only knew, but also disapproved?"

"No, Jacob."

He stopped as they came to the second floor. "You've heard, I guess, what happened this morning," he said. "That Hitler's armies have attacked the Soviet Union."

"Yes. I heard it on the radio."

"It was just like the Nazi attack on Poland, Maggie," he said. "There was no declaration of war. Hitler's tanks simply rolled across the Russian frontier—all the way from the Baltic to the Black Sea."

"It's all so confusing, Jacob—these changing loyalties. All I want is for the bombs to stop and this terrible killing to end."

He had always admired the simple fervor of her British patriotism—the fact that she saw the war in simple terms: Hitler was the enemy, British citizens were dying by the thousands, and the Nazis must be defeated.

Together, in silence, they turned down the hallway toward his father's apartment. Setting his overnight case on the floor beside the door, he began fishing in his pockets for the key his father had given him six weeks ago, when he began coming down every weekend to see Maggie.

He found it and, without bothering to knock, opened the door. He took his overnight case from the floor and went in. The living room was empty, but he could smell cigarette smoke in the air. He looked back at Maggie, who was still waiting outside in the hallway. "It's all right," he said. "They're here."

She followed him reluctantly into the room, closed the door, and stood looking around with wonder at his stepmother's antique French furniture and his father's books lining the walls.

Setting his overnight case by the coffee table, he called out, "Papa? Aloise? It's me, Jacob!"

There was the sound of a cupboard closing in the kitchen, and a moment later Aloise hurried into the living room. "Jacob!" she exclaimed with astonishment. "We thought you were staying in Cambridge for the weekend."

When she caught sight of Maggie behind him, a look of surprise came over her face. "Miss Ryder."

"Good evening, Mrs. Linz," Maggie said, trying to appear at ease.

Aloise turned to Jacob.

"Don't be angry, Aloise. I came because I'm worried about Papa, and I brought Maggie along to have a look at him."

"I see." Aloise turned away and took a cigarette from the silver dish on the coffee table.

"He insisted that he was all right, but I could tell that something was wrong."

"You're quite right, Jacob." Her hand shook as she lit a cigarette. "The raid began a little after eight and was over by eighty forty-five. Your father says he took shelter in the Marble Arch tube station, then walked through Hyde Park to get some fresh air. When he came home, it was twelve forty-five. He had a severe gash on his head. It was when I cleaned his neck that I . . ." She drew on her cigarette and looked away, as if remembering something that had horrified her.

"That you what?" Jacob asked.

"Nothing." She shook her head and returned the lighter to the table. "I could tell that the injury was worse than he thought," she said. "I tried to get him to go to the hospital, but he said he was perfectly fine and refused." When she turned to look at him, there was fear in her eyes. "I was going to call you myself, Jacob, but your father insisted that I keep silent."

"Where is Papa?" he asked.

"I don't know. I tried to phone him at the college about five o'clock, but they said he wasn't there." She caught sight of Maggie still standing by the door. "There's a comfortable chair by the fireplace, Miss Ryder," she said with annoyance. "Please sit down."

"Thank you." With a puzzled glance at Jacob, Maggie went obediently to the wing back armchair and sat down.

"I would have come down yesterday," he said, "but Papa ordered me to stay in Cambridge. He was worried there might be another bombing."

"I'm glad you're here," Aloise said, nervously fingering her cigarette. "Your father hasn't been himself for two days. Aside from staying out late last night, he's been acting very strangely here at home. He wanders about the apartment as if in a daze; he scarcely touches the food I prepare for him; and when he's not sleeping, he's working in his study."

He glanced at Maggie and said quickly, "When I told Maggie how Papa sounded on the telephone, she said he had all the symptoms of a concussion."

"I said he *could* have the symptoms of a concussion, Jacob," she cautioned. "But it would take a doctor to know for sure."

Aloise shot back with exasperation, "I've already said that your father has refused to see a doctor."

"This could be a simple case of overwork," said Jacob, trying to calm Aloise. "They've been pressing Papa to finish his critical-mass calculations, and when I talked to him yesterday, he said that Cockcroft—"

"It isn't overwork, Jacob!" Aloise interrupted angrily. "This evening, when I telephoned the college, they told me your father had left work at four o'clock!"

Seeing Maggie's look of misery, Jacob went and stood behind her chair. "You're saying that Papa lied to you," he said.

"Yes."

"But why? He's never lied to you before, has he?"

"No. Never."

"Could it have something to do with Tube Alloys? He told me he's worried about security," Jacob said, wondering, on the other hand, if it was beginning all over again: the whole pattern of deceit and lies that had destroyed his parents' marriage and had driven him and his father from Berlin. He hurried on, trying to offer encouragement. "But now that Russia and Britain are allies, Papa really has nothing to fear, does he?"

"I don't know about that, Jacob," she said, drawing nervously on her cigarette. "But I do know that this is the second night in a row that he has come home late and I can't go on living in a . . ." She left off and looked up as a key suddenly turned in the apartment's front door lock.

Maggie stood up as the door opened.

"I'm sorry, sweetheart," David said, removing his key from the lock. "I was held up in a meeting at Burlington House." He stopped with his hand on the door as he caught sight of Jacob and Maggie.

"Hello, Papa," Jacob said.

For a moment, his father merely stared at the two of them.

"Jacob decided to come down for the weekend after all," Aloise said.

"I see. I thought we agreed yesterday that you would stay in Cambridge for the weekend."

"I was worried about you, Papa."

"I told you I was fine," David said, looking aimlessly around the room. "I got hit by a small fragment of brick, not a bomb, and I'm perfectly all right."

Jacob saw the small gash, but the wound had scabbed and he wore no bandage to cover it. "I came to visit you, nonetheless, Papa," he said. "And I also brought along my friend Maggie."

"Good evening, Miss Ryder." His father nodded without looking at her.

"Good evening, Dr. Linz," she said, looking worriedly at Jacob.

"Do you realize, dear, that it's nine fifteen?" asked Aloise.

"I had a meeting at Burlington House," he said, placing his briefcase on the coffee table. "Concerning the MAUD Committee's report," he added.

"Even so," she said, glancing nervously at the briefcase, "you could have telephoned and told me that you were going to be late."

"There wasn't time." His father threw his jacket on the sofa, hesitated, then went to the bookcase next to the hallway door.

"You mustn't be angry with me, Papa," said Jacob. "Yesterday on the telephone you didn't sound like yourself. You said some things that worried me."

"You called when I was on my way out of the office, son," his father said, searching among the journals stacked on the shelf, "and I was in the midst of an important experiment."

"What did he say that worried you, Jacob?" asked Aloise.

Seeing his father stop thumbing through the journals, Jacob hesitated, wondering if he should go on. "When I told him that I was worried and wanted to take the next train down to London, he said there were things happening here that he couldn't talk about on the telephone. He told me I had to trust him and stay in Cambridge for the weekend."

"But things are happening here in London, son," David said. "We're about to finish the critical-mass estimates; and if we're right, we may have the go-ahead on the uranium bomb."

Maggie looked at Jacob with surprise.

"You were right, Jacob," Aloise said, shifting the briefcase on the coffee table. "Your father is under pressure at the college and he's simply over-worked."

David replaced the journal on the shelf and turned. "In any case, it's nice to see you again, Miss Ryder. You're doing well, I hope, with your studies at the Nursing Academy."

"Yes, sir. Quite well, thank you."

"You have what, a year more to finish?"

"Two years. I'm working for a fully registered license."

He shook his head. "At the rate things are going, you'll be needed."

"I'd like to be of use, Dr. Linz," she said, "but not at that price."

Glancing warily at Aloise, David went to the window and recklessly drew back the blackout curtain. "I take it, Jacob brought you here to have a look at me, Miss Ryder," he said.

"A look at you, sir?"

"He and Aloise think I'm suffering from a concussion."

"You seem perfectly fine to me, Dr. Linz."

"Good." He threw open the window and took a deep breath. "Then there's no need to continue with this examination."

Aloise shot Jacob a look of despair. "In any case, Jacob is here, sweet-heart, and I was about to make a nice pot of hot tea."

"Yes," David said, lowering the blackout curtain. "That's what we need . . . a nice pot of hot tea."

"I'll only be a minute," Aloise said, as she hurried toward the kitchen.

When she was out of earshot, David said in a low voice, "It was wrong of you to disobey me, son, and it was stupid of you to come here."

"But I was worried, Papa."

Motioning for him to lower his voice, David left the window and joined him and Maggie by the fireplace. "I want you to do as I say, Jacob. I want you to go back to Cambridge tonight and wait there until I contact you."

"Why, Papa?"

"I can't tell you why, son," he said, glancing at the open kitchen door. "You'll just have to trust me."

"If something bad has happened, I want to know about it," Jacob said. "It's time you trusted me, Papa. I'm not a child anymore."

Again, his father motioned for him to lower his voice. "But I can't give you any reasons. At least, not tonight."

"If you won't tell me what's wrong, Papa," he said, "then I won't go back."

His father glanced again at the open kitchen door, then said with a gesture of misery, "Believe me, I will tell you when the time comes, but for now, you must trust me and do as I say."

Trust, Jacob realized, had already been stretched to its limits. He looked at Maggie, knowing that he was violating the vow of secrecy he had made with his father, and said, "Does this have something to do with the War Office, with the people at MI5?"

From the kitchen came the sound of a cupboard door closing and the rattle of cups and saucers.

"Yes," David sighed.

In the kitchen, hurrying to bring David his tea while it was still hot, Aloise placed two cups and saucers on the tray. She could hear the murmur of his voice from the living room, lecturing his son. As she placed the silver cream and sugar salvers on the tray with the cups and the steaming pot of tea, she thought again of the disturbing remark Jacob had made minutes before: that there were things happening here in London his father couldn't talk about on the telephone. The boy was right, of course, about his father's strange behavior. Since Wednesday night, when he came home after the bomb raid with Rakovsky's first draft copy of the MAUD Committee's report in his briefcase, there had been endless excuses for not giving her the report. Last night, still stalling for time, he had said that there would be "major changes" in the final draft and she should wait until the report was completely finished.

She filled the cream pitcher and set the milk bottle on the kitchen counter.

Things happening here in London: she wondered if he was being watched now by British intelligence.

As she gathered up the tea tray and turned toward the hallway door, she suddenly remembered again the puzzling stain on the towel that night, when she sponged the blood from his neck. Last night, she had wondered if his unexplained absence could mean there was another woman in his life, but he had never shown interest in any other woman.

She drew up at the door, hearing David's muffled voice from the living room. "All I can tell you now, Jacob, is that I've made some terrible mistakes."

The first thought that came to her was the guilt he had always felt when he gave in to her pleas for still more Tube Alloys research.

Then she heard him say, "I can't explain this to you now, son, but the mistakes go all the way back to France."

Aloise felt something brush the back of her neck—like the fingers of an invisible hand—sending a chill through her entire body. She gripped the tray and stared at the steaming pot of tea.

Jacob said with impatience, "But I still don't understand what this has got to do with my going back to Cambridge tonight, Papa."

"I'll explain everything in a few days, son. But in the meantime," David went on, "for your own safety, you must go back to Cambridge tonight and wait for me to contact you."

Suddenly feeling faint, Aloise turned back into the kitchen and set the tea tray down on the counter. For a moment, she stood holding onto the counter, trying to make sense of what David had said. When she went back to the door, she heard David say, "No, I can't explain what I mean by suspicions. But I have documents to prove what I suspect."

It took a moment for her to realize what he was talking about. Then she remembered that he had brought to England the documents she had given him relating to Katherine and had placed them in his filing cabinet for safekeeping. Careful not to be seen, she edged her way out of the kitchen and turned down the hallway toward his study.

If she remembered correctly, he had stored the documents in a yellow file among his personal papers in the bottom drawer of his filing cabinet.

She slipped into the study, quietly closed the door, and took out the filing cabinet key from his desk drawer.

It was as if her hands were trying to postpone what her mind knew was inevitable: they shook uncontrollably as she labored to insert the key into its tiny lock. Racing back in her mind over the last two days, she recalled that he had made a point of taking his briefcase to his study the night he came home from the bomb raid. And the next morning, he had kept it beside him all during breakfast.

As she turned the key in the lock and opened the drawer, she thought with panic of the compromises she had made with Moscow to build a life for herself with David. Knowing that the Kremlin was merciless with those who betrayed them, she had risked everything—her membership in the Party and even her life—to marry David.

"If they're here," she said aloud to herself, "then I'm wrong and nothing has changed." She held her breath, trying to remember the Catholic prayer for a miracle that her mother had taught her as a child, and took the file from the drawer.

She quickly said, instead, the only prayer she could remember: the short little prayer that the French nuns of her convent school in the Ardennes had said every night during the Great War—the prayer for "lost causes." She opened the file and saw that it was empty.

In the living room, holding Maggie tightly by the hand, Jacob said to David, "Where's Aloise? I want to tell her goodbye."

"I don't know, but I'll tell her you said goodbye." He turned as he opened the door.

"Oh. One more thing." Glancing back at the open door, he reached into his trouser pocket and took out a small black box. "I want you to have this," he said. "You may need it during the next few days."

The boy said with surprise, "But that belongs to you, Papa. Your father gave it to you before you left America, and you've had it with you since Germany."

Mystified by the small black box in his palm, Maggie said, "What is it, Jacob?"

"A mezuzah. It's a kind of charm that Orthodox Jews put on their doorposts. There's a little scroll inside with a Hebrew prayer written on it."

"It's been passed down in my family from father to son for the last hundred years, Maggie," David said, dropping the box into the boy's jacket pocket, "and now it belongs to Jacob."

"I'm not very religious, Papa," the boy smiled. "But I'm proud to have it, just the same."

As the boy turned down the hallway, he offered Maggie his right arm. "I'll wait for you to contact me in Cambridge, Papa," he said over his shoulder.

"It won't take long," David called after them. "Just a few more days."

48

FEELING Jacob's racing heartbeat against her breast, Maggie thought of the dreadful question she had been asking herself for over a week. She had not seen a doctor yet, but she was now eight days, at least, beyond her menstrual period.

She opened her eyes and looked up at the moonlit ceiling overhead, wishing they could go on lying here together for the rest of the night. She didn't mind the endless cheap hotel rooms or even the anonymity of the fake married names they chose to register under. What she hated about these secret weekend trysts were the games they were forced to play to maintain their charade of innocent friendship—racing home before her parents' pub closed at ten thirty, never being able to spend a whole night together.

He kissed her forehead, then lifted himself and settled his body next to hers on the bed.

This was the first night they had ever stayed together past ten o'clock. She touched his hand where it rested on her naked breast.

She closed her eyes again, relishing the feeling of his body beside hers. Before Jacob came into her life she had always fancied she would meet and fall in love with one of the soldiers who frequented her parents' Greek Street pub—perhaps a handsome airforce lieutenant home on leave from Northumberland or Scotland. There would be a long respectable engagement, with flowers and boxes of American chocolates; a springtime wedding at St. Andrew's in Covent Garden, with a full dress military escort; and a romantic weekend honeymoon in a proper hotel on Brighton Beach. But then Jacob had wandered into the pub and changed everything. She had never imagined that the handsome student from Cambridge would return the following day and ask her to go with him to the new Clark Gable movie that had just opened at the Prince William on Piccadilly. Nor had she imagined that he would come back the following weekend and the weekend after that, or that she would fall in love with him. But the war had changed everything.

The window of their second-floor room was open, and an automobile horn blared in the street below.

Suddenly remembering Jacob's 12:20 train to Cambridge, she opened her eyes. It had been his idea to take a room at the small Waltham Hotel on Gray's Inn Road, for the hotel was only a five minute walk to King's Cross station. Turning to face him on the bed, she said, softly, "You'd better check the time, Jacob."

"Why?" He yawned, lazily. "It can't be much after eleven."

"I think it's close to midnight."

"It can't be. We checked in at ten o'clock." He ran his fingers across her neck and kissed the end of her nose.

"But it's the last train back to Cambridge tonight."

With a sigh, he reached back and took his watch from the bedside table. "Scheisse!" He sat up. "It's five minutes after twelve. That gives us fifteen minutes to get to the station." He swung his legs from the bed and began sorting through the pile of clothes on the floor.

She sat up, watching him dress and said, "You haven't told me the whole truth, Jacob, have you?"

"About what?"

"About your father's reasons for sending you back to Cambridge tonight."

"I've told you what I can, Maggie." He pulled up his trousers and reached for his shirt. "My father's involved in a secret project at the Imperial College."

"What you told me about spies at the college," she said, "you made it up, didn't you?"

"No, Maggie, I didn't make it up. Papa's working on a new kind of bomb, and there's always the danger of spies." He looked back at her on the bed. "You'd better get dressed. It's a five minute walk to King's Cross from here."

She left the bed and went naked to the open window.

She said, watching the traffic pass in the street below, "I don't believe that's what your father is afraid of."

Behind her, Jacob dropped one of his shoes on the floor. "What do you mean?" he asked.

"I'm not sure. But I think it's Aloise he's afraid of."

"That's ridiculous."

She felt suddenly, and for the first time, ashamed to be naked in front of him. Turning from the window, she went to her clothes on the floor beside the bed.

Hurrying to dress, she watched Jacob put his jacket on, take the room key from the bedside table, and grab his overnight case from the floor beside the bed.

"Don't forget your purse," he said as she hurried to join him at the door.

When she caught up, he had started down the narrow carpeted staircase to the first floor. "You forgot this," she said, handing him the little black box his father had given him.

"Thanks. It must have fallen out of my pocket."

"Yes. It was on the floor by the bed."

As they crossed the hotel's small shabbily furnished lobby, he said, "The room is paid for. I just have to return the key."

She continued to the front door, wanting to avoid the expression she knew would be on the room clerk's face.

Jacob joined her on the sidewalk outside the hotel and they turned north, keeping pace with the traffic heading toward King's Cross station two blocks away. "I wish you'd stop worrying about my stepmother," he said. "She loves my father, and she's only trying to look after him."

"I suppose so," she said.

He looked up at the clock on the station's dark façade, gave a sigh of exasperation, and picked up speed. "We'll have to run," he said. "It's twelve sixteen."

When they reached the station entrance, there were taxis lined along the street, loading and unloading late night passengers. "I have a round-trip ticket," he said, "so we can go right to the platform."

As they joined the people hurrying toward the various platforms, mostly late night revelers on their way back to the safety of the English countryside, she said, "Please don't be angry with me, Jacob. I'm afraid for you."

He shook his head and grinned at her.

As she kept pace with him across the lobby, she wondered again if she had only imagined what her body was telling her.

"The twelve twenty leaves from platform seven," he said, picking up speed.

Looking up at the station's bomb-shattered glass ceiling, she had a sudden and terrible premonition that they were racing to meet a deadline far more important than any train schedule, that this would be much more than a week's separation.

A voice called out the 12:20's departure, echoing through the vaulted station.

Jacob came to a halt as they reached platform seven. "Maggie, what's wrong!" he exclaimed. "You look scared to death."

Watching the carriage doors begin to close she thought to herself: If I tell him now he will refuse to go back to Cambridge tonight.

"Trust me," he pleaded. "There's nothing to be afraid of."

"I know," she said. "But I'm worried about how long you'll be away."

He smiled with relief. "I'll be back next Friday on the six fifteen. I promise."

As he turned away, she grasped his face and kissed him on the mouth. "I love you, Jacob," she said, "more than anything."

He returned her kiss. "And I love you, more than anything."

She saw the last carriage begin to move. "You'll have to run now, or you'll miss your train."

"Till next weekend!" As he started down the platform, he suddenly remembered the night he and his father raced to catch the train at Saarbrücken, the night they crossed into France and left his mother behind in Germany.

49

"THAT'S impossible, Linz," Michael Rakovsky said.

"Impossible or not, it's true. She's been living in London for over two years."

"Look, I've got a twelve fifteen meeting at the War Office." Grabbing his suit jacket from the clothes hook on the wall, Rakovsky started out of the physics laboratory.

It was 11:47 and David had told Katherine he would meet her at Rakovsky's office in the Administration building at noon. He left the physics lab and started after Rakovsky. He had timed Katherine's arrival at the Imperial College for the midday lunch break, when the quadrangle in front of the chemistry and physics buildings would be swarming with students and professors. Dodging his way through the crowd in the hallway, he caught up with Rakovsky as he reached the staircase. "For God's sake, Mike," he said, "I need your help."

Throwing his jacket over his shoulder, Rakovsky started down to the first floor. "I remember stories like this at the end of the last war—people coming back from the dead," he said. "There was a soldier in my company who was listed as missing in action in the Battle of the Marne. Two years after the war, he came home to America to find that his wife had remarried. A lot of strange things happen in wartime, Linz."

"It was one of those impossible accidents of chance," David said. "We met in the Marble Arch tube station during last Wednesday's bomb raid."

"And she's been living here in England for two years?"

"She came to London in January of '39."

Rakovsky stopped when they reached the landing. "I don't understand. You've always said that your wife stayed behind in Germany."

Wondering how he could bring himself to tell the truth he had so far

kept hidden from his friend, knowing that the whole fabric of his trea-
sonous deception would come unraveled, he continued down to the first
floor in silence. Last fall, when they first met, he had told Rakovsky the
story of his escape from Germany and of his marriage, a year and a half
later, to Aloise. Knowing that Rakovsky was a fiercely patriotic soldier,
who was proud to be an American, he had gone out of his way to conceal
the darker side of his life with Aloise: her membership in the British
Communist Party and, above all, his collaboration with her.

"Katherine left Berlin the same night that Jacob and I left. And instead
of going to France, she came directly to England. She's been living in
South Lambeth since then, working in a local library."

"This must have been something of a shock for Jacob," Rakovsky said.

"The boy knows nothing, Mike. Under the circumstances, we thought
it best to wait."

"Why? Because of Aloise?"

"Yes. Exactly."

"Then I take it, she doesn't know."

"No. I've said nothing."

Rakovsky continued out into the sunlit quadrangle. The eleven o'clock
classes had just ended, and students and faculty were pouring out of the
buildings. "Knowing Aloise, I can see why you would want to wait to
tell her," he said, as he started toward the gates leading out to Imperial
College Road. "But why keep this a secret from Jacob?"

David said, looking around at the faces of the people milling in the
quadrangle, "It's a long story, Mike; there are things going on in London
which makes it dangerous for the boy to know about his mother."

Rakovsky looked at him with surprise. "What do you mean, things
going on?"

Searching for some place to begin, David realized that the lies and
deceits ran back, like a chain reaction, all the way to Paris. "Funny,"
he said with a sinking feeling of dismay, "after waiting this long to tell
you the truth about Aloise and myself, I don't even know where to begin."

The word truth brought Rakovsky to a halt. He looked off toward the
clock in the Queen's Gate tower.

"I'm in a very dangerous situation, Mike, and I need your help. As a
rule, you usually hang around the college during lunch hour, so I asked
Katherine to meet me in your office at noon."

"This mess you're in with Aloise is a matter for a British court of law,

David. What you need is a good lawyer. Preferably one who's had experience with bigamy laws."

"You're wrong, Mike. This mess, as you call it, with Aloise involves the entire security of the Tube Alloys project."

Walking slowly, Rakovsky continued toward the college gates. "Go on. I'm listening."

David plunged on, saying the first thing that came to mind. "You won't believe me, I know, but on the eve of the Nazi invasion, when it was clear that Aloise and I would be separated, she forged Katherine's German death certificate."

"You're right," Rakovsky said. "I don't believe you." Then for a moment, as if weighing the statement he had just made, he stopped again and looked up absently at the gold summit of the Queen's Tower. "On the other hand, it's amazing what people will do for love," he said, and continued ahead.

The minute hand of the clock in Queen's Gate tower jumped to 11:52. "I haven't even begun to tell you the truth, Mike," David said, "and the worst is yet to come. I've been lying to you about Aloise for the last eleven months. She's a member of the Communist Party; she's been a Party member for over ten years."

Rakovsky's only response was a soft, almost inaudible, sigh.

"I wanted to tell you the truth when we first met," David went on, "but I couldn't bring myself to betray Aloise."

"The loyalty between a man and a woman can be a dangerous thing, David," Rakovsky said, staring thoughtfully at the quadrangle's patterned pavement. "It sometimes leads people to betray more important loyalties."

"Aloise isn't just a card-carrying member of the Communist Party, Mike," he said. "She's an agent for Soviet intelligence here in England. Her specialty is atomic intelligence, and I've been giving her classified Tube Alloys documents for the last eleven months. I've made myself indispensable to her work for the Soviets here in England. And if she finds out that Katherine is in England, there's no telling what she will do."

"I see," said Rakovsky. "In that case, I guess the prime minister will have to do without me." Motioning for him to follow, he turned back toward the administration building at the west end of the quadrangle.

50

KATHERINE turned the corner of Queen's Gate and started up Imperial College Road toward the college's front gates. Certain that the Soviet NKVD had been watching him closely, David had given her exact instructions for their meeting with Major Rakovsky: she should enter the college grounds through the main gates on Imperial College Road at exactly noon and go directly to the administration building on the west side of the college quadrangle. Without asking directions, she should then go directly to Rakovsky's office on the second floor, where he and the major would be waiting for her.

When she reached the wrought iron gates leading into the college, she paused to look up and down the Arkwright Road. David had said you could easily spot the NKVD by the innocuous gray Humbers they always drove, but there was only one car parked on the street—an old blue Morris Minor at the far end of the block.

Passing the tall brick and stone Queen's Tower, she looked around, feeling suddenly and comfortably at home. The redbrick Victorian buildings, the faces of the young people talking in animated groups: it was as if she were returning to her student days with David in Göttingen. Trying to appear familiar with her surroundings, she hurried across the quadrangle, and entered the four-story administration building.

On the second floor, she came to the room number David had given her and knocked twice.

When she opened the door, Major Rakovsky was just rising from his chair behind a desk piled high with papers. He was younger and taller than she had imagined he would be from David's description, with a neatly trimmed black moustache and salt and pepper hair cropped close to his head.

David was already on his feet in front of the desk. "This is my wife Katherine, Mike," he said.

"I'm Mike Rakovsky," the major said. "Please come in."

As she entered the large office, David stepped forward and quickly closed the door. "Did you have trouble finding your way?" he asked.

"Not a bit. You described everything perfectly." Turning to Major Rakovsky, she saw a look of startled surprise pass across his handsome face.

"Please sit down, Mrs. Linz," he said, pointing to the chair next to David's. "Or should I call you Dr. Linz?"

She smiled. "That was always our problem in Berlin—people calling us both Dr. Linz," she said, observing the haphazard stacks of papers and books on the shelves lining the walls. "So if you don't mind, Major Rakovsky, I'd prefer that you call me Katherine."

"You must forgive the mess," he said, trying to arrange the papers on his desk. "We're finishing up a government report and I don't have a secretary."

When he looked up, there was a curious expression of recognition in his intense hazel eyes. "Is something wrong, Major Rakovsky?" she asked.

"It's nothing," he said, seating himself in the metal chair behind the desk. "Your appearance here today comes as a surprise."

"I've told Michael everything," David said, stepping in to relieve Rakovsky's hesitation. "About Aloise's work for Soviet intelligence, about my own collaboration—everything."

The major sat forward and folded his hands resolutely on the desk. "As David must have told you, I'm an American citizen representing the United States government here in England. Officially, I'm here as a member of Roosevelt's National Defense Research Committee. Legally, I'm merely a foreign visitor and a guest of the British government. As a visiting foreigner, I have no authority to interfere with matters involving British war security."

She looked from Rakovsky to David and back again. "But surely you can see why David came to you, instead of Scotland Yard," she said.

"As I've told David," Rakovsky went on without looking up, "violations of the Official Secrets Act fall under the jurisdiction of the British War Office and the MI5 branch of British Secret Service. It would be a serious breach of British law if I made any attempt to help you and your family without the knowledge of the British authorities." As he sat back, still keeping his eyes lowered, a bead of sweat appeared on his forehead. "I'm very sorry, believe me, but there is nothing I can do."

David turned to her and said, "Michael tells me he must inform the British authorities about Aloise's Soviet intelligence work here in England and about my own violations of the Official Secrets Act."

"I have no choice," said Rakovsky, drawing himself up stiffly. "I'm an officer in the American Army, and it's my duty."

Duty: the word rang in her ear like a curse. "Your duty?" she asked.

"England is at war," he replied. "And acts of treason such as David has described threaten the security of the entire British nation."

David had warned her last night not to put too much hope in Major

Rakovsky—that his American friend was, before anything else, "a loyal and patriotic soldier."

She said, watching him nervously run his finger down the arm of his chair, "David came to you as a friend, Colonel Rakovsky. He told you the truth about his and Aloise's acts of treason, as you call them, because you are the only man in England who can help him. If you report him to the British authorities, there will be an investigation. Questions will be asked, and Aloise Frégand will know of my presence in England before the week is out."

"She's right, Mike," David said. "Aloise has made a dangerous compromise, and if she finds out that Katherine is alive and living in London, she will stop at nothing to keep her betrayal hidden from the Soviets."

"The fact is," Katherine went on, "there's no evidence, other than David's own word, that Aloise has broken any laws here in England. Do you think that she will sit back and do nothing to protect her standing with the Soviets?"

Rakovsky said, trying to avoid David's unblinking stare, "David is my friend. I would do anything to help him. But my hands are tied."

"Do you remember what you said when I told you about her experimental work with uranium?" asked David.

Rakovsky began fidgeting with the letter opener on his desk. "No," he said. "I don't, as a matter of fact."

"You said—and I remember your exact words—you said 'it's a pity your wife died in the service of Nazi science. She would have been very useful to our Allied atom bomb project.' "

A flush spilled through Rakovsky's face. "What are you getting at, Linz?" he asked.

David took a deep breath and sat forward. "It's no secret that you and the NDRC are here in England to keep Roosevelt informed about British progress on the bomb. And it's also no secret that Roosevelt, if he can bring America into the war, will do everything in his power to take over the entire Allied atom bomb project."

"America is not at war, and it's only idle speculation that Roosevelt wants to take over the Allied bomb project," Rakovsky said, suddenly defensive.

"Then why has the president arranged a job for you with the MAUD Committee?" David asked.

Rakovsky went on turning the letter opener in his hands and said nothing.

"The fact is, Mike," David said, "if Roosevelt plans to take over the entire project and build the bomb in America, he will need all the first-rate scientists he can find. A physicist like Katherine would be an invaluable asset to the president's American bomb project."

Katherine stepped in before Rakovsky could speak. "On the other hand, the experimental work I did in Germany would have been impossible without David's theoretical help," she said, picking up the momentum of his argument. "It was David who understood the theoretical meaning of my uranium experiments, and it was David who first saw that I had fissioned the uranium atom." She reached over and took hold of his hand where it rested on his knee. "My experimental work has always been meaningless without David's theoretical interpretations."

Silent for a moment, Rakovsky said without looking up, "You realize, of course, that a man who could be tempted to make such a betrayal once could be tempted again."

Katherine tightened her grip on David's hand. "My husband and I have both made mistakes. And considering the price we have paid, I can assure you we won't make them again."

He dropped the letter opener on the desk, stood up, and turned to the curtainless window behind him. "My first concern, David, is your problem with Aloise. She must know that something is wrong."

"So far, I'm sure she knows nothing, Mike. But she suspects everything."

For a moment, Rakovsky went on staring absently at the rooftop of the opposite building. Then he said, "You realize, of course, that you may have to wait a long time to prove your case against Aloise in a British court of law."

"All we ask is that you use your influence with the government to get the three of us safely out of the country," Katherine said. "In exchange for your help, David and I will, when the time comes, work for the American atom bomb project."

"I will help you and Katherine on one condition. That you continue to say nothing to Jacob about Katherine's presence here in England."

It was David's turn to grip Katherine's hand. "Katherine hasn't seen her son for over two and a half years, Mike. We can't keep her presence here in London secret from the boy much longer."

Turning from the window, Rakovsky took his seat again. "It may take a few days, but I have friends in the American military intelligence mission here who can arrange everything. The first problem will be in bringing you and Katherine and Jacob together without alerting Aloise."

"Someone must go to Cambridge and tell Jacob the truth," Katherine said. "Someone we can trust."

"I'll take the day off tomorrow and drive up to Cambridge. In the meantime, you must make some arrangements," Rakovsky said. He took a notepad from his desk, wrote down an address, and handed the paper to David. "This is a travel agency on the High Street in Hampstead. I want you to go there today and book passage for yourself, Katherine, and Jacob on the next ship sailing to America. Then go to your bank and withdraw enough money for your travel expenses."

"We'll do everything you say, Major Rakovsky." Katherine let go of David's hand and stood up.

"I think you should leave my office as you came," he said. "Separately."

She turned and offered her hand to Rakovsky. "If not for friendship, Major Rakovsky, then for the victory of Allied atomic science over the Nazi atom bomb."

As Rakovsky took her hand, the color rose again in his face. "We'll meet again," he said.

David stepped back and opened the office door. "I'll meet you at the corner of Queen's Gate and Imperial College Road in exactly five minutes," he said.

"I'll be waiting." She kissed him quickly on the cheek and went out.

"There's one more thing," said Rakovsky as David closed the door. "For the next few days, until we draw up a plan for your escape, you must make no changes in your life with Aloise. Everything must go on as before."

"I understand."

David crossed the college quadrangle and came out onto the sidewalk fronting the college gates. The only car parked along the Arkwright Road fronting the college, he saw, was an old beatup blue Morris Minor at the end of the block. Moving to the edge of the sidewalk, he caught sight of a taxi heading toward him in the westbound lane. Ignoring the loud backfire from the Morris Minor as the driver started up the car's engine, he stepped out into the street and waved his arm.

"Merde!" Aloise exclaimed as she forced the Morris Minor's ancient gears into first. Malotte, the embassy secretary who had loaned her his car for the day, had warned her that she would have trouble with its gears, but there hadn't been time to locate a decent car.

She watched as David got into the taxi he had flagged, then pulled out into the Arkwright Road's westbound traffic. Four cars ahead, she saw the taxi turn in once again toward the curb. Inching her way to the right, she caught sight of a woman standing on the northeast corner of Imperial College Road, the same woman she had seen enter and leave the College gates. As she pulled up behind the taxi, she saw the woman's face for the first time: the chiseled Germanic chin, the slender tapered nose, and the blonde hair tied in a knot behind her head.

51

T H E R E was only one telephone at Jacob's lodgings in Cambridge, located in the porter's room on the ground floor of Bishop's Hostel, and it took an eternity, it seemed, for the porter to summon the boy from his rooms on the third floor.

He came on the line and said, "Hello?"

It was obvious from his breathless voice that he had run to the phone. Aloise gripped the receiver with both hands, wondering if she was too late, if the boy already knew everything.

"Hello!" he shouted, raising his voice over the telephone static. "Who's calling?"

"It's me, Jacob," she said. "Aloise."

"Aloise?" he repeated her name with alarm. "Where are you?"

"I'm in London," she said. "At my office in the embassy. We have a bad connection."

For a moment, there was only the crackling noise of the telephone static. "Is something wrong?" he asked.

The question itself was the answer she was looking for. "I'm calling about your father, Jacob. Have you talked with him in the last three days?"

"No. Not since last Friday. Why? Has something happened?"

She reached for the notepad on her desk where she had written her instructions for the call. "First, tell me this—are you alone?" she asked.

"The hall porter, Mr. Simms, is here with me," he replied. "Why?"

She took a pencil from the ceramic holder on her desk. "I will tell you what I can," she said, checking off the first instruction. "But you must be careful what you say in front of the porter, Jacob. None of us is safe now."

"All right," he said. "I'm listening."

"I've made a terrible mistake," she went on, carefully enunciating each word. "You were right about your father, and I was wrong." She looked down at the notepad, searching desperately for the words she had prepared for him. "I mean, the things you said about your father the other night when you came to the flat with Maggie . . ." She raised her voice over the static and said again, "You were right, Jacob, and I was wrong. Your father isn't sick at all. The reason he's been acting the way he has is because he's trying to protect us both. The British authorities now know everything about his work for the Party, and he's being closely watched wherever he goes."

"Where is Papa?" the boy interrupted.

She checked off the second instruction on her list. "I saw him three hours ago at the college," she replied. "He told me to call you and warn you about what's going on in London. He wants you to—"

Again, he interrupted. "I'll phone him myself at the college."

"No, Jacob!" The point of her pencil snapped. "That would be the worst thing you could do! Now listen to me, Jacob, because our safety is at stake," she said, leveling her voice over the static. "Do you understand what I'm saying?"

"No," he said. "Tell me."

"Your father says that I am also being watched." She took a fresh pencil and checked off the next instruction. "I've talked with him and he wants you to follow my instructions to the letter." The static on the line rose and fell. "Are you listening to me?" she demanded.

"Yes. Go on."

She went on, reading what she had written on the notepad, "David tells me that the authorities have been asking questions about you, Jacob, as well. They know about the work you've been doing in Cambridge, and they're conducting an investigation into your German background." She heard a soft curse under the static and drew a check beside the next instruction. "Your father wants you to remain in Cambridge and make no attempt to contact either me or him. Do you understand what I'm saying?"

"Yes."

"In the meantime, David and I will draw up a plan for the three of us. This means, you realize, that you and your father and I will have to leave England," she said.

"And go where?" his voice broke over the static. "The Nazis have the whole of Europe, and if Papa is in trouble with British security we won't be able to go to America!"

"Your father and I will talk about that tonight, Jacob. It will depend entirely on what he decides to do, but I'm sure we'll be able to work out some solution." She drew the letters MAUD at the bottom of her notepad. "The fortunate thing is," she added, "Russia and England are now allies and I have friends in Moscow who can arrange passage for us to a safe place."

Again, he muttered something under the static that sounded like a curse.

"What did you say, Jacob?" she asked.

"Nothing. I was only thinking about my girlfriend, Maggie."

She dropped her pencil and sat back. "You must keep in mind that your father's safety is at stake," she said, "and you must make no attempt to contact Maggie. Is that clear?"

"Yes," he said.

"I've said all I can for now, Jacob. I will contact you again later."

"When?"

"Just as soon as I know your father's plans."

"I'll be waiting," he said. There was a click and the line disconnected.

She sat forward and returned the receiver to the hook. Taking a cigarette from the pack on her desk, she lit it and sat smoking for a moment, waiting for her racing heartbeat to calm. Through the window of her fourth-floor office she looked out across Hyde Park and watched as a flock of pigeons took flight from the top of Marble Arch. For the first time in hours, it seemed as if she could finally see a small light at the far end of the tunnel of her darkest fear, and that she might now find a way out of the labyrinth she had constructed.

She picked up the receiver and dialed from memory the local emergency number she had been given by the Commissar of the Soviet NKVD in Moscow—a number she had never used until now.

52

ALOISE put the kettle on at exactly 6:30, then took the tin of tea from the cupboard and spooned the usual amount into the teapot.

Returning the tea to the cupboard, she chose two cups and saucers and placed them on the tea tray.

She thought of how close they had come to a happy marriage. True, she had known from the very beginning that she would never be able to completely replace Katherine in David's affections—that she would always be the understudy for the role of David's wife.

Moving with calm deliberation, she filled the sugar bowl and the cream pitcher. There would be nothing different tonight when he came home. The pleasure would be in knowing that he did not know that she knew, in watching him squirm as she turned the screws and closed him up in the trap of his own lies, just as she had watched him do to her for the past four days.

She added a dish of English butter cookies to the tray. His favorite brand, she had always gone out of her way to buy them, even at their inflated wartime price.

The irony was that he had undoubtedly come across Katherine by accident during the bomb raid last Wednesday, and that their almost perfect life here in England—the life she had made for them at a such high cost to herself—had been ruined by chance.

The kettle had come to a boil. Pouring the steaming water into the teapot, she thought: I may have lost the battle, but not the war.

Returning the kettle to the stove, she took the tea tray and went to the living room. The clock on the mantelpiece read 6:34. She placed the teatray in its usual place on the table. In the past, before Katherine's untimely reappearance, he had always come home by six forty-five—seven, at the latest. She had done it a hundred times in the past, and it was as if she was reenacting an old and time-worn ritual: she went to the window and looked out across the rooftops toward Hyde Park to the south. She watched as two small birds playfully pursued each other from one tree to another, wondering to herself if the summers in Moscow could ever be as lovely as that first summer she and David had spent together in London.

Behind her, she heard a key turn in the lock. Feeling a sudden rush of nostalgic affection, she made no move to turn from the window.

"Aloise!" he said with a tone of forced cheerfulness.

She forced herself to smile and turned to face him. "David, sweetheart," she said, just as she had said so many times before, and went to meet him at the door. "How did things go today?" she asked.

"Pretty good," he replied, removing his key from the lock. "We made a little progress, for once."

It was amazing how one got used to the little habits of speech: he had said those same words countless times in the past. "That's wonderful, dear. I can tell you've solved a big problem," she said, presenting herself for his kiss. "You look relaxed for the first time in days."

He closed the door and turned to offer the old embrace.

Smiling up at him, she forced him to kiss her.

"What's that—?" he started to ask, but she drew him still closer, closed her eyes, and silenced him with her mouth. For one brief moment, knowing that this would be the last time she would ever feel the touch of his lips or the reassuring warmth of his embrace, she pressed his body against her own. When she drew back, she could read the puzzled surprise in his eyes.

Now, she thought, we can begin.

She let go of him and turned to the coffee table. "If you want tea, dear, I have some ready."

"Tea would be great, thanks," he said, placing his briefcase on the table—just as he had always done in the past.

"You know, you've really become quite an Englishman since we moved here," she said, laughing as she poured his cup. "Tea in the afternoons, picnics in the country on the weekends. It's funny how the accidents of place and time change us."

"I guess you're right." He took off his jacket and lay it across the back of the armchair. "I remember, in Germany I used to drink a beer in the evenings after work."

She put his teaspoon of sugar in and added the proper dash of milk. "And in Paris, it was always whiskey," she said, handing his cup.

He saw that she had bought his favorite butter cookies. "Is this some special occasion?"

"Not particularly. I just suspected you might be on time for a change, that's all," she said, pouring her own cup. "And considering how late you've been these last few days," she added with a smile, "that's something of an occasion."

"I told you, we've been trying to finish up the new critical-mass experiments."

She spooned a half teaspoon of sugar into her tea. "And you made a little progress today?" she asked.

"We finally have a clear estimate of the U235 critical mass."

"Excellent. And was it the same as your theoretical calculations?"

"Yes." He turned away and sipped his tea. "Roughly."

"By the way, dear," she said, seating herself on the sofa, "I tried to reach you this afternoon at your office. I phoned at two o'clock and again at three, but there was no answer."

"I had some errands to run," he said.

She sipped her tea and thought: That's true. For he had dropped

Katherine off at the Maiden Lane tube station in Camden Town at three thirty and had returned to the college at three fifty-five. She tried a different tactic. "It's so unlike you to run errands during work hours."

"They were things I had postponed that had to get done right away," he said, and began loosening his tie.

"Things do catch up with one, don't they?" she said, wondering how much of the truth she could force from him.

"What were you trying to say, Aloise?" he asked.

"I had a meeting this morning with my contact at the Soviet Embassy," she replied. "He said there had been inquiries from Moscow about the MAUD Committee's report. Commissar Beria, it seems, has sent an urgent message demanding to know when the final draft will be finished."

"Soon," he said, pulling his tie free.

"But how soon is soon?" she asked. "It's an important document for the Soviets. The future of Kurchatov's atom bomb research at the Lebedev depends on it, and I've promised Comrade Beria a copy of the report."

"Rakovsky says there'll be a finished draft by the end of the week," said David, unbuttoning his shirt collar.

"That's wonderful news, sweetheart. Moscow will be pleased to hear it."

"But it will take time for me to get my hands on a copy of the final draft," he said. "I can't promise anything, but maybe by the end of the month."

She said, stirring her tea, "Provided, of course, you're still here in England by the end of the month."

Caught in the act of draping his tie across the jacket on the armchair, he stopped and stood holding the tie with both hands—his mouth opened and his face frozen in a look of shock.

She sipped her tea and watched him slowly lay his tie down, relishing the sight of his helplessness.

"How did you find out?" he asked, quietly.

"I knew something strange had happened the night you came back late from the bomb raid," she replied. "But it was not until Friday night, when Jacob and little Maggie came to visit us, that I began to suspect the truth. That was the night I checked your filing cabinet and discovered that the documents you had brought with you from France were missing."

Amazing, he thought. He had lived in dread of this moment for four days, but instead of the murderous rage he had anticipated, he felt only relief. "I see," he said, and turned to face her. "Then your NKVD people have been following me all weekend."

"They've been following you since I learned about the MAUD Committee report, David, but this afternoon I canceled your surveillance. You see—" She sipped her tea again. "—I don't think it's wise to involve the NKVD in personal matters."

"So you found out about Katherine on your own," he said.

"Yes." Her teacup rattled in its saucer as she set it down on the coffee table. "Twice over the weekend I tried to follow you, but you lost me both times in South Lambeth. This morning, I borrowed my secretary's car and waited for you outside the college gates."

David went to the chest where the liquor bottles stood and poured himself a full glass of whiskey.

"She's more beautiful than I had imagined," Aloise said. She could taste her hatred of the woman in the bitter aftertaste of the tea in her mouth.

Already knowing the answer before he asked the question, David drank the entire glass of whiskey. "You knew all along that she was alive, didn't you?"

"Yes."

After all the elaborate precautions she had taken to keep him in ignorance, the easy candor of her statement astonished him. "And you arranged everything, didn't you?" he said. "Both the documents proving she had remained in Germany and her forged death certificate."

"Yes. Everything."

He thought of the slow death by radiation that she had invented for Katherine and the agonizing grief Jacob had suffered during those last days in Paris. "For God's sake, Aloise," he said, "what good did killing Katherine do?"

"You know the answer to that as well as I do," she said with maddening composure. "I would have been content to go on as we were—with nothing more than an affair—but the day the Germans invaded Holland, I knew I would either have to marry you or lose you."

"How could you hope to get away with such a fraud?"

She came up and stopped a few feet behind him. "I loved you, and with the Nazis about to occupy the whole of Europe, I was willing to gamble that Katherine would never reach England."

He could feel the heat of her body behind him. "So you lied to me from the very beginning," he said.

"I had no choice. I knew that you were in love with Katherine and that you would not give her up as long as you could hope she would join you in Paris." She moved still closer. "When it became clear that Jacob would never agree to our leaving France together, I decided to take the final leap and do what was necessary."

He uncapped the bottle and slowly refilled his glass. "You took a big risk, Aloise, when you accepted the job with Russian intelligence in England," he said. "Stalin is merciless with those who compromise their loyalty to the Kremlin."

It was as if he had reached out, without turning, and struck the one vulnerable place in her courage. She watched as he drank the whiskey in his glass, then said, "I risked everything for you. My career, my honor, my life—everything."

David turned the empty glass in his hand, wondering to himself at the choices he had made in the last twenty years.

The rage she had kept in check for the last four days came boiling up inside her. "I loved you more than Katherine ever did," she shouted, "and she deserved to die!"

"Katherine was my life, Aloise. You could never replace her." He set his glass down and turned to face her. "You knew what the risks were when you took them," he said. "You gambled everything on a lie, and now you've lost."

It was as if they were suddenly seeing each other for the first time. For a moment, they went on staring at one another in silence.

"It's finished, Aloise."

The time for arguments of the heart, she realized, had passed. "You're planning to leave England with Katherine and Jacob, aren't you?" she said.

"Yes. As soon as possible."

She turned away and went back to the coffee table. Taking a cigarette from the silver dish, she said, "This afternoon, I followed you and Katherine to Hampstead, where you paid a call on a little travel agency in the High Street—the P. G. Lawrence Travel Agency, to be exact."

He watched her light the cigarette and said nothing.

"You also paid a call this afternoon on the Kensington branch of the Westminster Bank. I know the manager, and when I got back to the embassy I called and made some inquiries. Mr. Grisholm told me you had removed a hundred pounds from our account. I also telephoned the travel agency. I identified myself as Mrs. Linz and asked a few questions about our travel plans." As she lit her cigarette, her voice, like her hand, began to shake uncontrollably. "Apparently, you and Katherine have booked three berths on an American freighter, the S.S. *Comstock*, sailing from Liverpool to Boston.

"Of course, I can't force you to try to save what we had in the past," she said. "But I can force you to do what's necessary to ensure my own future."

"What do you mean?"

"You can break the promises you made to me, but I cannot break the promises I have made to Moscow." She left the coffee table and went to the open window. "Moscow wants the final draft copy of the MAUD report, so I will make a bargain with you," she said, gazing out at the sunset's fading light. "If you will turn the report over to me, as promised, I will do nothing to stop you and Katherine and Jacob from leaving England."

"I was foolish enough to help you in the past, Aloise," he said, "I won't be again."

For a moment, saying nothing, Aloise looked out across Hyde Park toward the darkening horizon. "I spoke to Jacob this afternoon when I returned to the embassy," she said. "I was surprised to find out that he still knows nothing about his mother's presence in England." She drew on her cigarette and blew the smoke through the open window, watching as it vanished. "I told the boy that you were being watched by the British MI5 and that he was to stay in Cambridge and make no attempt to contact you. I said that you and I were working on a plan to get the three of us safely out of England, and that I would get back to him as soon as all the arrangements were made."

David took a step forward. "All I have to do is tell him the bloody truth to end this charade of yours!"

She said, watching the soft evening light fade away in the empty sky above the city, "I also had a meeting this afternoon with the head of the NKVD. And though I said nothing about Katherine's presence in London, I told him that you were having second thoughts about your work for Soviet atomic intelligence and that you were planning to defect with your son to America."

"You're mad!" he exclaimed. "What can you hope to gain from this?"

"My safe passage to Russia, David. I have promised to bring Moscow the finished MAUD report, and you have until next Monday to turn it over to me."

"I will make no bargain with either you or the Soviets."

She drew again on her cigarette and said, calmly, "The choice you have is very simple. You will either give me a final draft copy of the MAUD report by next Monday, or you will forfeit your son's life."

He watched in horror as she tossed her burned cigarette through the open window.

"If any attempt is made between now and then to contact Jacob in Cambridge, I will instruct the NKVD to kill him."

53

MICHAEL Rakovsky stolled up the west side of Greek Street, stopping here and there to examine the merchandise displayed in the shop windows. Aside from a group of workmen dismantling the charred walls of a burned brick house at the corner of Bateman Street, the narrow cobblestoned street was deserted. The middle-aged man in the mackintosh and bowler hat who had gotten off the train with him at Piccadilly had disappeared into the Shaftesbury Avenue Theater, and he was pretty sure that no one had followed him.

David had said that he would be able to find Maggie between the hours of five and ten at her parents' pub, where she worked in the evenings as a barmaid. It seemed unlikely that she might be the solution to the problem they now faced; but that morning, when David came to him with the news of last night's confrontation with Aloise, he had promised that he would leave no stone unturned in finding a way to bring Jacob safely to London.

Half a block away, on the opposite side of the street, the shades were being drawn up in the windows of the White Horse Tavern. Though spared a direct hit, the pub's old eighteenth-century wooden façade had been scorched by the fire in the neighboring building.

Aside from the fact that the girl was only eighteen and, from David's description of her, completely lacking in worldly experience, there was the added problem of loyalty. But, with a few carefully chosen questions, he would know if she could be trusted.

For the sake of appearances, he waited another minute, then he crossed the street and walked in a leisurely manner toward the tavern. Pausing at the door, he glanced back in the direction of Shaftesbury Avenue to confirm that no one was following him and went in.

"G'd evenin', sir!" the pubkeeper, a stout, bald man, greeted him from behind the bar with a thick Cockney accent.

"Good evening." Rakovsky nodded and continued toward the farthest table in the corner. Aside from a plump little woman with curly red hair and a soft Irish face who was stacking glasses, and one old man, hunched over a glass of Guinness at the bar, the pub was empty.

"Maggie!" the pubkeeper called out, sharply. "We've got customers!"

"Coming, Papa!" The melodic voice from behind the curtained-off room on the right side of the bar sounded like that of a child.

Rakovsky chose a chair with a view of the tavern door, sat down, and looked around. With its white tiled floors, its seasoned paneled walls and sturdy polished furniture, the White Horse, like so many of London's public houses, had a comfortable atmosphere of enduring tradition.

"Maggie!" the pubkeeper called out again. "Bloody hell!" he cursed. "She's late again!"

"Now Walter," the woman chided, "she's been at school all afternoon, and she's gettin' herself dressed."

"School or not, Coral, this is fourth time running!"

Rakovsky recalled David's description of the girl and her parents that morning. Though he had never visited the White Horse Tavern or met Maggie's parents, he had said that the Ryders were native Londoners who had been operating their Soho establishment for twenty-one years.

The curtain parted and the girl came out into the pub, hurriedly fastening the buttons down the front of a modest, gray dress. With her long blonde hair tied back with a ribbon behind her head, she bore a resemblance to Katherine.

"We open up here at five, Maggie," her father scolded, "not ten after five."

"I had an examination at school this afternoon, Papa," she said with exasperation.

As the girl came toward his table, Rakovsky saw that there were dark circles under her watery blue eyes.

"Good evening, sir," she said absently, without looking at him. "Would you like something from the bar?"

"A bourbon and soda, please, with a double helping of ice."

"Yes, sir." She started for the bar.

"By the way," he said, "aren't you Maggie Ryder, Jacob Linz's girl-friend?"

She turned and looked at him with startled surprise. "How do you know that?" she asked.

"I'm a friend of Jacob's father, Miss Ryder. When you get a moment, I'd like to talk to you about Jacob."

Her look of surprise gave way to one of fear. She came back to the table. "Where is he?" she asked. "Where is Jacob?"

"In Cambridge. At least, for now," he replied.

"Is he . . . is he in trouble?"

"You might say so, yes. That's what I want to talk to you about."

She looked back at her father behind the bar.

"I only have a few questions to ask. It won't take long," he assured her.

"A bourbon and soda?" she asked.

"Yes, please. With a double helping of ice."

She hurried to her father, gave him the order, then went to her mother at the end of the bar where she was stacking glasses. There was an exchange of whispers, then a questioning glance from her mother in his direction. "All right," the woman said. "But only for a minute."

Seeing that her father had turned away to talk to the old man at the bar, the girl took the drink he had made and came back to the table. "I only have a minute," she said, placing the drink in front of him.

"Won't you sit down, Miss Ryder?" Rakovsky asked, motioning to the empty chair beside him.

"Papa doesn't like me to socialize with the patrons," she said, nervously seating herself at the opposite side of the table.

"In that case, I'll come right to the point. My name is Michael Rakovsky, and I work with Jacob's father at the Imperial College."

She studied his face warily for a moment. "Rakovsky," she said, "that's a Russian name, isn't it?"

He sipped his drink, wondering if Jacob had told the girl of Aloise's involvement with Moscow. "Yes," he said. "My parents were Russian, but I was born in America."

"I see."

He said, trying to ease her sudden defensiveness, "Dr. Linz tells me you're studying to be nurse."

"Yes. I'm a first-year student at the Brompton School of Nursing."

"That's a very good school—the best in London," he said, smiling at her with encouragement. "I know that because my wife was a nurse."

She weighed his statement, then said, "What do you mean, was?"

"She was a nurse in America during the last war, but she's dead now. She died in childbirth, just before the end of the war. Come to think of it," he added to bring the conversation around, "my son would have been three years older than Jacob, if he had lived."

"I need to see Jacob, Mr. Rakovsky," she said. "I need to talk to him."

"Why, Maggie? Is something wrong?"

She glanced back at her father behind the bar. "I don't want to talk about it. It's something private."

"You can trust me," he said. "I'm a close friend of Jacob's father."

"But this has nothing to do with Jacob's father," she said with hushed vehemence, "and I can only talk about it with Jacob."

"I see." Watching her nervously turn the button at her midriff, he suddenly wondered if he had found the answer to his problem.

He sat forward. "Tell me, Maggie, when was the last time you spoke to Jacob?"

"On Friday night—when I took him to King's Cross to catch his train back to Cambridge."

David, he recalled, had said that the girl had heard Jacob ask him about the War Office and the people at MI5. He said, phrasing his question with caution, "When you saw Jacob on Friday, did he explain why he had come down from Cambridge?"

"He comes down every Friday. Usually, he takes the 7:15 express, but last Friday he came down earlier. He was worried about his father."

"Dr. Linz tells me you and Jacob came to his apartment that night. Can you tell me what happened?"

He had opened a floodgate. With sudden panic, she leaned forward as the words came pouring out. "Jacob came to the White Horse about six o'clock and begged me to go with him to his parents' flat. Since I'm studying to be a nurse, he wanted me to convince his father to see a doctor." She looked away and added under her breath, "But I didn't want to go with him to the flat."

"Why?'

"I had gone there the week before to meet his father and stepmother. His father was very kind; but his stepmother, I could tell, didn't like me."

He recalled David's account of Maggie's first meeting with Aloise: that Aloise had considered the girl an "ardent little patriot." "Why do you think Mrs. Linz didn't like you?" he asked.

"I'm only a pubkeeper's daughter, and she didn't approve of me as Jacob's girlfriend." She hesitated, turning the button on her dress, then said, "Not only that, I think there were things going on that she didn't want me to know about."

"Like what?"

"Get to work, Maggie!" her father shouted angrily from the bar. "We have customers!"

The girl looked back to see two middle-aged couples seating themselves at the table by the door. "I can't talk now," she said, and started to rise. "I have work to do."

"It's important that you answer my question, Maggie," he said, flatly. "Jacob's life may depend upon your answer."

She sat back down. "I felt that he was in danger last Friday," she said. "He should have never come down to see his father."

"What were the things going on here in London that Mrs. Linz didn't want you to know about, Maggie?" he asked.

"I can't tell you," she said. "I promised Jacob never to speak about it."

"You must trust me, Maggie, and answer my questions. I'm here to help Jacob."

There was terror in the girl's innocent eyes as she leaned forward. "The night I met Mrs. Linz, she took me aside and questioned me about my politics. She was trying to find out if I knew that she was a member of the Communist Party."

"And did you know?" Rakovsky asked.

"Yes. Jacob had told me soon after we met."

Rakovsky sipped his drink. "So what do you think was going on that Mrs. Linz didn't want you to know about?" he asked again.

"I don't know. But I think it had something to do with the work that Dr. Linz is doing at the Imperial College."

He watched as her father left the old man and hurried down the bar toward her mother. There was an animated exchange of whispers and an angry gesture in their direction. He said, quickly, "Last Friday night, you were alone with Jacob and his father for a few minutes. Do you remember what they talked about?"

"Dr. Linz wanted Jacob to go back that night to Cambridge and stay there. He said that there were things happening in London that made it very dangerous for him to be here."

"Did you understand why Dr. Linz wanted Jacob to go back that night?"

"Dr. Linz refused to give a reason. But later, Jacob told me that it had to do with his father's work and the spies that were operating inside the Imperial College."

Rakovsky smiled at her choice of words: it was the language of spy thrillers. "And did you believe him?" he asked.

"No. I was sure it had something to do with his stepmother."

"Dammit, Maggie!" her father barked. "You have two tables to serve!"

"I can't stay," she said. She got up and hurried away to take orders from the two middle-aged couples. Three men in gray overalls, workers from the demolition crew next door, had just entered and taken a table next to the window.

Realizing that he could not expect more than another half minute of the girl's time, Rakovsky sipped his drink and weighed the girl's potential usefulness against the danger her failure would cause. David was right that morning when he said that she would be worried about Jacob's safety. Her war loyalties were obvious, but the question now was whether she could be trusted with not only Jacob's, but also David's and Katherine's lives. On the other hand, given her youth and anonymity, she would never be suspected.

When she had taken the orders from the second table, Maggie came back to Rakovsky's table carrying a damp dishtowel. "I have only a moment and I can't sit down," she said and began wiping the table.

"What do you know about Dr. Linz's work at the Imperial College?" he asked.

"I only know what Jacob has told me. Dr. Linz is working on a government project called Tube Alloys. It's a top secret war project."

"And what did Jacob tell you about this top secret war project?"

"He only told me that they're trying to build a new kind of bomb," she said. "And if it works, it will end the war with Germany."

"Did he tell you that the Germans, and maybe even the Russians, are trying to build a similar bomb?"

"No." She stopped wiping the table and looked up. "He only said that his father and mother had discovered the secret of the bomb when they were working as scientists in Germany."

Rakovsky sipped his drink, then asked, "What has Jacob told you about his mother, Maggie?"

"He told me that she was a scientist in Germany, that she was a very beautiful woman and that he loved her very much. He told me that she died working as a scientist for the Nazis."

"The drinks are ready, Maggie!" her father called out.

She stopped wiping the table. "Look, Mr. Rakovsky, I'll do anything I can to help Jacob. All I want is to be able to see him and talk to him."

He thought to himself: What she lacks in knowledge and experience, she will more than make up for with love. "I understand, Maggie," he said. "But before I can let you talk to Jacob, there are some things about him I want to explain. Can you meet me later tonight?"

"I finish work at ten. Where?"

"Piccadilly is close. I'll meet you at the corner of Coventry Street at ten fifteen."

54

"IT'S a woman that's calling you, Mr. Linz," said old man Simms.

"Did she give her name?" Jacob asked.

Hard of hearing, Simms cupped his ear. "Did she what?"

"I said, did she give her name?"

"No, sir. I inquired, but she refused to identify herself."

"Never mind. I know who it is."

"It's not a voice I recognize, Mr. Linz." Puffing on his pipe, the old man followed Jacob into the porter's lodge. Guardian of the college's only telephone, Simms had always made a point of remaining in the room so that he could clock the students' calls and charge them for the use of his ancient phone.

"If you don't mind, Mr. Simms," said Jacob, "I'd like to talk to my stepmother alone."

He cupped his ear again. "You what?"

"I said I want to talk to my stepmother alone!"

His anger startled the old man. "Indeed, Mr. Linz. In that case, I will wait outside." Puffing with indignation on the unlit pipe, Simms turned and went out.

He took the receiver and said, "Hello, this is Jacob."

"Jacob?"

The voice at the other end took him by complete surprise.

"Jacob, this is Maggie calling!"

He had always said that she could call him in Cambridge for any emergency, but until now she had never dared to telephone him. "Maggie!" he said. "Are you all right?"

"I need to see you, Jacob. I need to talk to you."

"What's wrong?" he asked, hearing the terror in her voice.

"I need to see you," she repeated. "I need to talk to you."

"What's wrong, Maggie? Has something happened?"

"You've got to come to London, Jacob!" she yelled. "I need you here!"

"Now calm down," he said, "talk slowly, and tell me what this is about."

"I can't tell you on the telephone! I want you to come to London!"

Searching his mind for all of the possible catastrophes that could have happened, he said, "But Maggie, you know I can't come to London now. For God's sake, tell me what's wrong!"

There was a moment of silence at the other end. "I can't talk about it on the telephone, Jacob," she said. "It's something private . . . something personal . . ." She began to cry. " . . . and I need you here.

"Please come!" she pleaded. "I'm scared, and I need you with me."

Something private, something personal: as the terrifying implications of her words crowded in on him, he could only stare out through the lodge's leaded-glass window at the students hurrying through the Great Gate to their one o'clock lectures.

"I didn't want to tell you, Jacob, not like this!" she blurted out. "I'm pregnant!" She broke into sobs. "I'm going to have a baby!"

Pregnant. He tried to form the word on his lips, but it stuck like a fist in his throat.

"Oh God, Jacob," she cried out, "I'm so scared!"

In the last two days he had thought of a hundred reasons he could give his father and Aloise for refusing to leave Maggie behind in England—but never this! "Maggie, sweetheart, are you sure?" he asked.

She stopped crying and when she spoke again, her voice was cold and deliberate. "Yes, I'm sure," she said.

He remembered the fear he had seen in her eyes last Friday night when he left her standing on the station platform. "Why didn't you tell me this when I saw you on Friday?" he asked.

"I wasn't sure on Friday," she said. "And I didn't want to stop you from going back to Cambridge."

"Have you seen a doctor?"

"I can't see a doctor, Jacob, not alone. I'm not married." She began to cry again. "You've got to come to London and help me!"

Outside in the alleyway, four students hurried by, their blue college gowns flapping in the warm summer breeze.

He thought of the trap closing in on his father in London and the promise he had made to remain in Cambridge. "I made a promise to Papa, Maggie, you know I can't come to London."

There was fierce resolution in her voice when she spoke again. "You must find a way to come," she said. "I can't go to my parents and there's no one I can turn to."

"Today is Wednesday," he pleaded, "and if I can find a way to talk to Papa, maybe I can come on Friday."

"Friday is too late, Jacob! I need to see a doctor today, and we have to go together!"

He looked around, feeling suffocated in the small porter's lodge, and suddenly remembered the broken promises in Berlin that had destroyed his family and driven him and his father from Germany.

"Jacob!" Maggie called, and began to weep.

"All right, Maggie," he said. "I will come."

She caught her breath and stopped crying. "I checked the train schedule," she said, "there's a 1:23 express to London."

He looked at the clock on Simms' desk. "But it's already five to one, and the station is over a mile from here!"

"You must try, Jacob!" she exclaimed. "The next train is the local 5:15! It won't get here until after seven!"

He thought of his options for reaching the Cambridge station in time for the 1:23. It was a five-minute taxi ride from Trinity Street, an eight minute bus ride from Market Hill, and a twenty minute trip by foot at a fast run. "All right," he said. "If I leave right now, I might make it."

"There's a bookstore near the station where we can meet," she said quickly. "It's one block east of King's Cross, at the corner of Albion Street—the Whitney Bookstore on Pentonville Road. Your train gets in at two fifty-five, and I'll meet you there at three."

"Three o'clock," he repeated, "at the Whitney Bookstore."

"I love you, Jacob, more than anything."

"And I love you too, more than anything," he said, but the line had disconnected before he finished the sentence.

By the clock on Simms' desk it was 12:56.

"That will be t'pence, Mr. Linz!" Simms called after him, as he hurried across the Hostel's entrance hall toward the staircase.

"Put it on my bill, Simms!" Jacob shouted back. Darting between the students racing to their one o'clock classes, he bounded up the staircase to the second floor.

He kept moving, taking the steps three at a time, and seconds later burst into his cramped rooms overlooking Nevile's Gate. "Merde!" he cursed, searching for his wallet amid the chaos of books and papers on his desk. With exactly twenty-five minutes to reach the station, every bloody second counted! Grabbing his jacket from the chair, he stuffed the wallet into his pocket and raced back out into the hallway.

As he left Bishop's Hostel and turned down the alleyway toward Nevile's Gate, the bell in King Edward's Tower tolled the hour. Running as fast as he could, he continued down Trinity Lane past Gonville and Caius College and came out into crowded Trinity Street.

Damn! he thought. There's not a single taxi in sight.

The blood pounded in his face as he zigzagged his way through the dense pedestrian traffic. It took a minute and a half, roughly, to reach Market Hill, and it was 1:03 when he drew up at the corner of Market Street.

"Scheisse!" he cursed aloud. Again, there wasn't a single taxi in sight.

He took a deep breath and quickly calculated his shrinking options. There was no point in gambling on the appearance of a bus, and the next likely street for a taxi would be St. Andrews.

Fighting to hold back back the panic that was rising inside him, he cut a diagonal path across the crowded market place and turned west along the crowded Petty Cury walkway. Racing past the Lion's Yard market, he came out into busy St. Andrews Street. Again, pausing to get his breath, he looked up and down the street at the congested automobile traffic.

It's hopeless, he thought, gazing up at the clock in Christ College tower. It was 1:15 and, unless the train was late, he had exactly eight minutes to make the mile and a half run to Cambridge station.

Ignoring both pedestrians and street traffic, he began to run. He pictured Maggie pacing the floor of her Camden Town bookstore, waiting for the lover, the father of her baby, who would never arrive. And he thought of the hopeless months he had spent waiting for his mother in Paris.

Off to the east, near Romsey Town, he heard the screech of the 1:23's whistle. In the distance, as he turned the corner of Parker Street, he saw the train coming into Cambridge station. He had caught a hundred trains before, and they always stopped for exactly three minutes to load and unload passengers.

Ignoring the automobile traffic, he took the center of the long tree-lined avenue and began counting off the interminable seconds that remained until the train's departure. It took an eternity of seconds to reach the station, and as he raced across the gravel parking lot fronting the small redbrick building, the train gave a short whistle and began to move. Rounding the south side of the building, he pushed his way past the station agent on duty at the gate and began running down the platform alongside the moving train.

"I say, young man! Stop!" the agent called after him.

Searching for an open carriage door, he suddenly realized that he had done this same thing before: the night he and his father boarded the moving train at Saabrücken. Only now, there were no doors open for him.

As the train picked up speed down the platform, he glanced back to see the last car pulling up alongside him: with its last carriage door still open. Dropping his jacket on the platform, he reached up to grasp the door's metal handle, but the train gave a sudden lurch and picked up speed.

It was useless. He came to a halt at the very end of the platform and bent over, gasping for air. The blood pounding at his face sent an ache through his head. When he lifted himself and wiped the sweat from his eyes, all that was left of the train was a shrinking black dot on the horizon.

He thought of Maggie waiting for him, and with a feeling of hopelessness he turned and started back down the platform toward the station building. Between now and three o'clock, there would be no way to reach her in London, and he realized, no way to warn her that he would miss their three o'clock rendezvous.

As he stopped to retrieve his jacket from the platform, the thought that came to him was like a sudden liberating reprieve. Fishing in his pockets for a telephone token, he hurried into the empty station and closed himself up in the public telephone booth. Inserting his one and only token, he dialed the London number of his father's office at the Imperial College.

The line connected and began ringing.

"Damn!" he exclaimed. His father was never one to be on time, but he should have been back from lunch by now!

He let the line ring seven times, then hung up.

The next best solution came to him as he removed the token from the telephone box. Aloise disliked and disapproved of Maggie, but in the light of her own reckless affair with his father in Paris she couldn't possibly refuse her woman's help.

Reinserting the token, he dialed the London number of the French Embassy.

The line rang only twice. "L'ambassade française," answered the male receptionist.

"Madame Linz, s'il vous plaît," said Jacob.

"Ne quittez pas, Monsieur." There was a moment's delay as the receptionist connected him to Aloise's office.

"Allô?" she responded.

"This is Jacob, Aloise," he said. "I'm calling from the train station in Cambridge."

She had told him on Monday not to phone her in London, and he could sense her bewildered surprise. "Yes, Jacob," she said, cautiously.

"I had to call," he said. "This is an emergency."

"An emergency?" she asked.

"It's Maggie," he said. "She called me from London a half hour ago. She's in trouble, and I need your help . . ."

As he told of the announcement Maggie had made on the telephone and of her desperate plea for him to come to London, he could hear the steady rise and fall of Aloise's breath at the other end of the line.

"She's frightened," he said, "and she wants to see a doctor. I told her I would take the 1:23 express and meet her near King's Cross at three o'clock, but I've missed the bloody train!"

"Where is Maggie now, Jacob?" Aloise asked.

"I don't know," he replied, and began himself to cry. "She called me from a phone booth in Soho."

"Now calm down, Jacob, and answer my questions," said Aloise. "Have you talked to your father today?"

He caught his breath. "I phoned his office a moment ago, but there was no answer."

"And you're to meet Maggie in London at three o'clock?"

"Yes."

"Where?"

"At the Whitney Bookstore on Pentonville Road near King's Cross station."

The heavy sigh at the other end of the line sounded strangely like defeat. "I see," she said.

"You've got to help me, Aloise!" he exclaimed. "She'll be waiting for me, and I won't be there!"

There was a moment of silence, then Aloise said with calm resolution, "I will meet Maggie myself, Jacob, and do everything I can to help her. But only on the condition that you do exactly what I tell you."

"If you'll just take care of her until I can get there," he said, "I'll do anything you want!"

"I'll be there, Jacob," she said with motherly reassurance. "In the meantime, I want you to go back to your rooms at the college and wait there until I contact you. Don't attempt to phone your father or anyone else in London. I will get back to you just as soon as Maggie and I have seen a doctor."

"All right, then," he said with relief. "I'll wait for your call."

"You were wise to phone me, Jacob," she said quietly. "After all, there's nothing in the world I wouldn't do for you."

He breathed with relief. "I knew I could count on you, Aloise," he said, but the line had already disconnected.

55

THAT morning, knowing she would never return to her South Lambeth flat, Katherine left everything as it was. Taking only her purse, her passport, and the money she had on hand, she went to work at the South Lambeth public library. At 1:45, complaining that she felt ill, she excused herself from work, left the library, and went to the Vauxhall tube station where she took a northbound train to Oxford Circus across the Thames. There, she changed to the Central London line for an eastbound train to Holborn. Though certain that she was not being followed, she none-theless changed trains again at Holborn Station, this time to a northbound train to King's Cross.

Last evening, when Michael Rakovsky met with her and David to explain the plan he had worked out for bringing the three of them safely together in London, he had described in detail what she must do. She must arrive at the Whitney Bookstore at exactly 2:55, he had said, "not a minute before or after."

Turning east, fighting the fear now crowding in on her, she slowly walked the three short blocks to Killick Street, pausing here and there at a shop window to waste the extra four minutes she had gained between trains at Holborn Station. At exactly 2:55, she entered the Whitney Bookstore.

Specializing in second-hand technical books, the Whitney was just as Rakovsky had described it: a rabbit warren of shelves stacked to the ceiling with books in every language. Occupying the center of the big room were tables with books arranged according to the various technical dis-ciplines. Rakovsky was already present, browsing among the books on a table labeled Aviation.

She closed the door and quickly surveyed the other customers in the shop. A young man with close-cropped brown hair was at the Geog-raphy table next to the door. In the center of the store, a blonde-haired girl in a blue dress was browsing among the books on the Medical table.

From the description David had given her, she knew at once that the girl was Maggie Ryder.

Rakovsky's instructions had been exact. Ignoring the other customers, and with no acknowledgment from either Rakovsky or Miss Ryder, she went directly to the sales counter at the back of the store, where an old man wearing a gray smock was sorting books. Told by Rakovsky which book to ask for, she said, "Excuse me, sir. I'm looking for a German edition of Einstein's *Theory of General and Special Relativity.*"

Glancing up, the old man said with impatience, "You mean, *Die Theorie von allgemeine und besondere Relativität?*"

"Yes. The 1917 Leipzig edition."

"You'll find that in the first alcove of the science section, Madam," he said, pointing to a row of shelves against the far right-hand wall.

"Thank you." Wondering if Rakovsky had purposefully chosen the most secluded place in the bookstore, she went to a small alcove between two shelves extending at right angles from the wall. From there, though concealed from the rest of the store by the books stacked along the alcove's outer wall, the store's front door and windows, as well as the patrons moving among the tables, were in clear view.

Pretending to inspect one of the aviation books, Rakovsky was watching a customer who had just entered: a middle-aged man wearing round gold spectacles, a gray business suit, and a black bowler hat, who was browsing among the books on the Horticulture table in the center of the store.

She looked at her watch: 2:58. Last evening, explaining his plan, Rakovsky had said that there were always contingencies to any human plan like this. Jacob, he had calculated, would arrive at roughly three o'clock, provided his express train from Cambridge was on time; and then David in a taxi two or three minutes later, depending on the traffic.

She peered through the shelves, watching Jacob's young lover—a girl she had never met—nervously rummaging among the medical books. Two and a half years had gone by since she last laid eyes on her son, but it was the last week—these last seven days—that had been the hardest to bear. Lacking any photographs of Jacob, she had lived on David's verbal description of the boy. He would be as tall as David, with his father's black curly hair and her blue eyes.

He has inherited a little from each of us, David had jokingly said, but thank God it's only the best of both.

It was hard to believe that in two months he would be twenty years old.

She looked at her watch again—2:59—and thought of her miraculous encounter with David last Wednesday. It was as if God had driven them from the garden of Eden to punish her for the sin of pride and then, in his infinite mercy, had decided to give her a second chance at paradise.

In her nervousness, Maggie suddenly dropped the book she was reading. When she bent down to retrieve it from the floor, the ribbon holding her hair came undone and her long blonde hair fell about her face.

The sudden change in her appearance startled Katherine. In a different world, she thought, she could have been my daughter.

When Maggie looked up, their eyes met for an instant.

The terror Katherine saw in Maggie's pale blue eyes was contagious. She moved deeper into the alcove and took down what she immediately recognized as the edition of Einstein's *Theory* she had asked for. Rakovsky, she was sure, had chosen the title as an omen of good luck, for it was the first book David had given her when they were students together in Göttingen. She turned the familiar pages, wondering to herself at the relativity of human space and time: that after wandering so far away from one another, she and David and Jacob would come together again in a second-hand Camden Town bookstore.

When she looked at her watch again, it was 3:01. Panic overtook her, and her heart began to beat rapidly.

The gentleman in the bowler hat, she saw, began moving along the table in the center of the room, heading toward Maggie at the Medical table.

She could feel the sudden tension in the room.

Rakovsky checked his watch, then looked at the young man.

Pressing the book to her breast, Katherine looked out at the traffic passing in front of the store. Assuming that David was being watched by the NKVD, Rakovsky had taken the precaution of having Jacob arrive at the bookstore first. Once David entered, it would take only seconds to bundle the three of them out the store's back door to the car that would be waiting in the alley.

Something had gone wrong, though—an accident of human space and time, she realized, that was beyond anyone's control. With an overwhelming feeling of dread, she closed her eyes and began to pray.

There was the sound of another book striking the floor. When she opened her eyes, she saw Maggie watching the door with a look of fear on her face.

She saw what the girl was staring at. David, who had just arrived, was leaning forward in a taxi parked at the curb before the store's front door, paying the driver.

For once, she thought, he's on time. Katherine watched as David opened the taxi's passenger door and stepped out into the hazy afternoon sunlight.

It seemed to happen in an instant. The man in the bowler hat stepped forward and removed a gun from his breast pocket, as Rakovsky and the

American-looking young man left the geography table and took positions on either side of the door.

As David closed the taxi's door and turned around, there was a report like the backfire of a car. With a look of shock, David lifted both arms and took a single step forward.

It was as if he had been struck by a stone from behind. David reached out with his right hand toward the bookstore's door, then took another step and fell face forward on the sidewalk.

Rakovsky and his young companion began backing away from the door with their pistols pointed at the bookstore's windows.

Paralyzed by horror, Katherine watched as two men, with pistols drawn, converged on David where he had fallen just outside the bookstore's door.

A wail that came from Maggie—the wail of a lost child—broke the spell of Katherine's disbelief. Katherine screamed out, "David!" and raced from her hiding place in the alcove.

"No, Katherine!" Rakovsky stepped forward to intercept her.

"Dammit, let me go!" she shrieked as he grabbed hold of her arm. "He's my husband!"

"No, Katherine!" he repeated. "You can't help him now!"

"You've got to find Jacob!" Maggie yelled furiously.

"Peter, start the car. Alan, bring the girl and let's get out of here!" Rakovsky called to the man in the bowler hat.

Fighting to free her arms, Katherine felt herself being dragged backward toward the sales counter.

"Listen to me," Rakovsky said, grasping her savagely by the shoulders. "There's nothing you can do for David or Jacob, and if you go out there, they will kill you, too."

As the man in the bowler hat swept past them toward the store's back door, supporting Maggie in his arms, she began to weep, helplessly.

"Jacob is not going to come," said Rakovsky. "And you and Maggie must leave here at once." Closing her up in his arms, with his pistol raised in his right hand, he guided her through the store's rear door into a narrow cobblestoned alley. A large black foreign-looking car was parked in the alley, with its motor running and its passenger door open. The young man was in the driver's seat, and Maggie and the man with the bowler hat were already inside.

"Get in," Rakovsky ordered.

It was as if she had suddenly awakened from a terrifying nightmare, only to find that the nightmare had been real. Realizing that everything she had found was now lost again, this time forever, she absently let go of the Einstein volume she had been holding.

"Leave it," said Rakovsky as she reached down to retrieve the book from the pavement.

She obeyed.

Rakovsky put her next to Maggie in the back seat, then ran to the other side and got in. As the car pulled away, she looked back through the rear window at her omen of good luck lying amid the alley's trash.

56

S H E had made the trip from London by car only once before—the day she and David drove Jacob up to Cambridge to take his university entrance exams—but the ancient country towns they had visited were still vivid in her mind. Four miles north of Harlow, Aloise came to the small Hertfordshire farming town of Bishop's Stortford.

It was exactly four thirty when she parked her secretary's old Morris Minor in front of the town's small brick railroad station. Praying that Jacob had obeyed her instructions, she got out and hurried toward the station's waiting room. It had taken her less than forty-five minutes to contact Konstantin Volkov, the director of the NKVD in London, and arrange everything. She had never worked so fast or so efficiently. She had telephoned Jacob at 2:45, just before leaving London, and had told the boy to pack a single suitcase, bring his passport and any atomic research he had, and take the 3:55 London local as far as Bishop's Stortford. Refusing to give an explanation or talk about Maggie on the telephone, she had simply said that she would come to collect him from the Bishop's Stortford railway station at four thirty.

She smiled to herself as she entered the station. It was encouraging to think how swift Volkov had acted when she informed him of David's decision to reject the Soviet Union's demand for the British government's MAUD report. His plan, she had said, was to rendezvous that afternoon with agents of British MI5 at a bookstore on the Pentonville Road. There, in exchange for a complete list of Soviet intelligence operatives working in England, he was planning to demand safe passage from the country and asylum for himself in America.

Except for a uniformed railway agent behind the ticket window, the station's small waiting room was deserted. "Excuse me," she said, "could you tell me if the 3:55 local from Cambridge has passed through yet?"

The old man looked up from the tin box into which he was counting money. "Yes, ma'am. About ten minutes ago. The 3:55 train from Cambridge stops here at 4:19."

A feeling of panic came over her.

"Did you notice if a young man—a tall young man with black hair— got off the train here?"

"No, ma'am. I didn't look to see who got off the train," the agent said, and went back to counting his money into the box. "But you might check the station platform."

As Aloise turned toward the door leading out to the platform, she thought to herself: if Jacob has missed his train and stayed in Cambridge, then the police will have found him by now and told him everything.

The thought made her panic, for she had not, until now, considered the possibility that she might be forced to leave England without the boy.

She stopped just outside the door and looked down the platform: He was there.

He caught sight of her and started to rise, then sat back down.

She had debated with herself on the drive up from London whether she would tell him the news of his father's death here at the station or wait until they were alone in the car. But she could see from the expression in his face that he already knew that something terrible had happened.

As she began walking toward him down the platform, she tried to recall the speech she had practiced during the drive from London, but in the panic that had overtaken her in the station, she had forgotten it.

When she reached the bench, she said, "I'm sorry you had to wait, Jacob."

Shifting himself uneasily on the bench, he asked, "Where is my father?"

It was the echo of David's deep voice and the sight of the boy's blue eyes—his mother's blue eyes—that reignited the anger she felt. Now, recalling the speech she had practiced, she sat down and said, "I'm afraid I have bad news for you, Jacob. There's been a terrible accident." The word accident caught in her throat as she said it.

For a moment, he sat looking off toward something beyond the station platform, then said, "What do you mean, a terrible accident?"

She suddenly remembered the desperate grief he had suffered last year in Paris, following the announcement of his mother's death. Realizing that it was pointless to comfort him, she reached over and took his hand where it rested on his knee. "Your father is dead, Jacob," she said. "He was shot this afternoon by agents of the British Secret Service, trying to resist arrest."

The boy went on staring at the row of dilapidated council houses opposite the station and said nothing.

"I did as you asked me to do, Jacob," she said. "I went to the address you gave me near King's Cross station. I was ten minutes late, and when I got to the Whitney Bookstore there was a crowd gathered in the street. I couldn't see what had happened, but I heard people talking." She gripped the boy's hand. "They were talking about a man who had been shot trying to resist arrest. He drew a gun, and one of the British Secret Service agents shot him."

She could feel the rigid tension in the boy's hand. He said, "You're mistaken. It couldn't have been Papa." A whimper broke and caught in the boy's throat, then a shudder went through his body.

He said, trying to contain the quiver in his voice, "Maggie was terrified when she called me. When she told me she was going to have a baby, she broke down and cried."

It had taken Aloise most of the afternoon to construct her story, and she was sure that she had thought of every conceivable angle. "I warned you, Jacob, not to put your trust in a girl like Maggie Ryder," she said. "I warned you that she would think it her duty to report anything suspicious to the authorities. You told her everything, didn't you—about my membership in the Party and about your father's work."

The boy's silence was an admission.

Aloise went on with relentless determination. "Maggie was there at the bookstore," she said, "and when they took your father's body away, she got into a car and drove off with two Secret Service agents."

Saying nothing, Jacob withdrew his hand, got up, and walked to the very end of the station platform.

For a moment, Aloise watched in silence as he stood looking off down the line of railway tracks. Realizing that time was running out, she left the bench and went to him. "You must listen to me, Jacob," she said, "for your own life, as well as mine, may depend upon what you decide. When I left the bookstore, I telephoned Konstantin Volkov, the director of the Soviet NKVD here in England, and informed him of your father's murder. He told me what I already suspected—that warrants would undoubtedly be issued by the British authorities for our arrests."

The boy muttered something to himself in German, but she could only make out the word *Berlin*.

"At ten o'clock tonight," she said, "in exactly five and a half hours, a Portuguese merchant ship will be leaving the port of Plymouth, bound for Lisbon. The Soviet Embassy in London, Volkov tells me, will arrange passage for both you and me on the ship."

He said, looking off down the empty tracks toward the sunlit horizon, "It was Moscow, wasn't it, that arranged our passage last year to England?"

"Yes, Jacob."

"First, the Nazis," he said, "and now the British. I can't go on running forever, Aloise."

She suddenly remembered the words David had said the afternoon she confronted him with the fact of Katherine's return: You took a big risk, Aloise, when you accepted the job with Russian intelligence here in England. Stalin is merciless with those who compromise their loyalty to the Kremlin.

She moved closer to the boy, thinking of her own desperate hopes for a future in the Party after the costly compromises she had made in France and England.

Jacob turned away and leaned against the concrete post supporting the platform roof. "After Berlin," he said, "after what my mother did in Berlin, all Papa wanted was to stop the terrible thing they had started in Germany."

She reached out and gently rested her hand on the boy's shoulder. "Jacob," she said, "all those things that happened in Germany are finished now."

"Papa never admitted it, but he hated the work he was doing here in England," he said, and began to cry softly. "He hated using his scientific knowledge to build a nuclear bomb, but he couldn't forget what he and my mother had done for the Nazis in Germany."

She took Jacob by the shoulders and turned him to face her, just as she had done countless times with David in his moments of despair. "The past is finished, and you've got to let go of your father now and start building a future for yourself." She closed her eyes and drew the boy into her arms.

Like a small child, he lowered his head into the crook of her neck and began to weep, helplessly.

57

IT had taken Katherine and Maggie two and a half hours to make the drive from London to Cambridge in the dilapidated Humber Maggie had borrowed from her parents, and a misty twilight had already fallen over the Hertfordshire countryside as they drove up the King's Parade into the town's medieval center. Neither one of them had ever visited Cambridge, and they had stopped three times to ask directions to Trinity College.

As Katherine made a left turn into the narrow cobblestoned street that ran between Gonville and Caius College and Trinity College, Maggie spoke up. "It was foolish of us to come here on our own," she said. "We should have listened to Major Rakovsky and stayed in London."

Katherine shifted into first, searching the buildings on her right for the entrance to Trinity College. "That's nonsense, Maggie. We're doing what we have to do."

"But it's almost seven o'clock; and if Jacob missed the 1:23 London express, the NKVD will have found him by now."

The truth of her statement silenced Katherine. She pulled up to the curb, turned off the car's motor and headlights, and sat for a moment thinking of the hour and fifteen minutes they had lost at Michael Rakovsky's apartment in London, waiting for news of Jacob. Following David's murder, the major had driven her and Maggie to his flat in South Kensington, where he had insisted they remain until he could find a safe house for them. That was shortly after three o'clock. At 3:30, having promised that he would notify the Cambridge police of the danger that Jacob was in, he had set off to inform Scotland Yard of the facts surrounding David's murder. Then at 4:45, having waited in vain for Rakovsky's phone call, she and Maggie left the apartment and had set off on their own to find Jacob.

"There's a chance that he's still in Cambridge," Katherine said. "We can't just give up hope."

"I'm frightened, Katherine." The girl looked around at the darkening mist.

"It's all right, Maggie," Katherine said, opening her driver's door. "Let's take this one step at a time."

The girl left the car and joined her as she hurried up the sidewalk toward a vaulted archway between two huge stone-faced buildings. "Jacob's rooms are in Bishop's Hostel," she said, "but he never told me where the building is located."

"Never mind." Katherine turned down the dark passageway. "We'll ask directions when we get inside."

"Twice, Jacob invited me to come and visit him in Cambridge," Maggie said, her voice echoing from the cavernous walls. "But I was too ashamed to meet his university friends, and both times I refused."

At once, Katherine understood the guilt she heard in the girl's voice. In the hour they had spent together in Michael Rakovsky's flat, she had recounted the telephone conversation she had had with Jacob, and she insisted that she was responsible for everything that had happened that afternoon.

"You've got to stop blaming yourself, Maggie." Katherine reached out in the darkness and put her arm around the girl's shoulder. "The plan for bringing Jacob to London was Major Rakovsky's idea, and you only did what he told you to do."

"Jacob believed me when I told him I was pregnant!" she protested. "I'm sure of it!"

"Listen to me, Maggie." Katherine drew the girl closer. "Jacob loves you; and if he's here in Cambridge, we'll find him and tell him every-thing."

They emerged from the passageway into a large quadrangle surrounded on all sides by four-story stone buildings. Footsteps came toward them in the blackout darkness. "Excuse me, young man," she called out, "can you tell us the way to Bishop's Hostel?"

He came toward them, rounding a canopied fountain in the center of the quandrangle. "Follow me," he said. "I'm going there myself."

They joined the young man as he continued toward the southwest corner of the quadrangle. "We've never been here before," said Maggie, "and we don't know our way around the college."

The young man laughed. "Trinity's a labyrinth. And if you've never been here before, you'll have a hell of time finding your way in this blackout."

"I've come from London to see my son," said Katherine. "He's a first-year student at Trinity College."

"I'm a first-year student myself," he said. "What's your son's name?"

"Jacob Linz," she replied.

"Linz, of course! I know Jacob very well!" He picked up speed as they entered another long dark passageway. "We both have rooms at Bishop's Hostel."

Katherine felt a sudden sense of hopeful excitement.

"So you're the famous stepmother Jacob has told us about," the young man said.

The word stepmother instantly demolished Katherine's excitement. Realizing that she had neither the strength nor the courage to explain herself, she gave Maggie's arm a cautioning touch in the darkness. "Actually, I'm not famous at all," she said.

The young man drew up in front of a four-story brick building. "This is Bishop's Hostel," he said. "But I'm afraid you won't find Jacob in his rooms."

The statement brought Katherine to an abrupt halt. "What do you mean?"

"He stopped by my rooms about three hours ago," the young man said. "He had a suitcase with him, and he said he was going away on a short holiday."

Maggie spoke up, "A holiday? To where?"

"I don't know. He didn't say. But if you come this way, you can ask Mr. Simms, the porter, if he's seen Jacob."

They followed the young man into the hostel.

"If you ring that bell on the wall there, Simms will be out in a minute," he said, and continued across the room toward the staircase.

"Please wait!" Katherine called after him, but the young man had raced up the staircase and vanished before she could ask him anything more.

Katherine rang the bell, and a few moments later a wizened little man, wearing a threadbare tweed jacket, appeared. "Good evening, ladies. Welcome to Bishop's Hostel," he said, puffing on an unlit pipe. "I'm Wilfred Simms, the hall porter."

"We've come to see Jacob Linz," said Maggie.

"Who?" the old man asked, cupping his hand to his ear.

"Jacob Linz!" Katherine shouted.

"Ah! Linz!" A look of puzzled surprise came over the old man's face. "I'm afraid Jacob Linz isn't here."

Katherine moved forward and raised her voice. "It's most urgent that we find him. Can you tell us where he's gone?"

"The police were here looking for the boy," he said. "You're not from the police, are you?"

"No," said Katherine. "We're not from the police."

"This is a frightful thing, ladies," the old man said, puffing nervously on his pipe. "Bishop's Hostel has never had trouble with the police before."

Seeing the old man's muddled confusion, Katherine said, "I am Katherine Linz, Mr. Simms. Jacob's mother. And I've come here from London to find him."

"Ah!" The old man's face brightened. "So you're the woman who called here this afternoon."

The color drained from young Maggie's face.

"No, Mr. Simms," said Katherine. "I am not the woman who called here this afternoon. I told you, I'm Jacob's mother."

"His mother?" The old man shook his head.

"I don't have time to explain, Mr. Simms. You must tell me where Jacob has gone."

He stepped back and adjusted his bow tie. "As I told the police," he said, "I don't know where young Linz has gone."

In a sudden rage of frustration, Katherine shouted at the old man, "Then for God's sake, tell me what you do know!"

Startled, the old man dropped his pipe. "I only know what I told the police," he said. "Young Linz's mother phoned here at two thirty. I keep a record of the calls here, and I know that young Linz talked to his mother for a minute and a half. After that, he went up to his rooms, packed a suitcase, and came back at exactly three thirty. I remember the time because he told me he was in a hurry, that he had to catch the 3:55 London local."

Maggie looked with panic at Katherine. "I told you, we should have stayed in London."

"Did the boy tell you where he was going to in London?" Katherine asked.

The old man cupped his ear. "Did he what?"

"I said, did he tell you where he was going in London?"

"You're getting everything confused," the old man said. "The boy wasn't going to London. He said he was meeting his mother in Bishop's Stortford. He also said something rather idiotic about having to leave the country, tonight."

In the moment it took for Katherine to realize the meaning of the old man's words, she listened with growing horror as the clock in the college tower began to toll the seven o'clock hour.

58

A DENSE fog was beginning to roll in off the channel as Michael Rakovsky rounded the crest of the hill overlooking the port of Plymouth. In the foggy blackout darkness at the foot of the hill, where the town tumbled down to the water's edge, he could make out the faint shape of three ship funnels amid the warehouses of the port's congested waterfront.

As he braked to slow his car, he heard from somewhere far off in the darkness the plaintive moan of a harbor foghorn.

Wearily, he looked at his watch: 5:35. Over seven hours had passed since the alert had gone out from Scotland Yard to the port authorities at Southampton, Folkestone, and Plymouth to be on the lookout for Katherine Linz and Maggie Ryder. Inspector Collins had telephoned from Scotland Yard shortly after one o'clock to say that the two women had been identified and detained by the Plymouth harbor police. They had left Cambridge about seven thirty and had driven first to Folkestone, then to Plymouth, where they had arrived at approximately 12:30, an hour and a half after the *Cascais* had sailed for Lisbon.

At the foot of the main street, Rakovsky came to a long fenced-in wharf lined with newly built corrugated metal warehouses. The sign posted on the fence above the wharf's metal gate read Pier 4.

Pier 4, he remembered, was where Inspector Collins had said he would find the offices of Plymouth's harbor police.

As he steered his car toward the uniformed harbor policeman on duty at the sentry box, Rakovsky removed his American military I.D. card from his uniform pocket.

"Good morning," he said, handing the card through the window, "I'm Major Michael Rakovsky, U.S. Army Corps of Engineers, G2 Division."

"Good morning, Major." The young man saluted, took the card, and checked it in his flashlight beam. "We were told to expect you, sir. You can go right in." He handed the card back. "The harbor police office is at the end of this pier—the last building on your left."

"Thanks, son." Rakovsky moved on through the gate and drove past the pier's darkened warehouses. On his right, looming up in the foggy darkness, he passed three huge ships anchored prow to stern down the length of the pier. All three ships were flying American flags: merchant ships, he realized, from one of Roosevelt's hard-won arms convoys to the beleaguered British.

Just beyond the prow of the third ship, he came to an open mooring space at the end of the pier. Directly opposite the space, shrouded by the fog rolling in off the harbor, stood a small wooden barrack-like building with a sign, "Harbor Police," posted above the door. Parked in front of the building was a police car, and next to the police car an old four-door Humber.

He pulled up beside the police car, got out, and looked back at the empty mooring space opposite the station: the space, undoubtedly, where the *Cascais* had been docked.

For a moment, he stood listening to the steady clank of a fog buoy far out in the harbor's channel, thinking to himself of yesterday's chaotic events. Following his visit to Scotland Yard, he had tried to telephone Katherine and Maggie at his apartment to tell them that the Cambridge police were conducting an all-out search for Jacob. By then, the police had issued a warrant for Aloise's arrest, and it was clear that she had either fled the city or was in hiding. Realizing only then that Katherine and Maggie had left his apartment and were undoubtedly heading for Cambridge, he had notified Scotland Yard who, in turn, had ordered the police in Cambridge to be on the lookout for the two women. The frustrating thing was knowing that he and Scotland Yard were moving two steps behind the women, and it had taken them another two hours to assemble the pieces of the puzzle and post the alert in Southhampton, Folkestone, and Plymouth.

Far out in the harbor, like a clock tolling the wasted hours, the fog buoy went on clanking its warning to the passing ships. With a feeling of helpless frustration, he thought to himself: By now, the boy's ship will have reached the coast of France.

Turning his back on the empty mooring space, knowing that it was pointless trying to justify his failure to Katherine, he hurried into the harbor police station.

As he opened the door, the police officer on duty at the desk awoke with a start. "Good evening, sir," he said, looking up in groggy confusion.

"I'm afraid it's already morning, son," Rakovsky said, glancing around the empty room as he removed his ID card from his uniform pocket. "I'm Major Michael Rakovsky, U.S. Army Corps of Engineers, G2 Division."

"Ah. Yes, of course. We've been expecting you." The officer sat forward and took the card. "You'll have to excuse me, sir," he said, wearily. "It's been a long night."

"Yes, it has," Michael said. "For all of us."

"I take it, you're here to sign the release papers for the two women we've been holding in custody."

"That's correct."

The young man shook his head and sighed. "We've held all kinds of people in overnight detention before," he said, "but never the likes of these two."

"What do you mean?"

Handing the card back, the young man took a cigarette from his desk drawer. "We had a call last night from Scotland Yard about ten o'clock to be on the lookout for a German woman and a young English girl," he said, lighting the cigarette. "Around twelve thirty they appeared at the gate, asking questions about a Portuguese merchant ship, the *Cascais*, which had sailed from Pier 4 at ten o'clock. When we brought them in, they were pretty upset, especially the German woman. She kept insisting that her son was among the passengers who had sailed on the *Cascais*— and that he was traveling with a French woman who had forced him to board the ship against his will." He took a long drag on his cigarette, then said, "We checked with the passport control officer, and a French woman had boarded the ship with a German man; but the woman, they told us, was his stepmother. When we tried to explain to the German woman that we had no reason to stop him from boarding the ship with his stepmother, she became hysterical. It took an hour to calm her down."

"Where is Dr. Linz now?" Rakovsky asked.

"She came to me about four o'clock, saying she wanted to get some fresh air. This is a guarded fenced-in area, so I let her take a walk on the pier."

"And Miss Ryder?"

"The girl said she was pregnant and was having chills, so I let her sit by the stove in the canteen," he said, indicating the door behind his desk. "She's been there all night."

"If you'll tell Miss Ryder that I'm here," said Michael, "I'll go look for Dr. Linz and then come back and sign their release papers."

As he opened the door, the officer said, "When I checked on the German woman about an hour ago, she was walking along the empty mooring space across the pier."

"I'll find her," he said, and went out.

In the few moments that had gone by, the fog had rolled in, blanketing the entire pier. Leaving the station, Rakovsky walked out to the empty space where Jacob's ship had been moored. Off to the east, through the swirling fog, he could just make out the first faint glow of morning light. When he reached the water's edge, he turned along the mooring space and headed toward the open end of the pier. Guided only by the noise of the surf beating against the pier's wooden pilings, unable to see more than five feet ahead of him, he was almost to the end of the pier when he saw her faintly silhouetted against the rising light.

He stopped and watched Katherine stare off through the impenetrable fog toward the mouth of the harbor and the open sea.

She must have heard his footsteps, for she turned and looked back in his direction.

"It's me, Katherine," he said. "Mike Rakovsky."

Saying nothing, she turned away and looked back out at the faint ribbon of light that was spreading across the horizon.

Against the steady clank of the fog buoy far out in the harbor, her silence rang in his ear like an accusation. On a sudden impulse to justify himself, he said, "I did what I said I would do, Katherine. I went to Scotland Yard, and I told them about Jacob. But by the time the Cambridge police got to the college, he had gone."

"You should have at least telephoned to tell me what was happening, Michael," she said. "We waited for your phone call for almost two hours."

It was useless, he realized, trying to explain his failure to find her son, for the entire escape plan had been his, and he felt responsible for everything that had happened. "I didn't come here to justify what's happened, Katherine," he said. "I came to take you home."

For a moment, she went on staring at the light rising along the horizon. Then she said, her words barely audible under the wind, "The worst part of it is, Jacob doesn't even know I'm alive."

"I'm sorry, Katherine. It never occurred to me that Aloise would take him with her."

"Whether she decided to kill my son or take him with her, it comes to the same thing, Michael."

Alarmed by the defeat he heard in her voice, he quickly walked to the end of the pier. "Listen to me," he said. "You've been out here long enough. It's almost morning, and we've got to take Maggie back to London."

"This is the same port where David and Jacob arrived when they came to England," she said. "And I intend to see it in the daylight."

She looked down at the tide beating against the wooden pilings. "When I left Germany and came to England, I thought that I had destroyed everything and that my life was finished. Then last week—whether it was an accident or an act of God, I don't know—I thought I had been given a second chance." She lifted her head as the foghorn at the mouth of the bay gave off a long plaintive moan. "But it wasn't true," she said. "And this time, I have lost my husband and son forever."

He suddenly remembered the twenty-four long years he had spent grieving for his lost wife and son. With an impulse to comfort her, he reached out and touched her shoulder. "Your son is alive, Katherine," he said. "It may take time; but God willing, you will find him again."

"I've spent the last two and a half years praying that I would one day see my husband and son again," she said. "And I will not spend the rest of my life praying for something that God has taken from me, twice."

He moved an inch closer. Her hair had fallen about her shoulders. The wind lifted it and blew it against his face. "Jacob is your son, Katherine, your flesh and blood, and he's the only family you have left. You can stop praying, if you want; but you must never give up hope."

She looked back down at the water rolling under the pier. "I'm so tired," she said. "The war has gone on now for three years, and it seems as if it will last forever. I want to go to a place where I can forget Hitler and Germany and the nightmare I have made of my life."

"Where?" he asked. "The war is everywhere."

"I don't know. Just some place where I can rest."

He suddenly thought of the bargain he had struck with David and Katherine that afternoon in his office . . . and the hope of a new life in America he had offered them. "The fact is," he said, "I have so far said nothing to Scotland Yard about Aloise's involvement with the Soviets. I may be wrong, of course, but there's every chance that the Russians know nothing about your presence here in England. If they did find out that you're alive, however, and that you know everything about Aloise's and David's espionage, they will kill you."

She turned with astonishment. "I thought you would have told Scotland Yard everything."

"I told them only what they needed to know to issue a warrant for Aloise's arrest. I said it was a case of jealousy and passion—that Aloise had made a bigamous marriage in France, that you had reappeared in England, and that she had had David murdered rather than give him up. It will take them time to discover all the facts, but time is what we need right now."

"Time?" she asked. "What do you mean?"

He hesitated, listening to the tolling clank of the channel buoy, then said, "I made a bargain with you and David. I failed in part of it, but the offer still holds."

She stared at him, her hair blowing across her face, and said nothing.

"I'm offering you asylum in America, Katherine," he said.

She considered his statement, then turned away to look back at the light rising across the harbor. "I cannot go back to what I was in Germany, Michael," she said. "My ambitions as a scientist have been the cause of everything evil that has happened to me and my family."

He moved still closer. "I take it David told you that the Germans are working on an atom bomb."

"Yes. He told me that the Army has taken over the Kaiser-Wilhelm Institute and they're hard at work on a bomb of their own."

"If they build the bomb before we do, Katherine, they'll win the war."

Suddenly, from the direction of the harbor's mouth, came the deep moan of a ship's horn.

"With David, and now Jacob gone, the only responsibility I have left, Michael, is to Maggie," she said. "She is a month and a half pregnant."

She reached up, covered her face with both hands, and began to cry.

He said, quietly, "If to no one else, you owe it to David to carry out his part of the bargain and finish in America what you both started in Germany."

As she lowered her hands from her face, the fog bank rolling in across the harbor suddenly parted, like a curtain, revealing a long convoy of warships—three destroyers and four escorts—heading toward the mouth of the harbor and the open channel seas.

He sensed where her thoughts were running. "If it makes a difference, I will extend the offer to include Maggie. It may take months for Roosevelt to negotiate the American takeover of the Tube Alloys project, but in the meantime, while Maggie is waiting for her child, you and she can live in the house I own outside Washington."

He suddenly thought back to June of 1917, and the telegram that came to him in France announcing the death of his wife and child. "This time, Katherine, there will be no mistakes. I will arrange everything for you and Maggie from England; and when I've finished my work here for the president, I will join you in America."

FIVE

59

H E could see the face of the man opposite him clearly reflected in his own carriage window: the Tartar eyes and the large forehead. When he left the Lebedev a half hour ago, it was dark and raining, but he was sure that he had been the man amid the crowd in the street outside the Institute.

Jacob looked down at the bouquet of flowers he was carrying. It was three nights ago—the night he and Natasha Bolnitskaya dined together at the Aragvi restaurant on Gorki Street—that he first realized he was being watched by the NKVD. It had happened four years ago, when he and Aloise first arrived in Moscow; but this time, he was sure that the NKVD's sudden interest in him was not the result of Commissar Beria's well known suspicion of foreigners. This time, the NKVD's surveillance had coincided with the government's decision to build the new Dmitrov plutonium reactor north of Moscow—a project he had been promoting for almost a year now, ever since he first joined the Lebedev Institute.

Half the passengers in the carriage were workers heading for their nighttime factory shifts at the Lenin Suburb's Stalin Works. As the Metro pulled into the station at Krestyanskaya Square, they left their seats and formed a line in the aisle.

Krestyanskaya Square, he thought, is one stop early, but there's no law in Russia against taking a walk at night in the rain. Clutching his bouquet of flowers, he waited until the line began to move, then quickly got up, left the carriage, and merged with the crowd hurrying toward the station's escalator.

He had visited Natasha's apartment only once before, the evening he accompanied her home from supper at the Aragvi, but they had left the Metro at the next stop, and she had led the way. It would be a good

fifteen-minute walk from Krestyanskaya Square to her apartment on Len-
inskaya Sloboda Street.

When he reached the sidewalk outside the station, he stopped and
looked back at the sea of expressionless Russian faces moving toward him
through the marble station lobby. Maybe I was wrong, he thought. For
there was no sign of the Eurasian-looking man in the crowd.

He looked down again at the bouquet of spring flowers he had bought
for his celebration that night at the Lebedev. It was to have been a modest
little party to celebrate the government's approval of the Dmitrov plutonium reactor—a drink in his office after work with Igor Kurchatov,
the Institute's director, and three of his colleagues—but no one had
bothered to show.

To hell with them, he thought. If I can't celebrate the future of Russia's
nuclear industry with my colleagues at the Lebedev, then I can at least
celebrate it with Natasha.

Shifting the bouquet of flowers to his left hand, he took from his
raincoat pocket the bottle of Yubileinaya vodka he had brought to work
that morning. It was the best vodka you could find in Moscow—vodka
that only privileged Party members like Aloise had been able to obtain
during the war. Ignoring the disapproving stares from the people passing
him on the sidewalk, he uncorked the bottle and took a swallow of the
fortifying liquor.

It had been his dream since coming to Russia to complete the research
his father had left unfinished in England and, as a triumph of revenge
for his murder by the Allies, to help the Soviets build an atom bomb of
their own. Nonetheless, his colleagues' absence that night had been the
culmination of a year of frustration at the Lebedev. Since September of
last year, when he came to the Lebedev from the University of Moscow,
he had been urging the government to invest in the construction of an
atom bomb. At that first meeting with Igor Kurchatov, he had given a
full account of his father's work for the Tube Alloys project in England.
But that work had been done four years ago, and he had warned the
Institute's director that the Allies would be far advanced by now in the
experimental development of both the uranium and plutonium atom
bombs. Pleading his case for the post-war balance of nuclear power in
Europe, he had obtained permission to continue his father's plutonium
critical-mass calculations—the research that Aloise had brought with her
to Russia.

He drank another fortifying mouthful of vodka, then recorked the bottle. What had puzzled and disappointed him tonight was the fact that Kurchatov had not bothered to acknowledge the invitation to his little victory celebration. After all, it was he who had urged the government to build the reactor and it was he who, despite the criticism he had received from the more conservative scientists at the Institute, had backed him in his year-long battle with Beria's bureaucratic Commissariat of Atomic Sciences for experimental funding of his plutonium research.

Thrusting the bottle back into his raincoat pocket, he turned down the broad Krutitsky Val, heading toward the heart of Moscow's industrial district.

I should have planned to celebrate with Natasha in the first place, he thought. After all, she's the one who will carry out the experimental side of the critical-mass calculations. It would take maybe ten or eleven months to complete the reactor, but he had already explained his critical-mass theory to her, and she had agreed to ask for Kurchatov's permission to perform the experiments.

As he came to the end of the Krutitsky Val, he stopped and looked around at the brick apartment buildings Stalin had built during the war for the factory workers. Until three nights ago, knowing that he had experienced the luxuries of Berlin and Paris and London before he came to Russia, and that he now lived with his stepmother in a privileged government apartment building on Gorki Street, Natasha had felt too ashamed of her apartment to invite him home for a visit. Though a brilliant scientist, and one of the Lebedev's most promising experimental physicists, she was still, like himself, a newcomer to the Institute; and like all unmarried workers in crowded wartime Moscow, she had been allocated one small room for her living quarters.

As he started off down the broad Simonovsky Val, the Suburb's main thoroughfare, he thought to himself: So this is the paradise on earth Lenin promised the workers. As dismal as it was, Natasha's Russian worker's world was at least brighter than the Russian bureaucratic world in which he and Aloise lived, a privileged world of Stalinist dogma, of blind and mindless Party obedience, and of terrifying police suspicion, a world where you lived in the unrelenting shadow of Stalin's Kremlin.

Suddenly, the sound of rapid footsteps came from behind him. With instinctive caution, he quickly stepped back against the factory's fence and watched as a figure came toward him out of the darkness.

It took a moment for him to recognize the man in the rain. But despite the raincoat and the hat, he could make out the face of the man he had seen minutes before in the crowded Metro. Realizing that he had made no mistake, and that he was being followed, he suddenly wanted to laugh, for he had spent an entire year trying to attract the government's attention.

When his NKVD companion reached the corner, he stopped and looked around, as if debating with himself whether he should turn back.

With a feeling of defiance, Jacob stepped out from the shadows, lifted the vodka bottle, and took a long satisfying swallow. Replacing the cork, Jacob shoved the bottle back into his pocket and started off across the square, heading southeast toward the lights along the Moskva River's embankment.

Aloise will hear about this and she'll be angry. Remembering her warning that an important Lebedev scientist like himself was not free to run about Moscow at night, eating and drinking like a Western degenerate, made him laugh out loud.

A block from the river embankment, he came to Natasha's apartment building. Pausing at the entrance to shake the water from his bouquet of flowers, he thought to himself: *After being completely ignored by Beria's Commissariat of Atomic Science for a whole year, it's comforting to know that I've at least merited the attention of his Commissariat of State Security.*

A single dim light burned in the building's drab first-floor hallway. On the second-floor landing he paused, trying to remember which of the nine identical doors was the one to Natasha's apartment. The vodka had blurred his memory, but he was almost sure that it was the last door on the left.

Out of habit, knowing that there was always one tenant in every Moscow apartment building who kept watch over visitors, he tiptoed down the hallway and gave the door two soft taps.

There was the scrape of a chair across the floor. "Yes? Who is it?" Natasha asked.

"It's me," he said, "Jacob Linz."

He waited, but there was no response.

"It's me, Natasha," he repeated, "Jacob Linz."

Two doors away, there was the flush of a toilet in the second-floor public lavatory. "I know it's late," he said, "but I'd like to see you."

"You shouldn't have come here, Jacob," she murmured, "and you must go away."

The lavatory door opened and an elderly woman came out. She looked at him with suspicion, then hurried off down the hallway.

He said, making no effort to lower his voice, "I've brought some caviar and a bottle of vodka, and I was hoping we could celebrate our victory."

The latch turned and the door opened. "Come in, quickly," she said, hugging a quilted robe to her body.

The terror he saw in her blue eyes puzzled him. He went in and closed the door behind him. She had unbraided her long blonde hair and was already dressed for bed. "I brought you these," he said, and held out the bouquet of flowers.

She took the bouquet and laid it cautiously on the table.

"It's late, Jacob. You shouldn't have come here. I have to be in the laboratory at six tomorrow morning."

"I know it was wrong of me to come here without an invitation," he said, "but I wanted to see you tonight."

"You must leave, Jacob," she said.

He watched as she moved toward the door, then said, "You said last Saturday that you wanted us to be friends."

"I'm sorry, but I can't be your friend. I can't work with you, and I cannot ever see you again."

"Why?"

"I am, above all, a Soviet citizen, Jacob. I do not concern myself with government matters or with politics, and I know nothing about what goes on behind the walls of Stalin's Kremlin."

"So? What are you trying to tell me?"

"I may not be a member of the Party, but I'm a loyal citizen, and I'm a good Communist. I have lived in Moscow for four years, but I have never, before this, been the object of police surveillance." She began to cry, softly. "If you go on trying to involve me in your research, and if you keep seeing me outside the Institute like this, you will ruin my life."

The hopelessness he heard in her voice frightened him. "What do you mean by police surveillance, Natasha?" he asked. "I don't understand."

"Yesterday, two men came to see me at the Lebedev. They identified themselves as agents of the Commissariat of Internal Affairs. They took me into a room and asked me questions."

"Questions about what?"

"About you, Jacob. About the meetings I have had with you, about our conversation last Saturday at the Aragvi—everything."

"You have nothing to fear from the NKVD, Sasha," he said. "It's only my involvement with the plutonium reactor that they're interested in."

"It wasn't the plutonium reactor that they questioned me about. They wanted to know what you had told me about your parents, Jacob, and about the life you led in England, France, and Germany."

"What did they want to know about my parents?" he asked with amazement.

"First, they questioned me about your father, about his work for the Tube Alloys project and about his death in England. Then they questioned me about your mother. They also wanted to know if you had talked about a girl you once knew in England."

The rain went on tapping softly at the window. He felt his legs giving way from the vodka he had drunk. "Maggie Ryder?" he asked.

"Yes, that was her name. Maggie Ryder."

He tried to think how the NKVD had come to know about Maggie Ryder's existence. He and Aloise had agreed long ago never to speak of his foolish love affair in England.

He said, quietly, "Did they tell you what's happened to her?"

"No. They only asked if you had mentioned her."

Why, after four years of anonymity, he wondered, was the NKVD suddenly interested in the life he had left behind in England?

60

AWAKENED once again by the noise of the rain hammering against her bedroom window, Aloise hung for a moment in the twilight of half sleep, fitfully wondering if Jacob had returned home. Then suddenly, through her open bedroom door, came the rattle of liquor bottles from the living room.

She threw back the covers, sat up, and turned on her bedside lamp. The clock on her bureau read 12:55.

A chill ran through her body. This was the second time in four days that she had been awakened in the middle of the night by the sound of Jacob rummaging in the liquor cabinet.

She got up quickly, took her dressing gown from the chair, and as she reached up to draw the curtain across her bedroom window, she caught sight of a black government car, parked in the street below. It was last Saturday night, when Jacob came home well after one o'clock, that she finally realized how dangerously far he had gone in publicly displaying his private frustrations. And on Saturday night, she had learned that he was being watched and followed by Lavrenti Beria's Commissariat for State Security.

A bottle fell to the floor and shattered.

She quickly put on her dressing gown and hurried into the living room. Still dressed in his raincoat, Jacob had turned on the floorlamp next to the sofa and was pouring himself a glass of vodka. There was broken glass and a pool of red wine on the floor in front of the liquor cabinet. She said in English, trying to restrain her anger, "Jacob, dear, do you realize what time it is?"

"I do, indeed," he said, without looking up from the bottle. "I could have been home by midnight, but Stalin's Metros aren't reliable at night."

She continued into the room, tying the sash of her dressing gown. Sensing that he was on the the verge of launching into one of his drunken denunciations of Soviet bureaucratic incompetence, she said in a mollifying voice, "You should have told me that your party at the Lebedev was going to last so long. I cooked pyelmeni for supper, your favorite, and I waited up for you until midnight."

"My little celebration at the Lebedev didn't last till midnight," he said, filling his glass to the brim. "I invited Kurchatov and Skovorado and Kazakov and Gorodsky to have a drink in my office after work, but nobody came." He lost his balance and stumbled as he set the bottle on the coffee table. He took a drink, splashing the liquor down the front of his raincoat. "I bought flowers and set out the bloody vodka and caviar, but nobody came."

His words softened her anger. "I'm sorry, sweetheart," she said, remembering his excitement last night when he came home with the news that the government had agreed to build his longed-for plutonium reactor. That morning, when he told her about the victory celebration he had planned for his colleagues at the Lebedev, she had given him a bottle of Yubileinaya vodka and a tin of Black Sea caviar to take with him to work. "Perhaps there was some mistake," she said. "Or a misunderstanding."

"No. There was no mistake and no misunderstanding." He sipped his drink. "I wrote the invitations myself and I delivered them by hand."

"Then something important must have come up. Perhaps there was an unexpected meeting."

"No. There was no meeting tonight," he said, staring absently into his glass. "The reason they didn't come was because they were told not to come."

She thought at once of his experience last Saturday with the NKVD. "Told by whom, Jacob?" she asked.

"I don't know." He went on staring into the glass, turning it in his hand. "But since yesterday, when Kurchatov announced the government's plan to build the reactor, my colleagues at the Lebedev have been avoiding me. I noticed it today in the cafeteria at lunch."

She sighed again as he drank half the vodka in his glass, then said, "If your colleagues have been told to avoid you, Jacob, you have only yourself to blame. This is Moscow, not London or Paris, and no one in Moscow, least of all a foreign-born scientist at the Lebedev Institute, is free to stay out half the night drinking in public places."

"I don't think this has anything to do with my staying out late or my drinking in public places," he said.

She saw that he had opened the living-room curtains. Fighting to contain her anger, she turned away and quickly went to the window. As she drew the curtain over the window, she looked out across Gorki Street at the lighted windows in the opposite apartment building and wondered, with sudden panic, if any of the government officials living in the building had seen the boy stumbling about the room with his vodka bottle. The anger came boiling up as she turned from the window. "I have warned you in the past, Jacob. Considering who you are and where you came from, your public drinking and your criticism of Stalin will not go unnoticed by the NKVD."

He finished off the vodka in his glass. "I didn't go out drinking in a public place tonight. I waited in my office until eight thirty, then I took the vodka and the caviar you gave me and I went to see Natasha Bolnitskaya."

The name silenced her. She watched with dismay as he took the bottle from the coffee table and refilled his glass. Natasha Bolnitskaya, the young Ukrainian scientist he had met four months ago at the Lebedev, had been with him last Saturday night when the NKVD followed him home from the Aragvi. She had met Natasha only once, when she had met Jacob at the Institute one afternoon, but she had taken an instant dislike to the girl. The daughter of Ukrainian peasants, with a passionate loyalty to Stalin, she had brought back disturbing memories of Maggie Ryder.

She left the window and went to him. "It would have been better if you had brought the vodka and the caviar home to celebrate."

"I didn't want to celebrate at home, Aloise," he shot back angrily. "I wanted to celebrate with Natasha. She's the physicist I want to work with on my critical-mass experiments. And besides—" he looked away and drank again—"I was lonely."

Aloise took a cigarette and a match from the coffee table. "I know you think you have no freedom, and that you feel out of place here." She struck the match and lit her cigarette. "But you are no ordinary Muscovite, Jacob, and you must learn to choose your friends carefully."

He turned away and looked down into his glass again. "It's obvious that you don't like Natasha, Aloise," he said.

"It's not that I don't like Natasha, Jacob. Liking has nothing to do with it." She drew on the cigarette. "I simply don't trust her, that's all."

"Why?"

"I've told you already. There are police informers in every public institution in Moscow, and the Lebedev is no exception."

He said, turning his glass absently in his hand, "You're wrong to suspect Natasha."

"I think you're the one who's wrong, Jacob. There are women like Natasha at the Foreign Ministry. They work for Beria's Commissariat of State Security, and they report everything they see and hear to the authorities."

He turned back and looked at her for the first time. "I know why you don't trust Natasha. She reminds you of Maggie Ryder."

The name—which neither one of them had spoken in over three and a half years—silenced her. She turned away and went to the liquor cabinet. "Sometimes I wonder if you have any common sense left at all, Jacob," she said, and began gathering up the broken glass from the floor. "Natasha Bolnitskaya was with you last Saturday night when the NKVD followed you home from the Aragvi."

"That's true, she was." He took the bottle from the table and refilled his glass. "But she was not with me tonight, when the NKVD followed me to the Lenin Suburb."

"They followed you to the Lenin Suburb?"

"When I left the Lebedev, there was a fellow standing near the front steps. But it was raining, and I didn't get a good look at him." He got up and moved slowly toward the window. "Later, when I was on the Metro, I thought I saw him again. I wasn't sure, so I decided to get off one stop early, at Krestyanskaya Square, and walk the rest of the way. I was right, though. The fellow caught up with me and followed me to Natasha's apartment building. He was still there when I left and he followed me all the way here." He pushed the curtain back and looked down at the street. "It's raining like hell now, but for all I know he's still down there."

She left the glass on the floor, stood up, and went to him at the window. "I want you to listen to me, Jacob, and for once do what I say. I warned you last Saturday what will happen if you continue with this rebellious behavior of yours. You are a government-appointed scientist at the Lebedev, and on top of that, now that Commissar Beria has approved your experimental plutonium project, you are also a government security risk."

He let go of the curtain. "This has nothing whatever to do with my rebellious behavior, as you call it," he said, and started to turn away.

She took hold of his arm. "There are agents of the Soviet Secret Police everywhere, and you've got to stop making a spectacle of yourself in public places!"

"I've told you, this has nothing to do with my behavior in public places!" he shouted and pulled his arm free. "And it has nothing to do with my criticism of the government, either!" He left her at the window and started across the room to his bedroom door, splashing vodka on the floor as he went.

He stopped at his open bedroom door. "And it has nothing to do with Natasha. She told me that she didn't want to do my critical-mass experiments at the Lebedev. Not only that, she said she didn't want to see me outside the Institute, and the reason she gave was that the NKVD had come to the Lebedev yesterday and questioned her."

He turned his head and said over his shoulder, "They wanted to know what I had told her about my mother and father . . . and about my life in England, France, and Germany."

Aloise drew on her cigarette, nervously. "Why? They questioned you about those things when you first came to Russia."

"I don't know." He looked down again into his empty glass. "But they asked Natasha a lot of questions about Papa, about his work for Tube Alloys in England and about his death."

Feeling another chill run through her body, Aloise reached up and closed the collar of her dressing gown. "And what else?" she asked.

"That's what makes no sense," he replied. "They also asked her what I had said about my mother."

61

"You are to be congratulated, Comrade Linz," said the voice at the other end of the line. "The State Planning Commission has reviewed your recommendations, and they will be submitted at the next meeting of the Secretariat of the Central Committee."

For a moment, trying to remember Popov's position in the Defense Ministry's bureaucratic hierarchy, Aloise could only stare in astonishment at the homeward-bound Foreign Ministry office workers hurrying by her open office door.

"Depending on the Secretariat's response," the voice said, "the Defense Ministry's Deputy Secretary, Comrade Valerian Kaminsky, will submit copies of your recommendations to the Council of Ministries."

At the mention of Valerian Kaminsky, the name fell into place. Vladimir Popov, she recalled, was a Second Deputy Secretary of the Ministry of Defense and Valerian Kaminsky's assistant.

"This is a great honor, Comrade Popov," she said. "I had no idea that my modest report would be of interest to the Ministry of Defense."

"The Ministry was impressed by your recommendations for the Soviet Union's postwar economic recovery, Comrade Linz," Popov said. "Particularly your statements regarding the industries we have inherited from the Nazis in the newly occupied Balkan states."

"Ah, yes. Of course." Wondering which of her recommendations had aroused the Defense Ministry's interest, she quickly opened her desk drawer and took out the ten-page document. She had written the report almost three weeks ago, as a departmental exercise, and had submitted it to Gregorii Levshenko, the director of the Foreign Ministry's economics department.

"There was one statement in your report, Comrade Linz, that particularly interested our Minister of Defense," he said. "I'm speaking of your recommendations concerning the industries we have inherited in newly occupied Czechoslovakia."

She said, searching the document for what she had written about Czechoslovakia's industries, "The Bohemian coal deposits are, of course, some of the largest in Europe."

"I'm speaking of the Moravian Joachimsthal uranium mines, Comrade Linz," Popov said.

Her eyes came to rest on the three sentences she had written recommending the immediate takeover of Czechoslovakia's uranium industry.

"In my opinion, Comrade Popov, the Joachimsthal uranium mines could be of vital importance to the Soviet Union's military defense," she said, remembering that it was Jacob who had urged her to include the Moravian uranium mines in her list of useful foreign industries. "I'm referring, of course, to the government's recent decision to invest in a Russian atom bomb program. The Czech uranium mines are the largest in Europe, and the future success of the entire program may well depend on our supply of raw Czechoslovakian uranium ore."

"Precisely," he said. "And you are to be congratulated for the vigilance of your recommendations."

Aloise sat back, feeling suddenly lightheaded. Vigilance: the word was one of the Kremlin's new ideological labels and it echoed in her ear with the force of Stalin's own voice. "The Soviet Union's investment in a nuclear arms program has always been a subject close to my heart, Comrade Popov," she said, thinking of the goal she had set for herself when she brought young Jacob to Russia with her. "As you know, my stepson Jacob Linz is not only one of Russia's leading theoretical physicists, he is also a driving force behind the government's new atom bomb project."

"You are most fortunate to have such a talented stepson, Comrade Linz," he said. "Of course, everything will depend upon your absolute loyalty to the Party," Popov added.

She said, wondering where the Second Deputy Secretary was leading her, "I have served the Party for twenty years, Comrade Popov—first, as a member of the Comintern and a Communist deputy to the French Parliament, and then as a director of Soviet intelligence in England. If I may say so, I think I have more than proved my loyalty to the Party."

Popov chuckled softly. "Here in Russia, Comrade Linz, loyalty is not something one proves only once and then takes for granted. It must be constantly demonstrated with acts of selfless patriotism."

"I have always welcomed every opportunity to demonstrate my patriotism," she said.

"In that case, you have nothing to fear. Your report will be forwarded to the Central Committee's Secretariat, and I will inform Deputy Secretary Kaminsky of our conversation this afternoon."

"I look forward to the Secretariat's response, Comrade Popov," she said, but the line had already disconnected.

For a moment, she sat with the receiver to her ear and stared at the small framed photograph of Jacob on her desk. In the four years they had been together in Russia she had never spoken to anyone about the hopes she had for him. She had known, when she brought David's Tube Alloys plutonium research with them to Russia and arranged for Jacob to complete his doctoral degree at the University of Moscow, that his dream of completing his father's plutonium research would be the key that would open all the doors of power for her.

As she returned the receiver to the hook, she suddenly realized how much the boy had grown to resemble his father. The face in the photograph, taken in front of Lenin's mausoleum shortly after they arrived in Moscow, was that of a handsome, intelligent young man. But now, three and a half years later, he had come to possess the features that had belonged to his father and had drawn her to him.

The light from the window behind her desk had faded to twilight. She looked up at the clock on the wall above her desk. It was 5:25, there was shopping to do for supper, and the lines at the government food store would be long.

Rising from her chair, she looked up to see two men, strangers dressed in dark business suits, standing at her open door.

"Comrade Aloise Linz?" asked a heavy-set Eurasian man.

She knew at once who they were. "Yes," she replied.

The agent muttered something to his companion, a short blond-haired man in his mid-forties, then stepped through the door. "We are agents of the State Security Office, Comrade Linz," he said, surveying the room, "and we are here to accompany you to the offices of Comrade Lavrenti Pavlovich Beria."

She tried to speak, but the name Beria had silenced her. She went on staring at the papers she was holding, wondering if the Second Deputy Secretary's telephone call had merely been a coincidence, for Beria was not only the Commissar of Internal Affairs and State Security, he was also the director of all atomic research in the Soviet Union.

"If you will come with us, Comrade, we have a car waiting outside," the agent said, glancing impatiently at his watch.

"Yes, of course," she said.

She left her papers on the desk, quickly grabbed her purse, and joined the two agents in the hallway.

As they turned down the staircase to the first floor, Aloise raced back in her mind over the events of the last week, trying to think of some plausible explanation for Beria's summons. It had to do, she was sure, with Jacob's recent success at the Lebedev and his surveillance by the NKVD. But there had also been the NKVD's interrogation of young

Natasha Bolnitskaya and the disturbing questions they had asked about Jacob's life before he came to Russia: about his mother and father, and Maggie Ryder.

When they reached the street, a sleek black Volga with red government license plates was parked at the curb with its motor running.

The blond-haired agent joined the driver in the front seat and, as the Volga pulled out into the traffic circling Smolenskaya Square, he said, quietly, "The Lubyanka."

The name rang like an alarm in Aloise's ear. She gripped her purse, remembering the one visit she had paid to the dreaded prison in Dzerzhinsky Square. That was in October of '41, the day she and Jacob filed their application with the NKVD for permanent residence in the Soviet Union, and she had resolved that day never to enter the Lubyanka again.

She thought of Popov's words on the telephone: Here in Russia, Comrade Linz, loyalty is not something one proves only once. It must be constantly demonstrated with acts of selfless patriotism.

The memory of the compromises she had made, beginning in Paris, when she risked everything for love and arranged the forgery of Katherine Linz's death certificate, and ending with David's murder in London, had haunted her ever since she and Jacob arrived in Moscow.

The Volga came to a halt before the guarded door to the offices of the Soviet Commissariat of Internal Affairs and State Security. "We must not keep the Commissar waiting," the Eurasian agent said, and quickly got out.

Saying nothing, the two agents escorted her into the building and up a broad marble staircase to an unmarked door which resembled all the other doors lining the second-floor hallway. Without knocking, the Eurasian agent opened the door and motioned for her to go in.

"Comrade Linz!" he announced, then stepped back and closed the door behind her.

The Commissar's reception room was furnished in the same antiquated style as the ground-floor reception hall. There was a plain wooden bench against one wall, dominated by an official photograph of Stalin, and in the center of the room a large desk. Seated at the desk was a small bald man, writing busily in what looked like an old-fashioned clerk's ledger.

"Ah!" he looked up. "You can go right in, Comrade Linz," he said, pointing to the door behind his desk. "The Commissar is waiting."

Everything was happening too fast, and she had not had time to catch her breath after the hurried climb up the staircase. As she went to the door, the thought crossed her mind that she was about to meet, face to face, the second most powerful man in Russia.

"Don't knock, Comrade," the receptionist said, "just go in."

She obeyed and, to her astonishment, found herself in an immense oak-paneled room lavishly furnished with antiques.

"Ah! Come in!" a high-pitched voice called from a gilded armchair at the far end of the room. Barely visible in the room's fading light, Beria sat with his back to the window before an ornately carved gilded table. She had never been told how small the man was.

"Sit down, Comrade!" he called, motioning to the two chairs in front of the table.

As she closed the door and made her way down the long room, she looked up at the huge map of the world hanging on the wall beside Beria's desk. The recently occupied countries of East Europe were tinted red, and there were numerous brightly colored pins stuck in strategic places across the map.

As she took her place in one of the plain straightback chairs, Beria leaned forward and opened an enameled box on the table. "Cigarette, Comrade?" he asked with a pleasant smile.

The tiny steel-framed pince-nez perched on the Commissar's nose gave his plump pale face the look of a middle-aged Russian office clerk. She started to reach for the box, then drew back. "No, thank you," she said.

"We have never met, Comrade Linz, but your name is familiar to me. I'm told you work as an advisor to the Foreign Ministry here in Moscow."

"Yes, Commissar. I'm an assistant to Comrade Gregorii Levshenko, the director of the Foreign Ministry's economics department."

"They also tell me you were a deputy to the French Parliament at one time, and that you worked for Soviet intelligence in England during the war."

"That's correct. I served as a Communist deputy to Parliament during the Blum Administration." She shifted her purse nervously on her lap. "Then, following the Nazi occupation of Belgium, I moved with my husband and stepson to England, where I took charge of Soviet atomic intelligence for the Commissariat of State Security."

Beria reached forward and opened a thick brown file on the table in front of him. "You were married, they tell me, to an American atomic physicist, David Linz. Is that correct?"

"Yes. We were married in Paris in the spring of 1940."

He looked down at a typed page lying on the top of the file. "And before that, Dr. Linz was married to a German scientist, was he not?"

Her mouth had gone dry. She cleared her throat. "Yes. Her name, before they married, was Katherine von Steiner."

He turned a page in the file. "Tell me, Comrade Linz, how did your husband come to marry a second time?"

"Katherine Linz was a German Aryan and my husband was a Jew," she said, repeating the words she had said a thousand times before. "He left Germany with his son and moved to Paris. The following year, in May of 1940, David learned that his wife had died of radiation poisoning in Germany, and shortly thereafter, we were married and moved to England."

"With your husband's son?" he asked.

"Yes, that's correct."

"And it was through your scientist husband that you came to organize our Soviet atomic intelligence in England, Comrade Linz, was it not?"

"Yes. He began work for the Tube Alloys project in the fall of 1940. By then, there was scientific evidence that a uranium bomb could be developed, and I thought the Soviet Union should be alerted to the possibility. I had access to my husband's atomic research at the Imperial College, so I contacted Comrade Konstantin Volkov, the NKVD chief in London, and offered to supply Moscow with the latest atomic bomb data. That was the beginning of Soviet atomic intelligence in England."

"But then you directed our British atomic intelligence for only a year," he said, and smiled.

"Yes, that's correct," she said, hating the rhetorical repetitiousness of his questions. "In August of '41, when I learned that the British authorities were about to arrest my husband on suspicion of espionage, and that he planned to leave England, I went to Volkov and told him everything. I was faced with the probability that he would betray our entire operation to the British M15." She looked up at the fading light in the window behind Beria's desk, wondering how much he had been told about David's death in London. "When I explained my predicament to Volkov," she went on, "he told me that the NKVD would take care of everything and he ordered me to leave England that very night. I did, of course, what he told me."

"I see." Beria turned another page in the file. "And then you and the boy came here to the Soviet Union," he said.

"Yes."

"Until last year, when I received your stepson's application for a research position at the Lebedev Institute, I was unaware of his presence in Moscow." He took a loose sheaf of papers from the file. "In fact, it was not until March of this year that I learned about the critical-mass research he had been doing at the Lebedev and the proposal he had made for the experimental production of a Soviet plutonium bomb. Your stepson's predictions about the Allies' development of both a uranium and a plutonium bomb were quite accurate, Comrade Linz."

He got up and went to the map suspended from the wall beside his desk. He took a wooden rod from a rack on the wall and pointed to Berlin. "Our allies now occupy the whole of western Europe, and if they succeed in winning the war against Japan, the territorial boundaries of the capitalist powers will stretch from here to here." He drew the rod from Berlin, across the Atlantic and Pacific oceans, to the eastern coastline of China. "Russia has won her war with Nazi Germany, Comrade Linz," he said, "but she must continue to remain vigilant. America, as you know, is a vast country with unlimited natural resources and enormous industrial capabilities. We now know that the United States has been secretly at work on both a uranium and a plutonium bomb since 1942."

"But how is that possible, Comrade Commissar?" she asked. "When I left England in forty-one, Britain was the only country engaged in atom bomb research."

"Things have changed since you left England, Comrade Linz. When America entered the war in December of '41, Roosevelt immediately took control of the British Tube Alloys project. Full-scale research and production of both the uranium and plutonium bombs began in America in the fall of '43."

"Then they must be well ahead of us in its experimental development," she said.

"They are at least three years ahead of us, Comrade Linz. In approximately one month, the Americans will test their first plutonium bomb here, in the desert," he said, moving the rod down on the map.

"Forgive me Comrade Commissar," she said, "but I fail to understand why you are telling me these things."

Beria left the map and walked slowly toward the window behind the table. "I'm telling you these things, Comrade Linz, because I want you to understand that it will take the Soviet Union five years, at least, to develop an experimental atom bomb program comparable to the Americans'. And as a loyal member of the Soviet Communist Party," he added, "we will expect you to do what you can to help us close the gap."

"I will do anything I can to help," she said.

"It's truly amazing how our lives are changed by the accidents of war,

Comrade," he said, gazing pensively out the window. "For instance, it was an accident of war that brought you and your husband together in Paris. One accident, of course, can lead to another," he said, and chuckled. "For instance, it was only an accident of chance that our intelligence organization in America learned about the American atomic bomb project. One of our contacts in Washington accidentally came across a list of names of the scientists working on the American bomb project." He turned from the window. "And to our astonishment, Comrade Linz, among the names was that of Katherine Linz."

She waited a few seconds before she spoke, knowing that her voice would betray her, then she said, taking a breath between each phrase, "But that's impossible, there must be some mistake. Katherine Linz died in Germany."

"No, Comrade Linz. There is no mistake. Tell me, Comrade Linz, does the name Maggie Ryder mean anything to you?" he asked.

She hesitated, thinking again of the NKVD's interrogation of Natasha Bolnitskaya. "Yes," she replied. "Maggie Ryder was a British girl that my stepson knew in London."

Beria consulted the page, then said, "The girl was pregnant with young Linz's child when she moved with Katherine Linz to America."

She felt her heartbeat quicken, remembering the phone call Maggie Ryder had made to Jacob the afternoon of David's murder. "I see," she said. "I didn't know."

Beria flipped through the papers in the file and removed a small photograph from the back of the file. "This photo of your stepson was taken last September, following his appointment to the Lebedev," he said, and placed the photograph in front of her on the table.

She took the photo and held it under the desklamp. Jacob stood on the Institute's front steps, surrounded by his colleagues, smiling proudly at the camera. Above his head, carved in Russian letters into the building's stone façade, were the words USSR LEBEDEV INSTITUTE OF PHYSICAL SCIENCES.

He reached to the back of the file and took out a page typed on thin onionskin paper. "This is a letter we have prepared on your behalf, Comrade Linz—a personal letter addressed to Dr. Katherine Linz at the project headquarters in New Mexico. I will not bore you by reading the political arguments you give her for cooperating with our demands, but at the end of the letter you inform Dr. Linz that she is to turn over a complete copy of her plutonium critical-mass data to our intelligence operative. The letter, together with the photograph of Dr. Linz's son, will be sent to the Soviet Embassy in Washington and then delivered to her by our NKVD contact. She will follow his instructions to the letter."

He folded the page and placed it on the table in front of her.

She hesitated for a moment, then said, "From what I know of Katherine Linz, Comrade Commissar, I am certain she will never agree to your demands."

"The motives you give for her cooperation are quite simple, Comrade," he said. "First, we know that Dr. Linz and the man who brought her to America, a Colonel Michael Rakovsky, have conducted a tireless search for her son since they left England. Your letter informs her that young Jacob is now living in Russia, that he is a loyal Soviet citizen, and that he is working as a theoretical physicist at the Lebedev Institute in Moscow. Second, we know that Dr. Linz is deeply attached to her grandson, and that she would do anything to protect him from harm. You therefore end your letter by telling her she has a choice to make. She will either turn over her experimental calculations of the plutonium bomb's critical mass, or she will forfeit the life of her grandson." He leaned forward and smiled again, this time with malicious irony. "They tell me you are very fond of your stepson," Beria said.

She looked down at the photograph on the table in front of her, thinking with horror of that night in Paris, when she met David and Jacob for the first time. With all she and Jacob had been through together, she had grown quite fond of him. It seemed she would never be free from the compromises of her heart.

Beria reached out and pushed the letter toward her. "The choice, of course, is yours to make," he said. "But it would be wise to keep in mind the fate of those who have refused to demonstrate absolute loyalty to Stalin."

It wasn't necessary to ask what the punishment was for treason in the Soviet Union. She took a pen from her purse and signed the letter.

62

KATHERINE watched as the chart recorder's needle began to widen its path along the moving roll of paper. "You just made contact, Louis," she said. "I'm getting two neutrons per fission."

Bent over the metal disk in the center of the Omega Site's whitewashed assembly room, Louis Slotin, the group leader of Los Alamos's Gadget Division, went on rotating the lever of his worm gear, slowly drawing the subcritical halves of the nickel-plated plutonium sphere together.

"Easy, Louis, easy," Paul Morrison, Slotin's young assistant, cautioned as his Geiger counter leveled off to a steady rat-tat-tat. "You're approaching critical."

"The chemistry division says we were off on our last count, Paul," said Slotin, "and if we don't push it closer to critical, the Fat Man's gonna fizzle next Monday down at Trinity. There's two billion bucks, and maybe the war itself, riding on this experiment, and we're gonna tickle this dragon's tail till we get a decent reading."

Katherine glanced at her watch. Damn! she thought. She had promised Michael she would be waiting at the administration building at six for his phone call from Washington. It was 5:15, and the drive from Omega Site to the Tech Area took twenty minutes.

The chart recorder's needle suddenly swung out across the page. "Go slowly, Louis," she said. "You're now at three-quarters scale." She took hold of the recorder's moving page, trying to concentrate on the steadily rising neutron count, but her thoughts clung to Michael's promised call. On Saturday, he had phoned to say that he had been in touch by cable with his friend Matt Harmon, the military attaché at the American Embassy in Moscow, and that Harmon, who had been conducting the search for Jacob from the Russian end, had received "an interesting lead" from a contact inside the Soviet Academy of Sciences.

"I'll follow it up, sweetheart," Michael had said, "and get back to you on Tuesday."

"We've got to go the whole way, this time," Slotin said. "I talked to Oppie this morning, and Groves has refused to postpone the test." He looked up and laughed. "Believe it or not, we're gambling with very high stakes, you guys. Truman, he says, wants to know the results of our Fat Man test when he meets with Stalin next week at Potsdam."

"For Christ sake, Louis, watch what you're doin'!" Morrison shouted. "You're gonna blow us off the bloody Hill!"

Slotin muttered to himself and went on turning his worm gear lever.

"This is crazy, Louis," Morrison said, as his Geiger counter picked up speed. "We were told we had two days to make the final critical-mass measurements."

"That was yesterday, Paul, and things have changed. I got the order from Groves at noon today. The bomb core has to be ready by midnight.

It's leaving for Alamogordo at 3 A.M." He stopped turning his lever and looked up. "I'm sorry, you guys, but this is our last shot."

"It isn't fair, Louis," Katherine said, watching the needle's zigzag path across the page. "You should have warned us you were going to go critical."

"Good God, Katherine, make up your mind," Slotin said, and went back to turning his lever. "You've been badgering me for a week to go critical."

It was true. Since last week, when the metallurgists in the chemical division finally obtained enough plutonium to shape a finished bomb core, she had been urging Slotin to take the assembly experiment to the critical point. But that was last week, before she learned that Washington had made its final decision. Depending on the outcome of next week's plutonium bomb test at Alamogordo, they would drop both the Fat Man plutonium and the Little Boy uranium bombs over the Japanese mainland.

"Go real slow, Louis," Morrison said as the rat-tat-tat from his Geiger counter picked up speed. "You're almost there."

Katherine's hand shook as she held the chart recorder's moving page. God knows, they had tickled the dragon's tail, as Slotin called it, countless times in the last year with the uranium "Guillotine" experiments used to calculate the critical mass of uranium 235. But this was lethal plutonium, not uranium, and they had yet to determine its stability.

She kept her gaze riveted on the chart recorder's wavering red line and thought, as she always did in moments like this, of the promise she had made to Michael in London: that in exchange for his help in getting her and David and Jacob safely out of England, she would move to America and work as an experimental physicist on Roosevelt's atom bomb project. Things had not turned out as she and David had planned, but she had kept her side of the bargain and had carried out the experimental side of David's critical-mass calculations.

"Give me a reading at 3.8, Kate," said Slotin.

Katherine glanced up as Slotin reached for the screwdriver he kept on the metal disk. It was the makeshift device he had always used to maintain separation between the subcritical spheres.

When she looked again at the needle, she saw that he was moving faster than she had anticipated. "You've already passed 3.8, Louis," she said. "You're almost at 3.9."

"Good. Then we'll take it all the way."

What had always terrified her about their critical-mass calculations was the scientific uncertainty of their experiments: the fact that they could not know how far they had gone until they had reached the point of no return.

Across the room, Morrison coughed nervously as his Geiger counter leveled off to a steady buzz. "By the way, Louis," he said, "they tell me that death by radiation is very painful."

"I can't say from experience, Paul," Slotin said, as he centered the screwdriver between the closing plutonium spheres. "But if this screwdriver slips, I'll let you know."

Katherine smiled to herself, suddenly remembering that she had already died once before of radiation poisoning—six years ago in Berlin. She glanced up at the bomb core's small shiny halves. They looked, for all the world, like the innocent halves of a shiny silver apple. "Go very, very slowly, Louis," she said quietly. "You're approaching 4.0."

"Stop me at exactly four, Kate."

She watched as the chart recorder's needle swung back and forth in ever widening arcs across the page. Up to now, they had never pushed the experiment beyond 3.9 on the critical-mass scale. It was like watching a seismograph needle silently record the movements of a distant and devastating earthquake.

Over the last four years, the thought that she might be able to recover as a scientist what she had lost as a wife and mother had burned in her mind like a candle. She held her breath and prayed, as she had never prayed before, for success.

The needle hovered, then reached the critical mark on the scale. "Stop, Louis," she said, quickly. "You're at 4.0."

His response was instantaneous. He brought the worm gear's lever to a halt, then slowly began turning it in the opposite direction.

The buzz from Morrison's Geiger counter settled down to a steady rat-tat-tat. He stepped back and said in a shaky voice, "I should have volunteered for Red Cross duty."

"Think of it this way, Paul," Slotin said, "if our numbers are right this time, we may have just won the war."

A feeling of triumph came over Katherine. Scanning the recorder's chart, she said, "The numbers are here, Louis. We can't be off more than a fraction of a microgram."

"Great!" Slotin laughed. "Then we've done our part, and the rest is up to Oppie, Groves, and God." He left the spotlit metal disk and joined her at the chart recorder.

Katherine looked at her watch again. "Will you loan me your car, Louis," she said, "I'm supposed to be at the administration building for a phone call at six."

He smiled. "A phone call, I take it, from Washington."

Morrison looked up from his Geiger counter. "This is your third phone call from Rakovsky in a week!"

Slotin handed her his rabbit foot keyring. "You're a lousy driver, Kate, but I guess I have no choice."

"Thanks. When I finish with the call, I'll come back and pick you up."

"Never mind. I have to stay and pack up the bomb core, so I'll get a ride back with Morrison. You can leave the car in front of the administration building."

"You're lucky, Kate, to have a friend like Colonel Rakovsky," Morrison said. "He's been conducting this search for your son ever since you came to Los Alamos."

"Longer, Paul. Ever since I came to America." She found herself blushing as she hurried toward the assembly room's heavy steel door. In the two years she had worked with Slotin and Morrison, they were the only staff members at Omega Site who had read between the lines of her platonic friendship with Michael Rakovsky—that she, and not military duty, was the real reason for the colonel's frequent trips to Los Alamos.

"By the way," Slotin called after her. "It's six days to Trinity, and you still haven't made your wager!"

For a week now, the scientific staff at Los Alamos had been placing five dollar bets on the plutonium bomb's TNT yield at Alamogordo, ranging from zero to twenty thousand tons. She looked back and laughed as she pulled the door back. "I may be a fool, Louis, but I'm going to double your wager and say ten thousand."

"Good God!" he laughed. "You're getting reckless in your old age!"

"Maybe so." She swung the protective steel door closed and quickly hurried down the long cinder-block corridor to the lab's guarded front entrance. "Good night, Andy!" she called to the Army guard on duty outside the door.

"Sure thing, Dr. Linz!" he waved. "See you tomorrow!"

Slotin had left his Packard parked at the far end of the fenced-in lot. Katherine got in and headed for the administration building. She drove slowly, for she found the huge American Packard difficult to steer along the road's sandy ruts. Built two years ago for the Manhattan Project's dangerous uranium critical-mass experiments, the Omega Site laboratory had been situated five safe miles from the Tech Area at the lower end of Los Alamos Canyon, a deep gorge of volcanic tufa rock that ran along the southern edge of the Los Alamos mesa. In winter the canyon's road was perpetually blanketed with snow, and in summer the traffic from the Hill turned its loose clay into powder.

She kept the accelerator to the floor as she climbed the steep canyon wall and silently prayed again—this time, not for the success of their critical-mass experiment, but for a successful end to her four-year search for Jacob. It had so far led nowhere, but Michael was still convinced that Jacob and Aloise Frégand were living somewhere in the Soviet Union, concealed from the public eye and under the Russian government's protection.

As she rounded the last hairpin curve and reached the top of the mesa, the setting sun was poised just above the Jemez volcanic caldera overlooking Los Alamos. Sunset had always been her favorite time of day here on the Hill, and the warm golden reflection from the distant Sangre de Cristo mountain range reminded her of the loneliness she had come to feel between Michael's brief visits to Los Alamos. It was that first year here, when she realized that she was completely cut off from the outside world, that she found herself looking forward, instead of backward, and counting the days until Michael's next visit. It was her first taste of hope since she had come to America, and the feeling of longing and separation was mutual. Michael, with his new rank of colonel and his new job as General Styer's advisor on the President's Military Policy Committee, had begun to find excuses for more frequent visits to Los Alamos. Even so, it was not their mutual loneliness that had finally brought them together, but the truth: the fact that they could finally talk openly with one another about her inability, still, to let go of the past, to accept the fact that David was dead, that Jacob was now beyond her reach, and that he was living out his life in the terrible ignorance of the truth. The fact, too, that Michael could finally admit to himself—that it would be a long time, if ever, before she could love again.

With only two minutes to spare, she pulled into the parking lot next to the administration building. The thing about Michael she had come to rely on—the thing that David had never been able to acquire—was his military habit of punctuality. She left the car keys in the ignition, took her briefcase, and raced across the parking lot to the building's front steps. Nothing could shake the military and civilian staffs from their desks quicker than the six o'clock supper hour, and the dirt street fronting the building was crowded with groups of scientists, technicians, and military personnel heading off toward the cafeterias.

As she started up the steps, a voice called to her. She looked back as a young soldier wearing a corporal's uniform separated himself from a group of army personnel and came toward her. For one second, the man's dark face and close-cropped curly hair reminded her of David.

"If you can spare me a minute, Doctor, I'd like to have a word with you," he said.

"I'm sorry, Corporal, but I can't talk now," she said, continuing to the steps. "I have a six o'clock telephone call scheduled at the A.D. building, and I'm late already."

"I need to talk to you now, Dr. Linz," he said, following her up the steps. "I have some news for you about your son."

She stopped on the top step. "What do you mean, news about my son?"

"I have this letter for you, Doctor. It concerns your son Jacob."

The shock of hearing her son's name on the lips of a Los Alamos army corporal silenced her. She looked at his gray Class-B identification badge: Greenglass, Corp. David I. The name meant nothing to her. "How do you know my son's name?" she asked.

He looked around again and said in a soft nervous voice, "We can't talk here. If we can take a walk, I'll explain everything."

She looked again at the gray foreign-looking envelope in the man's shirt pocket and thought to herself: If he has news of Jacob, then Michael's phone call can wait. "All right," she said. "We'll take a walk." She went back down the steps and joined the corporal as he turned west, heading toward Trinity Drive.

He kept silent until they were out of earshot of the crowd. "I guess you're wondering who I am," he said, glancing nervously at two young technicians standing in front of the Housing Office. "My name is Greenglass and I work in the Ordnance Division. I'm a machinist in Dr. Kistiakowski's lens production shop."

"I see." She looked again at the envelope in his shirt pocket.

"My job with the Ordnance Division is to grind the implosion lenses for the plutonium bomb," he said.

She kept pace with him and said nothing.

He went on, as if compelled by a need to explain himself, "I tell you this, Doctor, because my work at the Ordnance production shop is closely connected with your own work at Omega Site; I know, for instance, that you're close to completing the experimental calculation of the plutonium bomb's critical mass."

"I fail to see what my work at Omega Site has to do with my son, Corporal Greenglass."

"We'll come to that in a minute." He stopped and looked in both directions down the laboratory's main dirt road, then motioned her to turn west toward the fenced in Tech Area. "I merely want you to know that the issues at stake here are much larger than you may imagine. I'm speaking, of course, of Fat Man and the test next week at Alamogordo. It's not just a question of using the bomb to end the war with Japan. The issues are political. If the test works, the bomb will give the United States a tremendous military advantage over her European allies, in particular the Soviet Union."

The words Soviet Union reminded her at once of Michael's "interesting lead" from his friend in Moscow. She stopped in the middle of the street. "You told me you had news of Jacob, Corporal Greenglass," she said. "What has America's military advantage over the Soviet Union got to do with my son?"

"I'm coming to that, Doctor. Please be patient," he said, suddenly rattled. "I merely want to remind you that Russia is far behind America in developing any kind of atomic defense, and the Soviets have no way, after what they have gone through in the war, of closing the nuclear gap with the U.S."

"I see," she said, recalling the rumors of espionage that had plagued the lab in recent months.

Greenglass looked around again, then started toward the deserted bus station across the street. "This letter will explain everything," he said, tapping his shirt pocket. "But before I give it to you, there're some things you must know. First, I've been told to tell you that the letter is absolutely authentic. It was personally delivered to me by an employee of the Soviet Embassy in Washington, and it was sent to Washington in the Embassy's diplomatic mail pouch."

Despite all the warnings and the precautions about secrecy on the Hill, she had never really believed that there could be "enemy agents," as General Groves referred to them, working inside the guarded gates of Los Alamos—especially a soldier of the United States Army. "I assume you realize, Corporal Greenglass," she said, breathlessly, "that the punishment for treason in the United States is death."

"There are risks we all have to take in times of war, Dr. Linz," he replied. "I'm a member of the American Communist Party, and it's my duty to do what I can for the Socialist cause."

As they passed the bus station, an army jeep came speeding toward them from the nearby Tech Area.

"This way," he said, and quickly drew her out of the street toward the bus station's covered entrance. The officer in the jeep's passenger seat, she saw, was Captain William S. Parsons, the head of Los Alamos's combat operations. "Don't say anything, Doctor. Just keep walking," said Greenglass, pretending to read a sign posted in the bus station window.

"I'm not interested in your motives, Corporal Greenglass," she said, and waved as the jeep sped by. "I want to know about my son."

He waited until they reached the fire station, then turned south down the narrow deserted dirt street leading to the outer rim of the mesa. "I've been instructed by my Washington contact to give you certain facts about him," he said. "Your son, Dr. Linz, is now living in the Soviet Union. He's a scientist—a theoretical physicist—employed at the Lebedev Institute in Moscow."

At that moment, a gust of hot dry wind blew past them from the rim of the mesa, throwing dust in their faces. Katherine looked away and covered her face with her left hand, feeling a sudden curious sense of relief come over her. A scientist employed at the Lebedev Institute in Moscow; it was as if the agonizing ignorance she had lived with for four years had been suddenly blown away by the wind. When her vision cleared, she saw that the sun was beginning to set behind the Jemez caldera.

"Your son now lives in Moscow with his French stepmother, a woman named Aloise Linz. I've been told to tell you that he's been carrying out research at the Lebedev in Moscow on the theoretical calculation of the plutonium bomb's critical mass."

The relief Katherine had felt suddenly vanished.

"Go on, Corporal," she said.

He kept walking, scanning the landscape around them, and said nothing.

"Why have you brought me here, Corporal? After what the Soviets have done to me and my family, I would be the last person on earth to give them anything."

"You have a grandson living in Washington, Dr. Linz," he said. "The baby's mother, Maggie Ryder, named the boy David, after his grandfather, isn't that right?"

"Yes," she said, knowing that it would be pointless to deny what he had said.

Greenglass took the envelope from his shirt pocket. As he removed the letter from the envelope a small photograph slipped from the folded page, fluttered in the wind, and came to rest on a narrow flat rock. He stepped forward and retrieved the photograph from the rock. "This photo was taken in front of the Lebedev Institute in Moscow."

Katherine's hand shook uncontrollably as she stared at the smiling young face in the photograph. It was a face, she saw, from her own distant past: David's youthful face, the same face she remembered that first year in Göttingen, when they met and fell in love.

"This will explain everything," Greenglass said, and handed her the letter.

As she unfolded the page, her eye came to rest on its neat academic signature: Aloise Frégand Linz.

Greenglass took hold of her arm again. "Never mind the first part of the letter," he said. "It only repeats what I have already told you. Read the last paragraph."

She let her eyes travel up the crudely typed page to the opening words of the last paragraph:

> Jacob knows nothing, of course, of your presence in America, your scientific work at Los Alamos, or the demands we are making of you. He believes, in fact, that you died years ago in Berlin . . .

She stepped back as a gust of wind shook the letter in her hands. "You must read to the very end," said Greenglass.
She forced herself to go on:

> Our demands are quite simple. The data we require of you is the experimental verification of the theoretical research your son has carried out in the Soviet Union. Namely, a complete and accurate copy of the Manhattan Project's experimental calculations of the plutonium critical mass. You will turn over the data to our contact at Los Alamos and follow his instructions to the letter. The choice, of course, is yours to make, Katherine.
>
> In the end, I'm sure you will agree that it is a small price to pay in exchange for your beloved grandson's life.

63

THE ring of the telephone awakened Michael with a start. For a moment, still half asleep, he lay in the sweltering darkness and listened to the insistent summons from the living room. Then he remembered his repeated attempts that night to telephone Katherine at Los Alamos and her failure to return the calls. He turned on the bedside lamp and looked at the clock: 3:55.

Christ! he thought. If that's Katherine calling, it's 1:55 in Los Alamos!

He got out of bed and hurried into the darkened living room. The floor was strewn with little David's toys, and on the way to his desk he banged his toe against the boy's mechanical construction set. "Damn!" he cursed, wishing for the thousandth time that he had had a phone installed in his bedroom.

He reached the phone on the seventh ring. "Hello!" he shouted.

There was a moment of crackling long distance silence, then Katherine came on the line. "Michael?"

"Katherine!" he called over the static. "What's wrong?"

There was a choked cry under the static, then silence.

"For God's sake, Katherine, answer me! What's wrong?"

The door to Maggie's bedroom was open, and before Katherine could answer little David began to cry.

"You've got to take Maggie and the baby away from Washington, Michael, and come here at once," she said. "Something terrible has happened."

The static on the lines to New Mexico was always worse at night. He shifted the receiver to his right ear. "Calm down, Katherine," he said, "and talk slowly. I can't hear what you're saying!"

He could hear her fighting to get her breath. He thought of the disturbing cable he had received that afternoon from Matt Harmon in Moscow.

Katherine raised her voice and said with deliberate slowness, "It's Jacob, Michael, I've had news of Jacob."

He heard the noise under the static quite clearly: the faint click of a second line being connected. He hesitated, remembering that the lines from Los Alamos were tapped day and night by security censors, then he reached for the switch on his desklamp. "It's almost four o'clock here, Katherine," he said, cautiously. "Where are you calling from?"

"I'm on the Hill," she replied. "In the public phones next to the bus station."

As he turned on the desk lamp, Maggie's soft voice came floating from her bedroom, trying to soothe the crying child.

Michael looked back at the open door, wondering if she could hear what he was saying. Though Maggie had never questioned him about the nature of Katherine's secret wartime work, or even asked about her real whereabouts, he was certain that she knew enough about David Linz's atom bomb work in England to piece together the truth here in America. In the past, to maintain the strict rule of secrecy, he and Katherine had always spoken to each other when he was at his Pentagon office.

He lowered his voice and said, "Listen to me, sweetheart. I want you to calm down, and tell me what's happened."

"I can't do that, Michael!" she called out, angrily. "I can't tell you what's happened over the telephone!" Her voice began to shake uncontrollably. "Where is Maggie?" she asked.

"She's here with me at home."

"And the baby, where is he?"

"It's the middle of the night, Katherine, and we're all here together."

"It's not safe for them there, David," she said, and began to cry. "I want you to take Maggie and David out of Washington. You have friends in Virginia, the Bagsters, I want you to take Maggie and David to the Bagsters and then come here at once."

The boy left off crying in the next room. For a moment, Michael stood staring out at the darkness beyond the window behind his desk, trying to grasp the implications of Katherine's words. In the two years she had been at Los Alamos they had devised a private language between themselves so they could speak on the telephone of the search for Jacob he was conducting in Russia. His "Uncle Joe" was the name they used to signify the Russians.

"I want you to answer this question, Katherine," he said. "Does this have something to do with my Uncle Joe?"

"Yes, Michael, it has everything to do with Uncle Joe."

"Is Jacob involved?"

There was a moment of silence as she struggled to stop crying. "Yes," she said. "And it has to do with our business operations in New York."

Their "business operations in New York" stood for the Manhattan Project. "This news of Jacob," he said. "Have you found out where he is living, Katherine?" he asked.

"Yes, Michael, I know everything now." She began to cry again. "Jacob is living with your uncle. He and Aloise have been there for four years. Jacob works for the government, and he does the same thing that his father was doing in England when he died."

He said, feeling a sense of dread closing in on him, "How do you know this, Katherine? Who told you?"

"I can't tell you now. I'm afraid, and I need your help!"

He heard little David say behind him, "Put me down, Mama. I want to talk to Grandmama on the telephone."

"Be still, sweetheart," said Maggie. "Uncle Mike has to talk to Grandmama first."

When he turned, Maggie was standing at her bedroom door holding David in her arms, staring at him. Knowing that his fear was plainly written on his face, he turned his back to her and said, "Listen to me, Katherine. I want you to calm down and answer my questions. Just say yes or no." The static on the line crackled. "Did you understand what I just said?" he shouted.

"Yes, Michael. I understand."

He raced back over what she had so far told him, wondering what he could safely say. "Does my taking Maggie and David out of Washington have something to do with our New York business operations?"

"Yes."

"Did you learn about Jacob from someone on the Hill?"

"Yes."

"From someone you know?"

"No, Michael. The man is a complete stranger."

"Just answer yes or no, Katherine," he said. "Is this guy a friend of my uncle's?"

"Yes."

He hesitated, remembering the statement General Groves had made about security at last week's Military Policy Committee meeting: that he had come to the conclusion that there were too many foreign scientists working at Los Alamos, and he feared there could be serious security leaks from some of the Soviet sympathizers. "Tell me this," he said, "did he come to you because he wants to make some kind of business deal?"

"Yes."

He looked up at the window as a car turned the corner at the end of the block, its headlights fanning the darkness. Groves, he remembered, had told General Styers that the Soviet Union was years behind the United States in the scientific development of an atom bomb, and there was mounting pressure from some of the MED project's scientists for America to share its atomic secrets with the Russians.

"Does it have something to do with the work Jacob is doing for my uncle?" he asked.

"Yes." Her voice broke.

As the car slowly passed by the house, David called out behind him, "Look, Mama! Someone's coming to see us!"

The boy's words and the creeping speed of the passing car suddenly reminded Michael that twice that week Maggie had seen the same car follow her home from the hospital.

"Is my uncle trying to use Maggie and David as some kind of bribe?" he blurted out before he could stop himself.

"It's not Maggie, Michael, it's the boy!" she shouted back. "He's being watched by friends of your uncle, and you've got to take him out of Washington!"

He thought of the four days still remaining before his flight with General Styers to Los Alamos on Saturday. "Listen to me, Katherine," he said. "I want you to do exactly what I tell you. I have a flight scheduled to the Hill on Saturday. For the next four days, until I can get there, I want you to go about your business as if nothing has happened. Do you understand?"

"Yes! But you've got to take David and Maggie—!"

"Leave David and Maggie to me, Katherine!" he interrupted. "I'll take care of everything." The static broke the line again. "Did you hear what I said?" he called out.

"Yes, I heard." She began to cry again. "They've given me a choice to make, and I cannot do it alone!"

The pain in her voice reached out like a hand across the fifteen hundred miles between them and gripped his heart. A choice to make. It took a moment for him to understand the meaning of her words.

"Michael," she said. "I need you now, more than ever."

When he looked back at the window, the car was turning the corner two blocks down the street. "You must not be afraid," he said. "I'll come there and we'll work this thing out together. You know that I love you . . . more than anything."

"I know, Michael." The static on the line rose and fell. "And I love you, too," she said.

"I'll be there on Saturday," he said.

"I'll be waiting."

When the line disconnected, he slowly lowered the receiver to the hook, then stood looking out into the darkness. She had never before said that she loved him.

Behind him, Maggie said, breathlessly, "Katherine has found Jacob, hasn't she?"

When he turned around, she was standing in the middle of the room, holding the boy tightly in both arms. "Yes," he said. "She's found him."

"Where, Michael?"

He thought of the long years she had patiently waited for the answer to that question. "He's where we thought he was," he said. "He's in Russia."

He couldn't tell if the sigh that came from her mouth was from relief or exhaustion.

"You asked Katherine if they were using me and David as some kind of bribe, Michael," she said. "What did you mean by that?"

He took a cigarette from the pack on his desk, thinking to himself that the truth about Jacob would inevitably lead to the truth about Katherine's work at Los Alamos.

"I have never questioned you about where Katherine is or what she's doing, Michael," Maggie said with anger. "But I have a right to know what you meant about David and me, and I have a right to know about Jacob."

It's true, he thought. Maggie, if anyone, had the right to know everything.

He lit his cigarette, then turned to face her. "I will tell you what Katherine has told me, Maggie," he said. "But you must first promise never to speak to anyone of what I'm about to say."

"Yes. I promise."

"Is Grandmama Katherine in Russia with my Papa, Uncle Mike?" the boy asked.

"No, son. Grandmama Katherine's here in America."

"Then I want to talk to her on the telephone," he said.

"Grandmama Katherine is in a far away place, David. And it's very hard for me to call her on the telephone."

"Here, sweetheart," said Maggie. "While Uncle Mike and I talk, I want you to play with your toys." As she set the boy down on the floor, her face caught the light from the desklamp, and the way her long blonde hair fell across her face suddenly reminded him of the photo of Katherine he kept in his bedroom.

Pulling at his pajamas, the boy hurried to his mechanical construction set on the floor near Michael's bedroom door.

For a moment, Michael smoked in silence, wondering to himself how much he should tell Maggie.

"Katherine tells me that Jacob is now a scientist," he said. "And he works for the Soviet government."

Maggie looked off absently at the darkened window behind him, as if weighing the implications of his words.

From across the room the boy called out with excitement, "Is my Papa a scientist like Grandmama, Uncle Mike?"

"Yes, son."

"I don't understand," she said. "What's Katherine's work got to do with Jacob's presence in the Soviet Union?"

He drew on his cigarette and began pacing the floor in front of his desk. "You know that Jacob's father was doing research on a secret military weapon in England."

"Yes. Jacob told me."

"What you don't know, Maggie, is that America has taken over the British war project. It's a huge scientific and industrial undertaking that extends across the whole of America, and it's been going on for two and a half years."

He stopped pacing and watched the boy artfully assembling the metal pieces of his construction set. "The laboratory where Katherine works on the project is at a secret installation, located in the mountains of New Mexico. Katherine is now at the final stages of her experiments, and if everything goes according to schedule, the weapon will be tested next Monday. Katherine was approached by someone who is working with the Russians. It seems the Soviets want Katherine to turn over her research and experimental data to them."

She came up and stood beside him at the desk. "Go on," she said quietly. "I'm listening."

"First of all, you told me last week that you thought someone was following you home from the hospital," he said. "Has it happened again?"

"Yes. I saw the same car again on Sunday."

"If I'm right, Maggie," he said softly, "the Soviets are using David to blackmail Katherine."

"Dear God," she murmured.

"Katherine says that the boy is in danger, and she wants me to get you and him out of Washington."

"But how? If we're being watched, they'll know and they'll follow us."

"Exactly." He put his arm around her shoulder. "Are you scheduled to work at the hospital this weekend?"

"Yes. I've been assigned afternoon shifts on both Saturday and Sunday, and I've arranged for Mrs. McCallister to stay with David both days."

"I'm going to New Mexico to be with Katherine on Saturday," he said. "And if the test on Monday is successful, I'll be back here on Tuesday." He gripped her shoulder and moved closer. "I think the safest thing for you to do is to stay in Washington. I want you to call Mrs. McCallister and tell her that you won't need her. Then on Saturday and Sunday, I want you to call in sick and stay here with David. Don't let him out of your sight."

"Good God," she murmured, "it seems like this will never end."

64

"You look tired, sweetheart," Michael said.

"It's been a nightmare waiting for you, Michael," she said, "and I haven't slept for four days." She noticed behind the tinted aviator glasses he was wearing that there were dark rings around his eyes. "You look tired as well."

"These last four days have been hell, Katherine. All I could think about was you being here alone." The soldiers saluted Michael as they passed, but he held onto her hand and only nodded.

"How are Maggie and the baby?" she asked.

"They're okay. Maggie told me to tell you not to worry, she's got everything under control."

"She always does, but this time—" She caught sight of Cyril Smith, the head of the Los Alamos metallurgy group, coming toward them up the street. She let go of Michael's hand. "Did you do what I said, Michael?" she asked. "Did you take them out of Washington?"

He shook his head. "No. I talked to Maggie, and we both agreed that the safest thing would be for them to stay in Washington."

"Hey, Mike!" Smith called as he passed. "How are things in Washington?"

"They're fine, Cyril!" he waved. "Just fine!"

"Did you just get in?"

"Yeah! About an hour ago!"

"Great! See y' Monday!" he waved and moved on.

"This is no place to talk," Michael said. "Let's go someplace where we can be alone."

"I found a new path where we can walk," she said. "It's just beyond the quonset huts at the end of town. We'll go out by the main road."

"Fine. You lead the way."

As they walked down Trinity Drive, he looked off toward the Jemez mountains above the laboratory, where a huge dark cumulus cloud was massing above the volcano's caldera.

He walked for a moment in silence, then said, "You told me on the phone that you think David is in danger. What kind of danger?"

A truck carrying boxes of tinned goods from the Commissary raced past them. She thought of the decision she had made last night, but it was too soon to talk of that. She had planned to tell him of Corporal Greenglass over supper at the cafeteria, and then later, on their evening walk, of the letter from Aloise Frégand and the demands the Soviets had made. But it was too soon to talk of decisions. "I'll explain that in a minute, Michael," she said, "but first, I want to know why Maggie and David are still in Washington."

"From what you've told me, they are probably being watched by Soviet agents in Washington. And not knowing what was going on, I decided that the safest thing to do was to keep them at home and not make any changes. While I'm gone, Maggie is going to stay with David at all times."

"I assume you've told Maggie everything," she said.

"Yes, Katherine. I told her about Jacob, and I told her about the work you've been doing here at Los Alamos."

She thought of the oath of secrecy he had kept for three years. "I'm glad, Michael," she said. "Maggie deserves to know."

He started to take her arm, but he saw they were being watched by a group of soldiers standing outside the Information Center. "You said that Jacob has been living in Russia with Aloise Frégand."

"Yes," she said. "He's been working on the theoretical calculation of the plutonium bomb's critical mass for the Soviets."

He waited until they were safely out of earshot of the soldiers, then said, "The thing that scares me, Katherine, is that the Russians must know about the MED project. Not only that, they must also know about the Trinity test and about our plans to use Little Boy and Fat Man to end the war with Japan."

She kept silent until they passed a group of Ordnance technicians milling in front of the bus station, wondering to herself how she would

ever be able to argue her case for her grandson's life in the face of
Michael's lifelong passion for honor and military duty. "Yes," she said.
"From what I was told on Tuesday, it's clear they know everything."

There was a flash of lightning from the clouds massing above the
mountain behind them. Michael waited until the thunder rolled by, then
said, "You told me on the phone that you were approached by someone
here at Los Alamos."

"Yes. The man's name is David Greenglass, and he's an Army corporal."

Michael's only response was a sigh. He walked in silence for a moment,
then said, "Is this Corporal Greenglass a member of Groves' staff?"

"No. He's part of the technical staff."

Michael shook his head and looked away. "For weeks I've been hearing
rumors in Washington of security leaks at Los Alamos, but I didn't believe
them."

She could sense from the distracted way Michael walked, with his
hands in his pockets and his gaze on the ground in front of him, that he
already suspected what she would ask of him.

"You told me the other night, Katherine, that you had a choice to
make."

There was a flash of lightning from behind, followed a second later
by a clap of thunder. She thought: He's moving too fast. It's too soon to
talk of choices. She wanted to talk about Jacob, first, to remind him of
the boy's innocent ignorance of what was happening here in America.
"On our walk last Tuesday night Corporal Greenglass gave me a letter,
Michael."

She had lived in dread of this moment for two days, since she made
her decision to cooperate with the Soviets. "Aloise ended her letter by
saying that the choice was mine to make," she said. "But if I refuse to
cooperate with the Soviets, Michael, if I refuse to turn over my plutonium
critical-mass data to their contact here at Los Alamos, they will not
hesitate to kill my grandson."

"I suspected as much, but I couldn't believe they would threaten the
life of a three-year-old child."

"Greenglass says that the Soviets want my plutonium critical-mass data,
at any price."

Another bolt of lightning streaked across the sky, and this time the
deafening boom of thunder was followed by a gust of cool wind.

"What sickens me," she said, "is that Jacob has been working all this
time for the Soviets in good faith, and that now, without my experimental

verification, he too may be in danger." She averted her face to conceal the tears that had begun to well up in her eyes. "I know my son, Michael, and I'm certain he knows nothing of the truth. He doesn't know what happened to his father, he doesn't know that Maggie gave birth to his son, and he still believes I'm dead."

Ignoring a small convoy of passenger cars speeding past them, Michael reached out and put his arm around her shoulder. "I remember an expression David used when he had doubts about his theoretical work. Theory, he used to say, without experiment is meaningless."

It was an old truth she had long ago mislaid and forgotten: the memory of that afternoon twenty-five years ago in Göttingen, when David first tried to convince her to share the work on his doctoral research project. "Yes," she said, "that was David's favorite expression in times of doubt."

They had reached the open space beyond the construction workers' quonset huts at the east end of town, where the mesa tapered off to a ragged finger of volcanic rock. Blown by the wind from the Jemez caldera, the storm cloud had rolled in above them, throwing its long shadow across the flat expanse of pinon and juniper trees. "The new path I found is over there," she said, pointing off toward the precipitous cliffs on the western side of the pajarito. "It leads to an Indian ruin on the bluff overlooking the canyon."

As a ragged bolt of lightning streaked across the sky, Michael let go of her shoulder. "Are you sure you want to go on?" he asked. "There's going to be a downpour."

"Yes. There are things I need to tell you, Michael."

"Then you lead," he said, "and I'll follow."

She waited until they had left the road and started off across the mesa through the scrubby trees, then she reached into her trouser pocket and took out the crumpled envelope she had carried with her for four days. "Aloise says that Jacob is in good health, that he lives a privileged life in the Soviet Union, and that he has a great future ahead of him as a nuclear physicist." She handed Michael the envelope.

He stopped and took out the letter and Jacob's photograph. "Amazing," he said, "the boy looks more and more like his father."

"Yes. He looks exactly like David did when we met twenty-five years ago in Göttingen."

A sudden gust of wind rattled the letter in Michael's hand. He returned the photograph to the envelope, unfolded the page, and began walking again.

The storm cloud was now directly above them, and another bolt of lightning streaked across the desert sky, shaking the air with deafening thunder. She had been terrified of storms like this all her life, but was determined to go on. She led the way, trying as he read the letter to rehearse in her mind all the arguments she had prepared to defend her choice.

They had reached the western side of the pajarito when he finished reading the letter, and the desert rainstorm was closing in, drawing a dark curtain of rain toward them. In the deepening shadows she could scarcely make out the footworn path.

He returned the letter to the envelope, then said, quietly, "If what Frégand says is true, he's a virtual prisoner in Moscow."

A fierce gust of wind swept by, throwing dust in Katherine's eyes. She looked away and said, "If he only knew the truth, he would leave Russia, I'm sure of it."

"That's easier said than done." Michael handed her the envelope. "If Jacob is one of their key atomic scientists, the Soviets would never let him leave Russia alive. Besides," he added, "it would take weeks, maybe months, to make contact with him in Moscow, and they've obviously given you a deadline for your decision."

Her hopes, she realized, were fading like the evening light. She paused and looked around, searching for the path. "Yes," she said. "But I persuaded Greenglass to wait. If the bomb test on Monday fails, my critical-mass research will be useless to the Soviets."

This time, the gust of wind across the mesa brought with it a few cold drops of rain. Michael took her by the shoulder and drew her close to him. "Strange, isn't it, that after waiting so long for success you should now have to pray for failure."

"I've been praying for failure for four days, Michael." She moved on, wondering if she had taken the wrong way.

"Sweetheart, I think we're lost," he said. "I think we should go back now."

She turned and looked at the approaching rain. "It's too late to go back. There's a rock over there on the bluff where we can take cover."

It was pointless, she realized, to go on postponing the inevitable. As she turned north, heading for the clearing beyond the trees, she said, "If the Soviets know about the American atom bomb, Michael, and if Jacob is already at work on the theoretical calculation of the plutonium bomb's critical mass, it will only be a matter of time before they solve the experimental problems."

"That's true," he said, keeping pace with her. "But if you give them your critical-mass data, they'll be able to build a plutonium bomb in half the time—maybe within two years."

There was an explosion of lightning above the opposite pajarito. "Compared to the alternative, Michael," she said, "what difference does two years make?"

He dropped back a pace behind her. "You don't understand, Katherine," he said. "Truman is in Potsdam right now, trying to negotiate the postwar map of Europe with the Russians; if Stalin knew that he could build a Russian atomic bomb in two years, he would not hesitate to demand the whole of Eastern Europe."

She continued toward the opening in the trees, but as she came out into the clearing, she saw that she had led them to a narrow rocky space between a row of trees and the pajarito's precipitous cliffside. "Stalin will draw his map of Europe with or without my critical-mass data, Michael."

He came up beside her and stood looking out at the vast landscape of volcanic rock that stretched as far as the eye could see. Off to the north, where the shadow of the storm cloud ended, the setting sun lit the ragged barrancas with a soft gold light. "I take it, Katherine, that you've made your decision," he said.

She hesitated, fighting to hold onto her failing resolve. "They want a few scraps of paper, Michael. It's a small price to pay for my grandson's life."

"I cannot argue the price," he said over the relentless wind. "But before you consent to their demands, remember this—one betrayal always leads to another."

"They've demanded my critical-mass data," she said, "nothing more."

He shook his head. "I don't like to remind you of this, but you are where you are today because of that one choice you made seven years ago in Germany."

The memory of that afternoon in Berlin when she went to her father at the Heereswaffenamt and turned over the paper David had written describing the theory of a uranium chain reaction was still painfully clear. She waited until the thunder rolled by, then said, "Greenglass promised they would not ask for more."

"You're wrong, Katherine. This is only the beginning. If you consent this once, it will go on and on. One betrayal will lead to another, and you will never be free again to refuse."

A gust of wind threw a chilling spray of rain against her face. "My loyalties belong to David!" she said, lifting her voice. "He's my grandson!"

This time, the sigh she heard from Michael was like an admission of defeat. "I came here praying that I had misunderstood you," he said.

"All I'm asking of you is to keep silent," she said, "and do nothing."

The wind rose and fell, beating against her face, shaking the trees behind them. He looked down at the darkening canyon floor far below them, watching a bird glide off through the empty space. "Treason is treason," he said. "It comes to the same thing. If I keep silent, knowing that you're engaged in espionage, I will be a worse traitor than Corporal Greenglass."

Lightning split the sky above them. "David is all I have left, Michael," she said and closed her eyes as the thunder rolled back and forth between the walls of the canyon. "And if I refuse their demands, they will kill him."

"Don't ask me to agree to anything now, Katherine," Michael said. "I need time to think.

The rain began to fall, touching her face like the fingers of a small child. She opened her eyes. "I need your help, Michael. I cannot do this alone," she said, and began to weep helplessly. "The choices they've given me are impossible."

He reached out and turned her to face him. "I love you, Katherine, but I cannot help you." He drew her against him and closed her up in his arms. "The choice is yours alone to make," he said, as the sky opened in a downpour.

65

FOUR miles past the sleeping village of San Antonio, the two Army buses left the paved Carrizozo highway and turned south along a rough unmarked dirt road. So this is it, Katherine thought to herself, staring out at the flat empty expanse of lifeless desert: the Jornada del Muerto— the Dead Man's Way.

The headlights of the two buses swung back and forth like searchlights in the night. Here and there along the road she could see the skeletal arms of a cholla cactus reaching up in the darkness. Off to the south, another bolt of lightning slithered across the sky, illuminating, for an instant, the jagged peaks of the San Andres mountains. After a six-week drought, it had finally rained at Los Alamos Saturday night, but the summer storm had quickly passed, leaving the mesa as dry as before. There had been talk that afternoon of a stormy gulf air mass moving in across New Mexico from the south. The sky had been clear when the two buses carrying the fifty laboratory-based scientists left the Hill a little before ten that night, but by midnight, when the convoy reached Belen, there were black, lightning-filled clouds rolling in from the direction of Alamogordo.

As the lead bus rocked across a dry arroyo, groaning to get a foothold in the desert sand, Edward Teller, the young Hungarian theoretical physicist seated in front of Katherine at the rear of the bus, awoke with a start. During the three-hour drive from Los Alamos, Teller had been the only passenger in the bus who had slept.

There was another glimmering explosion of lightning, this time above the Caballo Mountains to the southwest.

"Christ! Six weeks of drought, and now this!" someone called out from the forward end of the bus, shattering the anxious silence that hung over the group since they left Socorro.

In the darkness, murmurs erupted down the aisle.

Richard Feynman, one of the dozen scientists who had boarded the bus in Albuquerque, turned to Teller and said in a loud voice, "If Groves and Oppie postpone the test a third time, I'm gonna quit and go back to Princeton."

"They may have no choice," Teller said. "If there's a weather inversion, the cloud cover could trap the fallout and irradiate everyone from here to Colorado."

"That's assuming the damn thing is gonna work at all, Edward!" Feynman said, and laughed. "This could be a two-billion-dollar dud, you know!"

As the bus swayed around a sharp bend in the road, the silence returned, filling the air like an unspoken question.

Feynman looked back and grinned at Katherine. "By the way, Kate, what was your TNT wager on the bomb's success?" he asked.

She forced herself to smile in the darkness. "I was being reckless when I made my bet, Richard," she replied. "I said ten thousand."

"Wow!" he laughed again. "That would blow up half of Tokyo!"

"Yes," she said, "or Moscow."

Feynman stared at her for a moment, then went back to talking quietly with Teller.

Klaus Fuchs, a fellow German physicist from the theoretical division who occupied the seat next to Katherine on the aisle, sat forward and said, "Weather inversions or not, Edward, General Groves won't postpone a third time. The talks have started in Potsdam, and Truman, I'm sure, wants to have the bomb in his pocket when he sits down to negotiate with Stalin."

"Truman would be a fool to tell Stalin about the Trinity test at Potsdam, Klaus," Teller said over his shoulder. "He should wait until after we make the drop over Japan to tell the Russians about the bomb."

Fuchs sat back. "Truman should tell Stalin about both Fat Man and Little Boy, Edward," he said. "Secrecy and silence can only make things worse with the Russians. It can only create distrust."

She turned away and closed her eyes, thinking to herself of the president's appalling ignorance at Potsdam and the knowledge she carried inside her. She recalled the words Michael had said last night on their walk across the pajarito: You're wrong, Katherine. This is only the beginning. If you consent this once, it will go on and on. One betrayal will lead to another, and you will never be free again to refuse.

She took a deep breath, suddenly feeling that she would suffocate in the cramped cigarette smoke-filled space at the back of the bus. Wanting to be alone during the trip to Trinity, hoping she would be able to meditate on the choices she faced if the test was successful, she had taken the last window seat when they boarded at Los Alamos. But by the time the bus had pulled away at ten o'clock the empty space around her was filled to capacity.

She opened her eyes, realizing that Teller was speaking to her over the monotonous groan of the bus's engine. "Sorry, Edward," she said. "I was dozing."

"I was asking about your friend Rakovsky," he said. "I thought the colonel had been sent down from Washington to write a report on the shot for the Military Policy Committee."

She had pleaded with Michael to come with her, but he had insisted that she needed to be alone for the test. "Colonel Rakovsky had planned to watch the shot," she said, repeating the excuse he had given her to explain his absence. "But he took ill at the last minute and decided to stay behind in Los Alamos. Colonel Russak will write the MPC report for him."

"That's odd, Kate," said Feynman. "I saw Michael at supper this evening, and he seemed fine."

"He got sick after supper, Richard," she said, "just before Bethe's talk at the Conference Hall."

"Anything serious?"

"Stomach flu, he thinks." A bolt of lightning suddenly shot through the sky over the hills directly to the west of them, followed a few seconds later by a deafening clap of thunder. She turned back to the window, realizing that it was beginning all over again: the chain of lies and deceits in Berlin that had led to the ruin of her marriage, her family, and her life. Like the betrayals Michael had warned her about last night, the lies to protect her secret would go on and on.

As lightning flashed again, she opened her eyes and saw that they were now moving along the edge of a flat expanse that stretched as far as the eye could see.

"Look!" someone called out. "There's the shot tower!"

No one spoke as the bus suddenly slowed, then made a slow right turn up the slope of a steep hillside.

Then she saw it: a light far off to the south, sparkling like a beacon in the night. Ground Zero, they called it at the lab. The hundred-foot steel tower held, suspended in its steel cocoon, the bomb's uncertain critical mass core. The Trinity tower stood alone in the center of the desert floor, surrounded on three sides by earth-sheltered concrete bunkers: the control dugout ten thousand yards to the south, where the countdown would take place and the detonation switch would be thrown; in the west, banks of high-powered cameras would photograph the shot; and to the north, elaborate electrical instruments and cameras and searchlights would record for science the effects of the explosion and its aftermath.

"Those lights to the south of the shot tower," announced Teller, as the bus climbed higher, "that's the Base Camp."

Katherine stared at the tiny cluster of lights, wondering if Groves was there, restlessly debating with Oppenheimer and Bainbridge the pros and cons of a third postponement.

A bolt of lightning forked its way through the sky just south of Ground Zero.

Suddenly, as the bus rounded the crest of the hill, an excited murmur rolled down the aisle.

"We're here," Feynman said. "This is Compania Hill."

Flashlights fanned the darkness ahead of them.

Compania Hill, the site reserved for the Los Alamos-based scientists and an assortment of civilian VIP observers, was a safe twenty miles from Ground Zero. Katherine sat forward as the bus's headlights swept across a line of cars and trucks parked along the ridge, feeling as if she had come to the end of an incredibly long and slow voyage, that she had reached the crossroads of her entire life.

With a lurch and a groan, the bus came to a halt.

As the murmurs broke into excited shouts, with jokes about their chances for success or failure, a laughing voice came toward her down the aisle, reciting the poem that had been circulating around the lab in recent weeks:

> "From this crude lab that spawned a dud
> Their necks to Truman's ax uncurled . . .
> . . . Lo, the embattled savants stood
> And fired a flop heard round the world."

She closed her eyes again, trying to imagine how far the limits of their success would reach.

66

"FIVE minutes!" a voice shouted as a green Very rocket arched into the sky above Compania Hill, burst, and fell away into the darkness.

The first warning signal brought the forty scientists and VIPs on the hill to sudden life. The group which had assembled around the radio truck to wait for the decision from Base Camp separated and hurried off to their observation positions along the hillside.

Determined to be alone for the shot, Katherine left the group and moved off in the opposite direction, heading toward a narrow rocky promontory at the crest of the hill. The rain, which had begun in earnest soon after they arrived, had let up two hours later, and at 4:14 a radio message had come through from Base Camp that the test had been postponed until 5:30. It was 5:25, and there were streaks of pink dawn light in the clouds to the east.

A few paces up the sloping hillside, slowed by the weight of her Army-issued boots and coveralls, Katherine paused to catch her breath.

When she reached the spot she had chosen, a narrow declivity beside a foot-high granite boulder, she stopped, feeling dizzy from her climb. She took a deep breath, thinking of Jacob in Russia and little David, two thousand miles away in Washington.

This time, the voice from the darkness sounded lost and far away, "Zero minus one minute!"

Far out across the desert, the shot tower twinkled under the steady
white beam of a searchlight, looking like a child's toy in the vast desert
expanse. In the absence of moonlight, the desert floor stretched away
into nothingness. To the north, still veiled in mist, the Oscura peaks
were like black paper cutouts against the retreating lightning-filled clouds.
She looked up. The rain had stopped altogether. The clouds had separated, and the sweet odor of wet sagebrush hung in the air. Off to the
south, visible through a break in the clouds above the San Andres mountains, were two of Andromeda's stars.

"Fifty-eight . . . fifty-seven . . . !" the voice shouted out the passing
seconds.

A faint gust of wind from the desert floor passed over Katherine's face
like a cold hand. She drew back the damp hair clinging to her cheek,
suddenly aware of her total isolation. The beam of light at Ground Zero
resembled, it seemed, a tiny arrow—a compass needle pointing up at
the heart of a vast empty darkness. She stared at it, wondering at the
distance she had traveled from the innocent days in Göttingen to this, a
barren mound of indurated clay in a remote American desert named,
with prophetic cruelty, the Dead Man's Way.

"Fifty-three . . . fifty-two . . . !"

Like a condemned prisoner hurrying to telescope the last few seconds
before execution, she drew the welder's glasses over her eyes. As instructed, she turned her back to the shot tower and knelt down on the
crusted earth. She felt suddenly absurd: she had spent twenty-five years,
three-fourths of her life, racing to reach this very place, this moment in
time, and having arrived, she was helpless. Neither she nor any of them
knew what they had made out there in the desert.

"Forty-three . . . forty-two . . . !"

As she reached back in her mind, trying to imagine where it had all
started, she suddenly remembered that August afternoon in Germany,
twenty-five years ago, when the train from Berlin had pulled into the
station at Göttingen and she had looked out at the ancient brick walls of
the university for the first time—the afternoon she met David and made
her choice to defy her father and stay on at the Institute.

"Thirty-seven—thirty-six . . . !"

The opening words of the prayer for Divine protection she had said
every night of her life as a child in Berlin came back to her: O Gott, du
bist mein Herr, wenn du auf meinem Weg . . .

With sudden panic, she searched her memory for the words that followed.

"Thirty-one . . . thirty . . . !"

An eternity passed between each second. She would give anything now—her life even—for the chance to turn back the clock and choose another life for herself!

"Twenty-eight . . . twenty-seven . . . !"

Again, she tried to recall her childhood prayer, but without success. She had set out to reach the limits of human scientific knowledge, she had come to the end of human reason and certainty, but she could not remember the simple words of a child's prayer.

"Twenty-two . . . twenty-one . . . !"

Again, she thought of little David and the choice she would have to make, and realized that the time for postponement had run out. As she lowered herself closer to the ground, it was the weight of despair, not the weight of her heavy clothes, that dragged her down.

"Fifteen . . . fourteen . . . !"

Covering her ears with her hands did little to drown out the relentless sound of the passing seconds. After spending her life trying to prove to herself and the world that the power of human knowledge was limitless, all she had done was to come full circle to the ignorance of childhood— to the impotence of blind faith and gratuitous mercy of God's Providence.

"Ten . . . nine . . . !"

She closed her eyes and prayed again, with all the enormous power of her heart, for failure.

"Four . . . three . . . !"

If the scientific work of her lifetime now succeeded, she would be forced as a woman and a mother to commit yet another monstrous betrayal.

"Two . . . one . . . ZERO!" the voice broke with a desperate shout.

The silence went on and on, it seemed, for an eternity. She wondered with hope if her prayer had been answered. But the light that suddenly flooded her closed eyes was like the light of a hundred noonday suns. A feeling of warmth, like the warmth of a child's hand, caressed her neck.

She opened her eyes and saw that the hillside around her—the basalt rocks, the dry desert clay, the yuccas, the sagebrush and the Joshua trees— the entire desert was bathed in a brilliant yellow white light. Rolling over, she looked up at the blinding bell-shaped ball of yellow white fire rising up before her like the sun.

Out of habit, for one brief instant, she tried to calculate the physical force of the spectacle unfolding before her. Paralyzed, with her left hand raised in a reflex gesture of self-protection, she watched as the swirling fireball expanded, driving a huge cloud of earth before it across the desert floor. It seemed to her as if it would go on expanding, rolling in on itself as it grew, until it engulfed the entire world.

It was the silence that made her realize the enormity of it. Within seconds, the fireball's blinding yellow white light faded to molten gold, with swirls of luminous flames—orange and scarlet and green—blazing out from its center. Swallowed up by the roiling cloud of earth around it, the ball hung for a moment over the ground, then billowed out and began to rise like a gigantic parasol on a narrow column of fiery dust.

She thought of the chain-reaction force she had pictured from her plutonium critical-mass calculations, but the vision unfolding before her eyes was beyond anything she had dared to imagine. Boiling like a furious cauldron, the fireball turned an eerie spectral blue as it ascended, bathing the entire landscape—the flat desert floor and the surrounding mountains—with a kaleidescope of unearthly colors. She sat up and watched as the rolling balloon of radioactive fire rose up toward the heavens, pulling the earth behind it in a twisting corkscrew of burning dust.

She and David had dreamed of unlocking the door into the atomic nucleus for twenty-five years—from that very first day in Göttingen, when they talked about their future together as scientists. But neither of them had ever dreamed that the door would open on a new world of such power and magnificence.

She lifted her face to the sky, feeling suddenly dazzled by the human mind's boundless capacity for knowledge. Then, almost like an afterthought, the shock wave struck. The force of its silent impact thrust her backward, and it was followed a split-second later by a boom that detonated in her ear like the report from an artillery cannon. It shook the earth around her, then began rolling back and forth between the mountains, filling the entire Jornada del Muerto with the echo of its tremendous thunder. It was like a groan from the bowels of the earth that threatened to go on and on and never stop.

Katherine lifted herself to her knees and looked up at the darkening fireball above the earth. Still luminous with purple nuclear fire, it went on rising toward the heavens on its column of gray dust, taking the shape of a huge poisonous mushroom as it went.

She thought in the next instant of the future now awaiting their magnificent scientific discovery, and of Truman's plan to use the bomb to end the war with Japan. The irony of it horrified her: a bomb of this power and magnitude to end all war and bring peace. She had been born into a family dedicated to war, in a world that talked of war as a means to peace. She had lived through two world wars, with promises each time that it would be the last, and it was folly to think that a weapon such as this would be used as an instrument of peace.

She lifted her face again to the sky—toward the east where the pink light of dawn had just broken through the clouds—feeling amazed by the human mind's capacity for ignorance.

As the clamor of voices and laughter came toward her from the hillside below, she sat back and rested, thinking again of Jacob in Russia, struggling to complete the calculation of the plutonium critical mass that his father had begun in England. All along, ignorant of each other's dreams, they had been driven by the same ambition: to harness the energy of the stars and to build nuclear weapons to destroy one another. The capacity of the human heart for hatred and cruelty astonished and appalled her.

With feelings of hopelessness and despair, she bent forward and began to pray again, not for success or failure this time, but for the ones who had paid the price for her monstrous dream of fame and recognition: her husband and her parents. In the end, weeping, she prayed for little David, the child who would now be forced to pay for her folly with his life.

67

As the two Army buses carrying the laboratory-based scientists swung on to Trinity Drive, a cheer went up.

Parked in his jeep a block from the Los Alamos bus station, Michael Rakovsky watched as the crowd of welcomers, mostly wives and children, spilled from the station entrance into the street. Though Groves had made every attempt to keep the Fat Man "experiment" that morning a closely guarded secret, even from the staff members' families, it was impossible to keep anything secret from the scientists' wives here at Los Alamos. The light from the pre-dawn blast had been seen as far as Texas and Arizona, and the explanation that Groves had given to the press and radio—that a sizable military ammunition dump had exploded in the desert near Alamogordo—had only brought laughter on the Hill.

Michael waited until the buses passed the warehouse area, then he turned on his engine and sat watching the small group of lab technicians that had gathered in front of the Information Center opposite the station.

Last night, when Katherine boarded her bus for the Trinity test site, he had promised that he would be waiting in front of the station when she returned. But when he arrived at the station at 8:15, he decided to wait down the street out of sight. He couldn't be sure in the fading twilight, but the young man in civvies with the brown curly hair fit the description of Corporal Greenglass Katherine had given him.

Suddenly, as the two buses pulled up in front of the station, the man left his companions and started across the street. Mid-street he stopped and looked around at the people in his vicinity, then he continued on toward the public telephone booths next to the station. It was the rapid way he walked, like a man intent on a purpose, that confirmed Michael's suspicions.

"Damn!" he cursed aloud to himself. He had not counted on Greenglass's presence at the station, and the man's reckless appearance could only mean one thing. With a feeling of panic, he shifted into first and began moving toward the crowd. The Soviets, he thought, must already know about the success of the bomb test that morning, and they're now pressuring him for Katherine's reply.

Wondering how he could safely intercept Katherine before Greenglass got to her, Michael braked and came to a stop. Uncertain as it was, the success of the plan he had worked out last night to free Katherine from her dilemma of impossible choices depended on her willingness to play a dangerous game of deceit with the Soviets and consent to Greenglass's demands.

Ahead, blocking his view of the telephone booths for a moment, the welcoming crowd broke into shouts and surged forward as the passengers began to emerge from the buses. A squeal went up from the children as they darted back and forth, sharing in the excitement of their parents. It was like watching a homecoming for war heroes.

Michael pressed down gently on the accelerator and inched forward. His solution to Katherine's dilemma—impossible as it seemed—had come to him last night as he lay awake pondering Jacob's isolation and astonishing ignorance of the truth. Until then, he had not realized the advantage Katherine had over Greenglass. The fact was, Stalin would be bartering as America's ally at Potsdam, and the public disclosure of Soviet espionage within the Manhattan Project could blow Russia's negotiations off the map. Produced in the right place at the right time, Katherine's knowledge could be used as a bargaining lever for young Jacob's freedom. It was only an idea—an impossible theory, as she would say—but if he could wangle a trip to Moscow, preferably in some official capacity, they could, with careful timing and a little luck, turn his theory into an experimental reality. In any case, his solution would at least offer Katherine an option to outright treason.

Thirty feet away, he caught sight of her at the open door of the first bus. The last passenger to emerge, she stood searching the crowd for sight of him, then began making her way toward the cars parked on the north side of the street. She looked pale and lost and exhausted. He braked again and came to a halt. From the way she walked, ignoring the excitement around her, he could tell that she had reached her decision.

Suddenly, through a break in the crowd, she saw Greenglass. He had left the shadows of the telephone booths and had come forward into the light. Startled by the man's unexpected presence, she took a step backward.

With a knowing smile, Greenglass threw his cigarette on the ground and nodded at her.

She looked around again, this time with fear, as if seeing the crowd for the first time.

Michael thought: If he gets to her before we have the chance to talk . . .

Seeing the crowd suddenly surge forward, momentarily blocking Greenglass's view of Katherine, he reached forward, turned on his headlights, and pressed down on the accelerator. Oblivious of the approaching jeep, she stood scanning the crowd.

Michael braked and came to a halt as the people directly in front of him, all but Katherine, turned to stare. "Damn it, Katherine," he shouted, "it's me, Michael" and honked his horn.

At the sound of his voice, she turned around and stared at the jeep with surprise and confusion. It took an eternity, it seemed, for her to realize what was happening.

Seeing that the crowd was about to part for him, Michael leaned out of the jeep and called to her. It's now or never, Michael thought. Gunning his motor, he drove forward through the crowd and came up alongside her. "Do as I say, Katherine!" he commanded. "Get in!"

There was a moment's hesitation, then she obeyed. As the crowd in front of them parted, he thrust the jeep into reverse, backed out into the empty street behind them, and made a quick U-turn in the direction from which he had come. She reached out and took hold of the metal windshield frame, as he made a quick left turn into 17th Street. "Dear God, Michael," she murmured, "have you lost your mind!"

Except for a small group of people gathered outside the Personnel

Office, the street was deserted. He shifted into first and slowed down. "There's no harm done," he said. "The crowd was between us, and Greenglass didn't see me."

She let go of the windshield frame and sat back. "He's no fool, Michael. He'll ask questions, and he'll find out who you are."

"I had reasons for what I did, Katherine," he said. "Trust me."

As he made a left turn into Central Avenue, she turned away, looking out absently at the deserted office buildings they were passing.

He knew at once where her thoughts were. "I was on the pajarito this morning," he said, "and you could see the bomb's light all the way from Los Alamos." He reached over and grasped her hand on the seat.

"We wanted to know too much, Michael. We went too far, and we destroyed everything." She closed her fingers around his hand. "Pride is the most foolish sin of all."

The despair he heard in her voice startled him. "You worked in good faith to end the war, Katherine," he said. "You couldn't have known what the results were going to be."

She took her hand away and said, keeping her gaze averted, "When I wagered ten thousand tons, I thought it was only a joke. The blast was equal to at least twenty thousand tons of TNT."

Under the despair in her voice there was the sinking sound of surrender. He sped up to pass; the group of soldiers gathered in the street outside the Trading Post, then swung north alongside the meadow overlooking Ashley Pond.

She went on, raising her voice above the jeep's engine. "I've watched a hundred German bombs explode over London," she said, "but that was nothing compared to the destruction I saw this morning. The bomb's fireball was a mile wide, and it rose to a height of thirty thousand feet." Her voice broke and collapsed. "There was nothing left when it was over, Michael. The thermonuclear heat had turned the desert into glass. If Truman uses the atomic bomb to end the war with Japan, Michael, he will not bring peace to the world. The race with Russia for a balance of nuclear weapons will go on and on until one of us destroys the world."

As he made a right turn into the lab's residential area, lights were coming on in the women's dormitories. He took his foot from the accelerator and let the jeep slowly coast to a halt. The last of the twilight had faded above the mountains to the west, and a new crescent-shaped moon was rising above the grove of ponderosa pines to the east. "Katherine, have you decided to refuse Moscow's demands?"

"Yes, Michael. I must."

He recalled the statement she made last night during supper at the cafeteria: that there was no price she wouldn't pay for her grandson's life. His hand shook as he reached for the ignition key. "But last night, I thought you had decided to . . ." His voice died away with the motor.

"I was wrong last night," she said. "And I was wrong when I accepted your offer of a life here in America, Michael. I thought that things would be different—that I had left the nightmares of Germany behind. I told myself that I would find Jacob and make a new life for us here in America. But this morning, when I saw the bomb's fireball rising up in the sky, I realized that I would never be free."

Her defeat, he realized, went far beyond the destructive success at Trinity: she was speaking of life itself. "You're telling me that you've given up, aren't you?" he said. "You're telling me that I've waited all this time for nothing—that you and I are finished."

"Yes, Michael. You must go back to Washington, and you must tell Maggie why I did what I did." She let go of his hand. "You must forget that we ever met, and you must never try to see me again."

"But that's impossible, Katherine," he said, "I love you, and I think you love me. It may not be the kind of love you had for David, and it may not be the kind of love I had for Sarah. It isn't a perfect love, I know, but perfect love doesn't exist in this world. Love like that is a dream that belongs to the young, and neither one of us is young anymore."

Without saying a word she reached for the windshield frame to lift herself from the jeep.

"Do you think you can just walk away from here!"

"I have no choice. First my parents, then my husband, then my son, and now, my grandson. There's nothing left, Michael," she said. "I have destroyed everything."

He watched with horror as she rounded the front of the jeep, realizing that the separation this time would be forever. "No!" he said aloud to himself, remembering the long empty years he had spent between the wars, searching for what he had lost. It was not perfect, this love they had found, but it was a gift—a second chance to live again—that could never be replaced

He left the jeep and started after her down the long gravel path to the dormitory. "You're wrong, Katherine!" he shouted. "There is something left! And you do have a choice! Choice is the one thing you do have!"

Like a stone hurled at her out of the darkness, the words came echoing back from the distant past. She drew up outside the dormitory's front door, remembering a different door, and a picture suddenly flooded her vision: David following her down the hall at Welchzeckhaus, challenging her to defy her father, trying to convince her that she did have a choice.

She stood listening to the footsteps hurrying up the gravel path from behind. It was as if she had returned to the very place and time where she had begun, for she suddenly remembered the thought that had shaken her soul that first afternoon in Göttingen: that behind her, with David, lay all her hopes and dreams for the future; and ahead, with her parents, lay only hopelessness and defeat.

"You're wrong, Katherine, you do have a choice," Michael said again. "And there is something left. You have my love."

Caught between her memories of the past and her dread of the future, she could only stare with confusion at the dormitory's front door.

"It may be too late for you to stop what you started in Berlin," he said, "but you have the most powerful weapon in the world. You have the truth."

"The truth?" she asked, bewildered by the fervor in his voice.

"You said it yourself the other night, Katherine. If Jacob only knew the truth about his father, everything would be different. Good God, we've got all the evidence we need—" he gestured toward the ground-floor window of her room "—those documents you have in your room there!"

For a moment, she could only wonder at what he was talking about. Then she remembered the documents she had brought with her from England.

"I'm talking about your death certificate, Katherine," he said, "and the English warrant for Aloise Frégand's arrest! It's all the evidence we need!"

It was his boyish excitement that cleared her mind and brought her back to reality; and when she turned to face him, there was a look of resolute determination in his eyes.

"But you said it yourself, Michael. It would be impossible to reach Jacob in Moscow."

"Nothing is impossible if you want it badly enough. I have my contact Matt Harmon at the Embassy in Moscow, and if I can arrange a trip to the Soviet Union, I might be able to get through to Jacob."

She said, quickly, "If we could prove to Jacob that Aloise and the Soviets murdered his father, if he knew that he had a son here in America—" but then doubt came rushing back, crowding out her hopes. "It's useless, Michael," she said. "If Jacob is as valuable a scientist as Aloise says he is, then the Soviets will never let him leave Russia."

"It's a long shot, Katherine, but maybe without knowing it you have the one thing that could force them to let him go." He stepped forward and grasped her shoulders. She could see the excitement twinkling in his eyes. "Stalin is at Potsdam trying to negotiate with Truman and Churchill for his postwar piece of the world. The decks are stacked, so he's got to play his trump card as America's ally for all it's worth. And the last thing in the world he would want is for Russia's espionage inside the Manhattan Project to be known. Knowledge, Katherine, is the most powerful weapon of all—and you know enough right now to wreck Uncle Joe's entire gamble."

His hope began to overwhelm her doubt. "I will do anything to save my son and my grandson."

"Then you will have to trust me and do what I say."

"I said anything, Michael."

"What I need now is time, and to begin with you will have to agree to give Greenglass what he wants. You will have to give him bits and pieces of your research—enough to whet his appetite for more, but not enough to solve the plutonium critical-mass problem. Is that possible?"

"Yes. It's possible."

He drew her forward and closed her up in his arms. "It's only an idea, Katherine," he said, softly, "and I don't even have a plan this time. But if you will trust my love for you . . ." He grasped her head and gently kissed her neck.

She looked up at the new moon rising roward the star filled heavens, relishing the heat of his body against her own and the moisture of his sweat against her face, and suddenly felt all the years of accumulated grief and guilt and bitterness washing away on a tide of terrific joy. It seemed that all the hopelessness of this morning's failure and defeat now lay behind her, and all the possibilities of life once again lay ahead.

68

FOR once, the lines to Los Alamos were clear. "This afternoon, I had a meeting with Bill Hollins over at the State Department. He tells me that Secretary Byrnes came back yesterday from Germany and that there were a lot of questions left unsettled at Potsdam." He heard the familiar click of the security people cutting in on the line. He had kept her waiting now for three weeks, and it was pointless to go on playing cat and mouse with Groves' Los Alamos security. "It isn't public knowledge yet," he went on, "but Hollins says that Truman has agreed to negotiate the final settlement of the Potsdam Agreement through a Council of Foreign Ministers, and the four Allied Ministers will be meeting in Moscow in December."

There was a moment of silence, then she said in a cautious voice, "December is four months away, Michael, and we can't wait that long."

"If I play my cards right, sweetheart, we won't have to. Hollins tells me that Byrnes is sending an advance delegation to Moscow to arrange an agenda for the December meeting."

"When, Michael?"

"In eighteen days. They're leaving on August 26, and they'll be in Moscow for a week. If I can get Byrnes to appoint me to the delegation, our problem will be solved."

"Can you do that?"

"I don't know. Hollins says that Byrnes made the appointments before he left Potsdam, but there might be a military advisor's position open."

There was another faint click on the line. She hesitated, then said, "By the way, I ran into our friend yesterday, and he told me that the payments I've been making on the second-hand car of his aren't enough. He said he wants the entire sum, and he wants it in a very short time."

"Can you hold the guy off until the end of August?"

"I don't know, Michael, but I can try." She hesitated again. "He said Uncle Joe is broke and needs the money."

Michael shifted the receiver to his left ear and silently cursed himself for his delay in solving the problem of getting to Moscow. Counting yesterday, Katherine had met with Greenglass four times since he returned to Washington three weeks ago, and the Soviet demands for a complete experimental breakdown of the plutonium bomb's critical mass were becoming dangerously insistent.

There was another click, this time the faint metallic click of a tape recorder. "I'm afraid we'll have to talk about this another time, Katherine," he said. "The State Department is holding a welcome home reception for Byrnes and his Potsdam delegation over at the War Department this evening. I'm not invited, but I'm gonna crash the party and try to have a word with Byrnes."

"I understand, Michael. We'll talk again tomorrow."

"By the way," he said, quickly changing the subject, "was there anything in your newspapers today about yesterday's Little Boy bomb drop over Hiroshima?"

"Yes. They say the casualty figures may reach fifty thousand."

"The *Washington Post* reported the figure as closer to seventy thousand."

"What frightens me, Michael, is that there is still no sign of a Japanese surrender."

She was thinking, he knew, of the Fat Man uranium bomb that had left Los Alamos two weeks ago. "I told you yesterday, Katherine, it's out of your hands now, and you've got to stop blaming yourself."

"I can't help what I feel," she said. "I know that Hiroshima was only the beginning."

There was another soft click. "By the way," he said, "Maggie sends her love."

"How is she?"

"The girl is amazing, Katherine. I've never once heard her complain."

"And little David?"

"He's fine. Every morning, when I go to work, he asks me to tell you to come home."

"Tell Maggie and David that I love them, and God willing, it won't be long before I'll be home."

He looked at the clock on his desk. "It's ten minutes after six, Katherine, and I have to go now."

"Will you call me tonight and tell me how it went?" she asked.

"Yes. I'll be home by eight thirty, and I'll phone you at the Commissary between eight thirty and nine."

"I love you, Michael," she said, softly.

"And I love you."

It was 6:25 when Maggie and David pulled up at the east entrance to the Pentagon.

"I'm late, Michael," she called to him, "so you'd better drive."

"Right!" He got into the driver's seat as she picked up David and moved to the passenger side. "Hi there, cowboy," Michael said, tousling the boy's hair. "How's it going?"

"Okay. We played games today, and we listened to the radio."

"That's our new pastime," Maggie said with a sigh, as he pulled away from the curb. "We listen to all the news broadcasts."

"Mommy doesn't like to listen to the radio," the boy said. "She doesn't like to hear about Grandma's bomb."

Michael caught Maggie's eye and smiled. "I talked to your grandmother a few minutes ago, David," he said. "She told me to tell you that she loves you, and she's coming to see you."

"When, Uncle Mike?"

"I don't know, but maybe in a couple of weeks." As he passed the guard gate, he looked back at the traffic behind them in the rearview mirror. "By the way, Maggie, are we alone tonight, or do we have company?"

"I don't know." She turned around and looked back. "There was so much traffic, I couldn't tell."

"The reception is being held in the War Department building over in Foggy Bottom," he said. "It'll be dark when you get back to Arlington, so I want you to take the main highway and avoid all the side streets. Okay?"

"Right. I'll take the Falls Church road back." She took the boy and sat him in the seat between them. "I want you to sit here and hold your teddy while Uncle and I talk."

"Okay," the boy said.

"Now what's this you told me on the phone about a delegation to Moscow, Michael?" Maggie asked. "It sounds like the solution you've been looking for."

He looked at his watch, then took out a handkerchief and dabbed his brow. "It's a long story, but I'll make it short. I had a meeting this afternoon with a friend at the State Department. He told me that there were questions left unsettled at the Potsdam Conference, and the Foreign Ministers of the three Allied powers were planning to meet in Moscow in December to negotiate the final terms of the agreement. A preliminary delegation will be leaving for Moscow on the 26th of August."

"I see. And you want to ask Secretary Byrnes to give you a position with the delegation."

"Right. I'm going to ask Secretary Byrnes to give me a job as military advisor to the delegation."

"I don't see why he shouldn't, Michael," she said. "You've worked hard for the president's Military Policy Committee."

"I failed to turn in Byrnes' report on the Alamogordo test, and from what I hear, he was very angry."

"He's got to give you the job, Michael," she said. "Katherine is depending on you."

"I know. She told me this afternoon that Greenglass is demanding the rest of her research, and if I don't do something soon she's gonna be in serious trouble."

As he turned with the inbound city traffic over the Arlington Memorial Bridge, he glanced again at the rearview mirror and saw, four cars behind him, a green Ford with two men in the front seat.

"These State Department receptions usually run about an hour and a half," he said, and picked up speed. "But if I can cut through all the protocol and corner Secretary Byrnes for a few minutes, I'll be out in half an hour."

"Don't worry about us. We'll be fine."

"I don't want you to wait, Maggie," he said. "I'll get a taxi home."

"But Kelly Park is right across the street from the War Department building, Michael, and we could wait in the park for you."

He caught her eye and motioned with his head at the traffic behind them. "No. I think you'd better go straight home."

"Right," she smiled. "I understand."

As he left the bridge and started around the Lincoln Memorial, the green Ford edged up and moved in two cars behind him. "The War Department building is on 21st and Virginia," he said. "You can get back to the Arlington Memorial Bridge if you take 21st Street south to the Federal Reserve Building."

"Don't worry, Michael."

"If there's any trouble on the way back," he said, "don't be afraid to pull into a gas station and call the police."

It was pointless, he saw, trying to outdistance the Ford. The street was deserted, and the car was only two blocks behind him. He turned right into Virginia Avenue and pulled up alongside a line of limousines unloading passengers in front of the War Department building.

"Good luck, Michael," Maggie said. "I'll keep my fingers crossed."

"Say a prayer for me, Maggie. It's now or never."

"Can I go with you to the party, Uncle Mike?" David asked.

"No, son. You wouldn't like this party. It's for a lot of old grownups." He put the car into neutral, hugged the boy, and got out.

"Go on," he motioned her forward. "I'll wait here until you turn the corner."

It was useless, he knew, but he stood in the street and watched until she turned south into 21st Street. Then he joined the few remaining stragglers hurrying toward the entrance to the War Department building.

It was 7:05, and the welcome home reception for Truman's Potsdam delegation was in full swing when he reached the ground-floor reception room. Four uniformed Washington cops were on duty at the door. He took his Pentagon security pass from his pocket and handed it to one of the two State Department hostesses seated at the table next to the door. "Good evening, he said, "I'm Colonel Michael Rakovsky."

"Good evening, Colonel." The dark haired young woman took the pass as her blonde companion checked the typed guest list.

"I'm afraid you won't find my name on the guest list," he said, "but I'm here on official Pentagon business."

There was an anxious exchange of whispers.

The dark-haired hostess with the guest list surveyed the medals on his uniform breast pocket. "I'm sorry, Colonel, but we've been told to admit only the names on our guest list."

"I'm General Matthew Styer's adjutant, miss," he said, "and I have some Pentagon business to attend to."

The name seemed to register. There was another exchange of whispers, then the blonde hostess smiled and returned his pass. "In that case, Colonel," she said, "please go in."

Pocketing his pass, Michael moved on into the huge, noisy, flag-draped reception room. It seemed the whole of Washington's civilian and military establishment was present. Admiral Leahy, Truman's new military advisor, stood near the door, surrounded by a circle of State Department officials, Democratic Party bosses, and the now famous back-slapping pals that the new president had brought with him to the White House from Missouri.

As he entered, the orchestra broke into a slow stately rendition of the popular song "I Only Have Eyes for You." The humidity in the room was oppressive. Wiping the sweat from his brow with his finger, he began making his way toward the bar table against the wall, searching the crowd for Byrnes' familiar face.

Hollins was right, he thought. Almost every politician in Washington had showed up for the occasion—Republicans and Democrats alike.

"A double Dewars on the rocks," he told the barman, then turned back to search the crowd. He had not yet met the new Secretary of State, but he would recognize the man's famous face in the dark.

"The amazing thing about these Japs is their bullheaded stubbornness," the elderly man next to him at the bar table said. "You'd think after yesterday's atom bomb over Hiroshima they'd be showing signs of surrender."

"It's not stubbornness, sir," Michael said. "It's pride. If we had allowed the Japanese to keep their emperor, they might be showing signs of surrender."

"What's keeping their emperor got to do with it?" the man asked.

"The Japanese, sir, have a word they use—Matsuoko."

"Matsu—what?"

"Matsuoko. Roughly translated, it means honor."

"Your drink, sir," the bartender said, handing Michael's drink to him.

"Thanks," he took the glass and braced himself with a mouthful of scotch, remembering the frustration he had felt last week when he first read the terms of the Allies' surrender ultimatum. They had reminded him of the punishing terms of unconditional surrender that the Allies had imposed on the Germans at the end of the last world war. Peace with Honor—that was the expression the Germans had used in their plea for mercy at Versailles.

Taking care to avoid the faces he recognized from the Pentagon, he began making his way through the crowd, heading toward the far side of the room. The conversations he overheard along the way were invariably the same—the atom bomb drop yesterday on Hiroshima.

Blocked for a moment by a huge woman in a voluminous satin cocktail dress, he heard someone say, "The death toll in Hiroshima, they say, was fifty thousand, Senator Davies, and the final figures may be even higher."

"Those huge casualty figures you're reading in the papers are meaningless," the senator replied. "Our use of the atom bomb on Hiroshima may prevent a massive naval invasion of the Japanese mainland, and in the long run it may save a quarter of a million American lives."

Michael hesitated, feeling a sudden impulse to turn back and apprise the senator of the Pentagon's latest Japanese casualty figures. Coded radio messages of the Imperial War Command intercepted today from Japan had told of seventy thousand dead in Hiroshima, not counting the thousands dying from radiation poisoning.

The senator is right, he thought with dismay, and moved on. Now that Russia has embarked on building her own atom bomb, the huge Japanese casualty figures could, within a short time, be completely meaningless.

Suddenly, there was a burst of applause from the far end of the room, and when he looked around, Secretary Byrnes, together with a contingent of State Department officials, was making his way toward the reception room door.

Damn, Michael thought, glancing at his watch. It was 7:10, and the reception had only just begun. Knowing that he might only get this one chance, he kept moving, pushing his way through the crowd, and caught up with Byrnes as he entered the foyer.

"Excuse me, sir," he said, breathlessly. "I'm Colonel Michael Rakovsky."

Byrnes, a head shorter than himself, stopped and looked up at him with questioning surprise.

His name, Michael realized, meant nothing to the man. "I'm Colonel Michael Rakovsky, sir," he repeated. "General Styers' adjutant at the Pentagon."

"Ah, yes," said Byrnes. "You're the man behind Styers on the Manhattan Project."

"Yes, sir. I am General Styers' assistant on the president's Military Policy Committee."

"You were also the man who failed to write my State Department report on the test at Alamogordo."

"Yes, sir. That's correct."

Byrnes smiled and moved on. "So what can I do for you, Colonel?"

"Something urgent has come up, sir, and I need to speak to you in private," he said, keeping pace.

The circle of State Department officials closed around them as Byrnes started down the hallway to the building's front entrance. "I can't see you just now, Colonel," he said. "But if you will call my secretary at the State Department, she will make an appointment for you tomorrow."

"I'm sorry, Mr. Secretary, but tomorrow's too late. I have to speak to you tonight."

"That's not possible, Colonel. I'm due at the White House in twenty minutes." Without waiting for his reply, Byrnes pushed past him and hurried out of the building's front door.

Michael followed and caught up with Byrnes as he started down the walkway to his waiting limousine. "I need only five minutes of your time, sir," he said. "I want to talk to you about the delegation you're sending to Moscow on the 26th."

Byrnes came to a halt at the open door to his limousine. "That's not public knowledge, Colonel, but what about it?"

A half dozen State Department officials came up and closed around them in a circle.

"I have reasons to believe that the Soviets now have the means to force the United States to accept communist governments in the occupied territories of East Germany, Poland, Czechoslovakia, and Romania, sir," he said. "And I want to talk to you about a position on the State Department's delegation to Moscow."

"Get in, Colonel," Byrnes said. "We'll talk about this on the way to the White House."

69

"AND now that the war with the fascist powers of Germany, Italy, and Japan has been brought to a successful end, Colonel Rakovsky," Lieutenant Pershikov said, laboring through the stilted English of his Defense Ministry speech of welcome, "it is my government's hope that we will be able to negotiate the final settlement of the agreements we have reached at Potsdam. My government believes, Colonel, that these preliminary meetings of the Council of Foreign Ministers will be the first step toward a treaty of lasting peace with our American, English and French allies."

From the far end of Red Square, over the muffled noise of the Hotel Moskva's huge marble lobby, came the clank of the bell in St. Basil's church tower tolling the ten o'clock hour. "The American government is well aware of the importance of these preliminary meetings here in Moscow, Lieutenant Pershikov," Michael said. "And we are confident that we will be able to work out an agreeable agenda for the council's meetings next December."

With the formalities completed, the young Defense Ministry deputy quickly checked the notes he had brought with him. "Pending the arrival of the French delegation, Colonel Rakovsky, the opening meeting will take place the day after tomorrow in the Kremlin's Hall of the Supreme Soviet. In the meantime, the Foreign Ministry has designated tomorrow as a day of rest and relaxation for the American and English delegations. The Foreign Ministry's reception tomorrow night at the Grand Kremlin Palace is scheduled to commence at seven o'clock, but until that time you and your fellow delegates will be free to enjoy the many pleasures of the Soviet capital."

He had been watched every second since the American delegation's Air Force DC-6 touched down at Moscow's Sheremetyevo Airport two hours ago, and the lieutenant's deliberate emphasis on the word *free* brought a smile to Michael's face. "A day of rest and relaxation, Lieutenant, is exactly what we need," he said, eyeing the half dozen stony-faced NKVD agents milling about the hotel's lobby. "This is my first visit to Moscow, and I'd like to see as much of the Russian capital as I can. For instance, they tell me that the institutions of higher learning here in Moscow are worth visiting. If possible, I'd like to arrange a tour of the Lebedev Institute of Science."

There was a barely perceptible movement of the lieutenant's blue eyes—a faint expression of knowing recognition. "You are welcome, of course, to visit any place you wish to see in Moscow, Colonel," he said. "All you will have to do is inform Comrade Shvernika. She can arrange everything."

Comrade Shvernika, the attractive young government-appointed guide who had met him when he stepped off the plane at the airport, was conferring, he saw, with the hotel's receptionist. Until Lieutenant Pershikov's arrival at the hotel five minutes ago, she had never once let him out of her sight. "Comrade Shvernika, I take it, will be watching over me while I'm here in Moscow," he said.

"Moscow is a large and crowded city, Colonel Rakovsky." Pershikov's gaze rested for a moment on the briefcase in his right hand. "The government must take full responsibility for your safety and welfare during your stay in the Soviet capital. We have appointed guides for each of the foreign delegates to the conference, and yours will be pleased to look after your every need."

"That's very considerate of the government," Michael said. "Comrade Shvernika, I can see, is a very conscientious young woman."

"It's late, and you must be tired after your long flight," Pershikov said, looking up at the big gilded clock on the wall above the reception desk. "The Defense Ministry wishes me to extend you a warm welcome to the Soviet Union, Colonel Rakovsky, and our very good wish that you have success here in Moscow," he went on hurriedly, muddling his memorized English words. Retrieving his officer's cap from under his arm, he bowed and said with studied military dignity, "Goodnight, Colonel Rakovsky."

"Goodnight, Lieutenant, and thank Comrade Beria for his hospitality," he called out as Pershikov hurried past the two NKVD agents stationed at the hotel's front door. For the moment, to his relief, Comrade Shvernika was busy talking with one of the other government guides, and he was alone for the first time since his arrival. Across the lobby, the other five American delegates had grouped around Fred Cheever, the State Department's envoy to the conference and the leader of the American delegation, and they seemed to be arguing heatedly about a lost piece of luggage.

Michael looked around the hotel's crowded lobby, wondering if Matt Harmon had received the letter he had sent him twelve days ago in the diplomatic pouch from Washington. He had sent it the day after his appointment to the Moscow delegation, but it was possible, considering the irregularity of flights between Washington and Moscow, that his letter had not yet gotten through. In any case, Harmon had failed to appear at the airport with the welcoming delegation from the embassy.

He had explained in his letter that he was bringing a package of documents with him to Moscow and he needed to make contact with Jacob. He set his briefcase on the floor and lit a cigarette, pondering his chances of delivering Katherine's documents without Harmon's help. The Soviets may suspect that I'm here for reasons other than State Department business, and they will be watching me night and day. Not only that, he thought, I still don't know where Aloise and Jacob live, and I wouldn't know where to begin to look.

Seeing that he was alone, Shvernika came hurrying toward him across the lobby. "Ah, Colonel Rakovsky," she said, gesturing with the key ring she was carrying, "everything is now in order. I've instructed the porter to take your luggage to your room, and we can go up now, if you're ready."

He lifted his briefcase from the floor. "I'm ready, Comrade," he replied. "Lead the way."

"Come," she said, "the elevator is this way." Gesturing peremptorily at an old woman in blue kerchief and smock who was waiting near the reception desk with his suitcase, she set off at a fast clip for the hotel's single elevator.

As he kept pace with Shvernika across the lobby, Michael thought of meeting with Harmon that night and the chances he had of escaping Shvernika's company for an hour.

"Tell me, Comrade Shvernika," he said, "what's the nightlife like here in Moscow? Are there any bars or nightclubs around the Moskva where a guy could have a drink?"

The question failed to surprise her. "Yes, of course, Colonel," she said. "There are several excellent restaurants in the vicinity of Revolution Square. The famous Arbat restaurant on Prospect Kalinina, for instance, and the Aragvi on Gorki Street."

He suddenly wondered if he might not be able to contact Harmon at this hour through the American Embassy. "By the way," he said as they approached the hotel's elevator, "I was told we have telephones in our rooms here at the Moskva. Is that right?"

"Yes, Colonel. There's a telephone in every room. If you wish to make an outside call from the Moskva, simple notify the hotel operator and she will dial the number for you."

"I see," he said, realizing that it was pointless to think that he could arrange a clandestine meeting tonight with Harmon.

When they reached the elevator, Shvernika spoke a few words to the attendant, then motioned impatiently at the old woman who was struggling after them with the suitcase.

"Hey, Mike! Wait up!" a familiar booming voice called out in English. Startled, Michael turned to see Matt Harmon, dressed in his short-sleeved summer khakis, striding toward them across the lobby. Ignoring the stares from the American delegation and the hotel employees, the big flamboyant Texan waved and called out again, "Rakovsky, you old son of a gun! Why didn't you tell me you were comin' to Moscow."

Recalling the sobering letters he had received from Harmon during the last two months, Michael wondered at his friend's disarming bravura. Shvernika, he saw, had turned to stare at Harmon with shocked disapproval. "Long time no see, Matt," he said, and held out his hand.

"Christ, man, it was only this morning that I found out you were coming!" Harmon said, shaking his hand with hearty gusto. "Why didn't you write and tell me about this appointment of yours?"

Michael saw at once, from the knowing expression in Harmon's smiling eyes, the the ignorant bravura was a charade. "Everything happened so fast," he said, "the appointment and all, there wasn't time to write."

Harmon let go of his hand and stepped back. "You look great, Mike!" he laughed. "Not a day over seventy!"

The four years Harmon had spent in Moscow had taken their toll. The full head of sandy hair he had had in London during the war had thinned, and there was a hollow look of anxiety in his big eyes. "You look pretty good yourself, Matt," Michael said.

"So how's Washington treating you?" Harmon asked with a quick glance at Shvernika. "They tell me you had quite a hand in running the Manhattan Project."

"Washington is just like London was, Matt. I've been stuck behind a desk for the whole damn war." He turned to Shvernika and said, "Let me introduce my friend Captain Matt Harmon, Comrade Shvernika. We've known each other for twenty-five years. He's our military attaché at the American Embassy here in Moscow, and he was our attaché at the London Embassy when I was stationed in England during the war."

"Good evening, Captain Harmon," Shvernika nodded.

"Good evening, Comrade," Harmon bowed politely.

"Comrade Shvernika is going to be my government guide in Moscow," Michael said.

"That's great!" Harmon grinned and winked. "At least they gave you a good-looking young woman."

"Tell me, Matt, how are Alice and Paul?" Michael asked, wondering how he could lead the conversation around to the meeting he had planned.

"Alice is still Alice." Harmon chuckled and shook his head. "She hated the winters in London, she hates the winters in Moscow, and she's still nagging me about that embassy job in South America. Paul is nine now, and he wants to be a five-star general when he grows up." He caught Shvernika's look of impatience and went on. "I haven't heard from you since London, Mike, but I take it you're still enjoying the old bachelor's life."

The question, he knew, was a red herring. Harmon had been conducting his search for Jacob in Moscow for four years, and he knew from his letters of his love for Katherine. "I've been a bachelor for twenty-six years, Matt," he said, "and it's gonna take an act of God now to make a married man of me."

Harmon smiled. "That's what Alice said this morning, when I telephoned home and told her you were coming to Moscow."

Shvernika murmured a few words to the old woman with his suitcase, then stepped forward. "You will excuse me for a moment," she said to Michael, "I have a phone call to make."

"Sure, Comrade. Take your time." He waited until she was halfway across the lobby, then took Harmon's arm and drew him out of earshot of the old lady and the elevator attendant. "Did you get my letter?" he asked.

"Yes. It arrived on the fourteenth. What's going on, Mike? Is this another one of your crazy defection schemes, like the one you had in London?"

When Shvernika reached the hotel desk, she spoke to the receptionist, who handed her a telephone.

"We can't talk about this here, Matt," Michael said. "I have the whole day free tomorrow. Is there a place where we can meet and talk in private?"

"The ambassador is giving a lunch for the American delegates at Spaso House tomorrow. Tell your friend Shvernika that you want to tour the ambassador's residence, and come there at eleven thirty. The place is safe, and we can take a walk in the garden."

"What's the situation with Jacob?" Michael asked.

"I got in touch with my Russian contact the day after your letter arrived. Apparently, they know your relationship with Katherine, and the news of your appointment caused quite a furor at the Kremlin."

"The NKVD is going to be watching me like a hawk, Matt," Michael said, watching Shvernika's animated conversation on the telephone, "so I'm relying on you to find some way to make contact with Jacob. If the plan I have in mind works, there's every chance we'll be able to get him out of the Soviet Union."

"Look, Mike," Harmon sighed, "I've told Ambassador Harriman what I know of your plan, but he categorically refuses to involve the American Embassy in your scheme."

"I'm not asking the ambassador to involve the embassy in my scheme, Matt," Michael said, indicating the briefcase he was carrying. "All I'm asking is that you deliver a small package to Jacob, and the rest will be up to him."

Harmon shook his head. "You don't understand. It's going to be impossible for my contacts to get through to Jacob. He's got the security around him now of a Politburo member. He's driven to and from the Lebedev in a government car, there's a twenty-four-hour NKVD guard around his apartment building on Gorki Street, and his stepmother's telephone, you can be sure, is bugged. Aside from that, the Soviets would never allow one of their top atomic scientists to leave the country alive."

Michael said, watching Shvernika leave the reception desk and approach the NKVD agents near the hotel's front, "One way or the other, we've got to try. Like I told you in my letter, they've tried to blackmail

Katherine into turning over her bomb research at Los Alamos, and they're holding her grandson hostage in Washington. If they find out she's pulling the wool over their eyes, they'll kill them both."

"I can't promise anything," said Harmon, "but I'll speak to my contact again. In the meantime, bring your package of documents to Spaso House tomorrow, and I'll put it in the embassy safe until we need it."

"This may turn out to be another London disaster, Matt, but it's the last hope Katherine has of ever seeing her son again."

"What about the kid?" Harmon asked. "Is he safe?"

"Maggie has the boy with her at my house in Arlington, and they're being watched night and day by the NKVD. If everything goes according to schedule, Katherine will arrive in Washington the day after tomorrow. It's a gamble, but if my Moscow plan falls through, she will pay a call on the FBI and tell them everything she knows."

"You mean, she's gonna . . . ?" Harmon let the question die as Shvernika approached.

"Like I say, Matt," Michael lifted his voice, "we've got meetings scheduled every day from morning till night. But tell Alice I'll make every effort to stop by and see her."

Glancing suspiciously at Harmon, Shvernika joined the old woman with the suitcase by the elevator.

"Remember, now," Harmon said, lapsing back to his Texas bravura, "there's the lunch with Ambassador Harriman tomorrow at noon. And if you can manage to come early, I'll give you a tour of Spaso House."

"I'd like that, Matt," Michael said, joining Shvernika at the elevator. "I'm free tomorrow, and I can meet you there about what—eleven thirty?"

"Eleven thirty's just fine."

"They say Spaso House is one of the landmarks of Czarist capitalism here in Moscow," Michael said, and laughed.

"See you tomorrow, buddy!" Harmon grinned and lifted two fingers in the victory sign.

"If you're ready, Colonel Rakovsky, we will go up," Shvernika said, as she turned into the antiquated wood-paneled elevator.

Waiting for the old woman to join them with his suitcase, Michael watched as one of the NKVD agents at the door left his companions and followed Harmon out the hotel's front door.

70

HURRYING toward the staff members' lockers at the center of the building, Jacob took off his labcoat and turned down the Lebedev's main corridor. Except for a young man wearing a delivery worker's gray coveralls and a temporary security pass badge, the corridor was deserted.

"Good evening, Comrade," the man said, as he walked by, heading in the direction of the building's delivery entrance.

Moving down the long line of metal lockers, Jacob looked back, puzzled by the man's presence in this part of the building. The Institute's storage rooms were in the basement, and deliveries were made through a guarded door at the rear of the building. Remembering the sound of the locker door closing as he approached the main corridor, he suddenly wondered if the man had been rifling through one of the lockers.

Seventh from the end, with his name painted on the door in large black letters—J. E. Linz—his locker now stood next to Dr. Vladimir Bukovksy's. The Russian obsession with the outward signs of bureaucratic success had always amused him, and his rise up the scientific ladder at the Lebedev had been marked, step by step, by his change of lockers down the hallway. He opened the door, took his jacket out, and hung his labcoat on the metal hook. Reaching up to retrieve a notebook from the locker's small shelf, he noticed an envelope lying on top of it. He took the envelope out and looked at both sides. It was sealed and unmarked and made of thick foreign-looking white paper, with a short handwritten letter in English.

At the top of the page was the date: August 28, 1945.

And at the bottom, instead of a name, were the initials: M.R.

My dear Jacob,

You would probably know me by name, but we have never met. I am an American who lived in London from 1939 until 1941, and I was a close friend of your father's when he worked at the Imperial College. Circumstances prevent me from contacting you in person, Jacob, but I am visiting Moscow from the United States, and I have brought with me some papers that may be of interest to you. They are documents that tell the real facts about your mother's "death" in Berlin in 1939, about your father's marriage in Paris to Aloise Frégand in 1940, and about his tragic death in London in 1941 . . .

Jacob looked up, hearing voices at the far end of the corridor. His heart began to race as he recalled the unanswered questions that had lingered in his mind.

He read on, racing to finish the letter before his colleagues joined him at the lockers.

Watched and guarded as you are by the Soviet secret police, it will be impossible for me to deliver the documents to you in person. If you wish to examine them, a package has been left for you in a deserted building in the Golyanovo section of Moscow. The address of the building is 25 Rogozhskaya Street, and you will find the package in a small room on your right when you enter the building. The task of collecting the package must be your responsibility, Jacob, but keep in mind that the risk of your arrest is great and the State Security Police will follow you wherever you go during my stay here in Moscow.

With the hope of soon meeting you in person, I remain sincerely yours,

M.R.

Jacob replaced the letter in its envelope and placed it in his pocket. Closing his locker, he quickly walked to the Institute's main entrance, where he knew an NKVD agent would be waiting to drive him home.

71

JACOB struck a match, held it to the paper, and as the flame inched its way up the handwritten page, he read again the words his father's friend had written: a package has been left for you in a deserted building in the Golyanovo section of Moscow.

Twenty-five Rogozhskaya Street. He repeated the address to himself as he dropped the charred page into the wastepaper basket by his desk. The clock on his desk read 4:35. Calculating the time it would take to make the round trip to Golyanovo, he could still be back home before Aloise returned at seven. He changed clothes and, taking a map of the city from his desk, he hurried into the living room.

He drew back the curtains from the living-room window, opened the window, and looked down at the traffic moving along Gorki Street. The plainclothes NKVD agent who had brought him home from the Lebedev was now pacing the sidewalk in front of the building.

He closed the window, took his cap from the table in the foyer, and quietly left the apartment. A radio was playing in the Bolkovsky apartment, but the sixth-floor hallway was deserted and the building's ancient elevator, he saw to his relief, was where he had left it ten minutes ago. As he took the noisy machine to the eighth floor, he went back over the Metro route he would use to reach the Golyanovo district. Why his father's friend had chosen to leave the package for him at an address in Golyanovo was a mystery. From what he knew, Golyanovo was one of the old sections of Moscow.

A stairwell led to a small janitor's shed on his building's roof. Pulling his cap down over his forehead, he left the shed and began making his way across the roofs of the three adjacent apartment buildings. The sun had just set behind the tall concrete Izvestia building across the street, throwing a protective shadow across the roof of his own building. Certain that he could be seen from the office windows, he took his time, pausing to inspect an incinerator chimney on the first apartment building and a radio antenna on the second. When he reached the janitor's shed atop the third apartment building, he went in and took the building's elevator down to the ground floor.

The hallway was deserted, and he paused at the building's front door to roll up the sleeves of his loose-fitting gray shirt. He hoped his clothes would look like that of an ordinary factory worker. As he left the building, he saw that the NKVD watchdog pacing back and forth in front of his own apartment building had just turned in the opposite direction toward Pushkin Square. Luck is with me, he thought, and swung north, quickly joining the crowd heading towards Mayakovsky Square.

The Metro ride to the northeast side of Moscow took longer than he had anticipated, and it was 5:43 when he reached the Chtchelkovskaya station in the Golyanovo district. In a crowd of departing passengers, mostly workers heading for the nearby Goujon tractor factory, he emerged from the station into a street lined with ornately decorated brick apartment buildings.

Consulting his map, Jacob turned east down Golyanovo's main street, a broad avenue lined with government-owned shops selling rationed clothing and foodstuffs. Four blocks down the street, the huge apartment blocks ended, along with the pavement, at what appeared to be the remnants of a nineteenth-century Russian village. Beyond the village, the main street turned into a country dirt road that wound its way through a landscape of forested hills and carefully cultivated fields. Rogozhskaya Street, which had once served as the village's main thoroughfare, was a dirt street that ran south between a row of partly demolished wooden houses.

As he left the pavement and entered the village, Jacob caught sight of four boys playing soccer in the dirt road ahead. Dressed in short pants and short-sleeved shirts, they were undoubtedly tenants from the nearby apartment blocks.

The numbers above the doorposts of the houses that were still standing were painted in old Russian characters and ran down the road in descending order.

As he approached the boys, they stopped playing ball and stood staring at him with wary suspicion. Watching their small rubber ball roll into the ditch alongside the road, he suddenly remembered the afternoon in Berlin, when he followed his father to that first meeting with the Rote Kapelle, four boys had been playing ball in the street. It was foolish, he knew, but the coincidence struck him as an omen. He slowed his pace, feeling a sudden impulse to turn back.

Opposite the remains of what had once been a rambling nineteenth-century wooden dacha, the largest house in the village, he came to a wooden gate at the center of a crumbling stone wall. Behind the wall stood the burned-out ruins of a tall white-plastered building with a pitched tiled roof topped by the skeletal frame of a wooden onion-shaped dome. The building's front door was missing, and the slender windows on either side of the door had been broken. Suddenly realizing what the building had once been, he moved closer to the gate.

There was no number painted on the gatepost. He looked around, wondering if he had made a mistake. The houses on either side of the synagogue had been demolished, but there was no mistake. The number painted on the doorpost of the dacha across the street was twenty-five. The thought that he had come all this way to find himself in front of the burned-out ruins of an old Russian synagogue amazed him.

Watched by the four boys, he pushed the gate open and went in to what had once been a spacious entrance garden. Weeds had overtaken the walkway leading to the synagogue's front door. His instructions had said that he should enter the building and look for the package in the room on his right. He stopped just inside the door, recognizing the room that had once served as the synagogue's vestibule. Though the fire had blackened the room's walls, he could make out the familiar Hebrew letters inscribed across the lintel of the door leading to the synagogue's sanctuary.

A doorway on his right led to the room he was looking for. He went into the room and stood for a moment, waiting for his eyes to adjust to the dim light falling through the one small window high up on the opposite wall. He was standing, he realized, in the synagogue's registry. As he looked around the room, his eye came to rest on a small bookshelf directly under the window. There, lying on the bottom shelf, was what appeared to be a package wrapped in brown paper. Jacob took the package from the shelf. It was a large envelope made of brown paper, sealed with a hard colorless wax.

Outside, an argument had broken out between the boys. He could hear their voices at the synagogue's front door.

Breaking the seal, he opened the envelope and took out its contents. The first page seemed to be a letter written in the same upright hand as the note he had received yesterday at the Lebedev. Something slipped from the pages Jacob was holding. Reaching down, he retrieved what appeared to be two small photographs from the floor. Unable to make out the faces in the photographs, he stepped back and held up the first photo in the dim shaft of light falling through the overhead window.

A spasm gripped the muscles of his neck and ran down his back.

For a moment, he simply stared at the smiling face in the photo. The face was older now, but the eyes and the mouth and the blonde hair tied with a scarf were those of his mother. She wore a short-sleeved shirt, American-looking trousers, and was standing in front of what looked like a small clapboard military guardhouse. Painted on the wall above her head were the English words Los Alamos Army Laboratory.

Los Alamos, he remembered, was the name of the famous laboratory where the Americans had constructed their uranium and plutonium nuclear bombs.

Clutching the papers to his chest, he held the second photo up in the light. Again, though older, the face was unmistakable.

Dressed in a nurse's uniform, Maggie stood holding the hand of a small boy with large dark eyes and dark curly hair. The boy held a tiny American flag attached to the end of a stick. The two of them were standing in front of a place he recognized from newspaper photographs as the Washington Monument.

The face of the child, Jacob saw, was his own.

"This place is off limits," a voice behind him demanded. "What are you doing here?"

Startled, Jacob looked back to find the tallest of the four boys standing in the doorway to the registry. "Nothing," he said. "I'm looking around."

"It's forbidden to visit this place," the boy announced with officiousness. "You'll have to leave." And with that, he turned away and vanished.

Fighting to get his breath in the airless room, Jacob quickly returned the papers and the photographs to the envelope. A moment later, when he emerged from the synagogue, the four boys stood ranged in a circle around the front door, with the tallest in the center.

The boy holding the rubber soccer ball, a skinny adolescent with close-cropped brown hair and fierce hazel eyes, took a step forward. He wore a red Communist youth Komosol armband around the sleeve of his shirt. "Who are you?" he demanded with studied fearlessness.

"I'm a visitor from Moscow," Jacob replied. "Why do you ask?"

"Because it's forbidden to visit this place. The whole village is off limits."

He knew the game. He had played it hundreds of times with the Hitler Youth gangs in Berlin. "But I thought Golyanovo was open to the public," he said.

"This isn't Golyanovo." The boy pointed to the apartment blocks behind Jacob. "That's Golyanovo. This is the village of Kaliningrad, and outsiders are forbidden to visit here."

"Why?" he asked. "What's so special about Kaliningrad?"

"There's nothing special about Kaliningrad. It's an old Jewish ghetto, and the government has decided to demolish it."

"I see," Jacob said.

The smallest of the boys, a rugged-looking kid with a round pink face and chestnut hair, turned to the boy with the ball. "The man's a foreigner," he said, "and he doesn't belong here."

"Vinogradov is right," said the fourth boy. "We should report him to the authorities."

He meant, of course, the local NKVD.

The tallest of the boys stepped forward. "You're not from Golyanovo, and we want to know what you're doing here."

He took his wallet from his overall pocket and removed his Lebedev security pass. "I'm an official of the State Planning Commission," he said, "and I'm here on an official inspection tour."

The official-looking pass with its Gosplan State Security stamp brought looks of cautious uncertainty.

"That package under your arm," the boy called Vinogradov challenged. "You didn't have that when you arrived."

Precious seconds were ticking away. Holding the package clutched to his side, Jacob moved forward through the menacing phalanx. "No, I didn't," he said, fishing for a name they would easily recognize. "It was left for me by Comrade Lavrenti Beria of the Committee for State Security in Moscow." As he reached the synagogue's gate, the group closed in behind him.

"My father works for the Kaliningrad planning commission," said the boy with the ball. "If there was going to be an official tour of inspection today, I would have known about it."

There was a moment of silence as Jacob turned up the street, leaving the boys behind at the synagogue's gate.

"I don't believe he's an official of the State Planning Commission," one of them said. "He's dressed like a factory worker."

"Fadeyev is right," another boy agreed. "And he also looks like a Jew."

He kept moving, looking neither to the left nor to the right, turning the terrible question over and over in his mind: If my mother did not die in Berlin . . .

72

I T was 7:50 when Jacob retraced his steps over the Gorki Street apartment building roofs.

"Is that you, Jacob?" Aloise called out as he closed the apartment door.

"Yes," he said. "It's me." He set the envelope with the papers on the table by his bedroom door and went to the kitchen. She was at the sink, washing her supper dishes. A soup pot sat on the stove, with its burner unlit. "Sorry I missed supper," he said, trying to sound offhand. "I got held up at the lab."

"I see. Then you were at the Lebedev when I came home."

"Yes. I left a little after seven."

When she finally looked at him, there was fear and bewilderment in her eyes. "That's odd, Jacob," she said. "You weren't dressed like that when you went to work this morning."

"I spilled some chemicals on my jacket, and I had to change. I had these old clothes in my locker."

She said, forcing a pleasant smile, "I was worried. When I came home at seven, the apartment door was unlocked. I was sure I had locked it this morning when I left for work."

He suddenly remembered how, in his haste, he had grabbed his cap and raced out of the apartment. "You've had a lot of things on your mind," he said, "and maybe you just thought you locked it."

"You're right. I have had a lot of things on my mind of late." She took a dishtowel and began drying her soupbowl. "If you want, sweetheart, I'll reheat the borscht," she said. "You must be starved."

He had read through the contents of the envelope on the crowded Metro, and he desperately needed to be alone and think. "Thanks, but I'm not really hungry," he said. "It's been a long day, so I think I'll just go straight to bed."

"By the way," she said, "not only was the door unlocked when I came home tonight, but the living room curtains were also open."

She was testing him, he knew. "Shepilov, the janitor, has a key," he said. "Maybe Shepilov came in during the day to work on something."

"Maybe so," she smiled. "I'll ask him in the morning."

"Goodnight," he said and turned away.

"Goodnight, darling!" she called to him as he hurried toward his bedroom.

He heard a note of fear under the sweetness in her voice. Grabbing the envelope from the table, he went in and locked the bedroom door behind him. He turned on his desk lamp and removed the envelope's contents. He had quickly read through the small sheaf of papers during the long Metro ride from Golyanovo to Mayakovsky Square, but he needed time now to read them again and to think about what he was going to do.

Knowing that he was about to piece together the most important details of his life, he laid out the documents on his desk: his mother's German death certificate; the letter from the American Military Police in Berlin, dated July 9, 1945, confirming the fact that his mother's German death certificate was a forgery; the British warrant for Aloise's arrest, dated August 12, 1941; and the Scotland Yard investigation report, dated September 16, 1941, which described the evidence the Yard had collected supporting the arrest warrant issued against Aloise Frégand, a French citizen, for her complicity in the murder of David Linz, an American citizen residing in London.

Along with the photographs of his mother and Maggie and his son, he took Colonel Rakovsky's page of handwritten instructions on what he must do if he chose to act on the evidence, and set them aside on his desk.

Next, he sat down and took up the three-page letter his mother had written to him from her laboratory in Los Alamos. Dated August 18, 1945, it began:

My dearest Jacob,

Over seven years have passed since we last saw one another in Berlin, but when I look back over the terrible events that have separated us it seems to me that a century has gone by . . .

Moving the page closer to the light, he began to read again her account of the events that had led her to this appalling dilemma: her foolish and ambitious betrayal of his father's research in Berlin, and her flight from Germany.

. . . The night you and your father fled from Berlin, grandfather Eric telephoned the station authorities at Saarbrücken and ordered them to allow you and your father to pass the border into France . . .

He paused for a moment, remembering clearly that mysterious night at the railway station in Saarbrücken, when the German border guard came into the room where he and his father were being held and told them they were free to cross into France.

. . . Your grandfather was arrested for treason two days later and shot the following week at the Moabit Prison in Berlin. Your grandmother was sent to Auschwitz where she died in March of 1939 . . .

He thought with horror of the hatred he had carried inside him all these years, then turned the page and read again of his mother's flight to England, her two-year seclusion in the tenements of South London, and her miraculous meeting with his father in July of 1941.

He looked up from the page into the lamplight, remembering the night he and Maggie visited his father and Aloise following the air raid and the troubling feeling he had had afterward that his father had been trying to tell him something.

. . . Those last days I spent with your father in London, Jacob, were a nightmare. We wanted more than anything to contact you in Cambridge, but we were afraid that Aloise would discover my presence in London, and we knew that David was being watched by the NKVD . . .

As he read his mother's account of the events leading up to his father's death—the plans they had made for an escape to America and Major Michael Rakovsky's attempt to bring him safely to London—the puzzle of those last days in Cambridge suddenly came together: the telephone call from Aloise warning him to stay in Cambridge and make no attempt to contact his father; then the anxious call from Maggie, when she pleaded with him to meet her at the bookstore near Kings Cross station.

. . . Maggie was pregnant with your child, Jacob, and she was the only person Michael Rakovsky trusted to bring you safely to London. She loved you, and she wanted only to protect you. We still don't know what went wrong, but Aloise must have found out about Maggie's telephone call to you in Cambridge. The plan was to meet you at the bookstore near King's Cross station and go from there to a safe house in London. When your father arrived by taxi at one o'clock, Maggie and I were waiting with Michael Rakovsky in the bookstore. What I write now seems, in retrospect, unreal to me. I can see your father very clearly, leaving the taxi in front of the store. I heard the gunshot and I saw your father fall on the sidewalk in front of the shop's door . . .

He sat back and stared at the page, remembering his meeting that afternoon with Aloise at the station in Cambridge and their race to the port of Plymouth. With a sinking heart, he read again his mother's account of her drive that night with Maggie to the port of Plymouth, where they found that he had already sailed with Aloise for Lisbon, and her decision that night to accept Major Rakovsky's offer of refuge for herself and Maggie in America.

. . . We sailed for America on September 16, 1941, and arrived on September 21. Michael Rakovsky was a godsend, for he has given us everything and he asked for nothing in return. I had lost hope of ever learning your whereabouts in Europe for the duration of the war, but with Michael's help I began to search for your wherabouts in Europe and Russia. In March of that year Maggie gave birth to your son. Like you, he was taken to the synagogue two days later and given the name of his grandfather, David Albert Linz. As for myself, I left Washington for Los Alamos, New Mexico, the following year, in August of 1943, where I began my experimental work on the American atom bomb. . . . Six days before we tested the plutonium bomb at Alamogordo, a Soviet agent came to me in Los Alamos. He told me that the Russians were now determined to build an atom bomb of their own, but it would take them years to do so. It was only then that I finally learned of your whereabouts. He told me that you were living in the Soviet Union and that you were working as a theoretical physicist at the Lebedev Institute in Moscow. He gave me a letter from Aloise explaining what the Soviets wanted of me. Maggie and your son David are being closely watched by agents of the NKVD in Washington . . .

As he read his mother's account of the demands the Soviets had made and the choice Aloise had given her—the choice between her plutonium critical-mass data and the life of his son—the rage he had felt on the Metro came back.

He sat forward and closed his eyes. He thought of the vow Aloise had taken long ago in France to remain faithful to the Communist cause, and the extraordinary lengths to which she had gone to strengthen her position in the Party. When he opened his eyes, his gaze came to rest on the last words his mother had written in her letter:

> . . . I do not know if you will find the strength to accept the terrible truth I have brought you, Jacob, or the will to forgive the mistakes I have made, but the choice is now yours to make. I can only repeat those words your grandfather Jacob once wrote to your father in Göttingen: Gifted scientist that you are, you will one day come full circle to find yourself at the end of your powers to reason. Hopefully, you will then realize with humility that the answers to all the ultimate human questions can only be found in the darkness of blind faith.

Folding the pages of his mother's letter, he placed them with the photographs and Colonel Rakovsky's instructions in the top drawer of his desk. It was 8:55, and the long night still lay ahead of him. Opening the bottom drawer of the desk, he took out the tiny cardboard box he had brought with him to Russia from England. He had not opened the box for almost five years, not since that afternoon in Cambridge when he packed it in the overnight bag with his clothes. He removed the lid and took out the tiny black mezuzah that had once belonged to his grandfather Jacob: the gift his father had given him that last night they were together in London.

Holding the mezuzah clutched in his hand, he turned out the lamp, lowered his head, and wept.

73

AT 5:00 A.M., dressed as usual for work, Jacob carefully gathered up the evidence—his mother's handwritten letter and the four incriminating documents—and placed the papers in Colonel Rakovsky's brown paper envelope. Turning out his desklamp, he tiptoed into the living room. Though the curtains were drawn over the windows, he could see in the inky darkness that Aloise's bedroom door was closed. Taking care not to make a noise, he went out into the hallway and closed the apartment door behind him. This time, having no reason to conceal his departure, he took the elevator to the first floor and left the building by the front door.

"Good morning, Comrade," he greeted the startled NKVD agent on duty at the entrance with a wave, and turned south down Gorki Street, heading toward Revolution Square and the Kremlin.

There was a muttered protest, then the sound of scurrying footsteps as the man hurried inside the building. The nearest telephone would be in Shepilov's, the concierge's, apartment on the first floor.

Gorki Street, all the way down to Marx Prospect, was deserted, and only a single light burned on the top floor of the government apartment building across the street. A cold morning breeze was blowing up the street from the Moskva river beyond the Kremlin. Tucking the envelope under his left arm, Jacob set himself a brisk even pace.

To know the truth, he thought, is to possess the most amazing power of all. Overnight, the fear he had carried inside him for so long had vanished. He was free now, and beyond the reach of any harm.

As he came to Pushkin Square and started across the broad Strastnoy Boulevard, he could hear the fountains splashing in the nearby Naryshkin Gardens. This is the hour of peace, he thought, the silent hour of calm before the storm.

As he reached the enormous gray Central Telegraph Building at Ogareva Street, a car rounded the corner of Marx Prospect a block away, its headlights fanning the darkness, and came speeding toward him up the street. It was a black four door ZIS, the kind used by the NKVD. At a distance of fifty feet, just opposite the Yermolova Theater, the car suddenly slowed and swung in toward the curb. There were two men seated in the front seat, and as the car passed by he saw looks of puzzled anger on their faces.

The NKVD's response was even quicker than he had anticipated. The agent at the apartment building had made his call, and they had been sent, undoubtedly, from the State Security offices on Dzerzhinsky Square.

A moment later, the car made a quick U-turn, then came back and pulled in behind him. Shifting the envelope to his right hand, where it could be plainly seen, he continued on as the car followed behind him.

Ahead, at the corner of Marx Prospect and Revolution Square, the darkened façade of the American Embassy came into view. Rakovsky's instructions had said that his best opportunity would come on the morning of the 31st, when the foreign delegates to the Council of Ministers would assemble for an early morning meeting at the American Embassy. The delegates would begin arriving at the Embassy at 6:45 for the seven o'clock meeting, and he would have approximately fifteen minutes to make his move.

When he came to Revolution Square at the end of Gorki Street, the first light of dawn had just broken across the sky to the east, bathing the Kremlin's gilded onion-domes with a soft golden light. As he made a left turn up Marx Prospect, heading for Sverdlov Square, he looked back over his shoulder at the Kremlin's dark brick walls and recalled again the vow of loyalty Aloise had taken to the Communist Party. The wheels of Soviet justice grind slowly, he thought, but they grind very fine.

Behind him, with dog-like fidelity, the NKVD ZIS turned the corner into Marx Prospect and kept pace as he walked up the hill. He smiled to himself, amused by the thought that he was leading them back along the same route they had just taken to the very place they had started out from: to the Lubyanka Prison on Dzerzhinsky Square.

As he passed the ponderous stone monument to Ivan Fedorov and turned into Dzerzhinsky Square, the NKVD ZIS dropped back and made a slow wide circle around the square. A single row of lights burned in the prison's ground-floor windows, but the rest of the huge brick building was dark.

Except for the uniformed militiaman on duty at the door and a single NKVD receptionist, the Ministry of State Security's ground floor entrance appeared deserted. Greeting the militiaman at the door with a wave, Jacob continued across the huge gloomy room toward the NKVD agent seated behind the reception desk.

"Good morning, Comrade," he said, noticing that the receptionist had just awakened from a deep sleep.

"Good morning." The man leaned forward and began officiously arranging the papers on his desk.

"My name is Jacob Linz, and I'm here to deliver a package to Commissar Lavrenti Beria."

"You what?" The man's groggy eyes opened with surprise.

"I said I have a package for Commissar Beria."

The man picked up a pen and opened a leather-bound ledger. "Your name?" he asked.

"Jacob Eric Linz."

"Your place of residence?"

"Number 37 Gorki Street, apartment 17."

"Your occupation?"

They were the same questions he had answered a hundred times in a hundred other government offices here in Moscow. He glanced up at the clock on the wall behind the desk: Precious seconds were ticking away. It was already 5:31. "I'm a theoretical nuclear physicist with Lebedev Institute here in Moscow," he said, shifting the envelope impatiently in his hands.

"I'm sorry," the man said as his pen scratched its way across the paper, "but the Commissar does not receive visitors without an appointment. All business pertaining to the Ministry of State Security is handled by Comrade Secretary Gregor Golikov, the Commissar's deputy assistant. If you want to see Comrade Golikov, please take a seat there by the wall. The Deputy Secretary's office will open at seven thirty."

"You misunderstand, Comrade," Jacob said. "I don't want to see either Commissar Beria or the Ministry's deputy assistant secretary. I merely want you to deliver this package of documents to the Commissar of State Security."

The man opened a drawer and took out a single printed page. "In that case, you will have to fill out this form," he said.

"To hell with your bloody forms," Jacob said. "I've filled out enough bureaucratic forms in Moscow to last me a lifetime." He leaned forward, holding the package in his right hand, and rested his left hand on the desk. "I want you to listen very carefully to my instructions, Comrade," he said, staring fixedly at the man's astonished brown eyes. "Your boss Beria, I happen to know, arrives at the Lubyanka every morning at eight o'clock. At exactly eight fifteen, I want you to take this envelope up to his office on the eighth floor. Remember my name, Jacob Eric Linz. Tell Beria's secretary that the papers inside the envelope concern my stepmother, Comrade Aloise Frégand. It's a French name, Comrade, so you'd better repeat it to me."

Bewildered, the man obediently repeated the name.

Jacob placed the envelope in the center of the desk. "Remember," he said, "Comrade Aloise Frégand."

The receptionist lifted the envelope and nodded.

When he left the building, the NKVD ZIS was parked thirty feet away in the shadows of the prison's colonnade. As he started back across the square, the car pulled out and followed, keeping its steady distance. There was a soft golden light above the rooftops on the eastern side of the square. As he reached the corner of Marx Prospect, he looked up with a new feeling of hope at the cloudless blue sky overhead, then continued down the hill toward the Kremlin and Revolution Square.

74

IT was 5:55 when he arrived back at the Gorki Street apartment and found Aloise, as he had anticipated, pacing the living room floor. "My God, Jacob, it's six o'clock. Where have you been?"

Though it was already dawn, the curtains were drawn and the lamps were lit in the living room. "I had an errand to run," he said, quietly closing the door.

"I was awake when you went out. You left here at five o'clock."

"That's right," he said. "I had some papers to deliver." The ashtrays, he saw, were filled with half-smoked cigarette butts.

She watched in silence as he went to the living-room window and drew back the curtains. Lights were coming on in the apartment building across the street.

"Papers to deliver? Where?"

"To Dzerzhinsky Square."

He could see her reflection in the windowpane. He watched as she removed a cigarette from the package on the coffee table. "I want to know what's going on, Jacob," she said. "When I came home last night, I spoke to Shepilov in the hallway downstairs. He told me you had returned home from work a short time after four."

"The NKVD brought me home at four twenty-three."

"But you weren't here when I came home from work at seven."

"That's right. I came home, changed clothes, and went back out again."

"But that's not possible. Both Shepilov and your security guard would have known if you had come home and gone back out."

Your security guard: he smiled at her euphemism. "As my father used to say, Aloise, nothing is impossible if you really want it badly enough. I had some private business to take care of, some papers to collect. So I changed clothes and left the building by way of the roof."

"What are these papers you keep talking about?" she asked.

"Documents," he replied. "But I'll come to those in a minute. Suffice it to say that I collected them yesterday afternoon and delivered them this morning to Dzerzhinsky Square."

"What are you trying to tell me, Jacob?" she said. "You're talking in riddles."

"I think in riddles, Aloise," he said, "because my parents were both scientists and they taught me to think that way. The universe, they used to tell me, is a riddle, and the scientist's job is to ask questions so that he can solve the riddle and know the truth."

Gorki Street, he saw, was coming alive with early morning car traffic. Time was running out. "The thing is," he said, "I have answered all the scientific questions and I have solved all the scientific riddles I came here to Russia with. But what I want to know now, are the answers to some human riddles."

Behind him, there was a betraying moment of hesitation. "Like what, Jacob?" she asked.

"How, for instance, did you know that my mother was living in the United States and working for the American Manhattan Project?"

For a moment, the only sound in the room was that of Aloise's rapid breath.

"And how, for instance, did you know that Maggie Ryder was there, and that she had given birth to my son?"

The breathing stopped.

When he turned to face Aloise, the look of astonishment he saw in her eyes was almost childlike.

"I know that my mother is alive and living in America," he said. "You wrote a letter to her there in July."

Aloise's mouth opened, and her astonishment gave way to a look of horrified recognition.

He took from his jacket the photograph of his mother and the photograph of Maggie and his son. "As you can see, my mother is still beautiful. You always said that Maggie Ryder would amount to nothing, but she's a nurse now, just like she said she would be. Not only that, it turns out that she was telling the truth when she called me that afternoon in Cambridge and told me she was pregnant. She gave birth to my son in America, and she named him David, after my father. He's three and a half years old now, and he looks exactly like me." He placed the photographs on the table.

Aloise stared with disbelief at the two photographs for a moment, then said, "I was forced to write that letter, Jacob. I had no choice."

"What do you mean, you had no choice?"

"I was ordered to write it."

"Ordered by whom?"

She fidgeted with the sash on her dressing gown, hesitating. "By the Committee for State Security."

"You mean by Comrade Lavrenti Beria."

"Yes, by Beria. It was Beria who told me that your mother was living in America . . . that she was working for the American atomic bomb project."

"You wrote to her in America, and you told her she had a choice to make," he said. "You told her that Moscow wanted copies of the experimental research she had done on the American plutonium atomic bomb. You said if she didn't cooperate they would take steps to eliminate—those were the words you used—steps to eliminate Maggie Ryder and my son."

"Those were the words he wrote, Jacob," she said. "I had no other choice, I had to sign the letter."

"In other words, you were only carrying out the Commissar's orders," he said.

"Yes. He called me to the Lubyanka because he had learned that the Americans were about to test a plutonium atom bomb. He knew about your theoretical work at the Lebedev and your requests for experimental funding for a Soviet plutonium bomb."

He could see the lie taking shape in her face. "In other words, you're telling me you had no idea that my mother was alive when you met with Beria," he said.

"No. How could I have known?"

He left the coffee table and went to the bureau on the far side of the room. "I remember how guilty my father used to feel about his violations of the British Official Secrets Act. He came to you one time, I remember, and he told you that he wanted out, that he had helped you enough with your espionage work for the Soviets." He opened the bureau's top drawer. "Do you remember what you said to him that night?"

"No, Jacob. That was a long time ago."

"You told him that the Kremlin was an exacting master, Aloise. You told him that loyalty to the Party was everything." He took the cloth bag containing the revolver from the drawer—a Soviet 1.62 MM which the NKVD had given her last June.

She said, panic rising in her voice, "I may have said those words, yes. But your father was the key to our entire atomic intelligence operation in England. I couldn't have let him go, even if I had wanted to."

He removed the revolver from the bag and held it up. "Beria ordered the NKVD to give you this to use if I found out about his blackmail scheme, didn't he?"

"Don't be silly, Jacob." She edged back from the coffee table as he rotated the revolver's cylinder. "It was given to me for your protection."

The cylinder was empty. He placed the revolver on the bureau and removed the box of 7.62 MM cartridges from the drawer. "You remember, don't you, that expression my father used to use—that theory without experiment is meaningless? It was an expression he and my mother always used when they were faced with moments of scientific doubt."

"What are you trying to say, Jacob?"

He shook six cartridges into the palm of his right hand. "The first lesson my mother taught me as a scientist, Aloise, was to look for evidence. You can dream up all theories you want, but you can never prove anything until you have the experimental evidence." He replaced the cartridge box and closed the drawer. "Two days ago, someone paid a call on me at the Lebedev. I don't know who my visitor was, but he left a message in my locker saying that a package would be delivered to a certain address in east Moscow. The package, I was told, would contain some interesting evidence related to my mother's death in Germany in 1939, my father's marriage to you in 1940, and his death in 1941.

"The package interested me, of course," he said, "especially since there were so many unanswered questions about both my mother's and my father's deaths." He pulled the hammer back and examined the gun's barrel. "As it turned out, the address they had given was an old burned-out Jewish synagogue in the village of Kaliningrad." He released the hammer and gave the cylinder a spin. "And the evidence I found there was truly astonishing."

"Evidence for what?" she demanded.

When he turned from the window, she had retreated to the armchair on the far side of the room. At the sight of her there, fingering an unlit cigarette, looking as remorseless as ever, he suddenly wanted, more than anything, the satisfaction of avenging his father's murder. He took a single cartridge between his fingers and inserted it into the cylinder. "Evidence for the Soviet People's case against you for the crime of treason," he said. "Evidence that proves that you knew my mother was alive when you married my father in Paris . . . and when you took on the job of director for Soviet intelligence in England and made my father the key to your entire operation."

The cigarette broke in Aloise's fingers. "That's impossible," she said. "Your father and I had proof that your mother was dead when we married. We had her death certificate. It was sent to me from the Soviet embassy in Berlin."

Her capacity for offering a reasonable explanation for what seemed absurd had always amazed him. He took a second cartridge and inserted it into the cylinder. "You should have destroyed that document," he said with a feeling of relish. "Following the Russian occupation of Germany, the American military authorities in Washington sent a copy of the certificate to the Soviet occupation authorities in Berlin with a request that they verify its authenticity." His hand shook as he rotated the cylinder. He looked up and smiled at the helpless panic he saw in her eyes. "Among the papers I collected yesterday from the synagogue in Kaliningrad was a letter from General Vlasov, the head of our Soviet occupation troops in Berlin. It was dated July 9, 1945, and it confirms the fact that my mother's death certificate is a forgery."

As he took a third cartridge between his fingers, she asked, "Who gave you these papers, Jacob?"

He ignored the question and inserted the cartridge into the cylinder. "According to the Soviet military authorities in Berlin, the type used to print the document was not available in Germany in 1940," he said. "It was manufactured only in France."

"I assume you realize that the crimes of treason and bigamy are both punishable by death in the Soviet Union," he said.

She stepped back, staring vacantly at the revolver, and slowly lowered herself into the armchair.

He took a fourth cartridge between his fingers. "It wasn't until you married Papa and became the director of Soviet wartime intelligence in England that you finally won the Kremlin's recognition. Beria was in charge of Soviet atomic research, Papa was working for the Tube Alloys project, and he, not you, was the key to the Soviets' atomic intelligence operation."

He went on, slowly inserting the fourth cartridge as he spoke. "1941 was the year I met Maggie in London. The Blitz was still underway that summer, and I remember how I telephoned Papa in August to find out that he had been injured in a bomb raid . . ."

He took a breath and went on. "I came down to London the next afternoon, and Maggie and I paid a visit to you and Papa. He wasn't there when we arrived, and I remember how upset you were." He rotated the cylinder and took the fifth cartridge in his fingers. "That was the night you told me that Papa was under suspicion for espionage at the Imperial College and was being watched by the British Secret Service."

He tried to insert the cartridge, but his hands shook and he could not fit the point into the hole.

"When Papa came home that night," he said, "I remember how strangely he acted—as if he wanted to tell me something but couldn't." He braced his thumb against the handle and forced the cartridge into its hole. "Later, he took me aside and told me to go back to Cambridge and wait there until everything was arranged. I thought it all had to do with the threat of our arrest and some plan he had for getting us out of England." He rotated the cylinder to the last empty hole. "I went back to Cambridge that night, and that was the last time I saw either Papa or Maggie. Three days later, she called me in Cambridge and pleaded with me to come to London. She was pregnant, she said, and needed to see a doctor . . ."

When he turned to face Aloise again, she had left the armchair and was standing in the center of the room.

"You, of course, know the rest," he said, and looked away, thinking with anguish of all his father's tragic and misspent passion.

Still, she would not relent. "I've told you a thousand times, there was nothing I could do to help the girl!" she said. "Your father was going to be arrested!"

He swallowed again. He could taste his revenge, and it was sweet. He took the sixth and last cartridge and forced it into its hole.

"Among the papers I collected yesterday was a letter from my mother," he said. "It was written thirteen days ago in America and delivered to me here in Moscow. It explains how you found out that she had come back and how they planned to escape with me to America." He steadied the handle in his palm and let his finger come to rest on the trigger. "And how you discovered their plan and had my father shot by the NKVD."

She kept moving backward, watching him finger the trigger. "Your mother is lying, Jacob," she said. "She has no evidence to prove that I had anything to do with your father's death."

The temptation to rest his finger against the trigger's cold steel was irresistible. Slowly, he followed her across the room. "Among the papers I collected yesterday was a British warrant for your arrest. It was dated September 16, 1941, and it charges you with complicity in my father's murder." He drew the hammer back and locked it in place.

As she came up against the wall between the bookcase and her bedroom door, fury broke through her terror. "This is Russia, Jacob, not England!" she shouted. "Do you think that it matters one bit that the British have charged me with complicity in your father's murder?" She edged her way along the wall until her shoulder struck the corner of the bookcase. "He had planned to defect to America with the names of all the Soviet intelligence agents in England, and the NKVD would have killed him anyway."

The hatred that suddenly welled up inside him exploded with a power he had never imagined possible. He stopped and closed his finger around the trigger.

As he raised the gun and took aim at her heart, she turned her face away and shouted, "Don't you understand anything! I loved your father and I had lost him!"

He watched, holding the gun at arm's length, as she crouched back against the bookcase and lifted her hand into the air.

It was as if she had suddenly thrown a curtain back and flooded the room with light. He felt the rage drain from his body. And with it, all the fear and all the admiration that had held him bound to her for so many years.

He stepped back and lowered the gun. "You're right," he said. "What you did to my father in England doesn't matter here in Russia. What matters in Russia is the truth. The fact that you have built your entire career in the Soviet Communist Party on a lie, that's what matters," he said, releasing the gun's hammer. "The fact that you made my father the key to your atomic espionage operation, knowing that you were compromising the entire Soviet intelligence network in England—that's what will matter to the Kremlin."

She covered her face with her hand and began to weep.

The sight of her crouched against the bookcase sickened him. He turned away, gathered up the photographs from the coffee table, and thrust them into his jacket pocket. "In all, I delivered four documents to Beria at the Lubyanka," he said. "Your forged German death certificate, General Vlasov's letter, the British warrant for your arrest, and the letter from my mother."

She took her hands from her face and looked up at him with horrified astonishment.

He looked around, realizing that the apartment was filled with morning sunlight. "It's finished," he said. "I've done what I came to do."

As he started toward the apartment door, she took a step forward. "I was forced to do what I did, Jacob!" she cried out. "I had no choice!"

He stopped at the door, realizing that he was still holding the revolver.

A choice, he thought, is what she had made back in Paris, at the very beginning. And thereafter, it had only been the compromises she had made with her heart.

He turned and said, quietly, "You once told me that my father's death was one of honor, that he had made a great sacrifice to the Communist cause and that he died a hero of the Soviet Union." He pulled the hammer back and locked it in place again. "If that's true, then it's only fair that I allow you to make that sacrifice." He set the revolver down on the dining room table, then turned and left the room.

75

HIS watch read 6:32. In the morning rush-hour traffic a bicycle ride to the Marx Prospect would take roughly ten minutes. He took a deep breath to calm himself. The elevator passed the ground floor and bumped to a halt at the basement door. He had not used his bicycle since June, but he found it where he had left it, propped against the wall next to the water boiler. He loaded the cycle into the elevator and returned to the ground floor. Shepilov, the building's watchdog janitor, was on a ladder polishing the hallway's brass light fixtures.

"Good morning, Comrade Shepilov," he said, greeting the old man.

Mumbling to himself, the startled Shepilov watched from the ladder as he wheeled the bicycle out the front door.

The NKVD guard who had been on duty when he left the building at five o'clock, a heavy-set Karelian with a scar down the side of his face, was pacing the sidewalk in front of the building. He stopped at the sight of the bicycle.

"Comrade," Jacob said, wheeling the cycle out onto the sidewalk. Parked at the curb was the same four-door NKVD ZIS that had intercepted him on his way to the Lubyanka. Office workers hurried by, heading toward the nearby Izvestia newspaper building, and there was light automobile traffic moving in both directions along Gorki Street's six broad traffic lanes.

As he wheeled the bicycle to the curb, the other agent quickly left the car and came toward him. A tall muscular man with a fair Slavic face and glassy blue eyes, he opened his jacket to reveal the pistol holster strapped to his side. "What the hell's going on here?" he asked.

"I'm riding my bicycle to the Lebedev this morning," Jacob replied. "I need the exercise."

"You can't do that, Comrade. Our orders say you travel by car."

"Nonsense," he said, adjusting the bicycle's leather seat. "It's a fine sunny day, and I'm taking some exercise for a change."

The agent with the scar stepped forward. "You've caused enough trouble as it is, Comrade Linz."

Seeing that his hands were visibly shaking, Jacob reached down and began adjusting the bicycle's chain. "If the orders from State Security are to protect me, you can do that by keeping close to me," he said. "This is Moscow, not New York City, and nothing could conceivably happen to me between here and the Lebedev."

"State Security says you travel by car," the driver said, "and we can't make any exceptions."

Two young women hurried by, whispering to each other.

"You NKVD fellows carry excellent 7.65 millimeter pistols," said Jacob. "If there's any trouble, you can shoot from the car, just like they do in the movies. We'll take Gorki Street to Revolution Square; and then Karl Marx Prospect to Borovitsky Square. From there, we'll follow Frounze Street across the Bolshoi Bridge."

"I said you can't ride the damn bicycle without permission," the driver said. "It's against the rules."

Jacob stood up. "Fuck the rules."

His sudden and unexpected mutiny took them both by surprise. There was an exchange of nervous glances. "To make any exception to the rules we'd have to phone headquarters," the driver said.

"There's no time for that." Jacob rolled the bicycle off the curb into the street. "I have a seven fifteen appointment at the Lebedev." Seeing an opening in the northbound traffic, Jacob quickly mounted the bike. Without waiting for a reply, he pushed off and pedaled out into the empty space between the cars.

"They'll have our necks for this!" the tall agent yelled as they raced back to the car.

Jacob crossed the three northbound lanes, and drew up alongside the parked cars on the street. Jacob took another deep breath to slow his speeding heartbeat and then turned to look up at the apartment building for the last time. Aloise was there, he saw, watching him from the living-room window. The rage he had felt had left him, but the bitter hatred was still there and would always, he knew, occupy a place in his heart.

Behind him, the ZIS screeched to a halt in the outer lane. He looked at his watch again: 6:37. The Gorki Street morning traffic was heavier than he had anticipated, and it would take roughly twelve minutes to reach the embassy at Revolution Square. He glanced back over his shoulder, gave a cheerful wave of acknowledgment, and started off down the outer lane. With the hill's downgrade, he could coast all the way to the foot of Gorki Street, but what he needed now was not speed, but the appearance of a leisurely, early morning ride. He braked, keeping his speed down, and looked back in his handlebar rearview mirror at the two angry faces behind him. The stakes were high, and he was sure that the orders from State Security were to shoot to kill.

He slowed as he approached Pushkin Square. The cars and trucks feeding into the square from Tverskoy Boulevard were turning south, adding to the steady flow of traffic down Gorki Street. Motioning his intention to stay in the outer lane, he made a wide circle around the huge square and drew in behind a slow-moving truck loaded with construction machinery. The ZIS pulled in close behind him. The agent in the passenger seat, he saw in his rearview mirror, had turned to watch a sleek four-door Volga pull around them into the faster-moving center lane. The car's driver, a fat elderly Russian in a business suit, was undoubtedly a government official on his way to work.

The traffic in the outer lane plodded on. Jacob braked to slow the bicycle's downhill momentum. Calculating the speed of the traffic in all three southbound lanes, he would have to wait until after he passed the intersection of Arts Theater Street to make his move.

As he came alongside the Pushkin monument, a young woman and a small boy emerged from the square's fountained garden. Pausing on the sidewalk, the woman took the boy's hand, bent down, and wiped his mouth with a handkerchief. The gesture was that of an attentive mother, and the affectionate way she held onto the boy's small hand reminded him of the photograph of Maggie and his son in his jacket pocket. A feeling of longing gripped his heart. He braked again to keep his speed steady behind the truck, wanting to race ahead, but knowing that nothing beyond the next few moments was certain, that even if he succeeded in reaching the embassy it would be virtually impossible to arrange his exit from the Soviet Union.

As he approached the intersection of Ogareva Street, the white stone Czarist mansion housing the American Embassy came into view. A small crowd of men in business suits stood talking just outside of the embassy's open front door. Except for two black Volga limousines unloading passengers in the front of the building, the street in front of the embassy was empty.

At the intersection of Arts Theater Street, the truck in front of him suddenly slowed, stalled by a limousine waiting to take its place in front of the embassy. Motioning to the ZIS's driver that he would join the faster traffic, Jacob swung left into the center lane behind a small two-door Chaika. The ZIS followed, the driver waving his red NKVD badge, and pulled in behind him.

He took a deep breath, trying to slow his racing pulse, and scanned the traffic ahead of him. There was a six-foot space between the cars in the outer and middle lanes, too narrow for the ZIS to pass through but wide enough for him to have a clear straight passage down to the embassy at the corner. He gripped the handlebars, leaned forward, and quickly swerved to his right into the space between the cars. From behind him came a screech of wheels and the furious blare of a car's horn. For an instant, blinded by the morning sun rising over the rooftops of the Kremlin, he lost sight of his path between the cars and careened toward the center lane. In the next moment, a shot rang out behind him. The bullet ripped past his face and richocheted off the pavement ahead of him, throwing fragments of concrete into the air.

He swung left and began pedaling with all his strength toward the limousines parked in front of the embassy. Again, behind him, there was a screech of car wheels and the blare of a horn as the NKVD ZIS cut through the outer lane and came after him down the parking lane. The pedestrians along the sidewalk scattered like geese. Fifty feet ahead, the crowd of foreign delegates outside the embassy stood watching in silent shock as he hurtled toward the rear of the last parked limousine.

Holding his breath, he quickly calculated the angle of his approach to the sidewalk, then wrenched up on the bicycle's handlebars and leapt the four-inch curb. For an instant, following the impact of his rear wheel against the pavement, he lost control and swerved off toward the pedestrians who had drawn back against the embassy's wall. Righting himself, he bent forward and pedaled furiously toward the people assembled around the embassy's entrance.

Behind him the ZIS screeched to a halt and another shot rang out, this time grazing the embassy wall.

It was as if an invisible hand had reached out to clear a path for him: the dozen delegates at the door suddenly parted. It was only then that he saw the step leading up to the door, but it was too late to reverse his momentum. In the instant before his front wheel struck the step, he closed his eyes. Simultaneously, he felt a terrific jolt, heard the crash of collapsing metal, and felt himself flying forward. Then came a violent sensation of hitting the floor and, for a moment afterward, a numb and restful feeling of stillness. He opened his eyes, but the light blinded him and he saw only a confusion of moving images. A sound came from his mouth, followed by a streaking pain through his head and left shoulder. He lifted his right hand, but it belonged, it seemed, to another body. Voices broke the peaceful silence.

Opening his eyes again, he saw the room for the first time. Rolling over, he lifted himself with his right hand, drew his knees up under him, and crawled forward into the dark empty space. As he did, he felt his hand touch something cold and hard: the smooth surface of polished marble.

A voice above him said in English, "It's all right, son. You can rest now."

He looked up, and in the instant before he blacked out, he saw, framed in the light through the door behind him, a man in a gold braided military cap smiling gently down at him.

76

THE ambassador had warned him that the wheels of Soviet diplomatic machinery moved slowly. He had submitted his request for an interview with Foreign Minister Molotov at 11:00 A.M. that morning, four hours after Jacob entered the American Embassy, but twelve and a half hours had passed, and the embassy had already closed for the night, when Michael Rakovsky finally received the government's response.

"The Foreign Ministry regrets the delay in responding to your request, Colonel Rakovsky," Major Vladimir Rostov said, as he escorted Michael to a black government Volga limousine parked in front of the embassy. The major stepped aside and politely motioned for him to get in.

There were two other uniformed NKVD militiamen waiting in the limousine's front seat, and as Michael took his place in the passenger seat he quickly glanced at his watch. It was 11:26. His cable to Katherine informing her of Jacob's presence in the American Embassy had gone out at noon, and with the eight-hour time difference between Moscow and Washington, he would have to have Molotov's reply to his bargain for Jacob's release by noon tomorrow, Moscow time.

Rostov joined him in the limousine's plush passenger seat. "Your appointment with the Commissar is for eleven forty-five, Colonel Rakovsky," he said, as the limousine pulled away from the curb.

Michael sat back and looked out across Revolution Square. As the car swung past the Historical Museum into the broad dark expanse of Red Square, Major Rostov took a small badge from his uniform pocket and handed it to the officer seated next to the driver. The Volga swept past Lenin's monolithic tomb, its headlights fanning across the façade of St. Basil's Cathedral, and drew up at the opening of the Savior's Gate.

Two militiamen converged on the car from the sentry boxes on either side of the gate, their faces reflecting the red glow of the electrified red star at the top of the tower. Without lowering his window, the officer in the driver's seat showed the badge through the windshield. There was a brief exchange of words, and the limousine was waved forward.

As they passed through the gate, the bell in the tower above struck the half hour. He glanced at his watch again and thought of Katherine waiting at his house in Arlington. It was half past three in Washington, and her long vigil for Jacob's freedom would have begun by now.

"You have been given fifteen minutes for your interview, Colonel Rakovsky," said Rostov. "The car will wait for you and drive you back to the Moskva Hotel at midnight."

"I was told by Commissar Molotov's secretary that I would have at least a thirty-minute meeting with the Foreign Minister."

"I'm sorry, Colonel Rakovsky, but another meeting has been planned for midnight."

"A meeting at midnight?" Michael shook his head. "Good God, man, you'd think the war was still on."

Rostov smiled and said nothing.

As they reached the end of the avenue, instead of turning left toward Cathedral Square and the Kremlin, the car swung right into a narrow cobblestoned passageway. Twenty feet ahead, the passageway opened abruptly into a small square. The car slowed as it turned across the square, heading toward a long two-story brick building that resembled an army barracks. Lights burned on both floors of the building, and there was a line of black government limousines drawn up at the building's covered portico.

Before the car came to a halt under the portico, two uniformed NKVD militiamen had stepped forward into the open space between the limousines.

"If you will come with me, Colonel Rakovsky, I will take you in," said Rostov, as the car's right passenger door swung open.

Michael followed Rostov into a long red-carpeted hallway, where they were met by a man wearing the same NKVD major's uniform. The major nodded to Rostov. "Good evening, Colonel Rakovsky. I am Major Nikolai Mirovoy." Bowing politely, he pointed to an open elevator door at the far side of the hallway. "Please come this way."

The elevator was modern by Russian standards. On the way up, Major Mirovoy avoided his gaze and stared fixedly at the polished linoleum floor. When the door opened, he stepped out into another red-carpeted hallway and said, quietly, "This way, please."

They turned down a long hallway lined with identical oak doors on one side and windows hung with closed red velvet curtains on the other. Stationed at every second window was a young, smartly uniformed NKVD militia officer. Saluted by each guard along the way with a soft click of the heels, they came to a plain oak door at the end of the hallway. Indicating that he should wait behind, Major Mirovoy knocked once, opened the door, and went in. "Colonel Rakovsky," he announced, then stepped back and motioned for him to enter.

Removing his officer's cap as he stepped through the door, Michael entered a long, sparsely furnished room that resembled the waiting room of a Russian railway station. Just inside the door, he came to an abrupt halt. The short little man standing behind the desk at the end of the room was instantly recognizable from newspaper photographs as Laurenti Beria, the commissioner of internal affairs.

"Welcome to the Kremlin, Colonel Rakovsky," Beria said. "Please be seated."

Like Rostov, Major Mirovoy saluted, then turned and quickly vanished, closing the door behind him.

Expecting to see Minister Molotov, Michael was taken completely off guard by Beria's presence.

"I am Lavrenti Pavlovich Beria," the famous Police Chief went on, "Commissar for Internal Affairs, Deputy Prime Minister for Soviet Security, and Deputy Chairman of the Council of People's Commissars."

"Yes," he said as he sat down. "I know who you are."

The faint smile of contempt that played at the corners of the man's square-cut mouth accentuated the plumpness of his pale face. "You must forgive our delay in responding to your request for an interview with Foreign Minister Molotov," he said. "But since the interview concerns questions of Soviet national security, your request was turned over to the Commissariat for State Security."

"I see," Michael said.

"I confess that your appointment to the Foreign Councilors' conference came as something of a surprise, Colonel Rakovsky. I have known of you for some time, but I never anticipated meeting you face to face here in Moscow."

As Beria left the desk and slowly came toward him, Michael looked around the room, wondering where in hell they had brought him. Opposite the desk was another door. Above the door hung an old-fashioned metal clock. There was only one window at the far end of the room opposite the desk, a long narrow window hung, like the windows in the corridor, with red velvet drapes.

Suddenly, from behind the door opposite the desk came the sound of laughter. The smile vanished from Beria's face. He stopped and quickly glanced at the clock. "In any case," he said, "I can only spare you a few minutes, Colonel Rakovsky. I have a meeting to attend at midnight."

The clock on the wall opposite him read 11:46. "I don't know what you think I've come here to talk about Commissar Beria," Michael said, "but fourteen minutes is hardly enough."

"What puzzles us, Colonel Rakovsky, is the fact that the interview was requested for you, and not Ambassador Harriman," Beria said. "Under the circumstances, we would have thought that the ambassador himself would be conducting these negotiations."

Again, there was laughter in the next room.

Michael held his ground and said, "I assure you, Commissar, if Ambassador Harriman knew the full implications of Jacob Linz's defection this morning, he would be here conducting these negotiations himself."

"Commissar Molotov spoke with the ambassador by telephone this morning," Beria said, turning his hands in his pockets. "And the Commissar assured me that Harriman had taken a full statement from Comrade Linz."

"A full statement was taken," Michael said. "But not, I'm afraid, by the ambassador."

This time, from behind the door, came the muffled sound of a man's angry voice.

Beria's hands came to rest in his pockets. He stopped and waited until the voice died away. "Then by whom?" he asked.

Both the voice in the next room and the limousines parked outside gave Michael a feeling of uneasiness. "By me," he replied. "Linz asked for me by name and promised that he would make a full statement to me in private. I took young Linz's statement, but so far, assuming that your government will agree to my terms for the boy's release from the Soviet Union, I have said nothing to anyone about his real identity."

Beria's eyes widened with surprise. "What do you mean, you have said nothing about his real identity?"

"I mean that the ambassador is so far ignorant of the fact that young Linz is one of the Soviet Union's leading atomic physicists, and that he has been working for a year on the theoretical design of a plutonium atom bomb."

There was an angry shout from the room behind the door. The anger was contagious. A flush broke across Beria's pale face. Raising his voice, he said, "Issues of Soviet national security do not concern you, Colonel Rakovsky."

"Your mistakes go far beyond questions of Soviet national security, Comrade Beria. You are not only Commissar for Internal Affairs, Deputy Prime Minister for Soviet Security, and Deputy Chairman of the Council of People's Commissars, you are also head of the Soviet Union's atomic science program and the director of Soviet atomic intelligence. And as such, you must take full responsibility for appointing Comrade Aloise Frégand as the director of Soviet atomic intelligence in England."

Beria's face suddenly relaxed. Smiling up at Michael with malicious satisfaction, he said, "An order was issued this morning for Comrade Frégand's arrest, but fortunately she chose to spare us the embarrassment of a public trial. She shot herself this morning in her apartment."

The minute hand on the clock across the room jumped to 11:50. "I see," Michael said. "But Linz now knows the whole story, and he wants his freedom."

Again, there was the sound of the voice behind the door, this time like a scolding parent.

"It's impossible," Beria said. "Jacob Linz will not be permitted to leave the Soviet Union."

"I understand the value of Linz's work, Comrade Beria. This morning, when I took the boy's statement, he told me that approval has been given for the construction of a plutonium reactor outside Moscow, and that it will be finished within a year. He also told me that you had plans to build a plutonium bomb within two years, and that you would threaten his family in America to force him to complete his work at the Lebedev."

"This interview is a waste of time, Colonel Rakovsky." Beria turned away and started back to the desk at the far end of the room.

"I have a proposition to make," Michael said, following Beria to the desk. "And as we say in America, it's an offer you won't be able to refuse."

"As a minor officer in the American Army, you are in no position to negotiate this matter, Colonel Rakovsky."

"Knowing what I know about Jacob Linz's identity, Commissar, you can consider yourself lucky that I am conducting these negotiations," Michael said. "Moreover, I was told that I would have until midnight to present my statement."

"It's now eleven fifty-one," Beria said, seating himself in the chair behind the desk, "and I will give you exactly nine minutes to say what you have to say."

"First," he said, tucking his army cap under his arm, "you should know about today's decision regarding the agenda for the Foreign Ministers' Conference next December. With the consent of my government, the councilors have agreed to negotiate the settlement of the one major question left unanswered at the Potsdam Conference—namely, the kind of governments that will rule in the liberated countries of East Europe."

There was another burst of laughter from the room opposite Beria's desk.

"Yes, yes, I'm aware of the decision," he said, glancing nervously at the room's heavy oak door. "I fail to see what that has to do with Comrade Linz or his departure from the Soviet Union."

"It has to do with the question of trust between wartime allies, Commissar, and America's continued foreign policy of appeasement toward the Soviet Union."

Beria sat forward. "If you have come here to lecture me on American foreign policy, Colonel Rakovsky, you are wasting valuable time. It is now eleven fifty-four, and I have a conference to attend at midnight."

Michael stood directly in front of the desk. "In that case, I'll come straight to the point. The present foreign policy of the United States toward the Soviet Union is founded, I'm afraid, on ignorance. My government believes, for instance, that the Soviet Union only learned about the existence of its atom bomb following the detonation of the uranium bomb over Hiroshima, and it believes, moreover, that Soviet science has only now begun its atom bomb research and that it will take you five years, at least, to build a bomb of your own and close the nuclear gap with the U.S."

Suddenly, from the nearby door came the sound of a man's voice— the same voice, Michael realized, that he had heard five nights ago at the reception in the Great Kremlin Palace, when Stalin gave his speech of welcome to the conference delegates.

His realization, he saw, was reflected in Beria's own face.

"My country's ignorance of her Soviet ally's wartime betrayals is astonishing," he said, trying to remain calm. "When Truman met with Stalin at Potsdam, he was ignorant of the fact that Stalin knew of America's plutonium bomb test at Alamogordo, and he had no idea, when Stalin argued at Potsdam for Russia's rights as an equal ally, that the NKVD's intelligence apparatus had agents working inside the Manhattan Project. Had the president known that Russia was engaged in wartime espionage inside America's secret atom bomb project, he would have never conceded to Stalin's territorial demands in Eastern Europe . . ." He left off as his words were momentarily lost under a burst of loud applause in the next room.

When the applause died away, he said, "I will not waste valuable time recounting the story of your efforts to blackmail Katherine Linz into turning over her experimental calculations of the plutonium bomb's critical mass, Commissar Beria. Suffice it to say that, had it worked, your scheme would have allowed your scientists to complete a plutonium bomb within two years."

Beria sat forward. "Do you think that the Kremlin can be threatened by someone like you, Colonel Rakovsky—an unknown American soldier?"

"I may be an unknown American soldier," Michael said, "but I'm also an American gambler, and I like to play for high stakes. At this point, there are only three people who have knowledge of the Soviet Union's work on a plutonium bomb and your atomic espionage activities in America: Katherine Linz, Jacob Linz, and myself."

"This is a very foolish game you're playing, Rakovsky," Beria said, "and we are well equipped here in Moscow to promptly end it."

Choosing his words carefully, Michael turned away and walked back to the center of the room. "First, I will remind you that there is a growing feeling of distrust in America toward the Soviet Union. I need not describe what your own intelligence sources have reported to you, but there have been recent articles in the American press reporting the presence of Communist agents inside agencies of the American government."

The minute hand on the clock jumped to 11:58.

"Second, you should know that Katherine Linz has left Los Alamos and is presently visiting her grandson in Washington, D.C. This morning, I sent a cable to Dr. Linz in Washington informing her that her son had taken asylum in the American Embassy here in Moscow. If the Soviet government refuses to accept my terms for her son's release from Russia, Comrade Beria, she has instructions to go at once to the FBI in Washington and tell what she knows of Soviet espionage inside the Manhattan Project. If Katherine Linz tells what she knows of your espionage inside the Manhattan Project," he went on, "she will be called before the House Un-American Activities Committee in Washington."

The clock's minute hand jumped again: 11:59.

"The public outcry across America will, of course, force the Truman Administration to reverse its present policy of appeasement toward the Soviet Union, and if that happens Russia will have little hope of negotiating further concessions in Eastern Europe at the Foreign Ministers' conference in December.

"The terms of my proposition are quite simple. In exchange for her son's safe release from the Soviet Union and her grandson's guaranteed safety in America, Katherine Linz will agree not to reveal what she knows of Soviet espionage inside the Manhattan Project, and she will resign from any further involvement with atomic science. Jacob and I will likewise never reveal what we know of Soviet atomic bomb research and Soviet atomic espionage."

When Beria finally spoke, there was savage fury in his high-pitched voice. "You are in no position to make such a demand, Rakovsky, and the Soviet Government will not be made the victim of blackmail."

"Blackmail, Commissar, is the one diplomacy your government understands. The choice I give you is between the possibility of an atom bomb within five years and a negotiated settlement of Russia's future influence in Eastern Europe."

Suddenly, somewhere out in the darkness, a clock in one of the Kremlin towers began to chime the hour.

"A decision such as this will take time," said Beria, glancing at the door on his right. "We cannot give you a reply until you leave Moscow."

"I'm sorry, but there can be no delay," Michael said as a second bell began to ring. "It is now four P.M. in Washington, and if Katherine Linz does not have your government's response by eight o'clock tomorrow morning, she will go at once to the FBI. I must have your reply by noon tomorrow, Moscow time."

77

WHEN Katherine arrived with Maggie and David at South Brooklyn's Pier 26 on Sunday morning, a crowd of people had already gathered around the gate leading to the long fenced-in pier. Made up of many nationalities, the crowd had assembled to welcome the arrival of the Swedish liner, S.S. *Karlstad*. A week before, on September 14, Michael had cabled from Berlin that he and Jacob would try to book passage on the *Karlstad* sailing the following day from Bremen. The incoming ships from Europe had been booked to the gunwales since the end of the war, but she and Maggie and David had nonetheless driven up from Washington that morning on the mere chance that Michael and Jacob would be among the ship's passengers.

They had been told that the ship would dock at noon, but it was well after two when the *Karlstad* finally dropped anchor among the cargo ships moored along Brooklyn's crowded wharves. Customs and immigration, carried out in a huge fenced-in warehouse, had taken another two hours, and it was half past five when the ship's passengers began to straggle out of the warehouse to meet the welcoming embraces of their waiting loved ones.

"If they're not on this boat, there will be others," Maggie said, anxiously shifting David to her left arm. "I checked the paper this morning, and the *Stavanger* is due to sail from Bremen the day after tomorrow."

It was pointless, Katherine realized, to go on waiting. There had been no sign of Michael and Jacob.

"David's tired, Maggie, we should leave," she said, craning to see over the heads of the people in front of them.

"I'm not tired, Grandma," David announced as a young man and woman emerged from the warehouse carrying two large suitcases. Looking around with uncertainty at the waiting crowd, the couple continued on toward the warehouse gate.

The worst part of these last three weeks had been the uncertainty of

Michael's communications from Europe. There had been the cable from Moscow on September 1, informing them that the Soviets had agreed to his bargain but that the terms of Jacob's release from the Soviet Union were still to be negotiated. Then the cable from Berlin on the 4th, saying that they were being detained in the German capital while Jacob underwent an interrogation by the American occupation authorities. Even now, despite the cable on the 14th, it was not certain that Jacob would be allowed to enter the United States.

"Look, Mommy!" David shouted and pointed. "There's Papa!"

In excitement, Katherine pushed her way forward into the crowd.

"No, sweetheart," Maggie said behind her. "That's not Papa."

Again, for the hundredth time that afternoon, Katherine watched with longing as another dark-haired young man came out of the warehouse. Roughly Jacob's age, he was dressed in a baggy European-looking suit and appeared, like some of the other refugees, to be a Jew—a survivor, perhaps, from one of the Nazi death camps.

But even worse than the uncertainty of Michael's communications had been the uncertainty of Jacob's forgiveness. She had lived so long with the guilt of her betrayal in Berlin that it was difficult to believe that she could merit the boy's absolution.

As the young man passed through the gate and into the arms of his waiting loved ones, Maggie came up, clutching David in her arms, and joined her in the crowd. "If we stay until six," she said, "we can still be back in Washington by midnight."

"You're right," Katherine said. "We might as well stay."

"Look, Grandma," David said, pointing toward where they had parked the car.

When she turned, Katherine saw that the strange looking fellow who had followed them into the wharf area that morning was moving off arm-in-arm with a young woman carrying a small suitcase. "Yes, sweetheart, I see," she said, recalling the fear she had felt when she first saw the man among the waiting crowd. In the two weeks since she submitted her resignation from the Manhattan Project, it had been difficult to believe that she and David were no longer being watched and followed, or that she had been blessed, after all these years, with anonymity.

"Katherine?" Maggie said, quietly.

It was a both a statement and a question, and when she looked back, Michael Rakovsky had left the warehouse and was walking toward the open gate. He carried the army suitcase he had taken with him, but instead of the uniform she had been looking for, he wore a sleeveless white shirt and khaki trousers.

He was alone, she saw, but she had lived on his love alone for so long that it was enough to carry her forward. Seeing him, she remembered the words he had said the night she returned from Alamogordo: It isn't perfect love, I know, but perfect love doesn't exist in this world.

As she began pushing her way through the crowd toward the open gate, she realized that she had felt this same sense of completion only once before: the night inside the crowded Marble Arch tube station when, at last, she had found David. As she broke through the circle of people around the warehouse gate, Michael caught sight of her and waved. "Katherine!" he shouted over the excited voices.

She knew at once, from the smile that broke across his face, that all was well. She ran to meet him just outside the gate. Saying nothing, knowing that they had both come to the end of a voyage that had taken the whole of their lifetimes, they embraced amid the crowd.

78

"NEXT!" the immigration officer called out from behind a high wooden counter.

The elderly Czechoslovakian in front of Jacob took his stamped papers and moved on.

Jacob looked again at the two uniformed policemen who stood watching him from the warehouse door, then stepped forward and took his place at the counter.

"Papers, please," the immigration officer said, removing a printed form from one of the wooden boxes on the counter. The bureaucratic array of boxes and forms reminded Jacob of all of the government offices he had visited in Moscow. He handed the man the typed immigration document he had received from the occupation authorities in Berlin, with its tiny, badly developed photograph.

The officer scanned the document, then looked up, checking his face against the face in the photograph. "Name, please?" he asked.

"Jacob Eric Linz."

The man looked at the name typed at the top of the document. "Nationality?"

He knew the questions: he had answered them countless times in the last three weeks. "German," he said.

Taking up his fountain pen, the man quickly wrote his name and nationality in the blank spaces on the printed form. "Your age?" he asked.

"I'm twenty-four," Jacob replied.

The ease of his English surprised the man. He looked up, as if seeing him for the first time. "Your English is pretty good, son," he said.

"Yes. I learned English from my father. He was an American. He's dead now, but my mother . . ." He left off, realizing he was saying too much.

"I see."

As he watched the officer write something on the form, the questions that had kept him awake at night during the long voyage from Germany ran like water through his mind: Did the Americans now know who he really was? Did they suspect the terrible secret he carried inside him? And had they let him come this far only to arrest him?

Michael, of course, had insisted that his fears were unfounded. This is America, Jacob, not Germany or Russia, he had said when they passed the famous Statue of Liberty in the harbor, and you have nothing to worry about.

"Married or single?" the officer asked.

He thought of Maggie and his son, courageously waiting out the war for him. "I'm single," he replied.

"You say your father is dead. But what about your mother?"

"She's alive." He looked off at the warehouse door, wondering if she was out there waiting for him. "She lives here in America, in Washington, D.C."

"And your occupation?" the man asked.

Jacob swallowed, thinking of the answers he had given to that question in Moscow and Berlin, wondering again if telling only half the truth was the same as a telling a lie. "I'm a scientist," he replied.

It took an eternity, it seemed, for the man to write the word on the form.

Jacob shifted his weight, thinking of the terrible price he and his mother and father had paid for the glory of scientific discovery, and of the terrible new world they had helped to create.

"Your religion?"

The question, sudden as it was, startled him. He hesitated, remembering the fear he had always felt when he answered that question in Berlin and Moscow. "I'm Jewish," he replied.

The man saw his fear, smiled, and quickly wrote the word on the form. "As a resident alien, you'll be required to report your whereabouts to the authorities in America," he said. "There are immigration offices located in most American cities. If you reside in a place where there is no immigration office, you can report your whereabouts by letter." He scribbled his signature at the bottom of the form, then stamped the immigration document. "Keep this with you at all times," he said, and handed him the paper.

For a moment, in his confusion, Jacob could only stare at the stamped document in his hand.

"If you have baggage, you can claim it over there," the man said, pointing toward the far side of the huge room, where uniformed customs agents were inspecting the luggage.

Tucking the document in his jacket pocket, Jacob glanced back at the dozen people waiting to take his place at the counter.

"Next!" the man called out, and waved him on.

Dazed, still unable to believe that he would not be arrested, he crossed the room to the stack of luggage and parcels, removed his single bag, and joined the other immigrants at the tables along the wall.

"Open it," the customs agent said.

He opened the leather bag Michael had bought for him in Berlin.

The agent rummaged through the clothes and took out the tiny black box he had packed between his shirts. "What's this?" he asked.

Jacob watched him turn the box in his hand, wondering if he should tell the truth. It was the one possession he had brought with him from Moscow. "It's a mezuzah," he replied.

"A what?"

"A mezuzah. It's something Jews hang on their doors. It has a prayer inside."

"Ah." The officer shook his head and returned the mezuzah to its place between the shirts. "You can close it," he said.

He obeyed, wondering at the strange indifference of Americans.

Seeing his confusion, the agent pointed to the warehouse door. "The exit's that way."

Still dazed, he took his bag from the table and followed the other immigrants through a huge door into a fenced-in space between the warehouse and the wharf. The setting sun had cast a long shadow across the *Karlstad* moored alongside the pier. He stopped for a moment, scanning the crowd gathered around the open gate at the end of the wharf, wondering if he had only imagined that he was now free to leave.

Beyond the gate, there were cries of welcome in all the languages he had left behind in Europe. He searched the excited faces on the far side of the fence, wondering if his mother and Maggie and his son were waiting for him. Michael had said that he would look for them and meet him "on the American side of the fence."

He moved on, following the other immigrants as they passed between the guards posted on either side of the gate. It was difficult, after so many years and so many betrayals, to believe that he even had a family waiting for him. He continued through the gate, looking to the left and to the right at the sad, human wreckage of the war. It seemed impossible that there could be so much joy after so much suffering.

He kept moving, wondering to himself if the love he had known as a child in Germany could be his again, or if the hatred and betrayals he had experienced in Europe had destroyed everything.

Suddenly, like an echo from the past, came the musical sound of Maggie's voice—"Jacob!"—and when he looked around, she was coming toward him through the crowd with the boy clutched in her arms.

The sight of the two of them together filled him with sudden amazement. She was a woman now, he saw, and even more beautiful than he remembered. And the boy's face—he caught and held his breath—was his own!

It was as if he had suddenly and miraculously left the old world of war and death behind and had crossed over into a new and better world. With a feeling of joyful pride, he raced to meet them.

"Oh, Maggie . . ." He dropped his suitcase on the pavement and took the two of them in his arms.

"My God," she murmured, "it's been so long."

For a while, they went on holding each other and said nothing. He thought of the terrible distance they had traveled from one another and the miracle of God's mercy that had brought them together again.

Then Maggie let go of him and stepped back. "This is David," she said and grinned. "He's been waiting for months to meet you."

"Hello, son," Jacob said. "I've been waiting for months to meet you, too."

The boy smiled up at him, shyly. "Uncle Mike says you're a scientist, just like Grandma," he said.

"That's right."

"That's what I'm going to be when I grow up," David beamed.

Jacob caught Maggie's eye and shook his head, remembering his own childhood dreams and the terrible place it had led him. "You're only three years old, son," he said. "And you have all the time in the world to make that kind of choice."

"I'm not three," the boy corrected, "I'm three and a half, and Grandma says when she was a little girl she wanted to be a scientist."

"That's true," he said, thinking of the price she too had paid to realize her dream. "And is your Grandma here?" he asked.

"Yes." The boy turned and pointed off through the crowd. "She's over there."

For a moment, he could only stare at her in silent astonishment. Seven years had gone by since he last saw her in Berlin, and though there were lines around her soft blue eyes, her hair was as he remembered it in Göttingen—tied in a knot behind her head—and it was as if nothing else had changed. The look of questioning doubt he saw in her eyes reminded him of what Michael had said before they left Berlin: the one thing that has haunted your mother is the uncertainty of your forgiveness.

Maggie reached out and touched his arm. "Go to her," she said. "She's been waiting for this moment for seven years."

As she watched Jacob leave Maggie and David, and start toward them through the crowd, Katherine said to Michael, "You were right. He looks exactly like his father."

"And you were wrong," Michael said and smiled. "He loves you and he has forgiven everything."

It was as if God had suddenly answered her prayers and had given her a second chance at life. With a feeling of exultation, thinking to herself of the years she and David had spent searching for the key to unlock the power of the atom, she let go of Michael's arm and raced to embrace her son.

It had been a foolish and a useless search, for she now knew that the greatest force in the universe was not the power of the atom, but the power of love.

L